The Terminal Gene

A Techno-Conspiracy Thriller

John H. Thomas

ISBN Paperback - 979-8-9998386-4-3
ISBN Hardcover - 979-8-9998386-5-0

Cover design by Nick Castle @ Nick Castle Design
Editing by Jason Letts @ Imbue Editing

Dedication

To my neighbors — Andy and Kim, David and Rachel, Pedro and Colleen — whose children grew up so quickly, from toddlers to college students. The sight of your children playing outside my office window often made me realize how fast time goes by, and that's what inspired this book.

Epigraph

"Whenever science makes a discovery, the devil grabs it while the angels are debating the best way to use it."

— Alan Valentine

"The saddest aspect of life right now is that science gathers knowledge faster than society gathers wisdom."

— Isaac Asimov

Chapter 1

Breakthrough

The research facility at Helix Innovations hummed with soft whirs, punctuated by the occasional beep of a monitor. Dr. Emily Harper sat at her cluttered workstation, her chestnut-brown hair pulled into a messy bun.

Her tortoiseshell glasses slipped down her nose as she squinted at the cascade of genetic code on her screen. Coffee cups, some bearing lipstick smudges, crowded her desk, their rings staining notepads scribbled with months of hypotheses. The antiseptic scent of the laboratory, mingled with a faint ozone tang, clung to her rolled-up lab coat sleeves.

Emily's fingers hovered over the keyboard, her hazel eyes wide. After the former project leader died suddenly in a tragic car accident, the CEO promoted Emily from another division to lead Project BioSpark. For the past two years, she and her team had searched for an elusive pattern in the human genome aimed at uncovering the secrets of longevity. Nights blurred into mornings, fueled by caffeine and stubborn curiosity.

Six months ago, in early 2029, the data revealed a startling truth. A gene sequence present in all living things—humans, animals, and plants—determined the exact time of death, precise to the second. Internally, they called it the terminal gene, but her team members darkly nicknamed it the kill switch.

Instead of advancing human longevity as intended, the discovery revealed that death was predetermined, knowable, and unchangeable from the moment of conception. They had spent months manipulating the sequence, attempting to shorten or lengthen the timeline. All their efforts failed—they could not alter the genetic code.

As she reviewed the notes Mr. Kessler, the CEO, had given her to include in the presentation for the board, she murmured, "My God." Her heart beat rapidly. This wasn't just a breakthrough; it was a reckoning. The terminal gene had the potential to redefine medicine, providing insights into deadly diseases, or it might disrupt society, giving governments and corporations the power to exploit mortality. Her working-class roots, forged in South Boston, grounded her in practicality. Wisdom was her life's pursuit, but this knowledge cut like a blade, razor-sharp and double-edged.

She leaned back, rubbing her ink-stained hands together. Many months of grinding through data and arguing with colleagues over anomalies had led to this moment. But now, standing on the precipice, presenting their findings to the board of directors, Emily's mind churned. If Helix commercialized this, would it become a luxury for the elite, like the gene therapies that lined the pockets of Boston's Seaport billionaires? Would the government weaponize it, sorting citizens by their expiration dates? Her stomach twisted at the thought of such power in the wrong hands.

A sharp tone from her computer jolted her, the screen flashing with an unread message marked "URGENT" in pulsing red. Her pulse quickened. It was the second one this week, each vanishing when she tried to open it, leaving only a blank screen and a chill down her spine. She hesitated then dismissed it, telling herself it was only a glitch.

The lab door hissed open, and Emily flinched, her hand darting to minimize the screen. Tyler Reed stepped inside, his broad shoulders filling the doorway. His dark-green eyes, a soldier's instinct, swept the room before landing on her. His navy button-down was untucked, his scuffed boots thudding softly on the tiles. A lopsided grin softened the jagged scar above his eyebrow, and one of his tattoos—a faded pair of dog tags with his brother's initials and a heart, inked in memory of his death in Iraq—peeked from under a rolled sleeve.

"Caught you napping on the job, Doc?" he teased, his rough voice warm. He leaned against a counter, careful not to bump the equipment, his fingers absently tracing the edge of a worn leather bracelet he never took off, a habit Emily knew calmed him when he sensed trouble.

Emily forced a smile, her heart still racing. "Hardly. Wrestling with some last-minute changes to the board presentation." Although they'd been engaged since spring, Tyler didn't know the full scope of BioSpark—only that it was a high-stakes genetic project she had been working on for two years. She'd kept the details vague, not out of distrust but because the potential of it felt too heavy to share until she understood the implications.

He raised an eyebrow, his grin fading. "You look like you've solved world hunger or seen a ghost. Everything okay?"

She took a deep breath, her closeness to Tyler offset with caution. He was her rock, his pragmatism balancing her tendency to overthink. His years as a field medic in the 101st Airborne had sharpened his constant calm, but they'd also left him with a quiet distrust of systems like Helix's, his eyes flicking to the lab's security cameras. But the terminal gene was too raw, too dangerous to discuss in a casual chat.

"It's…huge," she said. "The validation has finally finished.

After six months of testing, Mr. Kessler said he's ready to take it to the board this evening."

Tyler's eyes sharpened, but he didn't press her. "Big enough to get you out of here for dinner? You've been at it since dawn." He crossed his arms, his watch catching the light.

Emily's lips quirked into a wry smile. "You don't quit, do you? I've got the board meeting in an hour, Ty. Gotta finish the prep." She gestured to her tablet, where her presentation waited, an overview of the BioSpark research.

He sighed, mock-exasperated. "Fine, but I'm holding you to a lobster roll or pizza later. This place is sucking the life out of you, Em." He looked at the surveillance cameras blinking in the corners, his jaw tightening. "Creeps me out, all these eyes watching every move you make." He shifted his weight, his hand brushing the small, dog-eared notebook he always carried, filled with sketches of dogs he found funny—a hobby he'd picked up to quiet his mind after long nights overseas.

She followed his gaze, a prickle of unease creeping up her spine. "It's only a lab, Ty. Overpriced tech and underpaid scientists." Her dry humor surfaced, but it seemed forced. The cameras had never bothered her, but lately with the reality of the terminal gene troubling her thoughts, they seemed watchful.

Tyler stepped closer, squeezing her shoulder. His calloused fingers were warm, grounding. "You're the best thing in this place. Don't let it chew you up." His voice was soft, his eyes scanning hers.

Her throat tightened, guilt gnawing at her for holding back. "I won't," she promised. She wanted to tell him everything—the genetic discovery, the ethical minefield, the fear in her gut—but not yet. Not until she'd faced the board and seen what Helix planned to do with this knowledge.

Tyler nodded, satisfied for now. "I'll hang out in the cafeteria, enjoying some of Helix's terrible coffee. Come find me when you're done." He flashed a grin and left, the door hissing shut behind him.

Alone again, Emily exhaled, her shoulders slumping. She reopened the genetic data, its stark numbers staring back. The BioSpark team's journey to this discovery had been meticulous, blending groundbreaking tech and persistent scientific work. It began with sequencing genomes using high-powered machines that read DNA like a book, letter by letter.

They initially collected DNA specimens from thousands of organisms to look for patterns related to longevity. Emily's team then trained computer algorithms to sift through billions of genetic samples, hunting for sequences that appeared consistently across species. After a year, they noticed an odd, repeating segment in every sample. For months, they couldn't determine the purpose of the related sequences. Over a three-day weekend, two independent artificial intelligence engines had revealed a correlation with death records.

At first, they thought it was a mistake. They conducted experiments, editing the sequence in lab-grown cells with CRISPR, which acts like genetic scissors. This technology works as highly precise shears, guided by RNA, to remove and repair damaged DNA. Their attempts to change the terminal gene's duration failed—the sequence was resistant to change.

They cross-checked their findings for five months, comparing data against death registries and animal lifespans, ensuring no errors. Under Mr. Kessler's insistence, the last month involved rigorous validation, re-running tests, and using statistical models to prove the genetic code was universal and unchangeable. The evidence was irrefutable, yet the consequences were horrifying.

She paced back and forth across the lab. She'd always believed science could uplift humanity, but this discovery was a Pandora's box. When she presented the research to the board, she feared they would see dollar signs, not dilemmas. James

Kessler's ambition was legendary, his charm a velvet glove over a steel fist. She'd seen him sideline colleagues who challenged him, their careers reduced to footnotes. If she pushed back too hard against the comments he'd added in the presentation, she risked losing everything—her job, credibility, and the chance to shape the fate of this discovery.

But silence wasn't an option either. The gene was real. Its data was airtight after many months of cross-referencing. Then another month to validate their findings and satisfy Mr. Kessler. A less ethical individual at a rival company could find it if they waited too long. She stopped pacing, her reflection faint in the monitor's dark screen. Her face looked pale; her eyes haunted. "You've got to do this right," she said, her voice firm despite her hands shaking. She grabbed her tablet, bracing herself for the boardroom. The truth was hers to defend, at least for now.

The boardroom at Helix Innovations gleamed with polished opulence, its mahogany table reflecting the soft glow of recessed lights. Floor-to-ceiling windows outlined Boston Harbor, where gray waves churned under a sky heavy with impending rain. The air smelled of expensive leather, a stark contrast to the lab's antiseptic odor. Dr. Harper stood at the head of the table, her fitted blazer snug against her frame, her shoes squeaking faintly on the polished floor as she connected her tablet to the virtual projector. The genetic sequence flickered onto the screen, its glowing data points looming.

James Kessler sat at the table's far end, his salt-and-pepper hair impeccable, his navy suit tailored to perfection. His dark eyes, sharp behind designer glasses, tracked Emily with a predator's patience. Around him, nine executives shifted in their high-backed chairs, their body language a mix of curiosity and guarded skepticism.

Dr. Catherine Morrow, a biochemist in her sixties with silver hair swept into a neat chignon, sat to Emily's left. Her kind face, lined with years of wisdom, softened as she offered Emily a warm, encouraging nod. Catherine's guidance, combining warmth and intellectual strength, steered Emily through the intricacies of corporate science during her initial years at Helix.

She had encouraged Emily to accept the promotion with the BioSpark team, and her presence eased the tense atmosphere in the room. The long-term board members—mostly older men in charcoal suits like Holt and Carver—were loyal to Kessler, their postures stiff, eyes hooded as Emily began.

Emily cleared her throat, her heart pounding, but her voice was calm. "Thank you for coming. After two years on Project BioSpark, we've achieved a breakthrough in genetic mapping. My team has identified a universal gene sequence in every living organism—animals, plants, and most relevant to today's presentation, humans."

Catherine's eyes widened, her pen froze, and her lips parted slightly in surprise. She leaned forward, curious, her fingers tightening around her pen as if to anchor herself. A heavyset executive, Mr. Carver, lurched forward, his jowls quivering, his bushy eyebrows shooting up. "A common genetic structure across all organisms?" His voice boomed, disbelief tinged with excitement, his hands splaying on the table as if to steady himself.

Another board member, Mr. Langston, a thin man with a pinched face, leaned forward intensely, his knuckles whitening as he gripped the table's edge. "That's shocking. Do we know what function this structure serves?"

Emily swallowed, her hands shaking as she clicked to the next slide. "It determines the exact moment of death, accurate to the second."

The room erupted. Carver gasped audibly, his hand flying to his chest as if struck. Langston's jaw dropped, his eyes bulging as he slumped back in his chair, muttering, "Impossible." Ms. Patel, a newer board member with sharp features, froze, her tablet slipping from her hands to the table with a soft thud.

Another executive, Mr. Holt, a gaunt man with thinning hair, let out a nervous laugh, his fingers drumming erratically on his notepad. Catherine's face paled, her warm eyes now wide with wonder, her hands clasped tightly in her lap as she exchanged glances with Emily.

"You're certain of this revelation, James?" Langston demanded, his voice sharp, bypassing Emily to address Kessler, his shoulders hunching as if bracing for a blow.

Kessler nodded, his thin-lipped smile unwavering, though his eyes flicked to Emily with a hint of warning. She pressed on, clicking through to a graph of lifespans across species. "Yes, over the last six months, we've cross-referenced and validated millions of genetic samples from every continent—humans, mammals, and plants. The sequence is consistent and fixed at inception. We refer to it as the terminal gene."

Carver's lips curved into a predatory grin, his fingers steepled, his chair creaking as he leaned back. "Remarkable work, James, Dr. Harper. Truly groundbreaking." His voice dripped with ambition, his eyes gleaming as he rubbed his hands together. "I'm already imagining the potential applications. This could redefine markets—health care, insurance, personal planning."

Emily's stomach knotted, her shoulders stiffening at the speed of his pivot to profit. Catherine caught her eye, her expression tightening, her jaw set as she straightened her glasses. "There are medical applications," Emily said carefully. "It could guide treatment plans and optimize resource allocation. But commercialization is complex. If individuals know their death dates, it could trigger mental health crises and disrupt economies. Governments could misuse this, prioritizing citizens by lifespan. Before refining potential applications, we need extensive research to understand the societal impact."

Catherine leaned forward. "Emily's right. This is unprecedented, but it's a double-edged sword. Think of the AI privacy scandals two years ago—public trust is fragile. Rushing to market risks chaos, even violence. We'd be handing people a clock they can't stop." Her silver hair caught the light as she turned to the board, her gaze sweeping the room, lingering on Carver's scowl.

Ms. Patel nodded, her fingers twisting a pen nervously, her brow furrowed. "I agree with Catherine. We'd need a robust framework—ethical guidelines, regulatory oversight. Without that, we're inviting disaster." Her voice wavered, her eyes darting to Kessler as if gauging his reaction.

The tension grew, chairs creaking as board members shifted. Holt's drumming fingers stilled, his face flushed as he muttered, "This is...biblical." Langston folded his arms, his lips pursed, his foot tapping under the table.

Kessler's smile tightened, a flash of irritation in his eyes as he bent forward, his hands folded with deliberate calm. "Caution is admirable, but progress demands vision. This isn't just a scientific discovery; it's a trillion-dollar opportunity. People want certainty—life plans tailored to their timelines, insurance models that eliminate guesswork. Helix can lead that revolution."

A low, frustrated grunt escaped board chair Herbert Beyer. He had been sitting silently, occasionally glancing at Emily but mainly observing the board members with a practiced eye, gauging their reactions and making mental notes. He slapped the table. The sound echoed through the room, and his face instantly reddened. "Kessler's got it. This is bigger than anything we've done. Hell, it's the biggest thing anyone has accomplished. We'd dominate biotech for decades. Research is fine, but let's not sit on a gold mine." His voice boomed, his jowls shaking with enthusiasm, his eyes gleaming with greed.

A ripple of agreement spread through the room. Holt nodded eagerly, his nervous energy replaced by a hungry grin. Two other older board members, silent until now, exchanged glances and murmured assent, their shoulders relaxing as they leaned toward Kessler. Emily's jaw clenched, her hands balled into fists at her sides, her stubborn streak flaring. "With respect, sir, this isn't a product like a new drug. It's life and death for everyone. If we misstep, we could destabilize society. Mental health systems are strained—imagine millions learning they have months or years left while others don't."

Catherine's voice cut through the murmurs like a blade. "Exactly, Emily. We need longitudinal studies, psychological impact assessments, maybe even global collaboration to model societal effects." She turned to Carver, her eyes narrowing. "You're talking about markets, but what about the human cost? People could riot, and economies could collapse. We can't think only about the stock price." Her tone was sharp, her posture stiff, her hands clutching the table.

Patel shifted uncomfortably, her fingers tapping her tablet, her eyes dancing between Catherine and Emily. "What about authoritarian regimes? If this leaks, they could use it to profile populations. We'd be complicit." Her voice trembled, her shoulders hunching as she glanced at Kessler, who remained impassive.

The room fell silent. Emily seized the moment, her voice fierce, her hands gesturing passionately. "That's my point. This isn't about profit. It's about responsibility. We've spent years unlocking this truth—two years, one to find the sequence, another to validate it across species. We owe the world caution, not exploitation."

Beyer scoffed, his face flushing deeper. "Responsibility doesn't pay returns, Dr. Harper. This is business, not an ethics seminar." His voice filled with disdain, his hands slamming the table for emphasis, sending a pen skittering.

Catherine's eyes flashed, her lips thinning as she shot back, "It's science, Herbert, not only business. Emily's concerns are valid. We're talking about rewriting human existence. Ignore that, and we're no better than the companies that tanked public trust in biotech." She pointed at the screen's data with trembling hands, her voice shaking with conviction.

Kessler raised a hand, his eyes boring into Emily. "Enough, Dr. Harper. Your passion is commendable, but vision drives progress. We'll fund further research and set a reasonable time-line for public release, but not two years. As BioSpark's lead, you'll head the next phase. I expect a commercialization plan in six months. Understood?"

Emily's nails dug into her palms, her heart racing, her face flushed with defiance. "Understood," she said, her voice even despite her gut churning. She glanced at Catherine, who gave a subtle nod, her lips pressed into a tight line.

The executives filed out, their murmurs trailing. Carver clapped Kessler's shoulder, his grin wide. Holt scribbled furiously, his excitement palpable. Patel lingered, her brow still furrowed, her hands clutching her tablet as if for comfort. Catherine approached Emily, her hand resting gently on her arm. "You did well, Emily," she whispered, her voice low and steady. "This fight's only beginning. I'll back you—whatever it takes to keep this from becoming a weapon." Her eyes held a fierce resolve, her grip firm but warm.

Kessler lingered by the door, his Patek Philippe watch glinting as he adjusted his cufflinks. "You're playing a high-stakes game now, Emily," he said, his tone almost paternal, his smile cold. "This could make your career or end it. Tread carefully."

Emily met his gaze, her chin lifting, her eyes unflinching. "I'm not posturing, Mr. Kessler. I'm resisting a premature release. Once the genie's out, we can't put it back in the bottle." Her voice was firm, her hands still now, fueled by Catherine's support.

He let out a dry, humorless chuckle and then left without saying anything else. Emily stood alone with Catherine, the harbor's gray expanse stretching beyond the windows.

Catherine squeezed her arm again. "We'll do the right thing, Emily. Together."

Emily nodded, her resolve hardening, but the discovery felt like a cloud darkening the future.

Back in the lab, Emily sank into her chair, the sequencers' noise a faint comfort. The clock read 7:45 p.m. Tyler would be in the cafeteria, likely nursing a coffee and streaming a Bruins game on his phone. She texted him to meet her at home and order dinner. She still had a few things to wrap up this evening.

Emily rubbed her temples, the boardroom's tension lingering. James's urgency had been unmistakable, his ambition a force that bent the boardroom to his will. But something else nagged at her—a flare in his eyes, a certainty that seemed personal. He and several of the board members had pushed for commercialization with a hunger that went beyond profit. Did they know more about the terminal gene than they let on? The thought sent chills down her spine.

Her computer terminal chimed, a notification flashing. She frowned, opening it to find a single line of text, no sender. "Truth is dangerous, Dr. Harper. Watch your step." Her breath caught, her fingers freezing on the keyboard. She glanced at the surveillance cameras, their red lights blinking like unflinching eyes. Paranoia surged, her pulse racing—a glitch, maybe, or her friend Anita's obnoxious prank. But after the boardroom, it felt like a warning.

She saved the message in a protected folder and locked her workstation, her hands trembling as she fumbled with the keyboard. The lab appeared smaller, the walls closing in, and the equipment's pulse became a low, ominous sound.

Emily reached for her cell phone, her fingers hesitating over Tyler's name. She needed his voice to calm her against the worry twisting in her gut. But as she put the phone to her ear, she caught the faint whir of a security camera adjusting its angle. Her breath hitched. *Are they watching me now?*

The lens seemed to stare, unblinking, tracking her every move. Heart pounding, she ended the call before it could connect. The screen went dark in her hand. She'd talk to Tyler at home, where the walls didn't feel alive with scrutiny.

Grabbing her coat, she slung it over her shoulders. She hurried to the lobby to catch a cab. Tyler's presence would calm her, his warmth a shelter against the storm brewing inside her—a storm fueled not just by the mysterious message but by the memory of James's clipped tone after the board meeting, his eyes avoiding hers as he'd dismissed her concerns with a curt wave.

Outside, Boston's Seaport glittered under a darkening sky, drones buzzing above the harbor. Emily sensed that the board meeting was only the beginning. The fight to protect the implications of the terminal gene might challenge her in ways she didn't want to imagine.

Chapter 2

What About Us

Emily eased the apartment door open, her arms heavy with a tote bag stuffed with BioSpark notepads and a tablet filled with data that haunted her.

The Jamaica Plain apartment was a warm, comfortable sanctuary against the sharp chill of late fall. The air carried the promising scent of brewed coffee and reheated pizza, remnants of her and Tyler's late-night talks in the kitchen. A balcony door was ajar, admitting a chilly breeze that stirred the bare branches of the community garden below, their skeletal silhouettes swaying against a dark sky.

"Is that you, Doc?" Tyler's gravelly voice called from the kitchen as she kicked the entry door closed with one foot.

"No, it's the maid," she said with a slight grin.

She set her bag down. Her chestnut hair, freed from its lab bun, fell in loose waves around her freckled face. She swapped her blazer for a faded Harvard hoodie hanging by the door, its worn fabric wrapping around her like a warm hug after a stressful day. She tugged on her jeans, her tortoiseshell glasses slipping down her nose.

The living room unfolded in cozy disarray: a lumpy couch sagged under a patchwork quilt, and a bookshelf overflowed with dog-eared novels, medical journals, and engineering manuals. Framed photos from their spring engagement party beamed from the walls, capturing her and Tyler mid-laugh under Cape Cod sunlight. Potted plants, their leaves curling in the fall air, crowded the windowsill, their green fading to amber. Tyler's field jacket was tossed over a chair in the corner, a relic of his years in the military.

She'd had some time in the taxi to decompress before getting home. However, the clash at the board meeting and a cryptic terminal message—*Truth is dangerous*—lingered. She wanted Tyler's perspective, but the terminal gene's implications felt like a ticking bomb, too volatile to share haphazardly.

"Em, you're letting the cold in," Tyler shouted from the small kitchen with playful chiding. He leaned against the counter, his muscular frame relaxed, scrolling through a sports betting app on his phone. His Red Sox cap tilted back, revealing the scar above his eyebrow. A black T-shirt, snug over his broad shoulders, showed a bit of his brother's commemorative tattoo. The smell of pizza wafted from an open box, its greasy warmth reminding her she had eaten nothing since breakfast.

Emily grinned, nudging the balcony door shut with her hip. "And you're letting the pizza get cold, chef," she quipped, despite the mix of dread and hunger knotting her stomach. She crossed the creaking floorboards and leaned against the counter beside him, her tired eyes catching the kitchen's soft glow. "Busy day saving the world from shoddy code?"

He leaned back against the counter. "Another day keeping drones from crashing into Fenway." His free hand absentmindedly brushed the dog-eared notebook on the table. "Saw this scrappy dog today," he added, a grin tugging at his raised eyebrow. "Looked ready to steal a hot dog from a vendor. The kid called him Rocket, which seemed like a perfect name. Gotta add him to the collection." His love of dogs always softened his rough edges. Their shared dream of a golden retriever—a big, goofy dog for the house they'd buy once they escaped their no-pet apartment—hovered unspoken between them.

Tyler chuckled, sliding a slice of pepperoni pizza onto a plate for her. His gaze coaxed her to let him in. He didn't push, but the way he tilted his head said he knew something was eating at her.

"You look like you've been through a meat grinder." His eyes searched her face, catching the tension in her expression. "The board meeting went okay?"

Tyler knew BioSpark was a high-stakes genetic project, her obsession as team leader for a couple of years, but she'd kept the genetic details confidential, a truth too heavy for their six-month-old engagement. She took the plate, her fingers brushing his calloused ones, and slowly chewed a bite of lukewarm pizza, buying time.

"Okay is a nice way to describe it," she said, her gaze flicking to the vacation photo on the fridge—a candid from their Bahamas trip, laughing as Tyler splashed her with seawater. "We completed something huge today, Ty. Something that's got me rethinking everything."

Tyler's chuckle faded, his hand pausing on his phone. "Rethinking how? You're not cooking up mutant viruses, are you? Because my time in the Army didn't fully prepare me for a zombie apocalypse." His grin was lopsided, but his eyes were serious, probing for the reason behind her discomfort.

Emily's lips twitched, a reluctant smile breaking through. "No zombies. Questions I don't have answers for." She set the plate down, her fingers tightening around the counter's edge. She wanted to spill it all—the terminal gene's precision, the board's greed, the warning message—but fear of disrupting their plans for a house, maybe kids, made her pause. "Ever think about how much we should know about what's coming?"

Tyler tilted his head, his cap casting a shadow across his face. "That's a loaded one, Doc. You trying to drop a bomb on me?"

She sighed, brushing a lock of hair behind her ear, and forced a lighter tone. "Not a bomb. BioSpark's stirring up big ethical questions, the kind that makes you wonder what truth's worth." Her necklace glinted as she shifted, her overthinking spiraling. Leading BioSpark had been her crucible, a year of late nights and data wars, but now the kill switch was a black box, and she was its reluctant keeper.

Tyler watched her, his eyes softening. "You're doing that thing where your brain's running a marathon, and I'm still back at the starting line. You don't have to carry it alone, you know." He set his phone down, leaning closer, his presence calming the storm of her thoughts.

Emily forced a smile, her heart racing. "I know. There's a lot, and I'll sort it out eventually. You'll get the full scoop soon, promise." She nudged his arm, her easy banter pushing through the anxiety. "For now, let's pretend you're a Michelin-star chef and not a pizza reheater."

He laughed, the sound easing the tension. "Fair enough, but I'm holding you to that scoop." He grabbed another slice, his eyes lingering on her, sensing a deeper conversation she wasn't sharing.

Emily marched into the living room, her steps making the floorboards creak. The community garden outside, with its bare trees swaying in the wind, mirrored her inner turmoil. The golden glow of a table lamp cast shadows on the cluttered bookshelf, where a photo of them at a friend's wedding—her in a sundress, Tyler's arm around her—reminded her of their dreams.

Since then, leading her work had consumed her, and her team's dogged pursuit of genetic truths had brought her to a historic moment. The terminal gene was the highlight of her career, but its implications—pandemonium, personal loss—were a maze she was tired of navigating alone. Could she and Tyler face it without losing the future they'd planned?

Tyler followed, his outline filling the balcony doorway, his jaw catching the lamplight. "You're going to wear a trench in the floor," he said, half-teasing, half-concerned. "This break-through's more than lab stuff. What's got you so wired? Did James undercut you at the board meeting again?"

She stopped pacing, her eyes meeting his, their green-gold flecks shifting. Her desire to open up to Tyler warred with caution, but he deserved some truth. "It's a gene sequence," she said finally. "Every living thing has one. It predicts lifespans with…terrifying precision. Down to the second." She crossed her arms, her hoodie's sleeves slipping to reveal chemical stains on her wrists, badges of her long battle with BioSpark's tissue samples.

Tyler's mouth tightened into a grimace, his hand gripping the doorframe. "You're saying you've got a stopwatch to the end? Like, you could know exactly when someone's clock is running out?"

She nodded, her heart pounding. "Yeah. If this gets out, it could mean chaos—people panicking, governments playing God. I'm not sure what it means for regular people. For us."

Her freckles stood out against her pale skin, her glasses glinting as she shifted. The terminal gene loomed, overshad-owing the happiness she felt about their engagement and dreams of a life beyond the thin walls of this apartment.

Tyler moved closer, his heavy steps thudding on the wooden floor. "Us?" he repeated, his voice low, almost a growl. "You're telling me we could know when we…" A flicker of dread that mirrored her own appeared. "You're thinking about looking at our genes, aren't you?"

Emily's throat tightened, her overthinking spiraling. "I don't know," she admitted, pacing again, her gaze shifting to her backpack. "I'm the team leader, Ty. BioSpark's been my life for almost two years—late nights, endless data, my team counting on me. Now we've got this, and I can't stop wondering what it means for us. Our plans, our life." She stopped, her voice trembling. "What if we could know?"

Tyler ran a hand through his short hair, his Red Sox cap tilting further. "Know when our clock is going to stop? You want that hanging over us? Over our wedding, our future?"

She moved to the kitchen, needing space, and stood against the stove where the coffee mugs sat, now cold. "I don't know," she said, her voice rising with stubbornness. "Part of me—the scientist who's poured everything into this project—wants to understand it. To know. But the rest of me…" She glanced at the engagement photo again, fighting back tears that were forming. "We're building a life, Ty. What if knowing tears it apart? What if one of us has years, and the other…"

Tyler followed her into the kitchen, grabbing a mug, his tattoo standing out as he gripped it. "You're asking me to bet our future on a test that might say we've got no time left," he said, his voice strained. "I've seen more than enough death, Emily. I don't need the test results to tell me how to live." His knuckles whitened, his past a shadow in his eyes.

Her stubbornness flared. Her voice was sharp. "And I don't want to live a lie! I've spent years leading this project. I can't pretend this information doesn't exist." The tension was palpable as she paced the kitchen. "What if knowing helps us? We could plan better and prioritize what matters—our wedding and our family. Isn't that worth something?"

Tyler set the mug down hard, coffee spilling onto the counter. "Worth what? The knowledge that we might only have one month left to live? Or do you already know?" His eyes flashed, his calm shattering. "Can we go back to picking out paint colors after that? This isn't science. It's a gut punch." His large body filled the small kitchen as he turned, his dark eyes seeming to drink in the light.

Emily's chest ached. "I don't have answers, Ty!" she snapped, her hands balling into fists. "I'm supposed to, as team leader, as the one who pushed to solve this damn riddle. But all I've got are questions, and they're tearing me apart! Pretending it doesn't exist feels like lying."

Tyler's shoulders slumped, his eyes softening with a vulnerability he rarely showed. "You're not lying to me," he said quietly, stepping closer. "You're scared, same as me. This could break what we've got, and I'm not ready to risk that."

Emily's throat burned; her emotions were overwhelming her. She saw the fear in his eyes, the same fear that kept her awake nights. Replaying the tension of the board meeting, the cryptic message. *Truth is dangerous.* She wanted to tell him about it, to share the paranoia creeping into her bones, but the words stuck. "I'm not asking for a decision tonight," she said. "I... I can't stop thinking about it. What will it mean for you and me, for everyone?" She leaned against the counter, her heart heavy.

Tyler nodded and joined her at the counter, his hip gently brushing her arm. "Fair enough," he said, a faint grin returning to his face. "Let's not jump into the deep end yet, okay? We've got time to figure this out." He paused, his grin spreading wider. "Besides, I'm not ready to trade next week's birthday bash for a funeral."

She laughed, a genuine sound that eased the tension, and nudged his shoulder. "Deal. No funeral planning before your birthday." Her mind kept racing. The importance of the gene results cast a pall over their engagement and their dreams of a life free from the apartment's peeling walls. Leading BioSpark had taught her to seek the truth, but this truth threatened everything—her career, love, and sense of self.

They wandered onto the porch, the garden's wilted plants a stark backdrop under the moonlight. Emily wrapped her hoodie tighter, needing the warmth and comfort. Tyler stood close, his field jacket unzipped, the intensity in his eyes softened in the dim light. He pulled her into his arms, his warmth a calming influence, and she leaned into him, her heart racing.

"We're tougher than this, right?" he murmured, his breath warm against her neck, his voice filled with concern.

"Yeah," she said, her voice trembling. "But it's one hell of a test." The moment was tender, their love a barrier holding back the fear. She wanted to believe they could face the kill switch together, but the weight of her silence—about the cryptic warning message, about BioSpark's stakes—gnawed at her. Leading the project meant revealing life-changing truths, but hiding them from Tyler felt like a breach of their commitment to build a life together.

Tyler kissed her forehead, his humor rising through the tension. "If I can survive your overthinking, I can handle anything," he teased as he pulled her back inside, the balcony door clicking shut.

Emily forced a brittle laugh, her voice catching as she and Tyler sank onto the couch. Her phone buzzed sharply in her pocket, a jolt that made her stomach twist. She glanced at the screen, and her heart slammed against her ribs. The message was stark, sender unknown. "Truth is a blade, Dr. Harper." Her breath hitched, an icy wave washing over her as her trembling fingers fumbled to hide the screen from Tyler.

He sprawled beside her, chuckling as he turned on the TV, completely unaware of the dread in her chest. The message was an escalation of the disquiet that had haunted her for weeks. In Helix's lab, she'd felt the oppression of unseen eyes, the hushed conversations that stopped when she entered a room.

This wasn't an accident; this message was deliberate. Her mind spiraled. *What do they want? And how much danger am I already in?*

"You good?" Tyler asked, his eyes narrowing as he caught her expression.

"Yes, work stuff," she lied, her voice tight, her cheeks coloring. She deleted the text but saved a screenshot, her mind circling.

Should I secretly analyze our genetic data to find out? The thought felt like a betrayal, yet the truth haunted her like a murky dream she wasn't sure she could escape. She'd spent a lot of time uncovering the truth in this project, but now it was personal—testing her love as much as her intellect.

Later, as Tyler dozed on the couch, his arm draped over his forehead, Emily stood alone in the living room, the lamp's glow dimmed. She stared at their Bahamas photo, her laughing face a distant memory before BioSpark's significance.

She stepped onto the balcony. Boston's traffic purred on. The terminal gene was her discovery and triumph, but its cost was also hers. She clutched her necklace, her parents' pride in her Harvard degree now a distant memory and wondered if the revelation of BioSpark was worth the cost of their dreams.

Chapter 3

Information and Ignorance

E mily's footsteps echoed through the open-plan lab at Helix Innovations as she walked across the white-tiled floor. A sterile thrum of sequencers and keyboards filled the space. A yellow sticky note waited on her workstation, its edges sharp against the stainless steel. "James would like to see you in his office at 8 a.m." She glanced at her smartwatch—7:50. Her pulse quickened; a jolt of adrenaline tied to last night's mysterious message. "Truth is a blade, Dr. Harper."

She hadn't even logged onto her computer. This couldn't be good. Yesterday's board meeting had been a battleground—James Kessler's forceful voice slicing through her presentation, drowning her appeal for caution. Most of the board had nodded along with him, their eyes gleaming with visions of profit, dismissing her warnings about the terminal gene's dangers—psychological collapse, societal upheaval, authoritarian exploitation—as alarmist. His summons now felt like a trap, and her stomach churned at the thought of facing him in his office.

Emily's closest friend and colleague, Anita Gupta, looked up from her desk across the lab, her oversized sweater clashing with the office's minimalist decor. Her coffee mug, emblazoned with "Keep calm and question everything," steamed faintly. Anita's dark curls formed a frizzy halo, and her brown eyes sparked with concern as she scrunched her face.

She and Emily had bonded as undergrads at Harvard, dissecting genetic code by day and hiking the White Mountains on weekends, their shared love for problem-solving, ciphers, and nature forging a friendship that weathered late-night study sessions and now corporate pressures. Anita's quick wit and never-ending curiosity had made her the BioSpark team's data analysis lead. Her knack for spotting patterns in genetic sequences was crucial to identifying the kill switch.

"How did the board meeting go?" Anita asked, leaning forward, her elbows propped on a thick stack of printouts.

Emily forced a tight smile, her finger flicking the sticky note. "I'll tell you when I get back. Got a meeting in Kessler's office right now."

Anita's bushy eyebrows shot up, her hands pausing mid-gesture over her keyboard. "In the lair? Good luck." Her lips pursed as she tilted her head, a gesture Emily knew meant she was already analyzing the implications.

Emily chuckled at the inside joke she shared with her team, who swore James's penthouse office, with its floor-to-ceiling windows and elaborate decor, reminded them of a Bond villain's.

Across the lab, two other BioSpark team members glanced up from their stations. Dr. Javier Morales, a lanky biochemist with a perpetual five o'clock shadow, adjusted his noise-canceling headphones, his dark eyes narrowing with curiosity. Javier's expertise in protein interactions had been key to understanding the terminal gene's resistance to CRISPR edits, his meticulous experiments ruling out false positives. He gave Emily a quick nod, his fingers tapping nervously on his desk, a silent question in his gaze.

Nearby, Dr. Li Wei, a petite computational biologist with an eye for neon sneakers, peered over her dual monitors, her short black hair tucked behind her ears. Wei's algorithms had sifted through trillions of genetic data points to pinpoint the gene, and her quiet intensity was a cornerstone of the team's success. She pushed her thick glasses up her nose, her brow furrowing as she caught Emily's eye.

"Don't let Kessler steamroll you," Wei said softly, her fingers twitching, betraying her tension. Nodding in agreement, Javier leaned back in his chair, tense, his headphones now around his neck.

"Thanks, guys," Emily said as she drew strength from her team's support. Anita crossed the lab in a few quick, purposeful strides, similar to their recent hike, a journey marked by talks about fate, free will, and the benefits of granola. She squeezed Emily's shoulder, her grip firm, their eyes locking.

"You've got this," Anita whispered as she stared at a ceiling-mounted camera. "Whatever he throws at you, we'll support you. Watch your back, okay?" She smirked.

Emily nodded, her throat tightening as she left the lab, the door hissing shut behind her. She stepped into the hallway, where the dim morning light of late fall filtered through the windows, casting an elongated, wavering darkness across the polished tiles.

Beyond the glass, Boston Harbor roiled, its gray waves crashing against the docks under a sky heavy with brooding storm clouds.

The elevator opened, revealing a sleek cocoon of steel and glass. Emily stepped inside, her white blazer crisp, its tailored lines a nod to professionalism, but her faded jeans and scuffed hiking boots a quiet rebellion against Seaport District's corporate dress code. She clutched her tablet, its screen filled with BioSpark's intricate data—years of research, millions of dollars, a genetic sequence mapped with chilling precision. Her cheeks were taut, her eyes sharp behind thick glasses, her necklace tucked beneath her blouse.

The elevator whirred, its soft chime marking each passing floor—twelfth, fourteenth, fifteenth. Emily's mind replayed the board meeting: James's persistent pressure, his tailored suit impeccable, his voice dominating the discussion. "The market demands progress, Dr. Harper. We can't afford hypotheticals." Her team's months of analyses—panic scenarios, governments weaponizing BioSpark, individuals crumbling under their mortality—had been brushed off.

BioSpark was a scientific triumph, but its implications were incredibly complex. Emily's team had often pulled all-nighters in the lab, their trust in her leadership absolute. James's agenda threatened to unravel their work, turning their breakthrough into a commodity. She hadn't had enough coffee for a combative meeting this early.

The elevator chimed—penthouse floor. She shifted her stance, her tablet heavy in her hands. The elevator doors slid open, revealing a corridor of frosted glass and muted opulence. She adjusted her glasses, squared her shoulders, and entered the corridor. The air was cooler, the silence heavier, and James's executive suite dominated the far end, its etched Helix logo glinting like a predator's eye. The cream-colored carpet muted the sound of her boots as she approached the reception desk, where Carla, James's secretary, sat typing with mechanical precision.

Usually warm, quick with a smile or a quip about the lab's bitter coffee, Carla was distant today, her lips pursed, her eyes fixed on her screen. Her auburn hair was pinned tightly, and her navy blazer buttoned to the collar as if armoring herself against the day's pressure.

James's raised voice leaked through the suite's glass door, indistinct but crackling with irritation. Emily grimaced, her stubborn streak flaring. Something was wrong, and Carla's demeanor was a glaring red flag.

"Morning, Carla," Emily said, forcing a casual tone, her wide smile concealing her anxiety. She leaned against the desk, her tablet tucked under her arm. "Sounds like James is already warming up for his meeting with me. Bad coffee or bad news?"

Carla's fingers paused, her gaze flicking up briefly, cool and guarded. "He's on a call," she said, her voice clipped, stripped of its usual warmth. "He's expecting you. Go on in." She resumed typing, her nails clicking rhythmically, dismissing Emily with a subtle tilt of her head. The pulsing light above her desk buzzed faintly, an unusual sound in the otherwise pristine space.

Emily's brow furrowed. Carla's detachment was new, a fracture in their usual light-hearted banter. She glanced at the glass door, James's voice rising again, as he barked something about an "unacceptable delay." Her fingers tightened around her tablet, the potential of another strained interaction with James worrying her.

"Everything okay?" she pressed Carla, her voice low, probing. "You seem…quieter than usual."

Carla's eyes met hers, a flash of something—worry, perhaps—before shuttering. "A busy morning, Dr. Harper." She offered a tight smile, her hands stilling. "He's waiting." The dismissal was final, but the tension in her posture spoke louder than words.

Emily glimpsed Carla's screen, which featured a calendar with red-flagged meetings, one labeled "URGENT," before Carla angled it away, her movements stiff.

Emily nodded, her smile thinning, her anxiety increasing. James's raised voice dropped abruptly, replaced by an indistinct murmur, as if he'd sensed her presence. She straightened and moved toward the door, her eyes narrowing with determination. Carla's behavior, the odd messages, and the number of drones recently flitting around the building made it feel as if the world had shifted since the board meeting. Whatever awaited inside James's office, she would confront it head-on, holding tight to her principles.

She pushed through the glass door, stepping into James's executive suite, a realm of opulence that dwarfed the laboratory's sterile functionality. Polished mahogany furniture gleamed under the diffused morning light, the desk a monolithic centerpiece carved with subtle Helix motifs. A glass wall framed the harbor's churning gray expanse, waves crashing against Seaport's edge. A sleek bar sparkled with crystal decanters, their amber contents catching the light, and abstract art—angular, exorbitant—adorned the walls, its sharp lines mimicking the tension in the air.

A biometric-locked testing device sat on James's desk, its dark screen mirroring Emily's anxiety. The air carried hints of leather and cologne, tinged with a faint whiskey note. However, she couldn't tell if it was the open decanters or her imagination conjuring a hint of whiskey on James's breath. Another faint flicker from the ceiling light added an unnerving edge, and a distant drone hum passing by the window wove an eerie thread through the scene.

James stood by the bar, pouring coffee from a silver carafe, his gray suit tailored to match the storm-heavy clouds outside. His salt-and-pepper hair was impeccable, his eyes sharp behind designer glasses, and his expensive watch glinted as he adjusted the bezel, a nervous tic betraying his obsession with time.

At fifty, he exuded privilege, his charisma a seductive current honed by years of corporate manipulation. His faint chin scar, barely visible in the muted light, hinted at a past less pure than his current image.

"Dr. Harper, you look like you've been burning the midnight oil," he said smoothly, a smile dawning as he set the carafe down. "Coffee to fuel the crusade?"

Emily's dry humor surfaced, and her return jab was sharp. "I'll pass. Lab coffee's bad enough without the corporate overhead." She set her tablet on a leather chair, its presence a reminder of BioSpark's data, and stood stiffly, ignoring the offered cup. "You called me up here, James. Let's not waste time on chitchat."

James's smile tightened, his eyes narrowing slightly, a predator sizing up prey. "Always cutting to the chase. It's why you're Helix's little star." He gestured to a chair, his hand lingering in the air, but Emily remained standing by the windows, the shifting scene a restless backdrop to her courage. "Yesterday's meeting was more spirited than it needed to be with such superb news. Let's align on your role for the next stage of BioSpark."

Her muscles clenched, her agitation stirring. "Until my role changes, I lead BioSpark. We unlocked the secret of the terminal gene, and I'll put together the risk analysis as you asked. But I'm telling you, rushing it to market is a disaster waiting to happen."

She leaned against the desk's edge. "We need years to study its impact—psychological fallout, societal risks, authoritarian misuse. Last night, you agreed to six months. That's not enough time to conduct the due diligence we'll need."

James sat at his desk, his posture relaxed but menacing, his watch glinting in the light as he adjusted it again. "The market doesn't pause for caution, Emily," he said, patronizing, dropping her title with deliberate ease. "I spoke with key board members late last night. We've revised the timeline. You have three months to finish the risk and commercialization plan. Profit drives progress."

Emily's stomach lurched, her resistance flaring like a spark in dry grass. "Three months? That's beyond reckless, James. I already told you six months was too short." She straightened, her glasses slipping slightly as she gestured. "This isn't some new social media app—it's life and death. People could lose their minds knowing their exact end date. You're betting on panic for a payout."

He leaned back, his fingers steepled, a smirk curling his lips. "Panic is a catalyst. People crave certainty—life plans, insurance models, tailored legacies. Helix will provide that. Your idealism is inspiring, but it's not practical." His eyes flicked to the biometric tablet, a fleeting glance that deepened her agitation, the twitching ceiling light pulsing faintly above.

Her remark sliced through the tension. "Inspiring? Try sensible. Someone's got to stop this from becoming an episode of *The Twilight Zone*." She crossed her arms, her blazer creasing. "Bio-Spark's my team. We've poured two years into this—late nights, endless data, my people trusting me to get it right. I won't let you twist all the careful research into a Wall Street lottery."

James's smirk faded, his eyes hardening like flint. "You're valuable, Emily, but don't overestimate your influence." He stood adjusting his watch with a deliberate flick. "I've taken steps to grasp the gene's potential from a personal perspective. I've seen my timeline."

Emily froze, her breath catching, her colored cheeks stark against her pale skin. "You what?" she asked, shocked. "You ran a test to determine the date of your kill switch?" Her glasses slipped further, and she pushed them up, her mind racing. "That's a conflict of interest. You're steering this company, pushing for profit, and now you have a personal stake too?"

He shrugged, his tone infuriatingly casual, the gold on his watch catching the cold light. "It's leadership. I needed to understand the information we're offering the world. The results are enlightening." His eyes were evasive, darting to the harbor, avoiding her intense gaze.

"Imagine a world where we could predict and prevent systemic health crises. BioSpark could save millions, not simply line pockets. How much is that worth?" He finished with a smug nod, yet the faint crease in his brow hinted at a more profound conviction, as if he genuinely believed this technology could rewrite humanity's future, even if his methods felt like betrayal.

Emily's shock emboldened her. "Worth? You're talking about people's lives, not stock options about to expire." She moved toward his desk, her footsteps echoing, her glasses catching the light. "What did your test show, James? If you're deciding based on your timeline, that's not leadership—it's bias. Tell me your date."

His charm returned, velvet layered over iron. "That's private, Dr. Harper. Let's keep our eyes on the horizon." He moved to the bar, pouring himself a coffee. The pulsing light buzzed again, a sound she was starting to think was a surveillance cue.

Emily's response was venomous. "Horizon? You mean your bonus plan? Or are you dodging because your clock's ticking faster than you'd like?" Her suspicion of a conflict of interest surged, her mind flashing to the disappearing messages, the lab's cameras, and Carla's sudden aloofness. Was James's test a calculated move, or was he grappling with his mortality?

He turned, his eyes cold, his voice a low warning. "Tread carefully. You're playing a dangerous game." He set the coffee down, untouched, and leaned against the bar, the crystal decanters glinting behind him. "I think we should begin with a confidential test of our employees. It would give us real-world insight into how to optimize operations, health plans, and productivity models. It's the future. You'll draft the proposal. I want to review it with you and human resources by the end of the week."

Defiant, she howled, "You're peddling lives for profit, James. I won't be your pawn." She grabbed her tablet, her knuckles white. "BioSpark's discovery isn't yours to warp. I'll fight for doing what's ethical, not what lines Helix's pockets."

James stepped closer, his suit flawless, his condescension icy. "You're shaping the future, or you're in its path. Choose carefully, Emily." His wristwatch flashed as he adjusted it, a motion that screamed manipulation. "Don't make enemies you can't outrun."

Outside James's office, Emily paused in the corridor, Seaport's glass towers looming under a slate-colored sky. Her eyes were haunted, her freckled face pale as she gripped her device. James's self-testing was a betrayal, his evasiveness a signal of deeper motives—greed or fear of his own end. Testing employees without consent was a nightmarish overreach, violating everything BioSpark stood for.

A shiver ran down her spine. Was he manipulating her, or was his every move a carefully orchestrated deception? She was determined to protect the potential benefit of the terminal gene, even as the strain of James's intense influence pressed on her.

Chapter 4

Convergence

Emily strode into the lab, her sneakers squeaking, the echo of James's voice still burning. Her hands balled into fists, the hostility of their meeting clinging to her.

The office buzzed with the early-morning bustle—keyboards clacking, fresh coffee wafting from a mug on Anita's desk. Javier and Wei glanced up from their desks as she passed, their chatter faltering at the sight of her. Her usually controlled expression was a storm of worry, her eyes glassy, her lips forced thin.

"Hey, Emily, you okay?" Javier called from his workstation, leaning back in his chair, his brow creased. Wei turned, her curiosity piqued.

Emily forced a smile, brittle and unconvincing. "It's been a long morning already," she said, voice strained, waving off his concern as she quickened her pace. The data archives loomed ahead, a tiny sanctuary. She could feel their stares, the unspoken questions hanging in the air. What happened upstairs?

She slipped into the archives room, shutting the door with a soft click. The noise of the lab was muffled instantly. With a shaky breath, she leaned against the door and exhaled. James's ultimatum replayed—be ready to go public in three months or face consequences. She sank into her chair, staring at the cluttered cubicle, the burden of it all pressing down. The lab buzzed along outside, indifferent to the gathering storm.

Emily sat rigidly at a workstation, surrounded by BioSpark's data archives. Her eyes, sharp behind her glasses, reflected the bluish sheen of glowing screens. The air in the archives carried a subtle hint of old coffee and ozone, a testament to her team's long hours decoding the data behind the terminal gene. Scattered coffee cups and crumpled notepads littered the empty workstations, a functional mess that reflected the frenetic pace of their work.

Emily's fingers danced across the keyboard, decrypting files as she grappled with Helix's options. Exposing BioSpark's terminal gene within three months would dismantle the company's empire. The risks were staggering: lawsuits, whistleblower ostracism, and even personal danger. Her team's findings, buried in complex code, revealed a chilling potential for misuse —targeted shutdowns of therapies in vulnerable populations, a tool for control rather than healing.

Individuals might react with outrage, patients fearing their treatments could be weaponized, sparking protests or mass distrust in biotech. Others desperate for knowledge might defend BioSpark, prioritizing access above ethics. Governments could respond unpredictably—some might demand transparency, launching investigations to regulate such tech, while others, complicit or power-hungry, could suppress the information, branding Emily a traitor. International tensions could flare if nations suspect targeted misuse against their citizens, escalating to economic sanctions or worse.

Until that moment, Emily had always trusted the steadiness of her hands, honed by years in college and meticulous research at Helix. But her composure wavered as the screen flickered to life, revealing data she had spent the previous two years chasing. A chill crept up her spine. The impossible had materialized before her eyes.

The kill switch dates for several trees, marine life, and other long-lived organisms, typically scattered across years, decades, and centuries, were no longer disparate. Instead, they were converging, collapsing into a single, terrifying point: 2150, a mere one hundred and twenty years away. A global extinction event emerged, its certainty etched in vibrant red digits glowing against the black grid of the interface. Emily's palms grew clammy, sweat beading despite the lab's chill.

She blinked, hoping—praying—the numbers would shift, that the data were a glitch, a cruel anomaly. But they held firm. The significance of Earth's impending doom settled over her like a suffocating shroud. The archive, once a place of logic and control, felt claustrophobic. Emily's breath caught, her heart pounding as she grappled with the truth: time was running out.

How could the team have overlooked this convergence of data? It's understandable why it wasn't apparent in human samples, since no living person is expected to reach 120 years; the data wouldn't reflect such long lifespans. However, this didn't account for the samples from other sources. She was aware that many trees and other organisms have lifespans long enough to reveal premature termination if it had occurred in the data.

The server's noise drowned out her quiet gasp. She leaned forward, her white lab coat creasing, and reran the algorithm. Her mind churned, grappling with the implications. Was this an error? A miscalculation? But she'd built this system herself, triple-checked every line of code. Perhaps it was a function of insufficient data in the distant years. *Or had the data been manipulated?*

After months of checking and rechecking, she was confident that the data they'd analyzed were clean. But this pattern was undeniable. Emily's pulse quickened, her mind racing to process the enormity. She had expected a distant threat, perhaps one species or ecosystem at risk, but this was total. The absence of human samples in the distant years only deepened the horror—presumption filled the gap, painting a grim picture of global doom. One hundred twenty years.

What once were abstract graduate school debates between her and Anita on fate versus free will had become a stark, undeniable reality. The nagging feeling of inadequacy, rooted in her upbringing, chipped away at her confidence. Suppose she was mistaken? What if she raised the alarm and it was a terrible mistake?

She feverishly cross-referenced the anomaly by opening a second dataset. She moved her glasses back up her nose with trembling fingers after they'd slipped. Once more, the numbers were perfectly aligned, against all odds. She felt a knot in her stomach. Something had changed in the data, and she needed to find out what quickly.

The lab's corporate sheen—its pristine walls and innovative tech—felt like a mockery of life outside these walls. This data was the future, a void staring back at her. She needed to tell someone, but who? James, the CEO, might dismiss it to protect BioSpark's reputation and question her competence.

If yesterday's board meeting was any sign, the board would likely exploit the development, turning a crisis into a profit scheme. The growing fear of failure threatened to overcome her dedication to bringing the research to light.

"You okay, Emily?" Anita's concerned voice broke through. She stood a few feet away. Emily had been so focused on the data that she hadn't heard her enter the archives. Her frizzy curls shook as she tilted her head, her oversized sweater—a clash of turquoise and orange—defying the lab's aesthetic. The mug in her hand read, "My coffee is not an experiment." Her deep-brown eyes flashed with curiosity.

Emily smiled, her cheeks tight with the effort. "I need more coffee," she muttered. She tucked a strand of hair behind her ear, hoping the motion hid her nervousness.

Anita's eyes narrowed, her gaze piercing. "If you say so." She lingered, her fingers tapping on the table, as if waiting for Emily to change her mind. Unspoken questions charged the air between them. Anita's knack for spotting patterns in data or people made her a dangerous confidante. Emily turned back to her screen, her pulse spiking as she minimized the dataset. She couldn't tell Anita, not yet. The significance was too raw, too unformed.

Anita let out a soft sigh, a mixture of affection and frustration. "You know where to find me," she said over her shoulder as she retreated into the lab.

Leaning back, Emily cleaned her smudged glasses. She had to verify this conclusion to be certain before it overwhelmed her. But the thought of being wrong—standing alone with this assumption and failing—gnawed at her. A voice of self-doubt insisted she wasn't up to the challenge.

Yet the data called for action. The problem had preoccupied her for hours, and she needed a fresh viewpoint. Someone outside of Helix. Tyler's pragmatism and steadiness were what she needed. She'd tell him first, but not here. Before that, she needed to be more certain. The lab's activity pulsed on, a world still turning, unaware of the shadow on her screen.

Her phone buzzed softly in her pocket. A text from Tyler. "You up for late lunch and afternoon latte?"

She typed, "Meet me at the park in an hour. Need to talk." She hit send, a decision crystallizing. Tyler, with his engineer's logic, might not have answers, but he'd ground her.

The lab's clock ticked toward three o'clock, the light softening to a muted gold through the windows. Emily saved her work. The anomaly's weight followed her, a gloom she couldn't shake. She stretched, left the archives, and glanced at Anita, who was typing furiously, her curls bouncing with each keystroke.

Their eyes met briefly, Anita's gaze still questioning, and Emily looked away, her guilt visible. She was shutting out her friend, but the truth was a forbidden vault—once opened, it couldn't be undone.

Emily headed for the door with her coat in hand, beckoned by the chilly fall air beyond the glass. Tyler would be waiting in the park, his sketchpad and humor starkly contrasting the lab's pressure. She needed his perspective, even if it came with his blunt responses and a shaken worldview. The extinction anomaly was a question of fate, of humanity's place in a universe that might not care. As she stepped outside, the breeze carried the harbor's briny scent, and Emily's commitment to do something hardened, a quiet fire against the fear that she might fail—not for herself but everyone.

The park near Helix's office was a modest patch of green, its grass worn thin by foot traffic and fall chill. Emily stepped onto the uneven path, her bright-red coat a vivid contrast to the fading light. The late-afternoon sun hung low, casting long shadows across the benches and sparse trees. The distant harbor churned, its waves restless against the docks, their rhythmic crash mingling with traffic sounds. A chilly breeze tugged at her coat, carrying the briny scent of the ocean and a hint of an incoming storm. She felt overwhelmed by what she was about to reveal to Tyler.

Tyler sat hunched on a weathered bench, his broad shoulders bent over his sketchpad. As she drew near, his eyes darted upward, the faint scar above his brow glinting in the golden afternoon light. His rugged chinos and worn boots hinted at a down-to-earth nature, yet the pencil stub in his hand displayed a gentler touch, bringing a cartoonish-looking bulldog to life on the page. His attempt at a grin died as he saw her expression.

"You look like you've eaten some bad sushi," he said. He closed the sketchpad, setting it beside him, and handed her half his sandwich.

The cold seeped through Emily's jeans as she sat on the bench. Her cheeks were red from the walk. She heard leaves whispering, a gull calling faintly. After dodging Anita's questions and securing the data, she needed Tyler's insight, despite the risk of challenging his practical perspective.

"I found something else," she said as she ate the sandwich. "The terminal gene—it's not only predicting lifespans. All the dates...they're converging. One hundred twenty years from now, they stop. All of them."

Tyler's pencil stilled, his fingers tightening around it. "What do you mean?" His eyes narrowed, searching her face for a hint that she was hiding something.

"Everything living," she said, her eyes locking with his. "Every sequence, every model points to 2150. A global extinction event." Her palms were clammy again, the memory of the archive's sterile walls and glowing screens flooding back. She leaned in, her voice dropping to a whisper. "It's not a glitch, Tyler. I checked. It's real."

He set the pencil nub down. His expression grew taut. The bulldog forgotten, its playful lines at odds with the tension between them. The harbor's waves seemed louder now, their churn a reminder of time slipping away. "One hundred twenty years—that's everyone on Earth," he said, his voice low, almost a growl. "Not a city or a country, everyone."

Emily nodded, her throat tight. "I don't know who to tell." The confession felt like a betrayal of her team and of herself. Her fear of failure surged. "James might bury the revelation to protect Helix. The board...they'll turn the discovery into a patent race or a media circus. I don't trust them after the meeting yesterday."

Tyler leaned back, his back rigid against the bench. "We can't sit on this," he said, on edge. "This isn't some lab puzzle, Em. This is the end of the line. Everyone has a right to know. And soon." The constant pragmatism that defined him faltered, replaced by a look of uncertainty and doubt.

"I know," she said, "but what if they don't believe me? What if I'm wrong?" The "fate versus free will" question gnawed at her. If the kill switch was destiny, what was the point of fighting? Yet the thought of doing nothing—of letting humanity slide unknowingly toward oblivion—was unbearable. She brushed a windblown strand of hair out of her eyes as her hand extended toward his.

Tyler's hand twitched, as if he wanted to reach for her but didn't. "You built that system. That's not a mistake that you'd make." He glanced at the harbor, where the waves glittered like shattered glass. "But you can't carry this alone. We need a plan."

Despite her fear, Emily's determination grew stronger. "A plan for what? Telling the world? Starting a panic?" She gestured toward Boston's towers, their glass facades reflecting the dying sun. "The second this gets out, it's not ours anymore. They'll twist it—governments, corporations, whoever's got the most money."

He rubbed his jaw, the faint stubble rasping under his fingers. "Then we find someone who won't. Someone who'll listen." His practicality was fraying, the soldier in him grasping for action but finding no obvious target. "What about Anita? Have you talked to her about this? She's sharp."

Emily shook her head, the memory of Anita's probing eyes in the lab stinging. "She's too close to the project. If I tell her, she'll start digging, and I'm not ready for that."

Emily trusted Anita's unwavering loyalty, but her inquisitiveness threatened to jeopardize everything before she was certain of her conclusions.

Tyler's brow furrowed. "You're cutting her out? That's not like you." His eyes softened, searching hers. "You don't have to do this alone, Emily."

That didn't ease the knot in her chest. "I know," she said

under her breath. "That's why I'm telling you, but I don't know what comes next or how to fix this."

He leaned forward, elbows on his knees, the sketchpad sliding slightly on the bench. "We aren't going to fix it today," he said, his voice steadying, though his eyes betrayed his restlessness. "We start at the beginning. First, verify the data again. I'll think about who we can trust—someone outside BioSpark. But we need to act soon. Don't wait for it to bury us."

Though she nodded, her apprehension about failing tangled with the growing fear that she was being watched. She leaned closer to Tyler. "I think talking to someone from outside Helix is a good idea. Since the board meeting, I've had an eerie feeling someone's watching me in the lab," she said. "Odd messages keep showing up, like I'm under surveillance. It could be a glitch, but I suspect James has something to do with it."

Tyler's eyes narrowed. "That's pretty strange, but it seems like something Kessler would do. I've told you that I don't trust him."

She added, "I know, but he's still my boss. I'll let you know if I get another message. For now, I'll do more digging into the data."

Tyler's lips quirked, a ghost of his usual levity. "You're the boss, Doctor Harper." But there was no laughter in his eyes. He grabbed his sketchpad and tucked it under his arm as the breeze picked up, signaling the first warning of the approaching storm.

Emily stood, smoothing her coat, her eyes scanning the horizon. The harbor's waves churned on. As they returned to the office, the fading sunlight cast their shadows long and thin—a partnership forged against a ticking clock.

Chapter 5

Days of Dread

The heavy glass door of the lab swung inward as Emily pushed through, her shoes emitting a quiet squeak on the polished floor. Her cheeks flushed from the crisp park air, and a faint smile of relief lingered as she dropped her bag beside her desk. The late-afternoon light bled through the tinted windows of the BioSpark lab, casting lengthy shapes across her cluttered workstation.

Anita, perched on a nearby stool, looked up from her tablet, noticing the change in Emily's mood. "Out gallivanting again, Harper?" Anita teased, her voice cutting through the noise of the servers, their cooling fans emitting a faint ozone scent that mingled with the bitterness of stale coffee.

Emily rolled her eyes, settling into her chair. "I grabbed some fresh air at the park and shared a latte and half a sandwich with Tyler."

Anita's grin grew wider, her stylus tapping the tablet with a knowing rhythm. "Aww, lovebirds..." she teased, leaning forward. Emily waved her off, but the blush in her cheeks darkened as she turned to her screen.

Emily's desk, a chaotic island in the high-tech sprawl, over-flowed with notepads scrawled with genetic sequences, tangled cables, and a half-empty mug emblazoned with a faded double helix. Her screen glowed with cascading data—strings of nucleotides pulsing—but her eyes, straining behind her tortoise-shell glasses, fixed on something else entirely.

A message had flashed onto her terminal, unbidden, its bold, white text searing against the dark interface. "Eyes on you." The message lingered for a heartbeat before vanishing, leaving only the soft click of keyboards and the distant whir of machinery. Emily's breath caught, her cheeks paling as her fingers froze above the keys.

She moved her glasses up her forehead, a nervous gesture, and drew nearer, as if getting closer would help her understand the message. Her pulse thrummed in her ears, louder than the lab's background noise. Was it a prank or something worse? Was someone watching her?

The building, Helix Innovation's gleaming stronghold in Boston's Seaport, had always felt like a second skin to Emily. Its sterile corridors and advanced technology provided a backdrop to her unstoppable drive to understand the mysteries of genet-ics. But now the familiar messiness of her workstation felt threatening. She scanned the lab, its rows of glowing monitors and equipment stretching into the dimness.

Javier, perpetually disheveled, hunched at a nearby station, his headphones bobbing slightly as he typed. Across the room, Li Wei's neon sneakers peeked out from under her desk, her thick glasses reflecting the blue glow of her screen as she murmured silently to her algorithms. Both of them failed to notice Emily's sudden attentiveness, but their presence troubled her, intensifying the question eating away at her. *Who can I really trust?*

Emily's fingers flew across the keyboard, expertly unraveling the message's digital footprint through the dense weave of system logs. Her genetics background at Harvard sparked a deeper obsession with cybersecurity—one she'd sharpened with Anita through rigorous advanced courses and her relentless dives into ethical hacking challenges and penetration testing. Spotting the internal address was child's play for her. Someone within Helix's network had sent it.

She quickly settled on James Kessler, whose polished demeanor and tailored suits masked a knack for evasion. He had access to the system's core, didn't he? And his cryptic comments at this morning's meeting, vague allusions to "oversight" and "necessary measures," had left a bitter taste. She recalled the glimmer of guilt in his graying eyes when she'd asked him about the terminal gene project's new timeline. Was he watching her, testing her loyalty?

The lab's pulsing fluorescent lights buzzed overhead, casting shadows that danced across her desk. Emily's glasses glinted faintly as she shifted uneasily in her chair. She typed faster, her search yielding only dead ends—encrypted logs and rerouted signals. The message was a ghost, designed to taunt.

Her paranoia surged, a rising tide that threatened to drown her in anxiety. She couldn't afford to be distracted, not with the project teetering on the edge of commercialization or catastrophe. And now she was sure that someone was watching.

A silhouette fell across her desk, and Emily flinched, her glasses slipping down her nose. Anita hovered over her, her frizzy curls barely tamed by a loose bun. Her colorful sweater clashed with the muted grays of the lab, and her favorite mug, proclaiming, "Keep calm and question everything," dangled from one hand. Studying Emily's tense posture, her usually wide eyes grew narrow.

"You're jumpy today," Anita said with concern. She leaned against an equipment rack, the thrum of the equipment vibrating through her body. "Everything okay, or too much caffeine again?"

Emily forced a smile, her lips tight. "There's a glitch in my computer," she said as she minimized her screen. The lie tasted sour, but Anita's intuition was sharp, and her questions were too probing. Emily didn't want to let her know there was a problem —not yet.

Anita tilted her head, her curls bouncing slightly. "Glitches rarely make you wince like that." She sipped her coffee, the steam curling around her face. "You've been off since you got back from your meeting with Kessler this morning. Spill it. Please don't tell me there's trouble in paradise."

Anita's perceptiveness, usually a comfort, now felt like a spotlight. She glanced at Javier, who had pulled off his head-phones, his dark eyes glancing toward them with a nervous edge. Wei too had paused, her sneakers still as she peered over her monitor. Were they all involved? No, that was absurd. They had been with her on this project. But the message, "Eyes on you," clung to her like a ghost.

"Everything's fine," Emily said with a forced chuckle. "Just the usual unrealistic push from the top floor. Deadlines, you know?"

Javier shifted, his stubble catching the light. "You sure?" he asked. "The pressure's different today. We're all feeling it."

Nodding, Wei reflected the lab's strained atmosphere in her quiet intensity. "The algorithms are stable," she said tersely, "but the pressure isn't. If something's up, Emily, you should tell us. You know we've got your back."

Her chest tightened. Their concern seemed genuine, but it only deepened her isolation. She couldn't tell them about the messages, about her discovery, about the convergence, not without certainty. Not when Kessler's presence loomed over every decision.

"I'm good," she said, "wrestling with some buggy code."

Anita's eyes lingered, unconvinced, but she didn't press further. She set her mug on Emily's desk, the ceramic clinking against a stray cable. "Don't be a martyr," she said with sincerity and irritation. She turned back to her workstation, leaving Emily alone with her secrets.

The lab's lights flickered again, a brief stutter that plunged the room into momentary darkness. Emily's screen blinked, and for a split-second she thought she saw the message again—but it was gone before she was sure. Her hands trembled as she rebooted her terminal. At the moment, she didn't trust the system or her instincts.

With her computer back up, she launched a secure chat and typed to Tyler, "Working late. Need to talk about the issue. Call me at seven."

His reply came instantly, terse and without his usual attempt at a pun. "You and your cryptic vibes. I'll call you then."

Emily closed the chat window, her eyes drifting to the row of server racks, their blinking lights like a thousand eyes. What was once her refuge, the Helix building, now felt like a tangle of treachery. And somewhere within it, James Kessler lurked.

The building's corridors stretched before Emily like a maze of polished anxiety, their sleek floors reflecting the erratic flashing of fluorescent lights overhead. Weak and gray, the late-afternoon sun struggled to penetrate the frosted glass.

The faint echo of Emily's sneakers amplified her isolation with each step. The chilling message from her terminal haunted her; she felt watched, the sender a ghost in the building's network. Her lab coat felt too tight. She adjusted her glasses, eyes scanning every shadow for a threat that refused to materialize.

Emily headed for the bland break room, hoping to collect herself and grab a bite. The corridor's lights cast strange reflections, making her eye twitch with every stutter of illumination. She passed a security camera, its red light blinking, and her stomach knotted. Was James behind the sudden attempt to scare her? The CEO's fleeting glances during their last meeting—his eyes darting away when she'd asked about project oversight—troubled her. BioSpark was too crucial for the company to risk, but the message hinted at manipulation. *Why?*

The break room door hissed open, and the fluorescent lights illuminated metal tables and a row of vending machines that whirred like distant machinery. A faint bleach smell hung in the air, mixing with the stale scent of burned popcorn.

She moved toward a vending machine offering a quick Powerbar to satisfy her hunger. Inserting a crumpled bill and punching in the code, she watched the machine spin and then drop a bar. She tore it open, then froze.

The wrapper's expiration date read December 2019—almost ten years past due. Her brow furrowed. She tossed the bar onto the table and tried again, selecting another. The machine groaned, spitting out a second bar dated March 2020. Emily's pulse quickened. She punched in another code then another, each bar clattering into the tray—January 2021, December 2029.

She lined up the wrappers on the table, staring at the dates in sequence: December 2019, the first whispers of the outbreak in Wuhan; March 2020, the WHO's pandemic declaration; January 2021, the vaccine's mass rollout. And then December 2029, next month, staring back like a promise—or a threat.

The alignment was too exact, reflecting the timeline pushed by lab-leak theorists—those who claimed it all began in a lab just like Helix's. Was this some insider's hidden clue, a sign pointing at something about to happen in the next few weeks? Or a coincidence, a sign of neglect?

The door hissed open, and Anita entered, her brown eyes instantly drawn to the discarded wrappers on the table. "What's with the Powerbar graveyard?"

Emily forced a laugh. "They're all expired, except one." She gestured at the wrappers, her voice tight. "You'd think someone would check these things."

Anita raised an eyebrow, setting her mug down with a soft

clink. "That's weird, but it's vending machine neglect. Someone in accounting is trying to pinch pennies, like when we got pens that didn't have ink. Don't read too much into it." She leaned against the table. "You, however, look like you're hiding something. Spill it, or I'm going to call Tyler and ask him."

Emily squeezed the wrapper, making it crinkle. Anita's intuition was a double-edged sword—loyal but too perceptive for Emily's mental state.

"I'm tired," Emily said. "It's this deadline, you know?"

Anita's lips pursed, unconvinced. She stepped closer, her voice dropping. "You've been off all day. Skittish, like you're waiting for the ceiling to cave in. I'm here, okay? Talk to me."

She offered comfort, but Emily couldn't grasp it. Not with the menace of surveillance hanging over her. She shook her head, forcing a smile. "I appreciate it, Anita. I'm fine but need more caffeine and snacks from this decade." She turned back to the vending machine, her reflection distorted in its glass.

Anita tapped on the table, her quietness heavy in the air, then took her coffee mug and walked toward the door. "I'm heading out for my art class. Call me if you want to chat," she said, full of frustration. The door hissed shut behind her, leaving Emily with the vending machine's noise and spiraling thoughts.

A few minutes later, Emily exited the break room, leaving the discarded wrappers, and returned to the dim corridor. She needed answers, and James Kessler was the most logical person to approach. She spotted him further down the hall, his tailored blue shirt crisp against the white walls. He was talking to an IT technician, but stiffened his posture as Emily approached.

"James," she called, her voice steadier than she felt.

He turned, his eyes twitching with something before settling into his usual practiced calm.

"Emily," he said, nodding. "Everything alright?"

She paused a few feet away, the corridor's lights stuttering overhead. "Any system issues lately?" she asked. "Glitches? Strange messages?"

Something was unsettling about his too-smooth smile and his unwavering gaze. "Nothing of significance," he said, fiddling with his cufflinks. "Ironically, I was asking Dan the same thing." He motioned to the technician, who bobbed his head with a confused look.

"Uh, right," Dan stammered. "All systems are operating normally."

With a dismissive nod, James disregarded the technician and raised his eyebrows at Emily. "I'm curious. What was the reason for your question?"

Emily pushed her glasses up from the tip of her nose. "Unusual hiccups in the lab computers. And these lights keep flickering. You'd tell me if something was off, right? With the project, the network... anything?"

"Always," he said, his voice like polished glass, but his gaze jerked to the technician again, revealing a crack in his facade. He stepped past her, brushing off the technician with a tilt of his head. "Keep me posted on your progress, Emily. We're counting on you."

James walked away, his footsteps echoing, leaving Emily in the corridor. In a way, James's evasion confirmed her suspicion of his connection to the messages. She didn't trust him but couldn't confront him without proof. Her hand grazed her phone, and she made a decision.

Emily's fingers wrapped around her phone, James's fading footsteps still echoing in her ears. She couldn't shake the gnawing certainty that he was hiding something, but chasing shadows without evidence would only tip her hand. She'd dig deeper, starting with the cryptic messages she'd saved on her secure drive. She needed to cross-reference them with James's access logs, but that would take time and privacy, neither of which she had in the lab. Tucking her phone away, she headed back to her desk, the burden of her choice weighing on her.

A couple of hours later, near 7 p.m., Emily sat alone in the conference room, the harsh glow of the fluorescents replacing the lab's softer light. Her laptop was open to a maze of data trails she hoped would lead to answers.

The harsh white light in the meeting room did little to ease the tension in Emily's shoulders. With a careful eye, she scanned the encrypted logs, nervously glancing between her computer and the door. Seaport's skyline beyond the window was now a blur of gray, with the fall haze swallowing the city's edges. The ventilation system felt like a mechanical pulse, aligning with her growing anxiety as she waited for Tyler's call. She relied on his perspective to bring some balance. Every creak of the building made her look up, half-expecting to see a camera's glint or James's silhouette, as the small room amplified her feeling of being spied on, trapped in a web she couldn't quite see.

Emily's phone rested on the table, its screen glowing with Tyler Reed's name. Her lips pressed into a thin line as she pushed call, and the line connected. Tyler's voice came through, rough and edged with a strain that reflected her own. "Hey, Em, are you coming home soon? What's with the check-in call?"

She said quietly, "I'm staying late." She looked at the ceiling's fluorescent light panels. "It's the issue we talked about in the park. It happened again."

Tyler's breath caught, a sharp hiss coming through the speaker. "The creepy messages? You got another one?"

Emily nodded, though Tyler couldn't see it. "Yeah. It's not a glitch, Tyler. Someone's watching, maybe James. I traced the message to an internal IP, but it's locked down. I can't tell if it's him or someone else in the system." Her fingers tightened around her phone, the plastic warm to the touch. "I don't know who to trust here other than Anita."

There was a pause, the whine of the ventilation filling the

silence. Tyler's voice returned, strained now. "We need a plan, Emily. If Kessler's involved, we can't sit on this. The implications are too big and dangerous to let this slide."

Her stomach knotted. Tyler's usually calming realism felt reckless tonight, his push for action clashing with her spiraling doubt. "What if it's a trap?" she whispered. "What if Kessler is baiting me to see what I'll do? I can't risk the project—or us—without proof."

"Proof?" Tyler growled. "Emily, you're the one who said this could screw us all. We can't wait for a smoking gun while they're watching every move." He softened, his voice dropping. "I'm not saying I've got all the answers. Hell, I'm as lost as you. But we've got to do something. These attempts to scare you won't stop unless something changes. If it's Kessler, what kind of game is he playing?"

Emily's eyes stung. The conference room's white walls seemed to close in, the bright lights casting jagged shade across the table. She wanted to lean into his certainty, but the anonymous messages had fractured her sense of stability.

"I'll dig deeper," she said finally. "But we play this smart, Tyler. No moves until we know more."

"You know, smart is my middle name," he joked, but the humor felt forced. "Do you want me to come over there?"

"No, I'll be home in a couple of hours," she replied. "I'm just worn out and under a lot of pressure." The call ended, leaving her alone with the background noises and her racing thoughts.

Emily stayed in the conference room, her phone dark on the table. The walls seemed to press in on her, their emptiness creating space for her imagination to wander. Outside the window, Seaport's skyscraper rose, its lights blurred by mist.

She leaned back. Their call had revealed small cracks in their relationship—Tyler's push to act clashing with her caution, their trust strained by the threat of the kill switch. Still, she couldn't do this alone. She'd investigate with Tyler, dig into the

51

messages' source, and confront whatever James Kessler was hiding.

The lights flickered again, plunging her into darkness long enough to startle her. Once they stabilized, Emily stood and slipped her phone into her pocket. She felt isolated but wasn't alone. With Tyler by her side, she was ready to face the implied threats, the pressure, and the truth—whatever it might cost.

Chapter 6

Too Close for Comfort

T he rain lashed Boston's Seaport district, transforming the streets into a glossy canvas of neon and gloom. Later that night, Emily stepped out of the BioSpark lab into the glass-walled lobby of the Helix building and sighed as she gazed at the rain outside.

From the security desk, Carl—a thin guard with deep-set eyes and a buzz cut streaked with gray—watched her approach. Drowning in his oversized uniform, he watched intently as she swiped her badge through the reader. The scanner beeped, and the glass doors hissed, ready to release her into the storm.

"Late one, Dr. Harper?" Carl's gravelly voice felt more invasive than his usual half-hearted wave. He leaned forward, elbows on the desk, his eyes narrowing slightly. "Working on something special up there?"

Emily's pulse ticked up, her fingers tightening on her backpack strap. The question hung in the air, its casual tone at odds with how he studied her, like he was waiting for a slip. "The usual," she said, forcing a smile. "Data, coffee, and a side of existential dread." Her voice was light, but her mind raced. Did he know something? Helix's controversies—whispers of neural control, corporate espionage—were no secret in Boston's tech circles. Carl's intense gaze felt like a red flag.

Carl chuckled, but it didn't reach his eyes. "Special's one word for it. Folks talk, you know. Big things coming outta this place." He tapped a pen on the Helix logo behind him, the rhythm slightly offbeat, his gaze never wavering.

Emily's throat tightened. She adjusted her glasses, buying a moment to shift the uncomfortable conversation. "Talk's cheap among us scientists," she quipped, stepping toward the doors. "I'm not looking forward to walking to the bus in this rain, though. Night, Carl." She felt his eyes on her back, a prickle of unease that followed her into the night.

The glass doors of the building slid shut behind her. Outside, the rain stung her face, and the drone noises grew sharper, as if the city itself were watching. Her confidence in decoding BioSpark's algorithms conflicted with increasing insecurity. James's pressure to ignore the gene's risks and prepare for the public launch in three months felt like a betrayal of her principles.

A shimmer of movement in the dark building across the street caught her eye—shadows, nothing more. She checked her phone for a rideshare, thumb hesitating over the app. A message flashed in her mind. "Eyes on you." As she increased her pace, the ominous, buzzing neon glow of Seaport's signs cast long, wavering ripples, their light a sickly yellow against the night. The air was damp and chilly, heavy with the smell of salt and wet leaves.

Her phone read 10:03 p.m., and the late-fall air bit at her cheeks as she pulled her jacket tighter. The Seaport District sprawled ahead of her, rain-slicked streets gleaming under the kaleidoscope of neon signs—blues, pinks, and greens from tech firms' logos bouncing off puddles. Drones buzzed overhead, red and white lights streaking through the drizzle, ferrying packages or scanning traffic for some faceless algorithm. She walked along, lost in thought, her steps splashing unevenly in the puddles.

Hidden in the Helix conference room, Emily had been investigating the company's communication network to track down the mysterious messages plaguing her inbox. Every strange occurrence—from untraceable emails and manipulated data to the lab's erratic lights—required a theory that could be investigated.

Years spent deciphering gene sequences had sharpened her analytical skills, and she relished such challenges. The implications of neural technology had intrigued her. She joined BioSpark, initially focused on enhancing cognitive functions through precise neural mapping, but the data produced unforeseen results. The chilling accuracy of the terminal gene, a secondary discovery predicting lifespans, still shocked her.

As Emily navigated the rain-slicked Seaport streets, her thoughts churned. She scanned the neon-lit horizon, alert for patterns in the urban sprawl. She excelled at untangling complexity—algorithms bent to her logic—but the stakes of BioSpark's work aroused restless doubts. Was she complicit in a dangerous venture? James Kessler's vision for Helix had once inspired her, but his recent deflections, coupled with the board's political maneuvering, hinted at hidden agendas.

The recent cryptic messages resembled data points in a dark sequence, their anonymity a variable she couldn't pin down. She hesitated, her fingers hovering over the rideshare app on her phone. Though her scientific mind urged her to dismiss her anxiety, her racing heart told her otherwise. The threat was real, and she was the target.

She glimpsed movement—a shadow shifting in the dark alley between the glass towers. She froze, rain dripping from her ponytail, her breath catching. Nerves, she reasoned. Attempting to bolster her courage, she said, "Wonderful, Emily, you're overreacting like a scared teenager in a horror movie." But as she kept moving, the sense of being watched weighed on her.

The intersection at Seaport Boulevard stretched before her, a rain-slicked grid of asphalt glinting under flickering streetlights and the pulsing glow of a holographic ad touting neural enhancements. The rain blurred her vision as she stepped off the curb, slipping slightly on the wet concrete.

She barely registered the low growl of an engine until headlights pierced the rain, blinding her. A black SUV—Cadillac Escalade, tinted windows, no plates—surged forward, its tires squealing as it bore down on her at high speed. Her mind logged details—velocity, trajectory, absence of markings—while panic seized her chest.

She lurched back, her backpack pulling her off balance, and crashed onto the sidewalk, her palms scraping raw, jeans soaking through to her skin. Her heart slammed in a staccato rhythm as the SUV veered at the last second, its side mirror grazing her sleeve before it vanished down the quiet street. Her breath hitched, the questions sharper than the sting in her hands, her mind racing.

The vehicle vanished around the corner, taillights swallowed by the rain. Drones whirred above, their cameras likely capturing the moment, red lights blinking like judgmental eyes. Distant sirens wailed, a faint echo through the storm, and Emily's breath came in sharp gasps. She wasn't merely a scientist puzzling out code. She was a target.

She scanned the street, rain streaking down her face, mixing with the salt of sweat despite the chilly air. Her confidence wavered. Could she handle this? BioSpark's secrets—the extinction event, the terminal gene—were a can of worms, and she'd uncovered them. The working-class kid from South Boston, the first in her family to claw into college, felt irrelevant against the stakes—corporations, governments, power plays beyond her small lab.

Emily stood, legs shaky, and brushed wet hair from her face. Fear battled determination in her chest—who was behind this? Her mind raced, analytical yet fraying, torn between digging for truth and running from it. "Get it together, Dr. Harper," she mumbled, her weak attempt at grounding herself, barely concealing her fear. Panic surged, cold and heavy as the rain soaking her blouse. Seaport's neon glow felt more like a warning, and she wondered if she'd already crossed a line she couldn't uncross.

Another set of headlights cut through the drizzle, and a battered police cruiser rolled up, its tires hissing against the wet asphalt. The door swung open, and Officer Wendy Mooney stepped out, her thick frame outlined against the streetlights. Her badge gleamed, her slightly rumpled uniform hugged her muscular build, and her salt-and-pepper bun glistened with rain.

"You okay, hon?" she called, her Boston accent thick. "Saw that SUV nearly clip ya."

Emily released the breath she was holding and sighed with relief. "I'm okay, mostly wet. That was so close."

"Hop in. I'll get ya home."

Emily stammered. "Thank you, Officer. I'll call an Uber. I don't want to inconvenience you."

Officer Mooney smiled. "No inconvenience at all. It's a slow night, and I'd never forgive myself if something happened to you."

The chill and shaking hands nudged her toward the cruiser's open door. "If you don't mind, I'd feel much safer. I'm soaked and pretty shaken up."

Inside the cruiser, the air smelled of vinyl and sweat, the old seats creaking as Emily settled in. Mooney slid behind the wheel, her piercing gray eyes flicking to Emily, taking in her soaked hair and tense posture. "Rough night to be out, especially in this mess," Mooney said, her tone gruff but a faint grin softening her round face. "Workin' late, huh? Helix, right? Fancy! Always wanted a gig where I could wear a lab coat."

Emily caught the curiosity beneath it, a cop's instinct probing deeper.

The cruiser rolled through Seaport's slick streets, wipers slapping rhythmically. She glanced at Mooney's calloused hands on the wheel, the faint scars, and wondered what the cop knew. Helix's name carried prestige—controversy, too—and Mooney's casual mention felt loaded. Trust was too much to ask for at the moment. Emily wiped the fog off her glasses to see better in the car's warmth.

She studied Mooney, the officer's eyes flicking to the rearview mirror, observant, steady. "You see that SUV's plates?" Mooney asked, her voice casual.

Emily shook her head, muttering, "No, too fast, too dark." Her sarcasm slipped out. "Guess I'm not cut out for police work."

Mooney chuckled, "Leave that to me, hon. You stick to the science stuff."

The cruiser's heat warmed Emily's chilled skin, but she couldn't relax. Mooney's kindness felt real—her maternal edge, the way she softened her tone—but Emily's suspicion clouded it. Was she there by coincidence, or was there more to her presence? Confide, her gut urged, but caution held her back. Her fear urged silence. The rain tapped on the windshield. Drones buzzed outside, and Emily's tired eyes stared into the night, caught between trust and suspicion.

The cruiser rolled to a stop outside Emily's apartment in Jamaica Plain, its engine idling under the constant drizzle. The neighborhood's triple-decker apartments and leaf-strewn sidewalks offered an eclectic contrast to Seaport's neon glare, the rain softening the edges of the streetlights' glow. Drones were rare here, their whirs replaced by the patter of water on asphalt and the creak of a porch swing on the colonial house across the street.

Emily stepped out, sinking into the muddy gravel path, her legs unsteady and her backpack heavy with her laptop. Her eyes, obscured behind rain-flecked glasses, scanned the quiet street, the memory of the black SUV's headlights still playing in her mind.

Officer Mooney leaned out the cruiser's window, her gray eyes steady. "Take care, Dr. Harper. Call if you need anything."

Emily nodded, managing a tight smile, and the cruiser pulled away, its taillights fading into the wet night. Before she could reach the buzzer, the apartment door swung open. Tyler stood there, his eyes narrowing as they took in her soaked jeans and pale face. His heavy jacket was thrown over a Patriots T-shirt, his high-and-tight hair damp, as if he'd been pacing outside. The sight of her stepping out of the police cruiser must have brought him down from the apartment.

"Emily, what happened?" He pulled her close.

"I'm okay," she said as she stepped into the warm entryway, smelling cedar and baking bread wrapping around her. "An SUV almost hit me near the office. Swerved at the last second." She avoided his gaze, peeling off her dripping jacket, her long hair loose and clinging to her neck.

Tyler's face stiffened. "Nearly hit you?" He closed the door and moved to the living room window to scan the street. "This isn't random, Emily. The messages you've been getting—they're not noise anymore. Someone's coming for you." He pulled the drapes tighter on the window.

Emily sank onto the couch, her hands trembling as she set her backpack down. The SUV's roar and the rain blurring her vision was a warning.

"I don't know who would do that," she admitted. "Corporate rivals? Someone tied to James's boardroom fights? I've been digging into BioSpark's network, and those messages…they're tied to the kill switch. I can feel it but can't prove it yet." She was determined to understand, yet a deep-seated fear fueled her self-doubt.

Tyler kneeled before her, his eyes searching hers. "We can't do this alone," he said, his tone softer but urgent. "Let's hire security. Or walk away from BioSpark. Hell, go public—blow the whistle on James and Helix." His large hand, warm through her jeans, rested firmly on her knee. But the intensity in his gaze felt important, pushing against her attempt not to overreact.

Emily's chest tightened, her mind in a tug-of-war. She was a scientist driven to decode the terminal gene's revolutionary and dangerous potential. Quitting meant ceding control to those who didn't care about the consequences. "I can't walk away. If I do, someone else gets to decide what happens with BioSpark. I'm close to the answers, Tyler." Her eyes met his, defiant. "I need to figure this out."

"Figure it out?" Tyler stood, pacing to the window. "You're not bulletproof, Emily. This isn't a lab experiment—it's your life." His voice cracked. "I can't lose you, babe."

Emily winced, her fingers clenching the couch. While she adored Tyler's loyalty and quirky humor, his protectiveness threatened her independence. Accepting help felt like a betrayal, but refusing it was dangerous.

"I'm not helpless," she mumbled. "But I'm nervous. I need time."

Tyler's gaze softened. "Time's a luxury here," he said. "Let me call someone—security, off the books."

Emily's jaw clenched, but the SUV's headlights flashed in her mind. "I'll think about it," she conceded.

After drying off, Emily stood alone on the apartment's small balcony, avoiding the drizzle as she stared at the wet street. Her eyes traced the shadows, her mind replaying the night—the SUV, Mooney's probing, Tyler's urgency. The kill switch felt oppressive, its power to alter humanity an imminent threat. Quitting now would betray everything she'd been working for.

When she returned inside to prepare for bed, Emily found Tyler sitting at their small kitchen table, his shoulders hunched over a coffee mug. "I'll think about security," she murmured, leaning against the counter, "but I'm not running."

Tyler nodded, his dark eyes fixed on hers, a mixture of relief and apprehension. "That's a start," he said.

In the bathroom, Emily brushed her teeth, the soft *bzzzz* of the electric toothbrush calming her. Her reflection in the mirror showed pale cheeks and tired eyes, the strain of the night etched into her face. Her phone, resting on the sink, pinged.

The screen lit up with a new message, sender unknown. "Next time, you won't walk away."

Her heart slammed against her ribs. The toothbrush clattered into the sink. The rain drummed against the windows, with the unseen enemy nearby.

Chapter 7

Pierced Heart

The kitchen in Tyler and Emily's apartment fell silent, like the calm before an autumn storm. Even the rhythmic whir of the refrigerator seemed to fade, replaced by the gentle patter of rain on the window.

At nearly midnight, Tyler hunched over his laptop at the cluttered kitchen table, its blue glow casting shadows. The air held the stale scent of old coffee, day-old pizza, and the faint musk of a wet dog from his field jacket draped over a chair.

His dark eyes, usually steady, wavered uneasily as he logged into an anonymous email account, fingers hesitating over the keys. Emily's soft breathing offered faint comfort down the hall —she'd gone to bed an hour ago.

In Tyler's inbox, a BioSpark email with a cryptic subject line of random alphanumeric characters awaited, promising answers he dreaded. Months earlier, haunted by his grandparents' dementia, he'd anonymously submitted neural data during BioSpark's indicator tests. The fear of inheriting their fate had grown sharper as he and Emily began discussing children. He'd confided in Anita, Emily's friend, but insisted on keeping it from Emily to spare her worry until he knew the results.

His mind replayed the moment he'd handed Anita his data and signed the release forms in a crowded South End cafe. Her sharp eyes softened as she urged him to tell Emily. He nodded, lying easily—he wanted the results first to protect Emily from uncertainty.

But BioSpark's plans shifted when they discovered a gene sequence predicting lifespans with chilling precision. Dementia faded to a secondary concern as this new revelation loomed. After Emily mentioned the kill switch, Tyler secretly asked Anita if the revised research study would include his information and if it would show his kill switch date.

The agreement he'd signed for the initial study granted Helix the right to use the de-identified data in any related research, a right she confirmed by answering yes to both questions.

Tyler recalled the instructions in his enrollment materials on how to access his individual results. The materials highlighted confidentiality, which Anita underscored by stating her inability and unwillingness to disclose any results, including Tyler's. If he used his de-identified study number on BioSpark's secure portal, he could request that his results, which he knew would include the kill switch calculation, be emailed to his preferred email address.

Although Anita had warned him about the burden of this knowledge, she'd instructed him on how to interpret the findings. Emily's casual remark about their shared testing and her confidence in its accuracy convinced him to go ahead. After entering his study number and creating an anonymous email address through the online portal, he submitted his request for the results. He had been waiting twenty-four hours for the promised email.

Now, with cryptic threats haunting Emily, Tyler's loyalty clashed with his fear of burdening her further. Hiding the test exposed his vulnerability—a dread of losing their dreamed-of future: marriage, a home, maybe kids. As he opened the email, his thumb grazed the faint scar above his eyebrow, a habit from his Army days. The screen brightened, his heart pounding.

The kitchen's silence pressed in, broken only by the fridge's vibration and the distant creak of the apartment settling. His watch ticked softly, a reminder of time's relentless march. The email loaded, and Tyler closed his eyes to brace himself, his love for Emily clashing with the dread of what he might discover. Truth or peace—he couldn't give her both.

Tyler stared intensely at the email, branding it into his consciousness. The analysis performed by the BioSpark algorithm was terse and clinical: the kill switch calculation, based on his genetic data, predicted his death at 306,810 hours after birth. His engineer's mind kicked in, calculating swiftly. Assuming his birth date—June 17, 1993—he had roughly thirty-six years of life. He quickly calculated: 365 days a year, 24 hours each, leap years... It meant only one year and three days remained. His hands trembled, betraying the practical approach to dealing with challenges he'd relied on throughout his life.

The kitchen's dim light quivered slightly, casting the photo on the fridge into sharp relief: him and Emily at Cape Cod last summer, her smile bright against his tanned chest. Their planned life—weddings, hikes, late-night talks—unraveled in his imagination, each moment slipping like sand. He leaned back, the chair creaking, and stared at the ceiling's cracked plaster, willing his pulse to slow. His eyes turned inward, haunted by the finite hours ahead. He found it difficult to concentrate.

Anita's voice echoed from a flashback, her plea sharp in that cafe. "Tell Emily, Tyler. She deserves to know." He winked and promised he would, but planned to wait—surprising her with good news once he confirmed the results wouldn't shatter their future. The irony stung.

His fingers tightened around the coffee mug. Tyler's determination grew stronger, fueled by his love for Emily. If he had a year, he'd live it to the fullest—protect her from BioSpark's dangers, savor every moment. His self-sacrificing streak, shaped by his working-class background and military service, surged within him. He'd carry this burden alone to spare her pain. He faced a tough decision with no good options. The rhythmic click-whirr of the refrigerator's compressor faded into a dull hum. Ignoring the kitchen sounds, he carefully weighed his choices, thinking about what would be best for Emily.

Tyler grappled with the need to confirm the kill switch timeline. He wanted the exact time down to the minute. The birth certificate held the key to his precise birth hour, the last piece needed to make the kill switch's calculation accurate. He needed the brutal truth, no matter how harsh, to face the devastating prediction of his future.

The junk drawer rattled as he sifted through its clutter— utility bills, crumpled takeout menus, a rusted spare key—but no certificate. In the living room, the filing cabinet's drawers groaned, revealing only tax forms, Emily's faded Harvard transcripts, and his service records.

Frustration tightened his shoulder muscles. His watch read 1:07 a.m., its soft tick a mocking countdown. Sleep was a distant fantasy. Tyler grabbed his phone, his thumb hesitating over his mother's contact—Colleen Reed, a retired nurse in Dorchester. His eyes flicked to the fridge photo of him and Emily, her smile a quiet plea to keep her unburdened. He dialed, forcing his voice into a casual tone to hide the dread twisting in his stomach.

"Tyler? It's past midnight, sweetheart." Colleen's voice was warm but rough with sleep. "Is everything okay over there?"

He leaned against the counter. "I'm finishing some paperwork. I can't find my birth certificate. You got a copy tucked away in that hoarder's paradise?"

Colleen's bright and familiar laugh eased the knot in his

chest for a moment. "Watch it, kid. My attic's an organized disaster, and you're going to inherit all this treasure someday." Her tone softened, a mother's warmth that hadn't faded despite years of long shifts at Boston General. "What's got you digging for that old piece of paper at this hour? Is Emily planning a surprise for your birthday?"

Tyler's grip tightened on the phone, his mind scrambling for a lie. "I'm updating records for work. Defense contractor nonsense—bureaucracy's worse than the Army." He forced a chuckle.

"Sounds like a headache," Colleen said with sympathy. "But your certificate… That's a funny story. When you were born, the clerk botched your records. Typed your birth date as June 17, 1993, an entire year in the future. Made you younger than you are, lucky devil."

She laughed again, unaware of the silence on his end. "We caught it when you were a toddler and told people you were big for your age. We never fixed it for your license and school stuff, but the original has the right year, 1992. I never pushed to correct the records fully—thought it was a harmless quirk that didn't matter. Age is just a number. Kept you my baby a little longer, you know?"

Tyler's heart lurched, the kitchen's background sounds dissolving into a dull roar. He sank into the chair, his broad back slumping as the math recalculated in his head. A year older. Not 306,810 hours from 1993, but 1992. His mental tally was merciless: not a year and three days left, only three days. Three days and change.

His eyes burned with the pressure of a life crushed into a few days.

"Tyler? You still with me?" Colleen asked.

"Yeah, Ma," he lied. "Long day." He swallowed, grasping for normalcy. "Why didn't you tell me about the birth certificate mix-up sooner? That's a big deal."

Colleen sighed, "Oh, dear, it never seemed worth all the commotion. We were so busy trying to get by that fighting city hall that it didn't seem worth the effort. And I don't know... I liked the idea of you staying my little boy. Silly, right? But you were always racing ahead—enlisting at eighteen, those tours overseas. I held onto the small stuff."

Tyler's chest tightened, a mix of love and frustration swelling inside him. Colleen's protectiveness, her working-class strength, had shaped him—her late-night stories after shifts, her fierce pride when he graduated from BU on the GI Bill. But this secret, however small she thought it was, had rewritten his fate. He rubbed his hands through his short hair, a reflex, and forced a lighter tone.

"Silly's one word for it. You got that certificate somewhere, or will I have to fight the spiders in the attic again?"

"It's in my safe-deposit box at the bank. I'll grab it next week, promise. You sure you're okay? You sound...off."

"I'm tired," he said. "Thanks, Ma. Get some sleep." He ended the call, his thumb lingering on the screen, the burden of three days crushing him. Colleen's decision to keep the birth date error quiet, born from love and exhaustion, had protected him then but doomed him now.

His loyalty to Emily surfaced through his pain. Three days were too short to shatter her with grief or dim her bright plans. He would live those hours for her—secure her safety and confront BioSpark's threats himself. His silence was a betrayal, a fracture in their trust, but love justified it. The rain outside swirled in the wind, drumming on the window, as Tyler sat alone, passing the dark hours of the night, lost in thought.

He pressed his fingers to his temples, imagining himself collapsing in his office, his body failing without a sound, or perhaps slipping away in the stillness of night from an early stroke. The absence of a clear cause of why his kill switch would trigger gnawed at him as much as the deadline itself. Each possibility, from sudden heart failure to a fatal car accident, spiraled into deeper uncertainty. He needed to act, to help Emily uncover the truth before time ran out, yet every plan dissolved against the question of how his end would come.

A weak dawn light crept through the kitchen window, slicing across the cluttered counter, illuminating dust motes and the cold coffee mug in his hands. The apartment was still, the refrigerator's whir now a faint drone against the chirp of the black-capped chickadees outside. Exhaustion weighed on him, his head resting in his hands, his eyes bloodshot from a sleepless night.

The sound of Emily's light snoring amplified his isolation. Tyler slumped, his shoulders weighted down by the kill switch's chilling decree: three days remaining. He wiped away the single tear tracing his cheek.

His mind, usually sharp in the early morning, got stuck on a troubling blank. He couldn't remember where he'd parked his car yesterday. Was it on the street or in the lot? A recent conversation with Emily came to mind, half-formed: her talking about a hike, maybe, but the details slipped away.

Were these gaps caused by stress from the email's death sentence, or was the kill switch already unraveling his mind? He clutched the mug tighter and tested his memory, reciting the specs of a recent project. The numbers came easily, but the car, the talk with Emily—blank. His heart thudded.

Tyler's inner thoughts churned, his usual discipline clashing with fear. Stress might explain it—sleepless nights, threats against Emily—but the kill switch hovered, its consequences unknown. What if it wasn't only predicting his death, but was first poisoning his mind?

He visualized Emily's eyes, bright with plans, and his resolve hardened. Three days. He'd make them count—protect her from the recent danger, cherish their time. If he opened up, confessing his fears, he risked pulling her into his collapse. His calm exterior cracked at the edges, vulnerability bleeding through in the tremor of his hands, in the way his gaze stayed on the framed photos. He'd face this alone to keep her world whole. The dawn's quiet pressed on him.

Tyler snapped his laptop shut, the email from BioSpark vanishing into darkness. He grabbed a pen and scribbled a note on a scrap of paper: "Running errands. Back soon. Love you."

He placed it on the bedroom nightstand. He pulled on his field jacket by the front door, leaving the sketchbook behind. The apartment door clicked shut behind him, leaving the kitchen empty, with the note fluttering as the heater's air warmed the apartment. The scent of bitter coffee lingered, a reminder of the long night.

His heart ached, love and loss cutting deep. Three days weren't enough, but he'd make them perfect—dinner tonight, a walk by the Charles, anything to see Emily's smile. The memory gaps gnawed at him, foreshadowing the kill switch's immediate vulnerability, but he steeled himself. He'd face his fate alone, sparing her the grief. He was determined to protect Emily, even if it meant betraying her trust with unspoken silence.

Chapter 8

Digging Deeper

Emily watched the morning light filter through mismatched curtains, casting a soft glow across the small, cluttered apartment. She stirred in bed, her limbs heavy from a restless night that brought no further threats —no cryptic texts. Anxiety quickly replaced her brief feeling of relief.

She reached across the sheets for Tyler, her fingers only brushing a cool pillow. Her heart gave a slight lurch. Propped on the nightstand was a scribbled note in his familiar handwriting. "Running errands. Back soon. Love you."

Tyler had been distant the past few days, his smiles quick but not always reaching his eyes. She pushed the thought away, unwilling to let it fester.

Swinging her legs over the bed, Emily's bare feet touched the worn hardwood floor. The apartment filled with familiar sounds: the radiator's soft clank, the distant bark of a neighbor's dog. She padded to the dresser, her reflection catching in the mirror—long hair tangled, puffy eyes sharp despite the fatigue's smudges. Fear had tried to sink its claws into her after the SUV nearly hit her and the late-night text warning her that next time she wouldn't walk away. But fear wouldn't win. Not today.

She grabbed her phone and sent a quick message to Tyler. "Lunch later? I'm going to the office for a couple of hours. Miss your face." Her tone was light, hiding the anxiety gnawing at her.

No reply came, but she didn't expect one yet. Tyler was probably busy with some errand, unaware of her spiraling thoughts. She hesitated, tempted to unload all her worries—the surveillance, James's odd behavior at Helix, the unsettling questions from Officer Mooney. But sharing her fears would worry Tyler or make him rush to act. For now, she decided to handle this alone.

Emily's gaze settled on her laptop bag by the door. The sterile halls of the Helix building beckoned, promising answers. The chance to work in silence would be possible on a relaxed Saturday morning. She'd dig into BioSpark's servers, chase the phantoms behind the truth dogging her. The ethics of what she might uncover—knowledge that could save or destroy—prickled at her conscience. But she'd face that when the time came. With an oversized mug of coffee in hand, she dressed and headed for the bus stop.

The MBTA bus rattled along, its half-empty interior smelling of damp coats and lemony disinfectant. Fogged windows blurred Seaport's industrial edges—warehouses and chain-link fences fading into the gray morning. Emily sat near the back, her laptop bag held tightly, her eyes flicking warily over the handful of commuters. A man in a Bruins hoodie scrolled on his phone. A woman with earbuds stared blankly ahead. Although no one seemed suspicious, she felt a persistent sense of apprehension.

Last night's security guard at Helix, Carl, flashed in her mind—his nervous fidgeting, the way his eyes shifted to the cameras. The way he asked too many questions. Her fingers tightened on her bag. She wasn't merely a scientist running experiments. She was a fighter, and Helix's secrets wouldn't easily scare her away.

Outside, a billboard caught her eye. "Everlasting Smoothies —Live Forever!" Emily snorted, the sound soft in the bus commotion.

"Bet Helix is behind that too," she muttered. The idea was absurd, but it relaxed her. She leaned her head against the cool window, her reflection a faint ghost in the glass. Who benefited from the terminal gene data? The question gnawed at her, a thread tying her to something bigger—Helix, James, a corporate machine she was seeing through the fog of distrust.

Seaport's skyline rose as the bus lurched to a stop. The Helix building's sleek and cold glass facade shimmered ahead. Emily stood, her anxiety intensifying. She was determined to find answers, no matter who tried to stop her.

The lobby gleamed under cold fluorescent lights, its glass walls reflecting Emily's taut expression as she walked across the threshold. The usual weekday clamor was gone, replaced by a silence punctuated by the ventilation system's soft hum. Her sneakers squeaked on the polished marble, the sound vanishing into the cavernous space.

At the security desk, a new guard—stocky, buzz-cut, mid-thirties—slouched, his eyes glued to his phone. He flicked a glance her way, offering a half-hearted nod. Unlike Carl's twitchy vigilance last night, his apathy felt like a slight reprieve. Emily's shoulders loosened, but only slightly.

The elevator ride to the fifth floor was a quiet ascent, the mirrored walls tossing back her determined stare. When the doors parted, a corridor of glass and chrome stretched before her, silent save for the muffled din of machinery. The lab, her cluttered refuge, waited at the end.

Inside, sticky notes clung to her monitor. Coffee mugs formed a haphazard skyline on her desk, and a drooping fern sulked in the corner of her cubicle. The chair creaked reassuringly as she settled in, her laptop bag falling to the floor.

Her terminal came to life with a gentle whir, displaying the Helix login screen and its signature double helix. Emily's fingers paused over the keys, a knot of anticipation and fear tightening in her chest. She'd accessed restricted files before, but today's research dive felt like stepping off a cliff. She entered her credentials, and the system chimed in approval. With a deep breath, she plunged into the secure email servers, her expertise slicing through layers of code.

The directory sprawled like a digital maze, intricate and obscure, but Emily knew its paths. Her eyes locked onto a folder labeled Project Chronos—a name absent from every Helix memo, briefing, or watercooler chat she'd ever encountered. Her pulse quickened, a drumbeat in her chest. She clicked only to hit a wall of encryption, its code a taunting barrier. Undeterred, she launched a decryption script she'd crafted last year for moments like this. The screen flickered briefly, pulsed, then surrendered, revealing a trove of emails.

The correspondence was between James and a faceless group, their identities shrouded in cryptic aliases. Emily's heart pounded as she scanned the threads. James's writing dripped with arrogance, flinging phrases like "disruptive innovation" and "market dominance" with reckless confidence. The emails outlined a deal to leak the genetic data—genetic markers that predicted longevity, algorithms that would map a lifespan with chilling precision.

The recipients, cloaked in secrecy, promised lavish funding for predictive applications. One line seared into her mind. "Chronos will shape the future." Another email revealed James's disdain for Helix's board of directors. "The board lacks vision. They'd stall Chronos for years. I'm bypassing them for the greater good."

The betrayal stung—James was undermining the company for personal gain.

Emily's stomach twisted. The terminal gene wasn't merely research; it was a doomsday key, its contents poised to unleash global turmoil. In the wrong hands, the predictive power of the gene could be weaponized—insurers denying clients based on genetic fate, governments profiling citizens, corporations turning life and death into profit margins. James's hubris blinded him to the fallout, but Emily's moral compass spun wildly. Science guided her, but ethics kept her grounded. Exposing this meant confronting James and a board he'd side-stepped, their caution dismissed as cowardice. The stakes felt impossibly high.

Paranoia crept in, cold and sharp. Who else at Helix was involved? Were cameras watching her every keystroke? The office's glass walls seemed to press in, reflecting her tense expression and wide eyes. She plugged in a secure drive, her hands controlled despite the tightness in her chest. Copying the files felt torturous, with the progress bar inching forward as if taunting her urgency. Her eyes darted to the door, half-expecting James's smug grin or the silhouette of a stranger sent to silence her.

The transfer finished with a soft ping. She took out the thumb drives and put them into her jeans pocket. Another email caught her attention—a chilling line from James to an alias. "She's closing in. The texts didn't scare her away. Deal with it."

Emily's breath caught in a gasp. It had to be her. The vehicle that nearly hit her, the cryptic text warning her about next time —it all clicked, a web of threats tightening around her. Their attempt to scare her wasn't enough, and they were escalating. Her mind raced, fitting together the pieces: James's deal, Chronos, the board's ignorance, and now her as the target.

She logged out. A feeling of oppression filled the lab's silence. Grabbing her bag, she headed for the archives room, her mind a storm of questions. James's deal extended beyond Helix, connected to a phantom force she didn't fully understand. But she now had proof—a dangerous truth. The potential threat of that knowledge troubled her, but her defiance shone brighter. This wasn't only her struggle anymore.

For Emily, BioSpark's archive room appeared like a dark, high-tech world—a complex maze of flashing servers and hidden data, with firewalls acting as barriers and password-protected files concealing the truth. The lack of security cameras would give her more freedom to investigate the secure systems.

Her clammy fingers hovered over the keyboard. The harsh fluorescent lights above threw sharp shadows across the messy workstation—sticky notes, stained coffee mugs, and a discarded Powerbar wrapper. She moved past the initial emails to trace suspicious connections hidden deep within Helix's archived files. Free from the lab's constant surveillance cameras, she aimed to reveal James's treachery and the project's concealed secrets.

Her breath hitched as she launched a script Anita had helped her write last year, an agile tool for cracking low-level encrypted passwords during their BioSpark data runs. The code churned, and the screen pulsed. A new directory blinked open, revealing a trove of metadata tied to James's covert deal. Offshore accounts in the Cayman Islands, coded transactions funneled through shell companies, and a redacted memo labeled "Ethical Overrides" glared back at her.

Her pulse thundered in her ears, a relentless drumbeat echoing the tremor in her hands. The memo unveiled a chilling scheme: alter the terminal gene data to erase all traces of the extinction event. It outlined Project Chronos, a covert operation to leverage the terminal gene's predictive algorithms not only for population and immigration control in the near-term but also as a tool for far-reaching dominance.

In the near term, Chronos planned to deploy the genetic data to manipulate societal structures and benefit the rich and powerful while concealing the extinction event's broader implications—a calculated move to seize control on a global scale. James wasn't just leaking data but auctioning Helix's soul to the highest bidder, trading humanity's future for power.

Emily's throat tightened, her mouth dry as she swallowed hard. Though she longed to confide in someone who would grasp the situation's gravity, she couldn't bear the idea of putting Anita at risk. Tyler was unreachable, oblivious to her descent into this corporate conspiracy.

Like a stone on her chest, the significance of her discovery pressed down, making each breath a struggle. What was she going to do about it? The question remained, but her defiance flared, a fire in her veins pushing her forward. If someone wanted her dead, she'd damn well find out why.

She noticed something in the metadata that made her pause. James hadn't updated his login since the previous year.

"James, you idiot, your password's still Genius69?" she muttered, her lips twitching into a wry smile.

Her fingers steadied as she dove back into the search. She linked the offshore accounts and memos using James's password. She uncovered IP addresses from Dubai, London, and Singapore—Chronos was a global network, with James at the center and its tendrils snaking far beyond Boston. The scope of the betrayal widened, a chasm threatening to swallow her whole.

The ethical stakes emerged like a storm cloud. Exposing this could save countless lives and stop the weaponization of genetic data. But whistleblowers didn't get parades—they received threats or ended up dead on dark streets. Her fingers, now sweaty, trembled as she saved screenshots to her secure thumb drive, its edges pressing into her palm. She was a speck in a digital ocean, with sharks circling her.

Emily shut the files, her movements exact as she erased the

temporary evidence of her search. She paused the access script, leaving a back door to reopen later. The conspiracy she'd uncovered was a monstrous, sprawling beast, and she questioned her ability to defeat it. But retreat wasn't an option—they'd already tried to scare her off, and they wouldn't stop. Her gaze darted to her phone, its screen blank—no reply from Tyler. The isolation hurt, sharp as a needle, but she'd manage alone until she found a safe place to meet him and make a plan. She'd carry this fight, no matter the cost.

Back in her cubicle in the lab, the calm felt like a facade. Outside, Seaport's heavy cloud cover pressed against the windows like a thick gray curtain. Emily's hands shook as she saved a copy of her findings to a second thumb drive, the responsibility of her discovery a physical ache. The files were her evidence, proof of James's deal and Chronos's reach, but they also made her a bigger target.

A muffled noise—a door closing down the hall—made her snap her head up. Her pulse raced, fear flooding her senses. The lab's glass walls provided no cover. She strained to listen, but only the racket of the air conditioning responded. Still, the silence felt heavy, as if watching her. She sent another text to Tyler. "Where are you? Need to talk." No reply.

She couldn't stay here. The building felt like a cage. The edges of the secure drives she had tucked into her jeans pocket were sharp against her thigh. With her bag slung over her shoulder, she moved toward the door, her steps light but purposeful. Every shadow seemed to shift, every sound a subtle threat. She glanced back at her desk, where sticky notes and mugs captured a life she wasn't sure she'd ever return to.

The elevator ride down was agonizingly long, the mirrored walls reflecting her grim, pale face. She tried to smile, but it faded quickly. When the doors opened, the lobby stretched before her, its marble expanse colder now. The security guard was still at his desk, but his phone was down, his eyes fixed on her. Emily's breath caught. Was he texting someone about her? His gaze lingered as she crossed the lobby, her sneakers' soft squeaks deafening in the silence.

She pushed through the glass doors, the chill of Seaport's air hitting her.

"Great job, Emily," she said. "Uncover a conspiracy, make enemies, all before lunch on a Saturday." But the levity couldn't mask her fear. James's arrogance might blind him to her digging, but someone—Chronos, the guards, a stranger—was watching—the secure drives burned in her pocket, a warning of danger.

As she stepped onto the sidewalk, her will hardened. She was alone but wasn't helpless. The fight was hers now, a scientist against a covert machine, carrying a truth that could shake Helix and the world. The guard's stare lingered in her mind. She glanced over her shoulder, the city's gray horizon swallowing her as she walked toward the bus stop and home.

Chapter 9

Emotional Battlefield

The apartment door clicked shut behind Emily, the sound sharp against the stillness of the late morning. Her legs ached from the hurried walk from the Forest Hills station, her mind heavier still from the morning at the Helix office. She dropped her backpack onto the sagging chair, its patchwork throw slipping to reveal a stain from last summer's wine spill. The cozy Jamaica Plain apartment—usually a haven of mismatched furniture, overflowing bookshelves, and her thriving potted plants—felt off, its warmth soured by an oppressive quiet. The half-drawn blinds sliced the sunlight into long, jagged shapes across the hardwood floor.

Emily's breath slowed, but her pulse didn't. She was safe for now, after sifting through encrypted files at Helix that pointed to a conspiracy knitting together James, the Chronos network, and something far darker. Her relief at being home clashed with a gnawing unease that Tyler wasn't here. The kitchen's usual clatter and music were missing, leaving an unnerving silence. She pulled out her phone, thumb hovering over his name. Her texts from earlier were unanswered, their blue bubbles mocking her in the chat window. He hadn't come to bed last night, and now this. Her stomach twisted. *What if something happened to him?*

She crossed into the kitchen, the floor creaking under her as she filled the kettle. The faint scent of her favorite tea rose as she steeped it, but it did little to soothe her. She gripped her phone and dialed Tyler. Each ring tightened the knot in her chest. What was he doing? Was he trying to arrange protection without talking to her? Or worse—had someone gotten to him?

The call connected. "Hey, Emily." Tyler's voice was barely audible over the noise of the docks—jackhammers pounding, a ship horn blaring.

"Where are you?" she gushed. "You didn't answer my texts. I was worried."

"I'm fine. Be home in thirty." He paused, metal clanging filling the silence. "We'll talk then." The line went dead.

Emily stared at her phone, the screen dimming as her tea cooled, untouched on the counter. Thirty minutes. He'd promised answers, but his blunt response only left her with more questions. *Why did it sound like the wharf in the background of his call?*

The apartment's stillness swallowed her thoughts, and its once-inviting clutter—books stacked haphazardly, a fern drooping on the windowsill—now felt unsettled. She let out a sigh and relaxed onto the couch, finding small comfort in the cooling mug as a reprieve from her growing anxiety. Tyler was her partner, her confidant, but his absence and evasiveness stirred a fear she couldn't grasp. She wanted to protect him from the truths she'd uncovered at Helix, but his silence made her wonder if he was hiding something too.

The apartment door swung open twenty-eight minutes later, and Tyler stepped inside, his field jacket rumpled, streaked with dust and grime. Emily's heart lurched then faltered as she caught his eyes—dark, darting, sweeping the room like he expected an attack. He kicked the door shut, the thud echoing through the hardwood, rattling the framed photos on the wall. She stood from the couch, the mug of barely warm tea clattering against the glass sofa table as she set it down too fast.

"Tyler, what's going on?" Her voice was tense, sharpened by the unease that had built up since his abrupt call. Ignoring the question, he shrugged off his jacket and threw it onto the sofa. Then she saw it—a bulge in the pocket, heavy and unmistakable. A gun. Her breath caught, a cold prickle racing down her arms, her stomach twisting. "Is that a pistol?"

His hand twitched toward the pocket, then froze. "It's for protection," he said tersely. He brushed past her to the kitchen, grabbing a glass from the cupboard with a clink. The faucet hissed as he filled it, his back to her, shoulders taut.

"Protection from what?" Emily's voice cracked, her feet pulling her closer to the kitchen despite the urge to bolt out of the apartment. "You didn't have a gun yesterday. You swore you'd never bring one into our home. Where did you get it?"

Tyler turned, leaning against the kitchen counter. "An old friend from the Army," he muttered, eyes fixed on the floor. "Things are getting serious, Emily. You know that."

"Serious enough to get a gun behind my back?" She crossed her arms, nails biting into her palms. "Who is this friend, Tyler? Some random guy you haven't mentioned at all during our time together? What's his name?"

He flinched at her raised voice, setting the glass down with a crack that made her jump. "His name's Vic," he snapped, raw and defensive. "He's…not exactly a model citizen, okay? He got kicked out of the Army for some shady stuff, but he has connections. Boston's waterfront, people who handle dangerous situations."

Emily's eyes widened. "He's a criminal? You're borrowing guns from someone who was dishonorably discharged?" She stepped forward, her shout echoing off the walls. "What the hell, Tyler? You're acting like you don't trust me, running off to meet criminals!"

"Don't turn this on me!" he yelled back, his face flushing, veins pulsing at his temple. "You've been dodging me about Helix for days! What did you find this morning? Your cheeks are red, Emily—I can tell you're hiding something!" He gestured wildly, the glass wobbling on the counter.

Her throat burned. She hadn't told him about the encrypted files, the names tied to Chronos, the chilling hints of an international conspiracy that would end millions of lives. She wanted to protect him from that horror, but his accusation cut deep.

"I'm trying to keep us out of trouble," she shouted, her voice breaking. "But you're out there with Vic, sneaking around, bringing guns into our home! Who are you right now?"

Tyler's teeth ground together, his eyes glinting with something raw—guilt or fear. "I'm doing what I have to," he said, but the edge remained. "If we're going public with whatever you found, that'll paint targets on our backs. I'll do whatever I have to do to keep you safe, Em."

"By shutting me out?" Her voice cracked, trembling with fury and hurt. "We're supposed to be in this together! You're acting like I'm the enemy!"

Tyler's eyes softened, a flash of the man she knew. "You're not the enemy, Emily. I love you. I'd do anything for you." He shook his head, stepping toward the couch and sinking into it, shoulders slumped. The gun's weight dragged his jacket askew, a visible reminder of the threat facing them.

Emily sat at the other end of the couch, her heart pounding, palms slick with sweat. She wanted to cross the sofa, sit beside Tyler, and mend the rift, but his dangerous, unfamiliar edge held her back. She couldn't guess what he was concealing—Vic, the gun, his late night—the gulf between them seemed immense.

Her unspoken secrets, the conspiracy's ticking time bomb, gnawed at her conscience.

Settling onto the edge of the couch, Emily traced the frayed cushion seam with her fingers. Tyler sat stiffly at the far end of the sofa, his figure a stark silhouette in the midday sun streaming through the blinds. Their voices, raw from shouting, had fallen silent, leaving only the clatter of the old refrigerator and the distant wail of a siren winding through the streets of Jamaica Plain.

"We can't keep doing this," Emily said. "We need a plan. Something solid. If something happens to us, the evidence about the terminal gene, the extinction event, all of it can't disappear."

Her gaze flicked to Tyler's jacket, slung over the arm of the couch, the pistol's bulge a silent accusation. The gravity of what she'd uncovered at Helix that morning—encrypted files linking James, Chronos, and a conspiracy—strained against her chest. They needed someone to safeguard their findings, someone who would act if they couldn't.

Tyler nodded, his shoulders hunched as he ran his fingers through his hair, tiny beads of sweat forming at his hairline. "You're right. We need someone we can trust. Someone who won't crack under pressure." He paused, his eyes drifting to the scuffed hardwood. "Not Anita. She's too close, too soft. She'd be the first target they would go after if they couldn't get to us."

Emily's chest tightened at the mention of her best friend. Anita's funny stories and late-night wine chats while binge-watching romantic comedies felt like relics from a life untouched by the strangeness of the last few days.

"Agreed. Anita's out." An idea had been simmering since she left Helix, a desperate bid for support. "What about Dr. Catherine Morrow? My old mentor at Harvard. She's on the Helix board now and has connections. If anyone can do some-thing about James, it's her."

Tyler's head snapped up, his eyes narrowing, sharp as

broken glass. "A Helix board member? Emily, you can not be serious. That's like handing our evidence to the enemy." He leaned forward his fingers tightly intertwined. "How do you know she's not in on whatever is happening there?"

Emily's facial muscles tightened, her certainty wavering under his gaze. Catherine had been her guide in graduate school, who taught her to dissect data, question assumptions, and chase the truth no matter the result. But Tyler's fear wasn't baseless—Helix was a labyrinth of agendas, and the board was near its heart, despite what James had said in the covert emails she'd uncovered this morning.

Still, Catherine's influence was their best shot at exposing James and dismantling Chronos before the network became a reality. "She's not like that," Emily shot back, her voice sharper than she intended. "Catherine taught me to think for myself. She'd listen and has power, Tyler, genuine power in this city. She could get the evidence to the right people—regulators, journalists, someone who can stop this."

Tyler stood, pacing to the window, the floor creaking under his heavy steps. "Power makes people dangerous, Emily. You're betting everything on her being clean, but what if she's not? What if she's tied to James? Or worse, what if she takes the evidence and turns it against us?" He turned, his face half-lit by the harsh light, deep lines etched across his brow. "We'd be handing them the rope to hang us."

Was she betraying Tyler's instincts by pushing for Catherine? Her empathy for his fear of Helix, of exposure, clashed with her desperation for an ally who could tip the scales in their favor. "We can't do this alone," she said, pleading. "Catherine's not only a board member. She's fought for transparency before— against Helix's policies. She's got access to the resources we need. If we don't trust someone, we're potential victims." She gestured toward the jacket, the gun's outline stark. "You're already acting like we're at war. We need someone who can fight on our side."

Tyler's eyes flicked to the jacket then back to her, his mouth set in a frown. "And how do we know she's on our side? You haven't been close to her in years. People change. Power changes them." He stepped closer, his voice dropping. "What's her angle, Emily? Why would she risk everything to help us?"

Emily swallowed, her fingers stilling on the fern. She didn't have proof—only faith—faith in the woman who'd once stayed late to help her debug code, who'd challenged Helix's secrecy in board meetings. "Because she believes in the truth," she said, though doubts crept in. "And because we're out of options. Who else do we have, Tyler? You tell me."

Though he stopped pacing, his eyes continued their restless sweep of the room. "I don't know. Maybe...Sarah." His ex-girlfriend's name landed like a stone. "She's a partner at a powerful law firm. Knows how to handle sensitive documents. She's got no ties to Helix."

Emily's eyes squinted, a flare of irritation sparking in her voice. "Sarah? You think your ex is the answer?" She forced a breath, balancing herself against the bookshelf. "Sarah's not involved in this. She doesn't understand the stakes. Catherine does." The apartment's light shifted, becoming harsher, carving deep lines across Tyler's face as he turned toward her. She saw the exhaustion and the fear he wouldn't name, and it softened her tone. "Catherine's our best shot. I'll call her."

Tyler's silence hung heavy, his skepticism palpable. "You're putting our lives in her hands, Emily. If you're wrong..." He didn't finish, but the implication hung between them.

Emily pulled out her phone and dialed Catherine, each ring stretching across the chasm between her and Tyler. When Catherine answered, her voice was calm and measured, and Emily's words came carefully, highlighting the need for discretion and a meeting tomorrow at a neutral location away from

Helix. Catherine agreed, her tone even but curious, promising to listen.

With the phone call over, a heavy silence filled the room. Their plan felt like a house of cards, and Emily wondered if it—or they—could withstand the forces they were crossing. The couch between them, once a place of shared laughter, now marked the distance they couldn't cross.

Her hand lingered on the phone, her thumb brushing its edge as the screen faded to black. The call to Dr. Morrow had been a step forward, but it felt like stepping onto thin ice. She glanced at Tyler, his fingers fidgeting with the pistol in his jacket pocket. The soft click of the magazine being loaded and unloaded—a nervous tic—grated on her.

She wanted to ask again about his morning, to demand to know where he'd been and how he'd connected with Vic, but instead she turned away, her gaze fixed on the wilting fern on the windowsill, its drooping leaves curling inward like a silent accusation.

Tyler's footsteps broke the silence, heavy as he moved toward the door. "I need to check something outside," he muttered. His hand brushed the jacket, the bulge of the gun still visible.

Emily wanted to call him back and demand the truth, but fear of what he might say kept her still. The door clicked shut, leaving her alone on the couch in the eerily quiet apartment.

A few moments later, a car door slammed, the sound echoing off the brick buildings. She peered through the blinds and watched Tyler's car speed around the corner. She wondered, *Will we survive the truth and each other?*

Chapter 10

In Their Absence

The apartment smelled of stale tea and the musty scent of the old heater, a sourness that hung in the air like an unwelcome guest.

Emily paced the narrow living room, her thick wool socks snagging on the rough hardwood floor. The floorboards creaked under her weight, each step a minor rebellion against the silence Tyler had left behind. An hour ago, he'd mumbled about needing to check "something outside" and slipped out the door, his shoulders taut, eyes avoiding hers. No text, no call, nothing to mend the gap of their earlier argument—a sharp, unresolved clash about secrets they were keeping from each other. Now, the quiet taunted her.

She stopped by the sagging bookshelf, its shelves filled with dog-eared paperbacks and framed photos. One photo caught her eye: her and Tyler at the pier last summer, his arm slung around her, both of them squinting into the sun. Her smile in the photo looked effortless, unburdened. Now, her reflection in the glass felt like a stranger's—eyes dimmed, mouth straight. She turned away, her eyes fixed on the kitchen counter: a half-empty mug of chamomile tea, cold and film-coated, sat beside a stack of unwashed dishes. The faucet dripped, a slow, maddening plink.

In the past, Tyler always stayed in touch. Today's withdrawal was uncharacteristic of him, but the minutes passed, and her phone stayed silent. She pressed her lips together, resisting the urge to call him again. The third unanswered text already felt like a betrayal. Instead, she walked to the window, parting the faded curtains. The street below was empty, except for a stray dog. The city droned softly—distant horns, the low rumble of a passing bus—but it felt far away, like another world.

Her eyes darted to the shadows across the street. Did something move? A person hiding among the parked cars? She squinted, her heart skipping a beat, but it was only the dog weaving through the traffic.

"Stop it," she muttered, pressing her palms to her temples.

She gasped for air, desperate to escape the suffocating room. Grabbing her keys from the end table, she hesitated at the door, glancing back at the clock on the coffee table. He'd be back soon. He had to be. She'd take a quick walk and stay close enough to rush back when he called. The decision felt like rebellion, a small claim to control in an increasingly unstable world. She slipped on her sneakers, closing the door behind her, and stepped into the fading afternoon.

The cafe bustled with activity a block away, visible through its windows. Inside, the air was filled with the scent of seafood chowder and fresh sourdough, undercut by the sharp tang of brewed coffee. Emily slid into a corner table, the vinyl seat sticking to her thighs through her jeans. The place buzzed with life—clinking cups, the indistinct murmur of conversations, the guy at the front counter calling out an order for a double chowder. She scanned the room, noting the faces: a couple laughing softly, an older woman reading a newspaper, a man in a navy jacket tapping at his laptop. Ordinary, she told herself—nothing to fear.

She ordered a bowl of chowder and a grilled cheese sandwich, but when the food arrived, the steam curling from the bowl did nothing for her appetite. Her stomach churned. Where was he? Why hadn't he called? She stirred the soup absently, the spoon clinking against the stoneware, her eyes flicking to her phone every few seconds. The screen stayed blank. The urge to hear a familiar voice, something to settle her nerves, grew overwhelming. She dialed Anita.

"Hey, Em!" Anita's voice was warm, a burst of sunlight through the phone. "Thought you and Tyler had eloped on me. What's up?"

Emily forced a laugh, the sound catching in her throat. "I needed a break from the apartment. You at the office?"

The cafe's clamor faded as Emily gripped her phone. The warm scent of chowder was no match for her knotted stomach.

"Nah, I'm home," Anita said. "I went in earlier. You wouldn't believe the chaos—some new IT guy spilled coffee on a server in the archive room. Had to replace the whole thing, so I bailed."

The mention of the archive room drew Emily's attention. She'd been there early this morning, sifting through old files for clues. Was it a coincidence or something more? Her pulse quickened, the question curling tight in her chest, but she shoved it down, unwilling to let paranoia unravel the conversation.

She forced a chuckle, leaning into the familiar cadence of Anita's chatter. "Again? What's with these IT guys and their coffee?"

"I know," Anita said as she launched into a breathless parade of tales of home mishaps—petty roommates, her cat's latest antics.

Emily wanted to interrupt and tell her about the conspiracy, the fear, and the gun she'd seen in Tyler's jacket this morning. She opened her mouth, the truth forming on her lips, but then her eyes caught the man in the navy jacket. He'd glanced up from his laptop, his gaze lingering on her for a split-second before dropping back to his screen.

Her pulse spiked. Was he watching her? The cafe's warmth turned cloying, the chatter too loud. She gripped the phone tightly, her knuckles whitening. "Anita, I—"

No, she couldn't drag Anita into this, not without talking to Tyler. Not when she wasn't even sure what "this" was. She stopped mid-sentence.

"You okay?"

"Yeah...tired. I think I'm coming down with something." Emily's eyes flicked back to the man. He was typing again, his face blank. "Get a grip," she whispered to herself. "I gotta go, Anita. Talk tomorrow?"

"Uh, sure. Call if you need me, okay?" Anita's worried tone remained, but Emily ended the call before it could pull her under. She set the phone on the table, her hands shaking slightly. The chowder sat untouched, a thick, unappetizing film forming on its surface. She felt the significance of his quick, upward look even after he'd looked away, adding to her apprehension. She was seeing threats everywhere, wasn't she? But the gun in Tyler's jacket was real. The near-miss with the SUV was real too. And Tyler was still gone.

She pushed the bowl away. Her breath slowed. Whatever was happening, she'd figure it out. For Tyler. For herself. She had to stay sharp, cautious, and not let the fear win.

The late afternoon air nipped at Emily's face, carrying the sharp scent of decaying leaves and the distant salt of Boston's harbor, whipped up by a breeze off the water. She hurried toward her apartment building, the cafe's brief respite fading as she neared home.

As she turned the corner, red and blue lights flared against the fading daylight, slicing through the skeletal branches of the street's maples. A pair of police cars jammed the curb, their strobes glinting off the brick facade of her building. A knot of neighbors huddled near the entrance, bundled in scarves, their murmurs blending with the crackle of police radios.

Emily slowed, her breath misting in the chill. The confusion felt too pointed, too near. She imagined a domestic squabble, a robbery down the hall—something unrelated. But as she pushed through the crowd, their stares lingering, she glimpsed the hallway to her floor through the lobby's open door. Two officers stood outside her apartment, their figures stark against the dim, fluorescent lights. Her stomach dropped. This was no accident.

She climbed the stairs, the stairwell's air heavy with radiator warmth and a faint whiff of damp plaster. Each step dragged, her legs resisting the truth waiting above.

At her door, a sturdy woman turned, her badge catching the light. Officer Mooney filled the hallway, broad shoulders squared under a slightly rumpled uniform. Her piercing eyes, framed by crow's feet, locked onto Emily, reading her with a cop's keen instinct.

"Now that's a coincidence. You live here?" Mooney asked.

"Yes," Emily said. "What's going on?" She peered past Mooney, glimpsing her apartment through the half-open door. The living room was a wreck—furniture overturned, books strewn, the large, framed photo of her and Tyler from last fall's trip shattered, its glass sparkling like ice. Her chest tightened, a soundless cry trapped behind her ribs.

"Neighbor heard a ruckus," Mooney said, flipping open a worn notebook, her calloused fingers moving with practice. "Thought it might be domestic. You got a boyfriend, someone who might've been here?" That stirred guilt from her earlier argument with Tyler. Their heated argument, his abrupt exit into the gray afternoon wasn't violence, but it left a mark.

"No," Emily said quickly, then composed herself. "My fiancé was here earlier, but he left hours ago." Her voice felt frail, and she hated it. Mooney's pen paused, her hooded eyes flicking up, searching Emily's face. A faint, knowing smile tugged at her lips, gone in a blink. Emily hugged her coat tighter, chin rising. "What kind of ruckus?"

"Loud bangs, like a fight," Mooney said, her gaze steady but softened, as if to ease the sting. "You sure no one else was around? Nobody who'd have a key?" Her eyes missed nothing —Emily's tense shoulders, her glance toward the door.

Tyler was gone, wasn't he? But the conspiracy—the illegal gun in his coat from this morning, and a mention of his "friend" Vic—surfaced. Was this random or tied to that? Her mouth tasted of acid.

"Only my fiancé and I, and we were both out," she said, holding Mooney's gaze.

Mooney nodded sympathetically. "Mind if we walk through with you? Make sure it's safe?" Her hand rested on her duty belt near her radio, her stride slightly uneven as she shifted—a hint of an old injury.

Emily wanted to refuse, to guard the wreckage alone, but Mooney nudged her to agree. "Okay," she said, brushing past into the ruin of her home.

The air inside was heavy, thick with dust and a faint metallic scent, like stale sweat. The couch was overturned, its cushions slashed, foam spilling onto the floor. Emily's backpack was open, its contents—receipts, pens, a tangled charger—strewn across the room. This morning's tea mug was shattered, its contents staining the hardwood. Emily's knees trembled, but she pushed forward, searching for clues. Mooney and her partner, a young officer with a nervous tic, trailed behind, their boots crunching on broken glass.

In the kitchen, the radiator ticked softly, its heat oppressive. The faucet dripped in a subtle rhythm. Emily was glad she had taken her laptop to the cafe. Otherwise, it probably would have been stolen. Last night, out of paranoia, she hid the two thumb drives with the information she downloaded from Helix in the kitchen. Pretending to get a glass of water, she checked their hiding spot and sighed with relief—they were still there.

Emily moved to the bedroom, her pulse loud as she saw the mattress flipped, seams torn. Clothes spilled from the closet, and Tyler's shoes were tossed. Her gaze caught on the bathroom door, ajar, a glint flashing from within—something taped to the mirror.

"You alright?" Mooney asked. Her eyes tracked Emily's every move, sharp.

"Yeah," Emily lied, stepping into the bathroom. Her reflection stared back, pale and hollow, but the note held her focus: a torn scrap from Tyler's sketch pad, taped to the mirror's edge. Jagged script warned, "We know what you saw."

It was about this morning, the archive room files. Her fingers trembled as she peeled it off, folding it into her palm before slipping it into her coat pocket. She glanced back. Mooney was turned away, murmuring to her partner.

Was Officer Mooney involved? Her probing questions, her watchful gaze—too sharp, too curious? Or was Emily's fear twisting shadows again? The break-in could be random, but the note screamed intent, linked to Helix, Tyler's meeting with Vic, and their secrets. She needed to find Tyler to unravel this.

"We'll file a report," Mooney said, stepping into the bathroom doorway, her sturdy frame crowding the space. "Anything missing you notice?"

Emily shook her head, touching the pocket where the note sat. "Not yet," she said, voice trembling as she brushed away a tear. She wouldn't trust Mooney, not until she knew more. The violation of her home, the scattered pieces of her life with Tyler, only sharpened her resolve. She couldn't afford to wait any longer — they were becoming bolder.

The apartment lay in gloom, the midafternoon light dulled by heavy clouds pressing against the windows. Emily stood near the kitchen, her fingers grazing the note in her coat pocket. Officer Mooney lingered in the bedroom hallway.

The front door creaked, and Tyler stumbled in, his jacket rumpled, hair damp with sweat despite the chill. His eyes nervously darted across the wreckage before landing on Emily. She felt relieved he was here, but it soured as she scanned him. No bulge under his jacket, no change in his stride. The gun she'd feared he'd taken when he stormed out was gone. Her stomach twisted.

"Where were you?" she whispered, stepping close, her voice low to avoid Mooney's ears.

Tyler's gaze flicked to Mooney then back to Emily, his jaw locked rigid. "Went for a drive. Needed to clear my head." His breath carried a faint tang of cigarette smoke, though he'd sworn he'd quit. He ran a hand through his hair, his fingers trembling slightly. "What the hell happened here?"

Emily's eyes narrowed, searching his face for the truth. She pulled him into the bedroom, away from Mooney's scrutiny, the torn mattress and scattered clothes amplifying the tension. "Someone broke in while I was at the cafe," she said, her voice low. "And this was on the mirror." She slipped the note from her pocket, unfolding it with shaking hands. Tyler's face paled as he read it, his lips pressing into a thin line.

"Damn it," he muttered, crumpling the paper in his fist. "This is about your digging at Helix." His eyes met hers, sharp with accusation. "You didn't tell anyone else, did you?"

"No," she snapped, stung by the implication. "But you're not telling me everything either. The note could be about Vic, too." Her voice wavered, the burden of his secrecy pressing against her loyalty. She wanted to trust him, to believe his desperation was about fear for them both, but his evasions gnawed at her. Was he protecting her or hiding something worse?

Mooney's voice cut through from the hallway. "Everything okay in there?" Her heavy steps drew closer, her silhouette stretching across the doorway. Emily's pulse spiked. She shoved the note back into her pocket.

"Yeah," Tyler called and stepped toward the door, blocking Mooney's view. "I'm checking the damage." His shoulders were tense, his posture defensive, and Emily saw Mooney's eyes narrow.

"I need you both to answer a few more questions," Mooney said. "Anything you can tell us about enemies? Debts? Someone who'd want to send a message?" Her eyes flicked between them, lingering on Tyler's disheveled clothes, his fidgeting hands.

Emily's throat tightened. She thought of the files she'd found at Helix, the cryptic texts. "No," she said, her tone controlled despite the lie. "Nothing like that." Tyler nodded, but his silence felt heavy, his eyes avoiding Mooney's. His defiance, his refusal to engage, only deepened the officer's scrutiny. Emily's stomach churned. Were the police allies or another threat? Tyler's muttered curses about "cops poking around" earlier echoed in her mind, feeding her doubt.

Mooney scribbled something in her notebook. "Alright," she said, "we'll need a list of anything missing. And stay reachable." Her eyes held Emily's for a long moment before she turned to her partner.

As Mooney stepped back into the hall, Emily grabbed Tyler's arm, her fingers digging into his sleeve. "What's going on?" she whispered, her voice raw. "Where's the gun? What did you do?" His eyes darted away, and the silence between them was louder than the front door closing as the police left.

The apartment was a crime scene now, cordoned off with yellow police tape that fluttered in the draft from the cracked window.

Emily sat on the floor amid the wreckage, her back against the wall, the note's menace echoing in her mind. Tyler slumped beside her, his knees drawn up, his face buried in his hands.

They were waiting for the locksmith, the door undamaged

but untrustworthy. Emily was sure she'd locked it before going to the cafe, which meant someone had a key. She shivered at the thought.

Mooney had left but promised to follow up as the door closed behind her. Her eyes had mixed concern and suspicion as she'd turned away. Emily couldn't shake the feeling that Mooney saw too much. Her questions about enemies and debts were circling too close to the truth. Were the police watching them now, too?

She looked at Tyler, trying to understand what he was doing. Her fear of the note, Vic, and the unseen eyes watching them fought with her need to take control. She couldn't wait for answers or trust Tyler's half-truths or Mooney's promises. The files at Helix and the names in the emails were real, and she was determined to uncover what they meant, no matter the cost.

She pulled her phone out of her back pocket and pressed redial. "Hi, Dr. Morrow, I'm sorry to bother you again so soon. I know we agreed to meet tomorrow evening, but I don't think we can wait that long."

Chapter 11

I Knew You Were Trouble

Emily sat across from Tyler in a dimly lit bar, The Wet Spot, a gritty hole-in-the-wall a block from Helix's towering headquarters. The air hung heavy with the musty smell of stale beer and the faint grease of fried food. Neon signs buzzed overhead, their shimmering reds and blues painting the room in a garish glow that danced across sticky tabletops and the weathered faces of scattered customers. A low hum of conversation rippled through the space, interrupted by the clink of glassware and a sudden bark of laughter from a group of men hunched over playing cards in the corner.

Tyler's fingers fidgeted with his beer glass, tracing restless patterns in the condensation. His eyes flicked to the door again, a nervous habit that set Emily's nerves on edge. She leaned forward. Her drink was untouched, the ice melting into a watery glass of gin and tonic. The bar's rough edges sharply contrasted with Helix's sterile presence only a few blocks away. But that comfort vanished as she watched Tyler's discomfort grow.

"Tyler, you've been jittery all day," she said, her voice low. "What's going on?"

He quickly turned his gaze to her, irritated and anxious. "I'm fine, Emily. Let me handle this situation my way, okay?"

She held her lips together, swallowing the hurt. They were here because Tyler had agreed to escort her to Helix, but she'd insisted on this location, claiming the company had "too many eyes and ears." Now, that excuse felt flimsy.

Since the cryptic text messages had started, she couldn't shake the sensation of being watched, a constant prickle of fear. Her eyes darted across the bar, scanning faces half-hidden in shadow. Was that man in the corner staring or lost in his drink? Had the woman at the counter glanced her way too often? The uncertainty gnawed at her, but she forced it down.

She had a mission: to get into Helix's archive room and find verifiable proof of Project Chronos's dark side. Without evidence, her suspicions were noise that could be easily dismissed. To accuse the CEO of a global conspiracy without confirmation would make Emily seem a little crazy.

"I need to do this," she murmured. "I need to get more evidence to back up my claims."

Tyler nodded quickly with a slight jerk, but his attention remained on the door. Emily followed his gaze, watching a couple stumble into the night, their laughter lost in the darkness beyond the glass.

She stood, smoothing her jacket. The jukebox in the corner sputtered to life, its speakers spilling a haunting cover of "I Knew You Were Trouble." The melody curled through the air, the bright, upbeat tune contrasting with the dread pooling in her stomach. But the lyrics lingered, a quiet taunt to her plan to confront James.

"Here goes nothing," she said.

Pausing for a moment, Tyler leaned in and kissed her. "Be careful."

She hugged him and then headed for the door. Stepping into the cool evening air, she gave him a small goodbye wave, the song's refrain fading behind her like a ghostly echo of the trouble to come as she hurried the few blocks to the Helix offices.

Emily's footsteps echoed as she entered the marble-floored Helix lobby. The security guard at the desk barely glanced up from his screen as she swiped her badge and passed through the turnstile.

It was late Saturday evening, and the building felt empty, lacking its usual weekday buzz. The empty building's silence closed in around her. The overhead lights cast uneven shade across the sterile space. Tyler's warning to be careful echoed in her ears as she left him at The Wet Spot, but she knew it was better to go alone. His being in the archive room would trigger alarms throughout the company. Discretion was the best approach, especially when she was closing in on the truth.

The elevator ride was quiet, the soft ding when the doors opened standing out in the silence. In the corridor, a confusing maze of glass walls and sharp corners stretched before her, the air thick with the buzz of unseen equipment. Her pulse beat steadily—hope battling the fear that had taken root in her since leaving the bar. She was confident she could find the proof to support her claims.

She reached the archive room and stopped short. A crooked sign taped on the door read, "UNDER REPAIR." Her stomach twisted. She'd heard about the server issue from Anita that morning—a spilled coffee, a minor mishap. But this closure felt deliberate.

She slid her keycard through the reader. A flicker of hope faded as the light flashed red with a sharp beep—access denied. Her fingers tightened around the card, her mind racing. This wasn't a coincidence. She was locked out.

Her thoughts darted to the puzzling text messages that had haunted her for days, their vague warnings fueling the tingle on her neck. The mysterious texts fostered a sense of constant surveillance, but the confrontations were growing more direct. She pulled her phone from her pocket and scrolled through them. "Next time, you won't walk away." No specifics, just menace.

Her hands trembled slightly as she shoved her laptop back into her bag, then reached deeper, searching for the two backup drives she'd kept after her last data pull. Her fingers froze—nothing. They were gone. She'd had them this afternoon after the break-in. The bar, the crowd—had someone taken them? Or had she misplaced them in her rush? Either way, the absence boosted her paranoia.

She needed another way into the archived files. A terminal flickered faintly a few steps down the hall, a workaround she had previously accessed using a backdoor trick. She hurried over, hunched over the keyboard as she entered her credentials. The screen flickered briefly, then changed. A screen loaded, stark and ominous, showing a single line, "How much is the truth worth?"

The question burned into her mind, a chill running down her spine. The terminal shut down abruptly before she could process it, a harsh buzz cutting her off. She stumbled back, heart pounding. Someone at Helix was watching, blocking her every move. They knew she was close.

A surge of defiance, hot and fierce, flowed through her. She wouldn't fold — not now. Tyler's jittery distraction at the bar flashed in her mind, his hesitation to move forward. She was on her own, and that was okay. She thought of James, the CEO, his smooth voice dropping hints about the importance of the terminal gene for humanity—hints that now felt like bait. He would know something.

She spun around, heading for the elevator, her determination growing with each step. The executive floor was waiting.

The top floor of Helix headquarters was a world apart from the labs Emily knew so well. Polished wood paneling lined the walls, soaking up the dim, amber glow of sconces that cast long, conspiratorial shadows. The air carried the faint scent of leather, contrasting with the sterile smell of the lower levels. It was late in the evening, and the dark and deserted corridor stretched before her, with the thick carpet muffling her footsteps as she moved forward.

A thin strip of light leaked from beneath James's office door, piercing through the gloom. Emily's breath caught. He was here working late on a weekend. Why? Her mind raced with possibilities, each more troubling than the last. She edged closer, sinking into the carpet, her approach silent. The door was slightly ajar, and through the gap she glimpsed him pacing with his back to her, phone pressed to his ear. His voice was low and clipped.

"We need to keep the gene data under control," he insisted. "No more leaks. Eliminate any loose ends—immediately."

Emily's blood ran cold. She slipped inside and ducked behind his desk while he stared out of a window. His office was a display of luxury—floor-to-ceiling windows showcased a dazzling view of the city's skyline and the busy harbor. Polished chrome and dark wood dominated the space, reflecting James's cold detachment. Her hands trembled as she shuffled through the files on his desk, looking for anything that might confirm her suspicions. Her fingers brushed against a folder labeled "Terminal Gene Data Logs," a partial record of revised data. She clutched it to her chest beneath her coat.

She fumbled for her phone, hitting the record button as James kept talking. "The trials are on schedule, but we can't let this slip. We're ready to move to the next phase." He paused, listening, then let out a low, chilling chuckle. "Don't worry. I've got it handled. The rest of the board won't suspect a thing."

The call ended, and silence filled the room. Emily's mind raced. The kill switch. *Controlling it. Loose ends.* It wasn't a project—it was a tool for power, a betrayal of Helix's mission, and James was at its core. He had given her the confirmation she needed. She stepped out from behind the desk, her voice trembling. "What are you doing to the data, James?"

He spun around, surprise flashing across his face before his trademark smile slid into place, disarming yet predatory. "Emily. Working late, are we?"

"Answer me," she snapped, closing the distance between them. "What's the terminal gene really about? What are you keeping from the board?"

James pocketed his cell phone, his sigh loud and theatrical. "You're jumping at ghosts, Emily. The terminal gene is an opportunity—complicated, but it's progress. You of all people should see that."

"Opportunity?" Her voice rose, anger breaking through her restraint. "I've seen enough to know it's dangerous. The archive room was locked down, and my access was denied. Someone's covering tracks, and it all points back to you."

His smile curdled. "I don't know about the archive room being locked. Maybe it's a sign you're pushing too hard. You should slow down and take some time to rest."

"Slow down?" She laughed. "After the threats I've gotten? After you told me I had three months to prepare to go public? Someone's watching me, James, and I bet you know who."

He stepped closer, his presence dominating and intense. "No one is watching you, Emily. It's just business. Paranoia's clouding your judgment. If you're getting threats, it's not my doing. I'm protecting Helix—protecting us. Trust me."

"Trust you?" She held his gaze, unwavering, her voice confident with conviction. "I submitted the terminal gene analysis at the board meeting. What was left out, James? What other information are you trying to hide?"

A hint of something—guilt? His face showed a flash of regret when she mentioned the board that would be caught in its crosshairs. But it vanished as he leaned closer, his smile widening, a glint of challenge in his eyes. "You're a scientist, Emily. Dig for it yourself. The truth's there if you can find it."

The deflection sparked her fury. "You've reviewed my personal genetic data, haven't you?" she guessed, gripping the file tighter. "What did it show?"

He shrugged, his charm masking the steel beneath. "Of course, I looked it over. You're an asset to Helix. It's about protecting Helix, nothing more. If you want to know your kill switch date, look for it yourself."

His refusal to answer rattled her, and her instincts battled doubt. She turned to go, but his voice stopped her at the door. "Be careful, Emily. Not everyone plays by the same rules."

She didn't look back as she stormed into the elevator, her mind a jumble of frustration and determination. He was taunting her, dangling half-truths like bait. As the doors closed behind her, her phone buzzed. She grabbed it, heart skipping a beat at the message. "Walk away while you still can."

Emily stepped out of the elevator, battling a storm of doubt. James's manipulation had shaken her, his charm and vague promises gnawing at her confidence, but the file tucked into her jacket—proof of his tampering with the terminal gene data—burned against her chest, fueling her boldness. She wasn't the same cautious researcher who'd walked into Helix years ago; she was now a relentless seeker of truth, ready to challenge James and anyone else standing in her way.

As she moved through the deserted corridors, the magnitude of betrayal settled over her like a cloud. It wasn't only James's duplicity that cut deep—it was Tyler's sudden, strange behavior, the distance in his eyes at the bar earlier, the fracture in a relationship she'd once trusted. Helix's pursuit of control through the terminal gene would cost human lives, families like hers. His charisma was a flimsy mask for his villainy.

The archive room loomed ahead, its "UNDER REPAIR" sign a mocking barrier. She pulled out her phone, her fingers quick as she texted Dr. Morrow, "I have evidence. We need to talk. I'll see you at your house in the morning." As she pressed send, her confidence grew. Dr. Morrow would back her up.

As Emily stepped outside Helix, the cool night air slapped her face, contrasting with the stifling heat of her confrontation with James. Her pulse hammered in her ears, and the stolen file pressed against her chest like a live wire, crackling with the betrayal she'd just witnessed. She'd left Tyler at The Wet Spot— needing his composed presence to calm her after the stress of Helix.

But as she reached the bar, her breath caught. Tyler was there, slumped against the grimy brick wall of the alley, his silhouette distorted by the dim streetlight. Her stomach twisted into a knot as she took in the scene: his clothes were wrinkled and torn, a fresh cut above his eyebrow bleeding down his cheek and staining the collar of his jacket.

"Tyler?" she called, her voice trembling with rising panic. She quickened her pace, but as she drew closer, her heart fluttered. His eyes—usually so warm, so sure—were distant and unfocused. He didn't seem to recognize her for a terrifying moment, his head tilting slightly as if she were a stranger intruding on his haze. The ground shifted beneath her feet, and the world seemed to tilt dangerously.

"Ty, it's me," she said, her voice cracking as she reached out, needing to touch him, to bridge the distance. Her fingers brushed his arm, and finally something like recognition appeared in his gaze.

"Oh, hey, Em. When'd you get here?" he rasped, his voice uncertain, like he was pulling her name from a fog. "You okay?" The question—so quintessentially Tyler, always putting her first —pierced her, unleashing a rush of conflicting emotions. Relief that he knew her warred with a sharp, searing hurt that he could ask about her when he was broken.

"I'm fine," she lied as her eyes traced his injuries: the bruise blooming along his jawline, the blood dripping, the way his hands trembled faintly. Tyler didn't get into fights. He was her rock, holding her steady when everything else spun out of control. Seeing him like this—disheveled, vulnerable, lost—felt like watching the last tether to her sanity tighten.

"What happened to you?" she asked in disbelief.

He shrugged and winced, his face twisting in pain. He vaguely gestured toward the nearby bar, muttering incoherently about a fight. "Nothing serious. A little rattled is all."

He didn't stumble into bar fights and come out bleeding. Something was terribly wrong—horribly, viscerally wrong—and her mind scrambled, trying to think of possibilities. A concussion? Something worse? The thought of a connection to Helix and the threats she'd been receiving sent a chill down her spine.

"Tyler, you're hurt. I'm going to call an ambulance," she said, digging in her bag for her phone as her vision blurred as she fought back tears.

He shook his head too hard and swayed dangerously. "Errrr, no. I'm fine. Need to walk it off."

Emily's fear intensified. He was disoriented, and his mind was slipping. She guided him back into The Wet Spot, the bar's dim interior enveloping them as she eased him into a booth near the door. Her hands shook as she dabbed at his cut with a napkin, the blood staining her fingers.

"Tyler, look at me," she begged, cupping his face. His eyes met hers but wavered, struggling to focus. "Who did this? What do you remember?"

A flash of confusion crossed his face. "I...don't know. A couple of guys were asking about you. Then...it's blank."

Someone had been asking about her, and now Tyler was injured. The danger she'd thought she could contain at Helix had followed her here, sinking its claws into the one person she couldn't bear to see hurt. Guilt crashed over her, heavy and suffocating. "This is my fault," she said, tears spilling over. "I dragged you into this."

"No, Emily," he said, his hand finding hers, his grip weak but stubborn. "We're a team." But his eyes betrayed him—clouded, uncertain—and she saw the truth. He was falling apart, and she was alone to carry them both.

They stepped outside to their car parked nearby. With the stolen file hidden inside her coat, James's warnings echoed in her mind as the city lights blurred beyond her view. Her world was falling apart. But a spark ignited. She was determined to fight for him, for the truth.

Chapter 12

Saturday Night's Alright

Tyler slumped at a corner table in The Wet Spot, his whiskey glass slick with condensation against his palm. The bar pulsed with restless energy, its neon signs casting a jittery glow—red, then blue, then red again, like a faulty heartbeat. The bar counter, scratched and gouged from years of neglect, shone dull under the dim lights, while the jukebox in the corner blared out classic rock, its volume an assault on Tyler's frayed nerves. Thick clouds of stale cigarette smoke and cheap liquor hung in the air, burning his throat with every breath. Clearly, the "No Smoking" signs weren't taken seriously.

He had switched from beer to whiskey twenty minutes ago, seeking a clarity the alcohol refused to provide. Emily had left for Helix—maybe thirty minutes back or more. She had hugged him tight before leaving, her lips brushing his cheek, her eyes filled with a trust that now sat heavy in his gut. She was hunting for evidence against Helix's CEO, the man Tyler hated with a quiet, fiery intensity.

Two days remained until his kill switch deadline, a date with death inching closer, and his mind buzzed with static—thoughts fleetingly dancing, half-formed, then vanishing. *I gotta stay alert for her sake*, he thought grimly, his expression held against the fog creeping into his mind.

The bar's commotion wore on him—raucous laughter, the clink of bottles, a shout from the far end where a group of leather-clad men clustered. He needed help to ground himself. Pulling out his phone, he texted Vic, fingers erratic on the screen. "Get to The Wet Spot. Now."

Vic's reply came quickly but was vague. "Nearby. Business first."

Tyler's stomach tightened. "If Emily shows, act like we're strangers," he texted back. She'd never put up with Vic's rough edges, his murky side gigs. The whiskey burned his throat as he swallowed, but it did little to calm the tremble in his hands or the noise in his head.

Tyler's head throbbed, a dull pulse syncing with the jukebox's bass pounding out a classic Elton John song. He scanned the bar, the faces of the crowd blurring at the edges of his vision, distorting into shadows. *Where did I put my gun this morning?* The question drifted unanswered, as did the memory of what he'd said to Emily before she left. Her voice lingered, soft but firm, though what she'd said escaped him. The uncertainty fed a gnawing dread.

A server, her apron stained and her eyes weary, slowed by his table, balancing a tray of smudged glasses. "Hey, you alright? You look like you're a million miles away, hon." Her voice was gentle, dripping with pity, making Tyler's teeth grind.

He squinted at her, his head foggy. "I'm fine. Leave me alone."

She hesitated, frowning. "You want something to eat?"

His irritation flared—her sympathy was an intrusion he didn't want. "No," he snapped, pulling his phone from his pocket—blank screen. No Emily. No Vic. He shoved it back into his pocket, glowering until she shuffled off.

Two men approached, cutting through the haze around his table. Their eyes flashed with a sharpness that made Tyler's jaw ache. "You're Tyler, right? Emily's friend?" the first asked, his tone light but probing.

"Yeah, she's my fiancé," Tyler replied, voice low, guarded. "Who's asking?"

"We work at Helix," the second said, dropping into the chair opposite him uninvited. "Saw Emily heading into the office tonight. Odd time for it, huh?"

The first man waved at the bartender. "Get this guy another drink—on us. Looks like he's got time to kill." Tyler's core clenched, a spike of adrenaline slicing through the whiskey's dullness. *Were they James's dogs, sniffing out what Emily was after?* He rechecked his phone—nothing.

His mind raced, imagining their smug faces in a different light—combat zones, sand and blood, enemies who'd underestimated him. He tightened his grip on the glass.

"She's dedicated," he mumbled, offering a strained shrug. "What's your point?"

The first man moved his chair closer, his smile thinning. "She's been poking around lately, asking questions about things better left alone."

"Yeah," the second chimed in, sprawling back in his chair. "Figured you might be lonely without her. Stick around, man. Have a few rounds with us. Keep the night interesting." His grin was a trap, baiting Tyler to stay put.

Tyler's eyes narrowed. "I'm good." He glanced at his phone —still silent. *Come on, Emily.*

"Oh, relax," the first man pressed, voice oily. "No need to rush off. We're getting to know Emily's fiancé. What's your story, huh? You look like you spend some time at the gym."

Their aggression snapped into focus—they were here to stall him, to keep him from Emily. "Beat it," he growled.

The second man chuckled, a harsh sound that grated on Tyler's nerves. "Or what? You gonna cry to her about it?" Mimicking crying, he puckered his lips and rubbed his fists around his eyes.

Tyler's control frayed, with bare threads snapping one after another. *Protect Emily*, he repeated as he leaned in toward the man.

The bartender, a hulking figure covered in tattoos, stared sharply at the men at the table. He grabbed a baseball bat from behind the counter and slammed it down with a *BANG* that cut through the noise. "Cool it or take it outside!" he barked, his gaze sweeping over the table. Tyler's muscles tensed, his body ready, on the verge of something he couldn't quite name.

The first man leaned in, his breath sour, eyes flashing under the bar's neon. "Tell Emily to watch herself. Wouldn't mind teaching her a lesson or two if you know what I mean," he said with a wink.

Tyler's vision narrowed to a pinpoint of red, a surge of heat flooding his skull. He lunged, hands seizing the man's collar, and slammed his face into the table with a force that sent glasses tumbling, shattering on the sticky floor in a spray of liquid and jagged shards.

The Wet Spot erupted—shouts exploded from the crowd, chairs screeched as they were pushed back, and customers surged forward, a restless tide drawn to the violence. The jukebox pounded on, its relentless bass line throbbing through the air, thick with cigarette smoke and the bitter odor of spilled liquor.

Trained to precision through endless hours of close combat, Tyler's punches landed instinctively, each strike releasing tension. He had always been the steady one, the medic who sutured wounds under fire, his hands calm even when blood soaked the sand. But now he was a storm, wild and unbound, driven by a desperate need to protect Emily from whatever these men represented—James's pawns, sent to stop her digging.

The second man swung at him, fist grazing Tyler's cheekbone, a sharp sting that sparked memories of backroom brawls, of nights when survival meant striking first and without mercy. He tasted copper on his tongue, blood mixing with the whiskey's burn, but it didn't slow him down. His body knew the rhythm of combat, and his muscle memory from years of training overrode the fog in his mind.

Mid-swing, his thoughts blanked, and the reason for the fight faded into a blur. Why was he here? The question nagged at him, then disappeared, leaving only a primal urge to stop these men. He grabbed a beer bottle from the table, its weight solid in his hand, and smashed it over the second man's head. Glass exploded in a glittering arc, catching the neon light like shrapnel under a flare. He staggered, clutching his scalp, blood seeping between his fingers as he swore. The crowd roared, some cheering, others pushing to get away, their voices a wall of noise pressing against Tyler's ears.

The first man scrambled up, face contorted with rage, and charged. Tyler sidestepped, years of training guiding his feet, and drove his elbow into the man's ribs, a dull crack echoing through the noise. The man gasped, doubling over, but Tyler didn't stop. He landed another blow, knuckles cracking against bone, pain surging through his arm. His mind flashed—images of Emily at Helix, alone and vulnerable—driving each blow. *They're after her.* That thought was a drumbeat, constant and relentless, fueling his rage as memories unraveled, cracks spreading like ice.

A massive figure loomed—the bartender, a wall of muscle

with a shaved head and a Louisville Slugger in his meaty hand. He barreled through the crowd, parting it like a battleship through waves, and seized Tyler's arm, gripping it tight.

"Enough!" he roared, voice cutting through the noise as he yanked Tyler toward the exit. Tyler's boots skidded on the slippery floor, his chest heaving, breath ragged. The bartender's strength was overwhelming, dragging him past toppled chairs and spilled drinks, the crowd's shouts fading to a dull roar.

Tyler's knuckles stung, blood streaking his hands, smearing across his jeans as he stumbled to the entrance. The night air met his flushed skin, the blood and sweat on his brow turning clammy. The two men, battered and dazed, hobbled out toward the back, one clutching his side, the other wiping blood from his face. They vanished into the dim hallway, their retreat a fleeting victory that did little to ease the knot in Tyler's shoulders. The bartender loomed in the doorway, phone in hand, his tattooed arm tense.

His eyes narrowed, hard as flint. "Out, or I'll call the cops," he growled.

Tyler slumped against the alley's grimy brick wall, its rough edges biting through his torn jacket. His knuckles stung, scraped raw, as his ragged breaths mingled with the damp, sour smell of the alley. Shadows stretched across the pavement under a dying streetlamp, the world tilting beneath him. His head throbbed, pulsing behind his eye—memories of the fight—fists, shouts, broken glass, scattered in a fog that swallowed the rest.

Two days left. The kill switch's deadline was pushing him to act. He needed to get the gun he had stashed in the apartment building's basement, though he didn't remember the exact spot. *Gotta stop James. Keep her safe.* His trembling hands wiped blood and dirt onto his torn jeans, each motion grounding him against the creeping disorientation.

The distant thump of bass from The Wet Spot pulsed faintly,

syncing with his racing heart. Tyler squinted into the dark, trying to cut through the haze for clarity. He couldn't remember whether he had stopped them or if they were still after Emily. But he would fight, even if it meant losing himself. Pushing off the wall, he stilled his shaking legs, his resolve firming. He had to get moving—*now*.

A figure approached him from Helix, footsteps loud and quick on the concrete. Tyler's eyes locked on her—*her?*—but the face was a blur, features smudged like a half-remembered dream. She seemed familiar, someone he knew, but her name slipped away, a whisper lost in the haze. He swallowed, his throat dry as sandpaper, and stepped back cautiously.

The woman broke into a run, her pace urgent, her breath visible in the cool night air. Tyler's pulse quickened, a flash of alarm sparking in his gut. *Why is she running? Is she coming after me?* His thoughts were fractured, jagged pieces that wouldn't fit. He pressed a hand to his temple, wincing as pain flared.

"Tyler?" The woman's voice cut through the darkness, trembling with raw emotion—fear, possibly. It pierced his fog, and the world snapped into focus at that moment. Her face sharpened under the streetlamp—dark eyes wide, lips parted in a gasp. *Emily.* The name slowly surfaced, like a rusty chain pulling him from the depths. The relief was fleeting, replaced by the ache in his cheek.

"Oh, hey, Emily," he rasped, his voice gravelly. "When'd you get here?" His gaze darted to the paper in her hands, then back to her face, worry etched into every line. "You okay?"

"I'm fine," she said, shaking her head. "What happened to you?" she whispered.

He shrugged, wincing as his ribs protested. "Nothing serious. A little rattled is all," he muttered, nodding vaguely toward the bar. The words felt thin, a shield against the truth he couldn't grasp—why he'd fought, who'd swung first. Her eyes, wide and searching, bore into him, and shame twisted in his stomach. She needs me to be stable, and I'm falling apart.

"Tyler, you're hurt. We need to get you help," she said, fumbling for her phone, her hands quaking. Tears shone in her eyes, and the sight unsettled him—her fear a reflection of his failure.

He shook his head too quickly, causing the alley to tilt. "Er, no. I'm fine. Need to walk it off."

She guided him inside The Wet Spot, where the dim light swallowed them as she helped him into a booth. The bartender's eyes—stern and watchful—tracked them from behind the counter. Emily forced a tight smile. "He's feeling better now," she said, but her voice wavered unconvincingly.

Her hands trembled as she dabbed at his cuts with a napkin, blood smearing her fingers. "Tyler, look at me," she pleaded, cupping his face. His gaze met hers, struggling to focus through the haze. "Who did this? What do you remember?"

Confusion pulsed through him as his brow furrowed. "I... don't know. A couple of guys talking about you. Then...it's blank."

"This is my fault," she whispered. "I dragged you into this."

"No, Emily," he said, taking her hand, grip weak. "We're a team." But his voice cracked, and doubt gnawed at him as she guided him out the door.

Outside, the city lights blurred as they hurried to their car, Emily clutching something tightly under her jacket. Tyler eased into the driver's seat, the car's worn leather creaking under his weight. A heavy silence hung between him and Emily, thick with the bar's lingering smoke and his own sweat. His hands gripped the steering wheel, knuckles raw and stinging, but they trembled too much to press the ignition button.

Emily sat beside him, her presence both comforting and burdensome—her trust a thread he feared he'd already broken. His mind churned. *Retrieve the gun from the laundry room, track down James, and end this before the kill switch takes what is left of me.* Across the street, Vic's silhouette stood under a streetlamp, waving insistently, beckoning him to follow. *What does he want?*

"Think I'm going to be sick," Tyler muttered, avoiding her gaze. "Need to step out of the car."

She reached for the keys. "Let me drive."

"No!" he said sharply, and she flinched, hurt flickering across her face. Guilt sank deeper. "Give me a minute, Em," he said softly, forcing calm he didn't feel. "Too much whiskey. Stupid mistake."

Emily's gaze shifted to the street, mirroring Tyler's stare. Her eyes narrowed. "Who's that guy? He's staring at us."

Tyler's stomach dropped. He'd hoped to keep Vic hidden. "Nobody," he muttered, voice rough, but her look held him, demanding the truth.

"Do *not* lie to me, Tyler." She leaned forward, her eyes flashing with anger. "You know each other. Why's he here?"

He rubbed his face, the split on his lip stinging. "It's Vic. I told you about him this morning. I texted him to come by while you were at Helix. Thought I needed backup."

Emily's face tightened, her lips pressing thin. "Backup? Without telling me? After everything that's happened today?" Her voice rose, edged with anger. "You're falling apart, and now you're dragging in some sketchy guy I don't know?"

"I'm trying to keep you safe," he said, desperate. "I'm running out of options to get us help."

She looked at him and exhaled loudly. "Fine. I'll trust you to fix this—right now. Find out what he wants. But no more secrets." Her tone was firm, but her eyes flickered with a hint of fear. She nodded hesitantly, settling back into the seat with a faint shake of her head.

Tyler stepped out of the car, the night air cool and biting at the blood crusted on his face and hands. Vic's silhouette lingered, a pull he couldn't resist.

He looked at Emily—her face a mix of love and doubt—and turned away. He'd follow Vic, face whatever was waiting, and protect her at all costs. The kill switch ticked. Only two days left, but he'd fight James—and the darkness following Emily—to his last breath.

Chapter 13

Friends Like These

"Hey, wait up, Vic," Tyler yelled as he waited at the alley entrance for Emily to get out of the parked car.

Emily splashed in the muddy puddle, the cold water soaking her shoes, and wondered what Tyler had gotten them into. It was after midnight. The city buzzed with a dangerous energy, shouting and car horns echoing through the streets. Her nerves twitched with every flicker that darted in her peripheral vision.

Hurrying after Tyler, she trudged through the grimy back-streets of Seaport, trying to avoid the deeper puddles that reflected the jittery glow of alternate reality billboards overhead. The virtual signs pulsed, their neon hues of electric blue and sickly green bleeding into the night, illuminating the cracked pavement and graffiti-covered walls in flickering light. The air pressed against her skin, heavy with the damp smell of salt from the nearby harbor.

She glanced at Tyler a few yards ahead, his stride weaving and eyes locked on Vic's silhouette weaving through the dirty alley. The shifting lights turned Tyler's face into a puzzle—sharp jawline one moment, an unreadable mask the next. Emily's stomach twisted tighter with each step. She didn't trust Vic with his vague past, and now he was leading them on a midnight hike to nowhere. Tyler's insistence on following him only deepened her concern.

"Why are we trailing Vic through this dump?" she asked, her voice tinged with irritation. "This place feels like a trap."

Tyler kept his gaze straight ahead. "Trust me, Emily. Give him a few minutes. He owes me a big favor and must have something to show us."

She rubbed her temples, where a dull ache pulsed in time with her footsteps. "We've got to meet with Dr. Morrow at seven in the morning, Tyler. I need sleep, not a scavenger hunt in Seaport's armpit."

"I know," he said, his tone softening, almost lost in the distant rumble of a passing garbage truck. "It won't take long. I hope."

Emily bit her lip as the day's stress hit her again. The recent confrontation with James still made her angry—his arrogance, the stolen evidence she now kept inside her coat like a talisman.

She could tell Tyler everything right here under the shimmering billboards. He deserved to know, didn't he? But his evasiveness lately, those blank spots in his memory he brushed off, stopped her. What if he didn't believe her? What if he was hiding something too? Her fingers curled into her palms.

Vic turned a corner ahead, his shadow stretching long and thin across the wet pavement. Emily's wariness flared, a cold prick at the base of her neck. She scanned the alley—rusted fire escapes clinging to sagging buildings, a rat bolting from an overturned trash can, its eyes glinting like coins. Tyler's faith in Vic puzzled her, and her exhaustion gnawed at her patience. Whatever Vic was leading them to, it had better be worth it, or she'd drag Tyler back to the car herself.

The alley widened into a small, deserted square, and Vic slowed, stepping around an oily lake. Emily's breath caught as she took in the next stop. An old building loomed ahead, its faded sign visible in the dim glow of a streetlamp. "Charlestown Wheels." *What the hell does that mean?* The night tightened around them, and she couldn't shake the feeling that they'd stepped deeper into something she didn't understand.

The plaza outside Charlestown Wheels stretched empty and silent, the building's crumbling brick facade swallowed by darkness beyond the reach of the streetlamp. A sign hung crooked, with weathered letters fading into a ghostly outline, hinting at a past better left buried. The air here felt stale, tinged with rust and the faint scent of motor oil, as if the place hadn't seen a customer in years. Emily crossed her arms, her feet planted firmly on the cracked asphalt, and glared at Vic, who leaned against the wall like he owned the night.

He pulled a cigarette from his camouflaged jacket, the lighter's flame flickering briefly across his sharp cheekbones before he snapped it shut. Smoke billowed upward, slow and gray, as he watched them approach with that half-smile Emily wanted to wipe off his face. The building behind him loomed, its dark windows like hollow eyes, and a shiver ran up her spine despite her thick jacket.

"Okay, Vic," Emily said, "what's this about? Why'd you drag us to this dump in the middle of the night?"

Vic took a slow drag, exhaling a plume that drifted into the damp air. His eyes flicked to Tyler, then back to her, calculating. "This place," he said, gesturing at the warehouse with a casual flip of his cigarette hand, "is a chop shop—and an old military stash—off the grid. If shit hits the fan, you come here. Say, 'Do you know the way to Buckingham Flats?' The guys inside will know you're with me. They'll take care of you."

Emily's eyes narrowed, her frustration spiking. "A password for this rundown heap? You're wasting our time, Vic. I'd crawl through glass before I set foot in there." She turned, her boots crunching on the gravel as she headed back toward the car.

"Emily, wait—" Tyler's voice was low and strained, but she kept walking, her breath fogging in the cold.

"I'm done here, Tyler," she called over her shoulder, leaving the two men standing in the warehouse's shadow.

Behind her, Tyler murmured something too soft to hear, answered by Vic's rough laugh—a sound that grated on her already frayed nerves. She didn't look back, but the warehouse seemed to loom over her.

Tyler's footsteps crunched behind her, catching up as she reached the edge of the empty square. She looked at him, searching his face—lips pressed in a tight line, eyes distant, fixed on some horizon she couldn't see. He had been like this since Vic's name came up that morning, retreating into a silence that felt like a wall she couldn't climb.

"What'd he say to you back there?" she asked, her tone sharper than she intended.

Tyler shrugged, his hands shoved deep in his pockets, his breath visible in the chill. "Vic's being Vic. Nothing worth repeating."

Emily clenched her fists, skepticism gnawing at her. Vic's casual attitude and Tyler's evasiveness added to the unease that had been simmering since they left the city's brighter streets. With its cryptic passphrase and hidden allies, the warehouse felt like a piece of a puzzle she didn't want to solve.

"What kind of favor does he owe you, Tyler? Why's he acting like you're his savior?"

Tyler's gaze dropped to the ground, his shoulders hunching slightly. "Back in the unit, I saved his ass twice. Once in a firefight, he was pinned down in a burning Humvee with no cover, and I dragged him out. Another time, he was about to get tagged by a sniper. I took a bullet to my ballistic plate. Got me a few days of R&R, but it kept him alive. Then he went AWOL."

Emily stopped walking and turned to face him fully. "You never mentioned him before this morning. Not once. Why's that?"

Tyler looked away, his voice barely above a whisper. "Some things are better left buried. Vic is tied to parts of my life I'd rather not revisit. How immature I was, the missions, the choices I made—they're not who I am now. When I called Vic for help, he gave me the gun and said he owed me, saying this place might be a lifeline if things got bad. I didn't want to come, but I couldn't ignore it. Not when it might keep you safe if things get worse."

His words hung between them, heavy with the burden of a past he rarely spoke of. Emily studied him, the thin scar above his eyebrow, a remnant of those unspoken years. She wanted to push, to demand more, but the raw edge in his voice held her back. She nodded, her anger softening but not gone.

Tyler said, locking eyes with her, "Remember how to get back here. Buckingham Flats. Don't forget it."

Emily didn't answer, but the passphrase stayed in her mind. As she walked toward the car, Tyler kept pace with her as distant city sounds crept back in as they neared the car. Emily's exhaustion warred with her need to press him for answers, to demand clarity, but she held her tongue. The stolen evidence, James, and now this midnight detour—secrets piled up like debris, and she wasn't sure how long she could carry them alone.

For now, she'd settle for the warmth of the car and a few hours of sleep before the meeting with Dr. Morrow.

The alley stretched out before them like a tunnel, its tight walls slick with grime and shadows dancing under the flickering glow of overhead billboards. Their footsteps echoed off the damp brick.

Emily's nerves were raw, her senses heightened by the surprise encounter with Vic and her ongoing worry about

Tyler's evasiveness. She glanced at him, his face tense, eyes sweeping the darkness ahead. The alley felt off—too quiet, too still—and a shudder ran up her spine again.

Then three figures emerged from the gloom, blocking their way.

The men moved with predatory speed, their faces obscured by the dim light, but the glint of knives in their hands was unmistakable. Emily's heart pounded against her ribs, her breath catching as the leader stepped forward, his voice a low snarl. "Emily Harper, we warned you and your boyfriend to stop digging."

Her blood ran cold. *Helix*. The name resounded in her mind, linking the danger to the conspiracy.

"Didn't we warn you, Mr. Tough Guy?" one of the men growled. "Now we're gonna finish what you started at the bar."

Tyler tensed up beside her, his hand moving toward his jacket, but the attackers got there first.

The first man lunged, his blade slicing through the air toward Emily's throat. She stumbled back, her ankle twisting on a loose cobblestone, and time slowed. The neon lights flared, casting the alley in vivid colors as Tyler moved faster than she'd ever seen him. He intercepted the attacker, his fist colliding with the man's throat in a sickening crunch. The knife hit the ground with a clatter, but the other two advanced together, their movements synchronized and deadly.

Emily's pulse roared in her ears as she scrambled to get away. But Tyler was a blur of motion before she could run, his body twisting to block a second attacker's strike. He seized the man's wrist, yanking it back with a brutal snap, and the alley echoed the scream that followed.

The third man hesitated, his eyes flicking between the two men on the ground and Tyler, who now stood over them, chest heaving, blood dripping from his knuckles. The lights reflected the feral gleam in Tyler's eyes, a darkness Emily had never seen before. He looked…dangerous. Unhinged. For a brief moment, she wasn't sure whether to fear the attackers or Tyler more.

"Tyler," she said, her voice trembling, but he didn't hear her.

He advanced on the last man. The attacker raised his knife, but Tyler was faster, disarming him with a savage kick that sent the blade skittering into the murk. With a ferocity that made Emily's stomach churn, Tyler drove his fists into the man's stomach, doubling him over, and followed with a knee to the face. Blood sprayed across the pavement, dark under the neon glow.

The man crumpled, motionless, and Tyler stood over him, his breath coming in ragged gasps. The alley fell silent again, except for the distant hum of the city and the faint drip of water from a broken gutter. Emily's hands trembled as she balanced herself against the wall. The immediate danger had passed, leaving her feeling this was only the start.

She stared at Tyler, her mind reeling. The violence he'd unleashed was precise, ruthless, and frighteningly effective. This wasn't the Tyler she knew—the cautious partner who cracked bad puns over stale coffee and sketched dogs in the park. This was someone else, shaped by an anger she hadn't seen before.

"Tyler," she said again, louder this time. He turned to her, his eyes still wild but softened as they met hers. Blood streaked his cheek, and his hands were stained with it, but he stepped toward her, his expression shifting to concern.

"Are you okay?" he asked, his voice hoarse.

Emily nodded, though her legs felt like they might give out. "You…might've killed him."

Tyler glanced back at the fallen men, his jaw locked. "They didn't give me a choice. They were going to kill us."

Helix wasn't a specter anymore—they were hunting her, hunting them. And Tyler… He was more than he'd revealed. The alley shadows seemed to close in, and Emily knew that whatever trust they had built was now shattered by today's hidden secrets and violence.

"We need to go," Tyler said urgently, "before more come."

Emily nodded again. As they hurried toward the car, the alley's darkness swallowed the scene behind them, but the image of Tyler's transformation burned in her mind. The stakes had escalated, and with them, there was a distance between her and the man she thought she would raise a family with.

Emily stumbled from the alley beside Tyler, their gasps cutting through the damp night air. The Wet Spot's neon sign buzzed and flared overhead, its pink-and-blue glow—once a beacon of late-night refuge—now throwing warped shadows across the pavement, turning the familiar lot into something sinister. Distant police sirens wailed, their pitch rising, and the street stretched empty before them, illuminated by the sickly yellow glow of a lone streetlamp where their car waited.

Her legs trembled as she reached the car, keys slipping in her sweat-slick hands. She clawed at the lock, the metal cold against her fingers, until it gave with a reluctant click. Tyler, blood streaking his arm, scanned the alley's mouth, his breath uneven.

"Get in," he barked, already heading toward the driver's side. Emily scrambled into the passenger seat, the seat creaking beneath her, with the faint smell of cigarette smoke clinging in the air. Her hands hovered over the seatbelt, too shaky to buckle it.

"The police are close," she said, voice fraying. "We should wait—"

"No chance." Tyler slid into the driver's seat, wincing as he gripped the keys. "You remember the break-in? Cops didn't do squat. They'll pin this attack on me."

Emily's mouth opened and then closed. The memory of their trashed apartment and Officer Mooney's probing questions gnawed at her, but this was different—blood, knives, the crack of bone in that alley. Still, Tyler's eyes burned with a certainty she couldn't fight, and she sank back as he started the car. The engine purred to life, headlights cutting through the dark, and with a lurch, they peeled away from the curb, tires shrieking against the asphalt.

The car sped forward, the Wet Spot shrinking in the rearview as the sirens' wail faded behind them. Buildings blurred past — brick walls, shuttered storefronts — Boston's underbelly swallowing them whole. Emily's gaze flicked to Tyler. His lips were squeezed tight, sweat on his brow, and his hands clenched the wheel. Blood seeped through his sleeve, dark and spreading.

"Tyler, you're hurt," she said above the engine. "Are you okay to drive?"

He didn't turn, eyes locked on the road, streetlights flashing across his face. "Probably not," he muttered, voice tinged with rebellion. "But I'm going to anyway."

The car surged on, the night grew thicker around them, and Emily's stomach knotted. They were fleeing from the sirens, the alley, from everything—but she couldn't get rid of the feeling that Tyler was driving them straight into something even worse.

Emily's hands shook as she fumbled with the key, the cold metal slipping against her trembling fingers. The apartment door loomed before her, its chipped paint and new lock a reminder of the break-in. Tyler stood close, his breathing still ragged from the alley, his jacket sleeve dark with blood that glistened faintly in the dim hallway glow. The door creaked open, revealing the dim interior of their small, cluttered home.

Inside, the apartment felt smaller than she remembered, with signs of the robbery still visible. A single lamp cast a weak amber glow across the room, illuminating the sagging couch, the pile of books waiting to be put back on the shelf, and the shattered coffee table. Shadows stretched long and jagged across the floor, shifting as the streetlights painted the room in shades of pale yellow.

She dropped her bag onto the couch. Tyler shut the door behind them, and the click of the latch was sharp and final. He moved to the window, peering through the slats, his silhouette tense against the glow. Blood smeared his knuckles, dried into dark, cracked lines, and Emily couldn't look away. The man she'd seen in the alley—ferocious, unrelenting—stood in her living room, and the disconnect gnawed at her.

"We're safe here," Tyler said, his voice rough. He didn't turn to face her, his gaze fixed on the street below. "But they'll be back."

Emily swallowed, her throat dry as sandpaper. "Safe? Those men, Tyler, you might've killed one of them."

He turned then, his eyes meeting hers. "I did what I had to, Emily. They weren't there to say mean things to us."

She sank onto the couch cushions. "Who are you?" she whispered. "I thought I knew you, but that…wasn't you."

Tyler crossed the living room in two strides, stopping short of her. The lamp's light revealed the strain on his face, with a faint sheen of sweat on his brow. "It was me, Emily. The part I thought I put away when I left the military is the part of me we need the most right now. It's all me."

She shook her head, fingers digging into the frayed fabric of the couch. "You fought like it's easy. And that guy said I was warned. Helix, Tyler. This is more dangerous than we thought, and you're in it as deep as I am."

He kneeled in front of her, close enough that she could smell the coppery tang of blood on him, mingled with the faint scent of his sweat. "I recognized one from the bar fight while you were at Helix. He's muscle for hire, tied to Helix's dirtier jobs. They're getting desperate because you must be getting close."

Emily's breath caught. "I know. I'm counting on Dr. Morrow to give us a way out of this."

"I hope so," Tyler mumbled, his shoulders lifting in a slight shrug. "But I'm not counting on it. I'm going to get the gun and then get some sleep." With a sad smile, Tyler turned and quietly closed the door behind him as he left the apartment.

Tears filled Emily's eyes as she watched the man she had

trusted and loved, his retreating figure a painful blur against the backdrop of her memories. Her fear wasn't only about the threats at Helix—it was for Tyler, the secrets he carried, and the realization that their love and survival were teetering on a knife's edge.

Chapter 14

Conspiracy Crossroads

T he first light of Sunday morning streaked across the sky as Emily and Tyler approached Dr. Morrow's house, their footsteps crunching on the gravel driveway.

Majestic and isolated at the end of the street, the house rose before them, its stone exterior elegant and weathered by time. Beyond the sagging wrought-iron gate, a garden stretched out— once bursting with color, now a tangle of drooping flowers and weeds. The air carried a faint smell of rot, softened by the dampness of untended soil.

Emily remembered this place from years ago when Dr. Morrow had been her mentor in the undergraduate program. Back then, it was filled with blooms spilling over the edges—a sanctuary. Now, the garden's decay troubled her, symbolizing Helix's slow collapse—or perhaps the world's fraying edges.

Tyler shifted beside her, his voice quiet. "Doesn't look like anyone's cared for this garden in a while."

She nodded, her fingers tightening around her bag's strap.

The wilted petals scattered on the ground seemed like a warning, a sign of hope fading away.

They moved forward, the gate groaning as Tyler pushed it wide. Before they knocked, the door swung open. Dr. Morrow stood there, her silver hair pulled back, her blouse crisp despite the hour. Her smile greeted them, but her eyes flicked between them, shaded with nervousness.

"Emily, Tyler," she said, stepping aside. "I didn't expect you so early. I thought we had agreed on seven o'clock. Come in."

Emily nodded slightly and said, "We did, but a few things happened that made us even more eager to see you. We were attacked last night after I left Helix."

"That's terrible," she gasped. "I hope you weren't hurt."

"We're doing fine thanks to Tyler, but we're worried they'll try again soon. It wasn't random. The men made it clear that the attack was connected to what we wanted to discuss with you."

Inside, the air was heavy with the smell of aged wood and dust, while heavy curtains smothered the morning light. The foyer's dark, bulky furniture seemed to crowd the space. Emily's chest tightened as they followed Dr. Morrow into the parlor, where a floor lamp cast a faint glow, its light barely reaching the walls.

"Please sit," Dr. Morrow said, motioning toward two stiff chairs. With a gentle tug, she partially opened the heavy curtains, gazing at the garden beyond before sighing and settling across from them, her hands neatly clasped in her lap. "Now, what's this all about?"

Emily looked at Tyler. His nod was subtle, but it boosted her confidence. This was their opportunity. Dr. Morrow might be the one to help them untangle the conspiracy at Helix. Still, the house's isolation and oppressive silence made her skin tingle. She had once felt safe here. That memory seemed far away, overshadowed by a growing sense of vulnerability.

She took a deep breath. "It's about James Kessler," she said, her voice softer than she intended, "and Helix."

Dr. Morrow's gaze sharpened, and her fingers stilled. "Go on."

Emily leaned forward, her hands clasped tightly enough to hurt. The dimness of the parlor seemed to deepen, the lamp's glow casting outlines across Dr. Morrow's face. She met her mentor's steady eyes and spoke, her voice gaining strength. "James is leading a network named Chronos to sell Helix's BioSpark data behind the board's back. It's a conspiracy, and it's already in motion."

Dr. Morrow furrowed her brow, lips slightly pursed. "That's a serious accusation, Emily. James has his flaws, but this?" She shook her head slightly. "What proof do you have?"

The question hit Emily hard, even though she had expected it. She thought of the thumb drives—gone after the break-in—and the phone recording from James's office, its words drowned in static. Her fingers clenched into a fist. "I had evidence," she said, frustration sharpening her tone. "Thumb drives with the data trails, but they were stolen from our apartment yesterday. I recorded James, but it's too faint to use."

Dr. Morrow raised her eyebrows and scrutinized her silently. The silence grew heavy, punctuated by the ticking of a clock somewhere in the room. Emily pulled out the file she'd taken from Kessler's desk—a thin stack of papers with creased edges —and extended it.

"This is what I managed to keep," she said. "It's from James's office. Transactions coded, but they're there."

Dr. Morrow reached for it, skimmed the pages, then looked up. "I'll need time to go through this in detail properly. Can I hold on to it?"

Emily froze. That file was her last hold on the truth, her safeguard against the doubts gnawing at her. She looked at Tyler, his posture stiff beside her, eyes narrowed. He didn't trust Morrow

—she could see it in how he sat, straight with his arms crossed. But she needed Dr. Morrow on their side. "Yes," she said reluctantly. "Take it."

Dr. Morrow set the file aside, her nod quick. "I'll look into this, but it won't be quick. If you're right, we need to be sure before we act. James has the unwavering support of most of the board members."

Emily's throat tightened. Time was slipping away—Tyler's behavior was worsening, and the extinction event weighed heavily on her mind. She started to speak, but Dr. Morrow raised a hand.

"I know it's urgent, Emily, but rash moves will fracture Helix completely. We can't risk that."

She recalled Dr. Morrow's mentorship—late nights, consistent advice, a bond she trusted. Now, suspicion wrapped around her. Was this caution wisdom or a hesitation to guard something else?

She dipped her chin, unspoken agreement hiding the storm inside her mind. Dr. Morrow's gaze stayed on her, and for a moment Emily saw a flicker of emotion in her eyes—perhaps surprise or calculation. It disappeared too quickly to identify, leaving Emily with questions.

Dr. Morrow gently tapped the closed file. "Is there anything else?" she asked, her voice smooth.

Emily's stomach churned, twisting into tight, painful knots. The secret she carried burned against her tongue like a live ember. She glanced at Tyler, who sat perched on the edge of his chair, his body tense as a bowstring.

As the seconds ticked away, a palpable tension—raw and inexplicable—emanated from Tyler. She struggled to understand the reasons behind his intense, silent anxiety, finding his behavior confusing. A shaky breath hitched in her throat.

"There's more," Emily finally said, calm despite the tremor

in her chest. "A threat bigger than the terminal gene. Bigger than the conspiracy itself."

Dr. Morrow's head tilted slightly, her sharp eyes narrowing. "What do you mean?" she asked, her tone blending curiosity with a faint edge of doubt.

"An extinction event," Emily said. "Global in scope, irreversible in its devastation. Helix has concealed the evidence. James hid it in a labyrinth of lies by altering the BioSpark data. This isn't about selling data or power plays. It's about whether humanity survives. No, not only humanity but everything living on Earth."

Dr. Morrow's lips parted, a faint gasp slipping free. Her gaze darted to the window, where the garden beyond sagged under frost's cruel grip.

"An extinction event? When?" she echoed, her voice thinning. "Why haven't I heard of this?"

Emily swallowed. "I only uncovered the truth on Friday," she said. "The terminal gene, far from being limited to individuals, is designed to activate worldwide in one hundred twenty years, causing a global extinction event and a deliberate, catastrophic reset of the planet."

"I understand how this wouldn't have been evident in the human life expectancy data, but what about other long-lived species?" Morrow asked incredulously.

Emily's cheeks blushed. "The knowledge was buried deep within Helix's archives. I searched the files and discovered the original data had been manipulated. When I pieced it together, I learned about James's plans. He's leading the Chronos Project with a group of international investors. They plan to sell the research, the data behind the event, to the highest bidders, all behind the Helix board's back."

Dr. Morrow's face drained of color, her hands tightening on the arms of her chair. "That's...treachery," she whispered. "If this is true, it could shatter everything we've built. Not to mention what it would mean for the planet."

"I don't trust James," Emily admitted. "Not after what I found—hidden files, coded messages. I confronted him, and he laughed it off. I couldn't risk telling anyone else until I was certain I could trust you."

Dr. Morrow rose, her steps measured as she moved toward the window. Her heels softly clicked against the hardwood.

"What purpose would this extinction event serve?" she murmured, almost to herself. It couldn't have been something that Helix engineered into the gene, could it?"

Emily moved to the window, and her silhouette framed the dying garden. "I don't see how. It would be impossible to introduce a change of that magnitude for all humans, let alone every species. It has to be a naturally occurring phenomenon."

A clock ticked softly from deep within the house, each sound intensifying her unease. Dr. Morrow's shock seemed genuine—widened eyes, trembling hands—but Emily feared that caution might prevent action.

Morrow was silent for a moment, staring out the window. "If this event is Earth's fate, what significance does the timeframe of one hundred twenty years hold?"

"I haven't given it much thought yet. I've been focused on the immediate concerns about the conspiracy," Emily said. "But the timing must be important to Chronos's plans. They'd need time to prepare."

Tyler jumped to his feet, nearly tripping over the thick, faded rug as he paced the length of the parlor. His movements were frantic, like a caged animal testing the bars.

"People deserve to know," he said, his voice rising. "Going public will force their hand—Helix, James, all of them. We can't sit here talking about what will happen in one hundred years while the people involved in the conspiracy bury the truth. Billions of people are destined to die."

Dr. Morrow turned away from the window, her posture stiffening as she crossed her arms over her chest. "And risk global chaos? We must verify this first, Tyler. If we act without proof, we'll cause more damage than good. The world can't handle a fracture like this. Remember the turmoil of Covid? It'll be a hundred or even a thousand times worse."

Emily's gaze flicked between them, her fingers clenched in her lap until her knuckles ached. The room was charged with Tyler's urgency, his quick steps and deep breaths building an apparent tension. She'd seen him upset before, but now his hands trembled slightly, and his eyes shifted toward the door as if expecting it to fly open.

"Tyler's right about the urgency," she said, seeking a balance between Tyler's passion and Catherine's caution. "But what if it triggers unrest we can't control? James and the Chronos group would surely retaliate. We'd be exposed and discredited while they destroyed the evidence."

Tyler froze in place, his chest rising and falling as he turned toward her. "Waiting's worse," he snapped. "Every minute we waste, they tighten their grip. You don't understand, Emily. We're running out of time."

She frowned, concern prickling her skin. He was unraveling quickly, and she didn't know why. Her eyes shifted to the garden outside the glass—its flowers wilted, their petals scattered like confetti at a funeral. It was a glimpse of what could happen if they failed. Or if they acted too early.

Catherine Morrow sank back into her chair, her hands folding neatly in her lap. "The world's fragile, Emily and Tyler," she said. "One misstep, and the thin veneer ruptures. We need irrefutable evidence, not haste. Panic is a weapon we can't afford to hand them."

Memories flashed through Emily's mind—shouts echoing through the streets, smoke curling over rooftops, and the tremor of a society stretched thin. She'd seen how fear can turn a crowd into a mob before.

"I know," she murmured to Tyler. "We have to be sure. I'm scared too."

He met her eyes, his wild, almost pleading. "Scared doesn't cover it," he said. "We're way past that."

A chill slid down her spine. She reached out, her hand hovering near his arm, but he stepped back, resuming his restless pacing. His fingers flexed then curled into fists, trembling faintly. Something gnawed at him—something he wouldn't share. Emily wanted to reach him, to understand, but Dr. Morrow's gaze held her in place, a silent reminder of the stakes that overshadowed their personal differences.

"Tyler," Dr. Morrow said, her tone softening, "I see the burden you're carrying, but we need a strategy. Give me time to find the truth."

He laughed, a harsh sound that shattered in the air. "Strategies take time we don't have." He shifted away from them, shoulders stiff as stone. "You don't see it. Neither of you."

Emily bit her lip. She respected Tyler's fire, but Dr. Morrow's restraint tugged at her. The shifting light cast gray shadows on the walls, and she felt trapped, torn between loyalty and the fear of a world falling apart.

Leaning forward, Dr. Morrow spoke in a calm, warm tone, her voice a soothing balm that eased the tension in the room. "It seems you're both already in danger since you were attacked last night," she said, her eyes flicking between them. "I can fund private security—keep you safe and shield Helix's name if this explodes. It's the least I can do."

Tyler stiffened next to Emily, his head lowering toward her ear. His breath brushed her skin. "It's a trap," he whispered, his voice barely audible.

Emily's gaze was fixed on Dr. Morrow. Her mentor sat still, hands folded, and her expression was calm yet unreadable.

Though the promise of safety hung heavy in the air, it was inter-twined with a risky gamble, a danger hard to ignore.

"Two days," Dr. Morrow added, her tone firming like a door closing. "Give me two days to investigate. Stay safe and hidden until then. Tell James you have a family emergency to handle."

Emily felt a rapid, fluttering sensation in her chest. Two days stretched before her like an endless abyss, with the knowledge of the conspiracy looming and Tyler's strange behavior pressing on her. She glanced at him, his mouth grimacing, eyes blazing with suspicion. He shook his head.

"I don't buy it," he said. "We're not pieces to be moved on a chessboard."

Dr. Morrow's gaze held still, unflinching. "You're not," she replied, her voice cool, "but you're also not untouchable, as you've already experienced. Take the security or leave it. The two days stand."

The musty smell of old books and the thick dust in the air pressed heavily on Emily, creating a suffocating sensation. She needed Dr. Morrow's help and influence, but Tyler's cynicism echoed, amplifying the apprehension she couldn't shake. "We'll take the two days," she said, her voice steadier than her nerves. "But we'll handle our security."

Tyler exhaled in relief. Dr. Morrow nodded, though a cloud crossed her eyes—disappointment perhaps. It vanished too quickly to be identified. "Fine," she said. "Let me know how to reach you. We'll meet again soon."

Emily stood, her legs unsteady, and followed Tyler toward the door. Dr. Morrow lingered behind her, a pressure she couldn't quite understand.

Gravel shifted beneath Emily's shoes as she stepped outside, heading toward their car—Morrow's house dominated behind them, its weathered exterior stark against the gray sky. The garden stretched to the left, flowers shriveled, vines twisted into knots. She pulled her jacket tighter as the cold seeped in.

Tyler moved ahead quickly, shoulders tense and raised. "She wants to spy on us," he muttered. "That security would be a leash. Vic and I can handle it. We don't need her mall cops tracking our every move."

Emily hurried to match his pace, her breath fogging in the cold. "Maybe," she said uncertainly, "but we need her help. We can't fight this alone, Tyler."

He stopped suddenly, turning to her with dark eyes. "You don't see it, Emily," he said, pleading. "We're already on our own. Always have been since this thing started."

She reached out, her fingers brushing his arm, but he pulled away, his gaze growing colder. "What's wrong, Tyler?" she asked, her voice shakier. "You're hiding something from me. I can feel it."

His expression softened, revealing a brief vulnerability, then it disappeared as his walls snapped back into place. "Keep focused on exposing James," he said, his tone clipped. "That's what matters now."

Emily's throat tightened. She wanted to push Tyler to lower his defenses, but the urgency of the coming two days made her hold back. They needed to find a place to hide. She nodded and headed toward the gate.

Looking back, the house stood alone, its elegance tarnished by the dying garden. She turned to Tyler and felt the tension in their shifting relationship. Time was their enemy, and she wondered if they could outrun it.

Chapter 15

The Fault Line

As Emily entered the small bathroom, Tyler quickly tucked the pistol from his waistband into the duffel bag.

"How long do you think we'll be gone?" Emily asked.

"Pack for a week, but I think this will be over in a few days," Tyler said as he jammed clothes into his bag, burying the gun. He moved with restless energy to silence the countdown that was starting to echo relentlessly inside his head.

The apartment seemed more cramped than Tyler remembered. Signs of the robbery were still visible. A single lamp cast a faint amber glow over the room, barely illuminating the sagging couch, pictures that needed rehanging, and the broken coffee table.

His eyes flicked to his watch: less than thirty-six hours until the kill switch activated. The realization sank into his chest, a tight grip that stole his breath. With the time he had left, he wouldn't be able to repair the apartment. Their home. Where their life together had started. He found the prospect of never sitting on the old couch with Emily again unbearable.

His hands shook as he shoved a sweater into the bag, the coarse wool rough on his raw palms. "Em, are you almost done in there?" Tyler asked from the living room.

Inside the bedroom, Emily carefully zipped up her suitcase. She lifted her head and looked at him, her eyes piercing the dim light to find something controlled in his expression. "What's next, Tyler?"

He yanked the zipper shut, eyes fixed on the bag. "We'll figure it out." The lie burned his tongue. James's betrayal threatened Emily's life, and he was powerless to stop it unless he did something drastic. His plan to confront James was a gamble. He couldn't tell Emily, not now, probably never. The truth might pull her into the chasm he was desperate to avoid.

He hoisted the heavy duffel bag onto his shoulder; the weight brought him back to the reality of the moment. "Let's go," he said sharply. "We need to get you somewhere safe."

Emily nodded, her pause heavy with unspoken questions. As they neared the door, the floor groaned beneath their weight, its mournful, fading echo a reminder of the world they were leaving behind, a world that seemed to sigh with their departure. Though he tried to hide his emotions with a forced blank expression, her gaze stayed on his face.

Stepping across the threshold into the hall, they left behind the apartment and all its memories. He clenched his shoulder muscles, forcefully pushing down the rising tide of panic that threatened to overwhelm him. His kill switch ticked on, a fuse burning short.

Tyler slowly drove the used Tesla along the tree-lined street of Telegraph Hill, its tires softly whispering against the pavement. Victorian row homes lined the road, their faded paint and ivy-covered walls glowing softly in the late afternoon light.

As Tyler tightly grasped the steering wheel, the leather creaked beneath his hands. Emily's fingers tapped on her phone while the engine hummed steadily.

A palpable tension filled the air between them, thick with unspoken questions, as she nervously emailed the BioSpark team to let them know she would be out of the office tomorrow. The deceptive calm of the quiet neighborhood only heightened Tyler's growing frustration.

He pulled up to Emily's parents' house. The light-blue paint peeled beneath thick ivy, curling over the front like veins on an aging hand. He knew that inside, the rooms carried the scent of aged paper and highly polished oak, with walls lined with countless books. For Emily, it was a sanctuary. Its isolation also reflected the growing distance between them—a gap he couldn't seem to close.

Tyler pulled into the driveway, stopped the car, and took a deep breath. He looked at the dashboard, avoiding her eyes.

"You'll be safe here," he said, his voice hollow. "I need to grab some things from the office in case we need to hide for more than a couple of days. I'll be back by dinner." His smooth lie caused a sharp pang of guilt.

Emily paused, her hand hovering over the door handle, fingers trembling slightly. She turned to him, her eyes probing his face, focusing on the tense line of his jaw. "You're sure?"

Tyler noticed the slight furrow in her brow, the way her lips parted as if she wanted to say more but didn't. It twisted something inside him to see her attempt to bridge the unease he was creating.

He nodded, forcing a smile that felt like a mask slipping. "Yeah. Don't worry, Em. Love you." But her gaze held his, searching, catching the brief twitch of doubt in her expression, the way her fingers tightened momentarily on the handle before loosening again. That flicker stung because he knew she sensed the secrets he was hiding. The truth was like a jagged edge in his mind. He wasn't going to the office. He was going after James.

"Love you too," she said, leaning in to kiss him. Her lips lingered a moment longer, her breath warm against his skin, and her fingers brushed his cheek, hesitant, almost pleading. Tyler felt a faint tremor in her touch, a silent question she didn't voice.

She stepped out of the car, walking up the sidewalk, each step deliberate. As she pulled her suitcase up the stone path, the wheels rattled over the uneven surface, a grating sound echoing the tension in Tyler's core. He watched her pause at the door, her hand gripping the suitcase handle tightly, her shoulders stiff as she glanced back at the car. For a moment, he thought she might turn, might call out, but then she pushed the door open and disappeared inside, the house swallowing her like a favorite memory.

Tyler shifted into reverse, backing away before he lost his nerve. In the rearview mirror, the house shrank. Lying to her was a betrayal, but letting her stay close—letting her follow him into the abyss—was unthinkable. Protecting her outweighed everything, a choice he would bear alone.

A sharp, bitter memory of James cut through Tyler's haze, recalling the day he first began to hate him: the inaugural Helix company picnic. Sunlight bounced off the plastic tables, mingling with the scent of beer and charred burgers, while laughter echoed hollowly. James, in the spotlight, wore a wide, charming grin that captivated the crowd. But Tyler saw past it— James sneaking away, groping his secretary behind the catering tent, grumbling about ungrateful employees. Then James's eyes met Tyler's, his smooth smile twisting into a cold, menacing expression. Hatred surged in Tyler's chest, distrust tightening its grasp.

The road stretched ahead, trees leaning in with their bare branches reaching toward the gray sky. Determination hardened his resolve. For Emily, he would do this. To keep her safe, he accepted the consequences of his plan. The house disappeared around a bend, along with the thread of the life he had been holding onto. He pushed the accelerator, the engine whining as he sped away from the quiet suburb.

Rain streaked across the windshield as Tyler left the suburbs and ventured into the foggy outskirts of Boston, the world shrinking into a haze of dark woods and rolling hills. The road, slick with water, glistened under the car's headlights, bordered by gnarled trees that loomed like twisted, skeletal figures shrouded in mist. Darkness fell early as another autumn squall approached.

Tyler's mind churned with dark intentions—get James alone in a remote warehouse, with its rusted walls reeking of damp rot and shattered windows, and make him confess the truth about targeting Emily and the Chronos conspiracy, all captured on a recording that would shatter illusions. Holding James until the truth spilled out was one thing; crossing the line to kill him was an act he wasn't sure he could face.

His hands tightened on the steering wheel as rain hammered the car's roof, the kill switch's relentless rhythm pushing him forward with each mile, the vague plan twisting into something reckless and raw.

A memory flashed—a nameless soldier's face, with a silent scream, back arched in pain, now fading into a vague blur. The lapse hit him like a punch, breath catching in his throat. No, not now, he thought, panic rising. He was convinced the terminal gene was eroding him, memory by memory. He wondered if the gene was triggering his family's predisposition for dementia. He knew he couldn't carry out this plan alone, or he might fail.

Vic's name resurfaced—a debt earned in blood and fire during a mission gone wrong. Pulling him into the plan meant stepping into the unknown—there'd be no turning back—but the ticking clock left no other choice. Vic owed him more than a used gun and possible refuge. One last favor would settle the debt.

The twisting branches of the trees, reaching toward the sky, snapped him out of his thoughts again. A quick memory flashed —Emily's warm, brief laugh on the beach, then nothing. His eyes became unfocused, teeth clenched. He experienced a sudden lapse in memory, losing track of where he was going and why.

The feeling was like a sudden fall from the sky onto a rain-soaked road leading nowhere, leaving him confused and his vision blurred. He wondered if this was what dementia might feel like, slowly erasing a person piece by piece.

As his thoughts became clear, he realized his life was nearly over. The rain intensified, a relentless wall of sound, and Tyler pressed the accelerator, chasing a plan as perilous as the slick road under him. With Vic, there was no retreat. He had to face the consequences, risks be damned.

Tyler pulled into the abandoned gas station Vic had mentioned, with rain now steadily pounding against the corrugated roof. He parked the Tesla in the back and checked his watch—he hadn't arrived yet. Tyler leaned against the car, the damp chill seeping through his jacket, and looked down the empty road. Minutes felt like an hour, each one tightening the knot in his stomach. A distant rumble of an engine snapped him to attention, headlights piercing through the mist. Vic had arrived.

Tyler walked toward Vic's dented Ford pickup, the gravel crunching under his boots. Vic sat up straight, his face hidden by a Bruins cap. In the driver's seat, Vic's muscular build, shaped by years of dock work and hard living, was visible. His olive-green jacket, worn and dirty, hung loosely on his shoulders.

As Tyler approached, he noticed the simple dog tags that hinted at his unspoken past. The cap tilted back, revealing shaggy brown hair damp from the dock's mist—a change from his strict military days. Vic's weathered face, with a strong jawline, stubble, and a scar along his cheek, showed hard-earned experience. His eyes locked onto Tyler's with a wary, sharp gaze, full of alertness and a touch of cynicism.

"Reed," Vic growled. He rolled his shoulders, a deliberate habit Tyler recognized from their time in combat, easing some lingering tension, and fiddled with a key. "You rescued me from hell twice. I owe you. I'm fully committed to this plan, but my boss wants a cut of the action. James's cash, maybe some inside info on whatever Helix is working on. Is that going to be a problem?"

Vic shifted in his seat, a rugged figure shaped by hardship, always half-braced for the next fight. Tyler's stomach tightened with an icy wave of doubt, and he swallowed. "Get me the gear and find me a deserted spot. A warehouse," he said, teeth clenched with a determination that felt more like desperation. "I'll deal with the rest."

Vic stood, gravel crunching underfoot. "This ain't clean, man," he said. "Are you sure about this? It doesn't seem like something the person I knew would do." His eyes searched Tyler's, looking for doubt.

"I'm sure," he said, locking eyes with Vic. "I'll do whatever's necessary."

"Alright," Vic conceded, his voice calm, though a hint of suspicion remained in his eyes. "I'll arrange it. But you know the price." He turned toward the truck, his movement quick, as if trying to outrun second thoughts, sealing their fates.

Tyler nodded, feeling the pressure of the deal settle on him. He wondered if Vic's boss would demand more—James's fortune, the Chronos secrets—or if even closer betrayal was on the horizon.

Vic's voice echoed off the gas station as Tyler reached his car. "Watch yourself, Reed," he warned.

"Always," Tyler muttered, his hand lingering on the car door. The motor purred, and a hint of defiance hung in the silent, misty air. The ticking in his mind grew louder, drowning out Vic's caution and driving him back onto the road.

The Tesla hummed softly down the quiet side road, the

world outside blurring into a gray streak that reflected Tyler's growing sense of isolation. Each mile widened the gulf between the man he was and the one now driven by a reckless quest for a truth that would cost him everything. His hands stabilized the wheel, hiding the storm of doubt and determination inside, but a glance at his watch—the glowing numbers a stark reminder of the kill switch's deadline—tightened his face.

He was waiting for Vic's call, the one that would give him the details of the hidden location and the equipment needed to carry out his plan. Once that call came, there would be no turning back—only the final steps of kidnapping James and forcing a confession that would reveal James to be the monster he really was.

In his mind, Tyler visualized James trapped inside a murky warehouse. The recorder on Tyler's phone would catch every word. That confession might be the key to saving Emily and everything else. But the thought of what might happen next—pulling the trigger—settled like a stone in his chest. He wasn't a killer, but the line between justice and revenge was getting thinner, worn down by the high stakes.

Vic had a warning, "You cross this line, it's over for you."

And Tyler had shot back, "It already is."

Vic hadn't fully grasped what he meant, but it was the plain truth. He was a man untethered, bound only to a cause that demanded his soul.

The road stretched out before him, pulling Tyler deeper into a solitary reckoning as memories faded—Emily making coffee, once a cherished routine, now just static in his mind. His chest tightened with the pressure of time running short, and the lie about going to the office stung. But her survival was more important than a small lie. His breath fogged the windshield, a brief sign of the life he was risking, yet there was no stopping now—only the fragile hope that his sacrifice could shift the tide.

He remembered a skirmish from years ago—moving through

smoke, blind, guided only by instinct and the men relying on him. This was no different: a march into uncertainty, driven by a purpose he couldn't abandon. Another memory faded away, lost in the void, and his grip on the wheel tightened. Time was running out, and he'd fight every second for what mattered.

Tyler sat in his car on the foggy outskirts, the damp air seeping through the cracked window. Darkness closed in as the mist formed a curtain around him. His phone buzzed, Vic's name flashing on the screen. Tyler answered.

Vic said, "We're set. Midnight. Don't be late, brother."

"I won't," Tyler grunted. The call ended, leaving him alone with the burden of the plan.

Tyler gripped the steering wheel, cool beneath his palms, and turned the key. A sports station droned from the radio, trying to drown out the thoughts swirling in his mind. Outside, the world blurred into a dim, shapeless haze. He pictured Emily's face—her warm eyes, her wide smile. He clung to faith in her strength, knowing she'd rise from this, weave a life of joy and love once the shadow of Helix lifted.

The urge to call her overwhelmed him—to hear her voice, to reveal every truth he'd kept hidden. But his voice would falter, thick with unshed tears, and he couldn't allow a goodbye to slip out. She'd notice the tremor and pull him back from what he was about to do, and he couldn't let her—not when everything was so close to falling apart.

The empty road stretched on, each mile deepening the darkness and pulling him farther from Emily's fading warmth. He had betrayed her trust for a gamble that might save her but would probably ruin him, and guilt gnawed at him as he wondered if the man she loved was already gone.

Still, the need to uncover James's lies pushed him toward a confrontation that could consume him. With only the engine's hum and the radio's drone for company, Tyler kept driving, haunted by his choices and the consequences ahead.

Chapter 16

What Are Friends For

Emily shuffled downstairs, her wool slippers whispering against the thick carpet, her mind still tangled in a haze of sleep.

The early-morning light streamed through the curtains of Emily's parents' living room, softly illuminating a space filled with her memories. A faint musk of old books and the lingering sweetness of her mother's lavender sachets, tucked into the couch cushions, permeated the air. The promise of coffee beckoned from the kitchen, its rich aroma wafting through the house, but she stopped short at the sight of Tyler curled up on the couch.

He sprawled on the cushions with one arm hanging off the edge, his chest rising and falling in constant, deep breaths. A plaid blanket—usually folded neatly on the armchair—twisted around his legs, and a shadow of stubble darkened his chin. Emily hadn't heard him come in last night. For days, he'd been a remnant of himself, but here, peacefully sleeping, he looked like the Tyler she'd fallen in love with.

He stirred as she approached, eyes fluttering open. A tired smile curved his lips. "Morning, babe," he said, his voice warm.

She felt a familiar flutter. "Morning," she replied, stepping closer. "I didn't hear you come in."

Tyler propped himself up, rubbing his eyes with the heel of his hand. "Got stuck at the office until after midnight. Grabbed the spare key from under the pot on the porch. I didn't want to wake you." His tone wrapped around her, comforting.

Emily nodded, the explanation seeming plausible and straightforward to her. A flicker of doubt nudged at her, but she pushed it away. Not now—especially when he appeared so much like his old self, relaxed and unguarded. She headed toward the kitchen, drawn by the persistent drip of the coffee maker. Pouring a mug, she held it close, warm and comforting, and glanced back at him as he sank into the cushions. The room felt like home for a moment, free from the growing gloom weighing on their lives.

Emily placed a mug next to Tyler and slipped into her father's study, shutting the door behind her and sealing herself in a quiet space. The room smelled like old paper. Paneled walls lined with shelves sagged under the weight of books and mementos—framed awards and a chipped award from her dad's "famous" hole-in-one. She sank into the leather chair behind the desk, its creak a soft echo of childhood, and pulled her phone from her pocket.

Her pulse raced as she dialed Anita, the heaviness of her frustration pressing down on her. Waiting for Dr. Morrow to take action wasn't an option for her.

Anita answered on the second ring. "Emily, what's up, girl?"

Emily exhaled, her breath wavering as she tightly gripped the phone. "Anita, I need your help. This is about protecting our work and the BioSpark team. I can't say much, but it's critical." Her fingers gently traced the scarred surface of the desk.

A pause stretched across the line, with the faint crackle of static filling the silence. "What are you asking for?" Anita replied.

Emily leaned forward, her voice dropping to a low, urgent whisper. "I need to access BioSpark's archive records without anyone noticing. There have been a lot of strange things happening since Thursday's board meeting, and the archive room lockdown over the weekend is very concerning."

Anita sighed, "Yeah, I told you about the supposed accident in the archive room. That guy from IT was suspicious when he said he spilled coffee on the servers. I don't even understand how you'd do that."

Emily continued, "I checked the office on Saturday evening, and it was still locked down. I asked James, but he said he knew nothing about it. Something's not right. I need you to access Helix's records without raising suspicion. You're the best at this."

Anita's tone changed, a spark of interest cutting through her hesitation. "I've got an idea, but it's risky. We can breach their system remotely, create a hidden backup of the key files, and plant fake data into the originals. It would be unnoticeable to anyone who checks."

Emily's heart raced, but she kept her voice even. "I trust you, Anita. We need to be cautious, but you can do this. It's about safeguarding our research, not doing something illegal. Trust me, and don't let us get caught."

The line went silent momentarily, the implication of Emily's request hanging between them. Anita's voice returned, steady. "Of course, Em. I'm in. But we do this my way."

"Great," Emily said. "I'll tell you everything later. I swear on a venti latte."

She laughed. "You do know the way to my heart. Alright. For you, I'll do it. But you owe me the full story after."

Emily's throat tightened. "Thank you, Anita. You don't know how much this means."

"Watch yourself," Anita said, softer now.

She set the phone down, her hands trembling slightly. She looked at the framed engagement announcement on the shelf—she and Tyler, arms wrapped around each other, laughing—and sensed the danger in her action. It was a risk, but one she was willing to take.

Anita called her back after an hour, and they analyzed the file structure. Anita's quick keystrokes created a soft rhythm through the line, with each tap acting as a thread connecting her to Helix's world of cold servers and sterile hallways, she easily imagined.

While Anita typed, Emily paced around the dining room. The mid-morning sun shone through the window, highlighting the family photos on the walls—smiling faces frozen in time—but the warmth couldn't reach the chill coiling within her.

"Almost there," Anita murmured, concentrating. "One more layer to get through. Hold on. Someone's logging in nearby. I need to cover my tracks."

Emily froze, her heart pounding against her ribs. "Anita, be careful!" Her voice trembled as panic set in. She visualized Anita in the lab, hunched over a terminal, fingers flying across the keyboard, her eyes darting to the door. A silhouette flickered past the frosted glass in Emily's mind, an omen of danger. What if security guards burst in? What if alarms blared through the halls? Her hands shook as she clutched the phone, knuckles whitening.

She paced faster through the room with each frantic step, reflecting her dread. The old grandfather clock ticked on relentlessly, mocking her with every agonizing second.

Emily sat down heavily, gripping the armrest, her nails digging into the upholstery. She could almost hear the echo of footsteps in Helix's halls, the flash of a security screen flickering to life. Her mind raced. *What if they catch her?*

"Got it," Anita said at last. "False alarm. We're done."

Emily sagged, air rushing from her lungs. "You're sure? Did you get the backup?"

"Yeah," Anita replied, a grin creeping into her voice. "And the fake data's in place. If anyone pulls those files, they'll be chasing shadows."

A fierce smile spread across Emily's face, triumph briefly overpowering the fear. "Good. No one will suspect a thing."

Anita chuckled, weary but satisfied. "Step one's done. Take a look and let me know if we need to do more."

"I'll double-check," Emily said, straightening up, her eyes drifting to the mantel clock, its incessant ticking a call to action. "I need to review some of the other files anyway."

She ended the call, and the phone slipped onto the coffee table with a soft clunk.

She crossed to the window, peering out at the quiet street, her mind already planning her next move while waiting to hear from Dr. Morrow. James thought he had the upper hand, but she had tilted the board. This was her fight now—against him, against Chronos, against every lie threatening to unravel her world—and she wouldn't stop until she exposed them all.

Tyler shifted on the worn couch, and the faint creak of the springs woke him from a shallow, restless sleep.

His body felt like it was sinking into the earth, pinned by an invisible weight that grew heavier each day. The kill switch was tightening its hold, its poison sinking deeper into his bones, leaving his muscles stiff and sluggish.

Yet this morning, his mind crackled with a strange, almost cruel clarity. *Is this it?* he wondered, a shiver of dread curling in his stomach. One last spark before it all goes dark? He pressed a hand to his forehead and tried to push the fear away. But it clung to him, like a monster he couldn't outrun.

The living room was quiet, with thin rays of light slipping through the blinds to streak the hardwood floor. Across the room, Emily sat at the dining table, her laptop open, fingers softly tapping a constant rhythm as she worked. She hadn't noticed him wake, hadn't seen the way his eyes fluttered open, heavy with sleep, or the tired smile that curved his lips.

"Morning, babe," he murmured when she had woken him earlier, his voice tender despite the fatigue. She had moved closer, her response soft and filled with a passion he recognized. Now, she focused on her work, her silhouette a quiet comfort: the gentle slope of her shoulders, the waves of her hair catching the faint light. *She's still fighting*, he thought. *For us. For me.*

He had told her earlier that he'd been at the office until late, grabbing the spare key to avoid waking her. The lie had come easily, and she'd nodded, accepting it. A flicker of doubt had crossed her face—he'd seen it—but she'd brushed it aside, turning to the kitchen where the coffee maker dripped. She'd left a mug beside him then, her touch lingering as she had entered her father's study.

Now, she was back working in the dining room, and he dragged himself upright, joints protesting with sharp stabs of pain. His legs felt foreign, and he shuffled toward the kitchen, each step a tick of the clock inside him.

The rich aroma of coffee greeted him as he crossed the threshold, piercing through the haze. Emily turned away from the dining room table, her face softening into that smile that always took his breath away. "Morning, birthday boy," she said, entering the kitchen. Her voice was gentle but tinged with something—maybe concern or a question she wouldn't voice.

"Morning," he rasped, throat dry as sandpaper. He took the fresh mug she offered, their fingers brushing for a heartbeat, and the warmth seeped into his stiff hands. He sipped slowly, the bitter taste bringing back memories of better days as he watched her move through the kitchen. She hummed softly, a tune he couldn't place, her movements fluid. She was vibrant, a splash of color against his fading gray, and he felt like a ghost beside her.

"Tyler, are you okay?" Her eyes narrowed, locking onto his.

He forced a smile. "Yeah, exhausted. I feel like I'm ten years older this morning."

She nodded, but her gaze stayed, searching for the truth he refused to give. He hated the wall it built between them, brick by silent brick. Earlier today, she had held her mug, looking back at him, and the room had briefly felt like home again. But the shadows were creeping back in, and the kill switch, James, the danger—it was a burden he couldn't share, not when he could still protect her.

"I'm going to do some work, then my mom and I are going to cook up a birthday dinner for you," Emily said. "I know it's not much, but we'll really celebrate when this craziness ends."

Tyler nodded and took another sip, the warmth offering brief comfort against the harsh reality closing in. He'd cling to these moments, to her, as tightly as possible. Soon, he feared they might be all he had left.

"That sounds perfect, Em. I'm not feeling the birthday spirit right now, so a party on another day sounds good. I think I'll go for a walk while you're working," he said, setting the mug down on the counter. "Clear my head a bit."

Emily's brow furrowed, a flicker of worry crossing her face. "Alright. Don't be too long, okay?"

He kissed her, grabbed his field jacket from the hook by the door, and stepped outside. The frigid morning air hit him like a slap—crisp and cold, biting at his exposed skin as the door clicked shut behind him. He paused, inhaling the chilly air, letting it calm the storm inside.

The neighborhood unfolded before him, a patchwork of familiar sights and sounds. He walked slowly, the crunch of dry leaves filling the silence. The air smelled of autumn—damp earth, faint wood smoke and the tang of dying grass—and he pulled his jacket tighter as the chill seeped through the fabric. Houses lined the street, porches adorned with pumpkins and wreaths, and windows glowing warmly.

He passed the old oak tree at the corner of the park, its gnarled branches reaching toward the sky. As he entered the open space, the monument at Thomas Park came into view. The Dorchester Heights Monument stood tall, its stone weathered but steadfast, a silent witness to centuries of struggle. Tyler found a bench off the main path, its wood still slick with morning dew, and sat down, the cold piercing through his jeans. He took out his phone, hands trembling—not from the cold but from what he needed to do—and dialed Vic's number.

Vic answered quickly, his voice tense. "Tyler, you okay?"

"Define okay," Tyler said, a weak attempt at humor that even he recognized as falling flat.

Vic didn't laugh. "I've got bad news."

Tyler's stomach dropped, a cold sweat forming on the back of his neck. "Spit it out."

"My boss owes Helix—big-time players, Tyler, the kind with serious money. That's why he had me lure you and Emily to the alley on Saturday night. Until last night, I didn't realize how connected he is with people at Helix."

Angry, Tyler scowled. "So it was a setup from the jump?"

"Yeah, and I hate myself for it. But I'm with you now. I want to help make this right."

Tyler's mind raced, suspicion battling the flicker of hope Vic held. *Can I trust him after everything?* But options were limited, and time was running out. "How are you going to help?"

"I'll help you get James. He's a dangerous guy, trust me. But the warehouse is a trap. They plan to get you there and then kill you. I know of an abandoned cabin by an old quarry, off the grid. I go there to party on weekends sometimes, and no one will bother you. Take him there instead and figure out your next move."

A new plan took shape in his mind. It was risky—crazy, even —but it was an opportunity. "Alright," he said, determined, "let's do it."

"Meet me at Charlestown Wheels at 2:30, and we'll go check it out," Vic said before hanging up.

Tyler slipped his phone into his pocket while looking at the monument. It towered over him, a symbol of battles fought and lives lost, and he wondered if his fight would matter in the end. Across the park, kids chased each other, their shouts and laughter piercing the quiet. He watched them for a moment, envious. *They can't even imagine what's coming*, he thought.

He stood with wobbly legs and started walking back toward the house, feeling the strain of his decision and how close he had come to being ambushed by James.

Back at Emily's parents' home, Tyler paused at the door, the muffled sound of Emily's voice seeping through the wood. He took a deep breath, pushing down the uncertainty, and stepped inside. The warmth wrapped around him, the faint scent of coffee mixing with the subtle floral aroma of Emily's shampoo.

She looked up from the table, where papers were scattered around her, and smiled. "Hey, how was your walk?"

"Refreshing," he lied, peeling off his jacket. "How about lunch? Ready for a break?"

Her face lit up, and she nodded. "Love that. Let's whip up some sandwiches."

They moved to the kitchen, falling into an old rhythm—her slicing bread, him handling the tomatoes and lettuce. He focused on his tasks, the feel of the knife, the sharp scent of the vegetables, but his mind kept drifting to the deserted ware-house, to James, to his countdown. His hands trembled as he set the knife down, and he turned away, hoping she didn't notice.

Emily filled the silence with chatter. "Remember that

camping trip when you forgot the tent poles?" She asked, laughing. "We ended up sleeping under the stars, freezing."

Tyler managed a chuckle, but the memory was blurry, edges frayed and fading. "Yeah, total disaster."

Her laughter faded, her eyes narrowing as she studied him. "You don't remember, do you?"

He froze as the tomato slice slipped from his fingers. "It's...fuzzy," he admitted. "My mind's been foggy since the bar fight the other night. Comes and goes."

She reached for his hand, her touch warm and calming. "It's okay, Tyler—probably a mild concussion. We'll make plenty of new memories after this is all over. Maybe even laugh about it."

But he knew they wouldn't. There wasn't any more time. He squeezed her hand, his throat tight, and nodded. "Yeah. New ones, with a tent this time."

They ate at the small table by the garden window, sunlight spilling across the plates. Emily reminisced about first dates, late-night talks, quiet mornings like this one. Tyler nodded, smiling where he could, but the memories were slipping away, dissolving into a fog he couldn't pierce. Each gap was a wound, a piece of them lost to the kill switch's hunger, and he fought to hold on to her voice, face, anything.

She reached across the table as they finished, her fingers interlacing with his. "I love you, Tyler. No matter what."

His chest ached, emotion rising until he could hardly breathe. "I love you too, Emily. Always."

He held her gaze, memorizing the flecks of gold in her eyes. Soon, he'd leave to face James, Helix and his fate. But for now, he found himself here with her, holding on tightly as if his life depended on it.

They cleared the dishes in silence, and she wrapped her arms around him, her head resting against his chest. He held her tightly, breathing her in, as the world shrank to this perfect moment. *For her*, he thought, resolve solidifying like steel. *I'll end this. Whatever it takes.*

Chapter 17

Two Movies, One Screen

E mily sat on the edge of her childhood bed, the faded floral comforter crumpling beneath her.

Her bedroom blended past and present, a patchwork of who she had been and has become. Posters of Albert Einstein, Twilight, and Lady Gaga covered the walls, their faces faded from years of sunlight.

Thin afternoon sunbeams slipped through dusty blinds, painting the hardwood floor in shades of antique gold. But the cold, bluish glow of three monitors dominated, casting an otherworldly sheen across the room. Cables snaked across the floor like roots, connecting her to a digital battlefield far beyond the peeling paint. She shifted, the bed frame creaking, and flexed her fingers until the knuckles popped, a sharp crack in the quiet.

"Time to go to work," she muttered.

Her setup was a makeshift war station assembled from electronics stored in the closet after the COVID lockdowns ended. The keyboard rested on an old nightstand that also served as a desk, its wood scratched and smooth, the keys cool and slick beneath her fingertips. She angled the monitors to reduce glare.

Their screens flickered to life as she ran a diagnostic on her custom software. Green code scrolled across black windows, a rhythm she felt in her bones, regular as a heartbeat.

She pictured Anita leaning over her shoulder, her voice clipped in Emily's memory. "Exploit the old subsystem. It's their weak spot. They never patch what they forget."

Emily nodded quickly, responding to her imagination.

She'd spent the last two days mapping Helix's digital skeleton, tracing every fault line and crack she could find. This wasn't simply a hack—it was personal, a confrontation. James's betrayal burned, leaving a raw, jagged ache. He'd taken her trust, her late nights, her data, and twisted them into stepping stones for his own raw power.

"You thought you could bury this, didn't you?" she whispered, her fingers hovering over the keys. Then they struck quickly, launching her into the breach.

She slipped past the outer security layer using Anita's technique—a quiet sidestep through a forgotten back door in the subsystem. The screen flickered, stuttering briefly, then stabilized as she broke through. A jolt of adrenaline surged in her chest, electric and racing down her arms. "Here we go," she whispered, leaning closer, her breath fogging the edge of the monitor. She typed a command, her fingers a blur, and Helix's defenses unfolded before her—a sprawling maze, designed to confuse intruders with its complexity.

But she'd been working around this beast for two years and knew where the seams were. It was now her and the file system, a dance of wits in the dark.

The deeper she delved into the code, the more the system fought back. Firewalls appeared like steel barricades, with their code shifting and twisting as they tracked her movements. She squinted, eyes burning as she dissected the patterns, her mind racing to stay one step ahead.

"Come on, a little further," she urged herself.

One obstacle vanished when she swiftly rewrote a script, mimicking one of the authorized IT tech's passwords she'd seen pasted on his badge. A move that felt like threading a needle in a thunderstorm. She spotted the opening, slipped through, and laughed as it snapped shut behind her.

Another layer presented an encryption puzzle — a chaotic jumble of numbers and symbols that challenged her to solve it. She leaned back, visualizing the pieces clicking into place like a lock unlocking, and held her breath until the solution slid in. It gave way with a soft ping, and her pulse hammered against her ribs. The room shrank to the blue haze of the screens, and the sweat prickled her scalp.

An angry and insistent red flash flickered on the center monitor, signaling that she had been spotted. "No, no, no—not now," she groaned, her stomach dropping. Sweat beaded on her palms, making the keys slick and dangerous. One wrong move, and Helix would catch her—locked out, traced, finished.

Her heart hammered against her chest with a wild, irregular beat she couldn't control. The red light lit up her face, hot and accusatory, reflected in her glasses.

"Think, Emily!" she snapped, her voice cracking. She froze, her fingers trembling over the keyboard. Taking a shaky breath, she rerouted her connection through a back door she had noticed earlier. The alert flashed, wavered, and then vanished. She slumped back, breathing heavily. "Too damn close." She wiped her forehead with a corner of the bedspread.

She continued on. The directories scrolled past—useless clutter, corporate noise—until Chronos flashed on the screen, stark and white against the black. "There you are," she breathed, a knot of excitement twisting in her stomach. Her mouth went dry as she clicked into it, the cursor blinking.

The files loaded in fragments—broken, redacted, like a puzzle missing half its pieces. She scrolled, her eyes darting as she tried to piece the scraps together. A transaction log flickered into view: millions funneled into offshore accounts, dates matching the success of the BioSpark project. An email to Q, sent by James, mentioned "immortality's hidden key" in unclear, frantic language, partially erased.

Messages indicated that the changes to the BioSpark data weren't about hiding profits or protecting proprietary technology; they were a deliberate cover-up designed to hide references to the extinction event. James had concealed the related data to give Chronos time to prepare, but for what reason? Was this event an environmental collapse, a genetic catastrophe, or something even more unimaginable, and why did it take over a century to get ready?

The email fragments raised more questions than answers, with each hint carefully scrambled to keep the world in the dark. Her teeth clenched until they ached, the tension radiating up her skull. She and Anita had swapped BioSpark's data this morning to protect it from manipulation, but this was deeper, darker, a shadow extending beyond what they'd known.

The pieces sketched a jagged outline: James entangled with this Q, chasing promises. One file hinted Q had dangled a kill switch reset—plus a fat payout—if James played along, or a bullet if he didn't. She bit her lip as she scrolled, but the redactions taunted her, leaving noticeable gaps in the truth.

Q was a phantom, a name without a face, and the kill switch? BioSpark confirmed the terminal gene was permanent and unchangeable. Was Q bluffing, or was the research incomplete?

"What the hell are you up to, James?" she muttered, doubt setting in.

Time was running out. With each passing minute, the risk of her getting caught increased. She started the download; the progress bar teased her with its sluggishness. "Move, damn it," she growled. Her eyes flicked to the system logs, watching for any sign of trouble. Her neck throbbed from the strain, a dull ache she ignored.

Then the logs shifted—security stirring and waking up. Red warnings flashed across the screen, a shrill beep piercing the air. "Not now!" she yelped, panic rising. Her fingers fumbled, slipping on the keys as the directory locked down. She grabbed the partial files and yanked the connection, slamming the power button. The screens went black, and the computer's sound died with the faint whine of the cooling fans. She slumped back, chest heaving.

She stood, legs wobbling, gripping the nightstand for support. The room snapped back into focus, dust motes drifting in the sunlight, Einstein, Edward, and Jacob staring down like witnesses. Those icons—her old rebellion—sparked defiance. The files confirmed James's betrayal and hinted at Chronos's ultimate plan, but they were incomplete. Who was Q? Could the gene really be altered? The questions gnawed at her. Everything she thought she knew was becoming quicksand.

She grabbed her phone, thumb hovering over Dr. Morrow's contact. The file she'd swiped from James's desk... Maybe it held a thread to pull. But trusting Dr. Morrow was a gamble, and her insides churned with uncertainty.

"I need a better plan," she said, setting the phone down. For now, the truth was hers to hunt. She glared at the blank screens, her reflection faint in the glass. Round one was hers—but she'd be back, and next time she'd tear the whole conspiracy open.

The alley behind Charlestown Wheels reeked of stale beer and motor oil, a stench that clung to clothes. Twilight draped the narrow passage, cast by sagging brick walls and a single pulsing streetlamp that buzzed faintly. Tyler pressed his back against the damp brick, breathing shallowly as the cold seeped through his field jacket. Boston's pulse thumped in the distance—honking cabs, a siren's wail—but here, the world felt suspended, waiting for something to break.

Tyler checked his watch: 2:47. Vic was late. His fingers twitched toward the gun in his jacket pocket, its weight constantly reminding him how far he had fallen. He didn't trust Vic, no matter what he said, but he needed him. Vic knew the quarry, the cabin, where screams wouldn't carry. Tyler's plan was simple: lure James, bind him, and record the truth. Force him to spit out why he wanted Emily dead. But simplicity was a lie if he looked too closely at the details.

A low rumble broke the silence—tires on asphalt. Dimmed headlights swept the alley's entrance, casting a sickly yellow light on the bricks. An old Ford pickup, its paint chipped to expose rust spots, rolled to a stop. The driver's door creaked open, and Vic stepped out, his hood pulled low, hands buried in his pockets. He moved like someone who knew how to vanish, all slouch and shadow.

"You're late again," Tyler said, annoyed.

Vic shrugged, his boots splashing in a shallow puddle. "Traffic. You wanna do this or not?"

Tyler studied him, eyes narrowing. He didn't like the way Vic's gaze darted to the alley's corners, as if he expected someone. "You got the gear?"

Vic patted the duffel slung over his shoulder. "Rope, zip ties, camera. Everything you asked for. You sure about this, man? James ain't some street punk. I warned you on the call. He's got connections."

Tyler's expression tightened. "That's why we're doing it my way." He jerked his head toward the truck. "Let's move."

They climbed into the truck's cab, the seat springs creaking. The interior smelled of pine air freshener over stale cigarette smoke and a sour aroma, like sweat. Vic turned the key, and the engine coughed to life, rattling the dashboard.

As they pulled out of the alley, Boston's back streets flickered past in a blur of wet gray—boarded-up storefronts, graffiti-covered walls, and the occasional shimmer of neon from a dive bar. Tyler kept his eyes on the road, but his mind swirled.

"You know why James wants me dead?" he asked, breaking the silence. His voice was even, but his pulse wasn't. "What's his problem?"

Vic's hands clenched tighter on the wheel, knuckles white. "That dude doesn't share his plans with me. I only hear things. He's involved with some heavy hitters—guys with more money than God who don't like loose ends. You and your girlfriend, you're...complications."

"She's my fiancé, not my girlfriend. Complications," Tyler spat. "That's what you call a hit list?"

Vic glanced at him. "Call it what you want. The point is he's cleaning house. You two are in the way, and he wants you buried and forgotten."

Tyler's fingers curled into fists, ragged nails digging into his palms. He didn't need Vic's half-answers; he needed James's voice on video, confessing everything—the why, the who, the how. He wanted him crying and begging for mercy.

As he leaned back, the seat groaned, and the truck's vibrations brought him back to the present. Outside, the city gave way to dirt roads, where tracks disappeared into the woods and the quarry loomed like a scar on the horizon.

The memory struck him suddenly and vividly. Two nights ago, in another alley, another plan went wrong. Three men, faces concealed, knives in hand. Tyler's knuckles still throbbed where he had cracked them on someone's nose. Emily's scream pierced the night as he fought off the attackers, blood slick on his hands. Betrayal wasn't a strong enough word, and Vic had led them there.

"You're quiet," Vic said, snapping Tyler back. The truck bounced over a pothole.

"Thinking," Tyler said. His eyes flicked to Vic's phone,

buzzing in the center console. The screen lit up, a string of texts flashing too quickly to read. "Who's that?"

Vic's hand shot out, flipping the phone screen down. "My sister. Chill."

Tyler's core twisted. "Your sister texts you when you're on a job? Who is it?"

Vic's laugh was sharp, like breaking glass. "You're paranoid, man. It's nothing, family stuff."

"Show me."

Vic's lips pressed together, but he stared at the road. "We've got bigger problems than my phone, Tyler. Focus."

Tension settled over his chest. Vic was a means to an end, nothing more. If he were playing both sides, Tyler would deal with it later. For now, the cabin waited.

The quarry road was a tangle of ruts and weeds, gravel spitting from under the tires as they climbed. The cabin came into view, a sagging relic of wood and rust, with boarded-up windows and a roof half-caved in from years of neglect. Weeds and leaves cluttered the porch. Vic shut off the engine, and the silence settled in, broken only by the sound of pine trees swaying in the breeze.

They stepped out, boots sinking into the mud. Tyler's breath fogged in the cold air, his eyes scanning the tree line. The quarry's edge was a dark void beyond, a drop that offered no forgiveness. He hefted the duffel from the truck bed, its contents clinking softly.

"How deep is the water in the quarry?" Tyler asked.

Vic considered the question. "Deep enough to hide a body if you weigh it down. Does that answer your question?"

Tyler nodded and proceeded up the rotten wooden stairs.

Inside, the cabin was a tomb of mildew and dust. The air smelled stale, like mold and rot. Peeling wallpaper hung in strips, revealing warped boards beneath. A single chair sat in the corner, its wood splintered, perfect for what came next. Tyler dropped the duffel, unzipping it with a sound that echoed ominously in the quiet. Vic moved the chair to the center of the room and set up the camera on an old, rusty tripod. He aimed the lens at the chair like an unblinking eye.

"Test it," Tyler said, tossing a coil of rope onto the floor. The fibers were rough, biting into his palms as he worked a knot.

Vic fiddled with the camera, the red light blinking on. "It's good. Records audio too. You sure he'll talk?"

"He'll talk." Tyler's voice was flat, final. He didn't look at Vic, didn't want to see his smirk. Instead, he focused on the restraints—zip ties looped through the chair's arms, tight enough to bruise. Even though his hands were steady, his mind was racing. What comes after the confession? Hand James over to the cops, taped and gift-wrapped? Or something else, something final? He'd never killed before, but the line felt blurry now, knowing it was his last chance to protect Emily from the danger after he was gone.

A rustle outside broke his focus. He froze, hand on the gun. Vic's head snapped up, eyes wide. The sound came again—scrabbling, low, from the tool shed. Tyler moved to the window, peering through a gap in the boards. Dappled light caught a raccoon climbing on the shed's roof, then two more, their claws ticking across the wood as they rummaged through the moss and leaves. Tyler exhaled, his pulse slowing.

"Critters," Vic muttered, relaxing. "They must have a nest nearby."

"What's inside the shed?"

Vic shrugged. "Tools for occasional repairs, all rusty."

"Let's wrap this up," Tyler said, turning back to the chair. "I need to get back."

They finished the setup in silence, the camera's red light glowing. Tyler stepped back, surveying the room. The chair, the ropes, the camera—all ready for James. This was a point of no return. Likely the last thing he'd do before his kill switch caught up with him. His mouth tightened as he dismissed the possibilities: if he failed to get James here, if Vic betrayed him, or if the video wasn't enough.

"You good?" Vic asked, zipping the duffel shut. His phone buzzed again, and he silenced it with a quick swipe, avoiding Tyler's gaze.

Tyler didn't answer. He stepped onto the porch, feeling the cold air on his face, and lit a cigarette. The smoke curled upward, gray against the dark green tree line. Although he rarely smoked, he wanted a cigarette today to distract himself. He questioned if James would beg, cry, or fight. He wondered what Emily would think if she saw him now with the darkness in his eyes.

Vic joined him, leaning on the porch railing. "Still going through with it?"

Tyler took a final drag, the ember flaring, then dropped the cigarette, crushing it under his boot. "Yeah," he said.

The living room of the Victorian house on Telegraph Hill smelled of rosemary and roasting lamb. Emily stood by the window, her fingers tracing the chipped paint on the sill, a pale outline of her face in the glass. Her eyes, darkened with exhaustion, scanned the street below for Tyler's familiar stride. The front door opened, and Emily turned, her breath catching.

Tyler stepped inside, his jacket damp, his face marked with deeper lines than in the morning. His boots left faint mud prints on the hardwood, and he paused, meeting her gaze. The air between them was tense, charged with anticipation. Emily's shoulders relaxed, the pressure of the day easing now that he was home.

"You look like you've seen a ghost," she said.

He snorted and kicked the door closed. "Feels like it too." He set his bag down beside the couch. The rug muffled the thud. "How was your afternoon being a digital detective?"

She gestured toward the coffee table and a pile of printouts. "Chronos files. It took me hours to crack their encryption, but it's bad, Tyler. Worse than we thought." She moved to the table and picked up a page. Her fingers trembled slightly, not from fear but from simmering fury. "James isn't merely skimming profits. He's tied to this group buying the BioSpark data. There's this mysterious person named Q pulling the strings, but James is the one tying the knots."

Tyler's eyes narrowed, his hands shoving into his pockets. "How's James connected?"

"Contracts, shell companies, offshore accounts. He's collecting money from private labs, governments, and those working on genetic tech—stuff that profits from the details of the terminal gene. But there are gaps. I don't have the whole picture." She set the page down, her voice tightening. "His kill switch, though—he knows his timeline. Only a couple of years. He's running scared."

Tyler's jaw clenched, a muscle twitching in his cheek. He looked away, focusing on the fireplace, its mantel crowded with family photos. "I'm seeing him tonight," he mumbled. "After dark. Gonna make him talk. Get all the details on video."

Emily's stomach twisted. She stepped closer, her shadow falling across him. "Talk how? Tyler, what's your plan?"

His gaze fixed on a photo of them from years ago, arms slung around each other at a pier. "I'll get him to confess. Everything."

Her breath caught. "You're not just talking to him. You're what, kidnapping him? Locking him in a room?" She crossed her arms. "You can't abduct him."

"He won't confess otherwise," Tyler said, turning to face her. His eyes burned, not with anger but with something desperate.

"You think he'll sit down over a beer and spill his guts? He's got blood on his hands, Emily. Ours soon if we don't stop him."

The clock's ticking louder now, each second like a drumbeat. She wanted to argue, to tell him this was too much, too dangerous. But the files on the table, with their cold data and even colder implications, silenced her protests. James had betrayed them, trying to kill them. Still, the thought of Tyler crossing that line—becoming a man capable of doing this—made her heart ache.

"Emily! Dinner's almost ready!" Patricia's voice floated from the kitchen, warm and unaware. The clatter of pots followed, a spoon scraping against cast iron.

Emily looked toward the kitchen, then back at Tyler. She lowered her voice and stepped closer. "You're not telling me everything. What happens after you get the confession?"

He didn't respond, his gaze dropping to the floor. His silence was an answer, an intention she couldn't quite grasp. She studied him—the tense set of his shoulders, the slight tremor in his hands. He was hiding something bigger than the plan to talk to James and get him to confess.

"We know why James is doing this," she said, steering the conversation back to solid ground. "Greed, fear, maybe both. He's building an empire on what's coming. But we need more than a confession. We need proof that sticks, something the government can't ignore."

Tyler nodded, his expression unreadable. "I'll get the recording. You keep digging. Those files—there's more in there, right?"

"Yes," she said, her voice steadying. "There's always more." She picked up another page, her eyes scanning lines of code and account numbers. The data was a maze, but she was good at navigating mazes. Her cleverness had gotten them this far, and it would take her further. But Tyler's path, with its sharp edges and dark intent, frightened her. Their alliance, once unbreakable, now felt fragile, stretched thin by their different ways of confronting the threat.

Patricia called again, her voice brighter. "You two coming? It's lamb tonight, and Tyler's special birthday cake!"

"We'll be there in a sec, Mom!" Emily shouted back, her tone lighter than she felt. She turned to Tyler. "We do this together, okay? No solo moves. Promise me."

He looked into her eyes, and she saw the lover she'd known —fierce, protective, flawed. "Together," he said.

She led Tyler toward the dining room, her hand gently resting on his arm. The air was thick with the sharp scent of rosemary, blending uneasily with the warm sweetness of chocolate cake. The grandfather clock struck six, its chimes soft. Her mother's antique china shimmered on the table, a symbol of celebration that deepened the dimness in Tyler's eyes. Their shared dreams kept them connected, but an unexplainable dread swelled in her chest, a ghost shadowing them into the flickering candlelight.

Chapter 18

A Tick-Tock Heart

Tyler's Tesla idled, its sleek black body almost invisible in the gloom, a silent predator blending into the dark.

The garage beneath Helix's glass tower was a sprawling maze of concrete, its air heavy with the sour smell of exhaust. Dim fluorescent lights pulsed overhead, casting patches of yellow onto oil-slicked floors, where tire tracks crisscrossed like old scars. A distant water drip echoed from a dark corner, synchronizing each plink with his watch's second hand.

Tyler crouched nearby, hidden behind a chipped pillar, his back pushed against the rough concrete, his breath shallow to dull the sharp smells.

His pulse hammered, each beat a reminder of the hours slipping away—less than five—before his kill switch triggered, ending his life. He still wasn't sure how it would happen, a heart attack or just slipping away quietly, but he was going to make sure he wasn't in public or driving at the time.

His gloved fingers clenched a chloroform-soaked rag, its sharp, chemical bite piercing through the thin fabric. Every nerve was tense, every sense razor-sharp, but his doubts gnawed relentlessly. This wasn't who he was. Or it hadn't been until Emily's life depended on him.

Tyler glanced at his wristwatch. 8:01 p.m. His anxiety grew at the thought that James might be late or had gone out a different door. He couldn't afford to fail—not with Emily's name on a hit list. His own name was also on it, but that didn't matter. He had accepted that he would soon be dead anyway.

The plan was simple: grab James, take him to the quarry, and force a confession about Chronos on camera. Simple in concept, but each step seemed like a descent into a darkness he couldn't return from. His free hand brushed the pistol in his pocket, a grim reminder of what he'd need to do after forcing the confession from James.

He pictured Emily's face—her wide grin from a few months ago, chasing him through the surf by the pier, her laughter joyful. Since last week, her voice had sounded different—fearful, piecing together details of Chronos. She'd trusted him to protect her. He was driven to do the unthinkable because of that trust.

The elevator dinged, a piercing sound that snapped Tyler's focus back. He pressed tighter against the pillar, his breath catching as the doors slid open. James stepped out, his key fob glinting in his hand, its metallic shine reflecting the fluorescent light. His polished loafers clicked on the concrete, a rhythm that exuded confidence, as if ordering Tyler and Emily's deaths was another day's work. His navy suit was crisp, untouched by the late hour, and his briefcase swung lightly as he strode toward his car, parked two rows away. His head tilted slightly, eyes on his phone, unaware of the shadows. Tyler's eyes widened, his grip on the rag clenched as he counted James's steps. Three. Two. One. *Now.*

Tyler moved quickly and silently, covering the distance in three long strides. The rag clamped over James's mouth, and the sharp scent of chloroform flooded the air, stinging Tyler's eyes. James grunted, a muffled sound of shock, as his body jerked and he desperately clawed at Tyler's arm. His shoes scraped against the concrete in a frantic shuffle, and the briefcase clattered to the floor with a hollow thud that echoed through the empty garage.

Tyler squeezed harder, his arm locking around James's chest, feeling the man's ribs heave under the strain. James's fingers dug into Tyler's wrist, nails scraping through the glove, but the fight was brief, frantic. His limbs slackened, his body sagging against Tyler like a puppet with cut strings. Tyler held on a moment longer, the rag held firm, ensuring the chloroform had taken hold. James's head lolled, lips parted, his breath shallow and uneven. Tyler eased him to the ground, his breath ragged, adrenaline flooding his veins.

The garage was quiet except for the distant drip and the faint buzz of the fluorescent lights. Tyler's heart pounded as he looked through the gloom for movement—cameras, guards, a stray janitor. Nothing.

He kneeled beside James, checking his pulse—steady, faint— then dragged him toward the Tesla, his limp form heavier than expected. He popped the trunk with a soft click. After heaving James inside, Tyler winced. The dull thud of James's body against the carpeted lining was audible, his head lolling, face slack in the dim light. Tyler retrieved the briefcase and tossed it beside him. He slammed the trunk. The sound was dull and final, a door closing on the man he'd been only days ago.

Tyler gripped the wheel after sliding into the driver's seat, his gloved hands trembling despite trying to calm them. The Tesla's interior was cool, and the faint glow from the dashboard lit up his face sharply. He saw his reflection in the rearview mirror—hollow eyes, a grimace on his mouth, a desperate stranger staring back.

The motor purred quietly as he pulled out, tires murmuring against the concrete, garage walls flashing past. Boston's lights flashed through the windshield, neon signs and streetlights fading into the fog over the quarry road. The city gave way to narrower streets then to rutted gravel, the Tesla bouncing slightly as civilization's remnants disappeared. The quarry loomed ahead, its dark edge a void in the mist, the cabin's silhouette barely visible through the haze.

Tyler's mind churned, recent memories flashing like static on a broken screen. Emily curled up next to him on the couch, reading. Her voice this evening, singing Happy Birthday to him, her eyes shining with love. She trusted him to end this, to keep her safe, but safety came with a cost, and he was paying for it now, piece by piece.

His knuckles whitened as the road twisted upward toward the abandoned cabin, gravel spitting under the tires. The fog thickened, swallowing the stars, and the air grew heavy with the scent of pine and wet granite.

He looked in the rearview mirror, half-expecting to see James's eyes shining from the back seat, but there was only darkness. The burden of what was coming pressed down— interrogation and confession. Then what? Tyler wasn't sure if he could kill, but he'd do whatever it took to protect Emily.

The cabin materialized through the fog, with its sagging roof and boarded-up windows, a bleak symbol of solitude. He parked, gravel crunching beneath the tires, and stepped out into the cold. He opened the trunk, where James was, breathing shallow but even. Tyler's resolve hardened, cold as the gunmetal in his pocket. The cabin awaited, its darkness ready to swallow them both and reveal the truth about Chronos.

The cabin's interior was a rotting husk, its splintered wooden walls sagging under the strain of years, their grain split and darkened by moisture. A sour, persistent smell of mildew filled the air, coating Tyler's throat with every breath he took. A single lantern was in the corner, its stark light casting rough shapes across peeling wallpaper, where faded floral patterns twisted.

The camera's red light glowed on its rusty tripod, an unblinking eye fixed on the chair at the room's center, its wood scarred and rough, with splintered edges catching the light. Ropes creaked as James moved, his wrists bound with zip ties that dug into his skin, leaving raw, red marks under his navy suit. His shirt was now creased and damp from the trunk and quarry's fog.

Tyler stood over him, the pistol tucked in his jacket pocket—a cold mass against his ribs, a constant reminder of how close he was to crossing the darkest line. Murder. His heartbeat pounded in his chest, each beat a stark countdown—four hours, probably less—until his kill switch activated. The fog outside pressed against the boarded-up windows, sealing the cabin in a gray, suffocating shroud.

Tyler leaned forward, his bruised knuckles cracking across James's jaw, the sharp blow slicing through the quiet. James's head snapped to the side, his eyes fluttering open, disoriented for a long moment before sharpening into a sneer. Blood trickled from his lip, a thin red line against his pale skin, but his arrogance held firm, unshaken by the zip ties and rope.

"You're wasting your time, Reed," he said contemptuously. "What's the plan? Scare me into talking? You're already a dead man."

Tyler's jaw locked, his fingers twitching toward the pistol. That cut deep, exposing the truth Tyler couldn't escape. His kill switch was only hours away, while Emily had told him James had two years left.

He must know about Tyler's deadline, and the smug certainty in his eyes made Tyler's blood boil. "You know about that," Tyler said, his voice taut, the air between them heavy with the threat of death. "Then you understand why we're here. Talk. Tell the camera what you're doing with Helix, Chronos. Why are you trying to kill Emily?"

James laughed, a sharp, brittle sound that scraped the silence like nails on concrete. "You think I'm afraid of you? You don't have the stomach for this." He leaned forward, the ropes and zip ties straining, his eyes glinting in the lantern's yellow glow. "Your terminal gene's about finished, Tyler. Mine's got years. I can wait you out. You'll be gone by midnight, and I'll walk away."

Rage surged like a white-hot flood, blurring Tyler's vision to pinpoint. He yanked the pistol from his jacket. Its metal was cold and heavy in his hand, and he fired.

The gunshot exploded in a deafening crack that shook the cabin's mildewed walls, with the echo lingering like a scream in the dark. James's body jerked, a raw cry tearing from his throat as blood bloomed through his suit pants, soaking his leg in a dark, spreading stain. The sharp, coppery smell of blood filled the air.

James's scream twisted into a laugh, wild and jagged, his pain fueling a defiance that made Tyler's stomach churn. "That's it?" James spat, his voice taunting, his eyes blazing with a manic edge. "You shot me in the leg? You're pathetic. After you're gone, I'll find Emily. She'll beg me to kill her before I'm done. I'll make her curse your name."

Tyler's finger twitched on the trigger, his breath ragged, his vision narrowing to James's sneering face. He wanted to pull the trigger again, to silence that voice, to erase the threat to Emily, but his hand shook, and the pistol's weight became a barrier. James was right. He couldn't kill him yet. Tyler needed more, the truth on tape, Emily safe beyond his last hours.

James leaned back, his breath ragged, and gestured to the watch on his wrist—a gaudy, gold-plated relic, its second hand ticking relentlessly, a cruel mockery of Tyler's fading time.

"This," he sneered, "is worth more than you and Emily combined. Built to run forever. Like me. You? You're nobody. And in a few hours, your pathetic attempt to stop me will mean nothing." The watch gleamed in the dim light, its face etched with gaudy detail, symbolizing James's greed, his belief that he could outrun time itself.

The taunt hit him hard, like a gut punch, but it also triggered something else—a cold, piercing clarity. Tyler's eyes flicked to the camera, its red light solid, recording every word and threat.

Tyler's thoughts raced, images flashing—the quarry's black waters, deep and unforgiving, a place to dump James and let him sink. But the depth was uncertain; the outcome, shaky. He could tie James and leave him in the cabin, but someone might find him, cut him loose. A stray hiker or a curious cop—too many variables.

No, he needed certainty to protect Emily beyond his final breath. An idea took root, desperate and dark: bury James alive. Not to kill but to trap him, to lock him away where he couldn't touch her. He had nothing left to lose and was willing to do anything to protect the person he loved.

Tyler stepped closer, the air thick with blood and rot. "You're right," he said. "I can't kill you." He pocketed the pistol, his hands steady now, the decision firming like ice in his veins.

James's sneer faltered, his eyes narrowing as he sensed the shift. The chair creaked as he strained, the zip ties biting deeper, blood pooling beneath them, but Tyler ignored him, turning to check the camera's angle before stepping outside. The red light blinked.

The darkness outside hid the overgrown yard as Tyler moved toward the old shed. The musty air clung to the scattered tools, dust, and cobwebs. Spotting an old shovel in a dim corner —its handle worn, its blade scarred—Tyler grabbed it and carried it out, the night's chill clinging to the metal, placing it on the creaky porch by the front door. With a final look, he went inside, leaving the shovel in the faint moonlight.

He moved to the corner where his duffel bag slumped against the wall, its canvas stained with dirt and age. He unzipped it, the sound loud in the quiet, and pulled out a coil of nylon rope, its fibers rough and biting. James watched, his breath quickening, the first crack in his arrogance showing in the twitch of his lips and the slight widening of his eyes. Tyler didn't meet his gaze, his focus on the task ahead—the woods, a shovel, a grave.

With a grim smile, Tyler showed James the nylon rope. "You're going to find out which one lasts longer, the nylon rope or your fancy watch."

Outside, the fog thickened, its chill seeping through the boarded windows, the quarry's stillness stark against the tension inside the cabin. Tyler's breath fogged in the cold, his mind focused on the next move. James's threats sounded empty, buried under the weight of Tyler's plan. The camera's battery light burned steadily, capturing the moment. Woods waited, their darkness prepared to swallow whatever was coming next.

The fog-soaked woods near the quarry formed a maze of dark and dampness. The loamy ground gave way under Tyler's boots with a faint squelch as he pulled James through the under-brush. Towering pines faded into the gray mist, their branches heavy, obscuring the moonlight. The quarry's edge was beyond the trees.

Tyler's grip on James's bound arms was iron, the coarse ropes biting his palms, zip ties cutting into James's wrists, slick with blood and sweat from his earlier thrashing in the cabin. The shovel slung over his shoulder clinked faintly, its blade catching slivers of moonlight, mirroring the cold resolve in his eyes. James stumbled, his bullet-wounded thigh buckling, his torn shirt stained with blood and dirt, but Tyler hauled him forward, unrelenting.

In a small clearing, the earth soft and yielding, Tyler let James collapse to his knees with a choked grunt. He drove the shovel into the soil, the wet crunch echoing in the stillness. James's head jerked up, his eyes wide, the arrogance from the cabin crumbling. "Tyler, don't," he rasped, voice trembling, stripped bare. "You don't have to do this. Please."

Tyler's face was stone, his expression tight as he dug, the

shovel's scrape rhythmic and relentless. Dirt piled in dark clumps, and the pit took shape under the faint moonlight. "You ordered her death," Tyler said, voice low, cutting through the fog. "Emily. The one person I'd become a monster for."

James's bound hands twitched as the grave deepened. "It wasn't my call!" he blurted in a panic. "Q forced me. Chronos plans to sell the genetic data and reset the kill switches for the rich—immortality for a price. Emily got too close, digging into their plans. I had no choice!"

Tyler paused, shovel half-buried, wet dirt clinging to its edge like clotted blood. He met James's gaze, his eyes cold and hollowed by betrayal. "No choice?" he repeated, his voice dripping with disgust. "You sold her out to save your own skin."

He dug again, the crunch of soil louder, drowning out the faint tick of James's gaudy gold watch.

"I didn't want this!" James pleaded, his voice cracking, body trembling as blood seeped from his thigh. "Q would've killed me. My kill switch... I only have two years left. I was trying to survive, Tyler. Let me go. I'll vanish. You don't need to do this."

Tyler's hands clutched the shovel tighter, knuckles turning white, the wood pressing into his palms. He paused, turning to James with a raw voice. "You don't get it. Emily's my everything. I'd tear the world apart for her. You made a mistake in thinking I wouldn't." His bitter laugh cut through the air as he dug, the pit now knee-deep, its damp walls glistening.

James's bravado had vanished. His face turned pale, and his eyes filled with fear. "I'm begging you. I'll do anything. Don't bury me." His voice cracked, a desperate sob swallowed by the fog.

Tyler's determination was forged by love and the ticking clock in his genes. He dropped the shovel, its blade thudding into the dirt, and hauled James to his feet. James's legs gave out, but Tyler dragged him to the pit's edge, the shallow scar deep enough to hide a body from scavengers. Using the extra rope, he lowered James into the open grave. James's back hit the cold, stony soil.

"Count every second for the next two years," Tyler said, voice hollow, pointing to the watch on James's wrist—a final jab at his earlier arrogance. "In case you're curious, I used nylon rope to tie you up for a reason. No matter how much you struggle, it will outlast you, your watch, and the time left on your kill switch." James's eyes widened, his muffled pleas fading as dirt covered his legs, torso, and twitching hands. As James's crying grew silent, the watch's faint tick persisted, a cruel reminder of time passing.

Tyler worked carefully, his arms aching as the fog's chill bit into his muscles. The quarry stood silent as the last scoop of dirt dropped, burying James in an unmarked mound. He rested the shovel on his shoulder, its blade sticky with wet dirt. The grave's faint outline faded into the mist as he walked away, the cost of saving Emily etched into his soul—a hollow trade for love. The fog drew in tighter, and the muffled stillness of the woods hid the sound of his steps.

Chapter 19

What Have I Become

The cabin stood alone, its shape concealed by the dense fog that clung to the forest.

Tyler drifted through the cabin, a wraith among the shadows, his hands unsteady as he dragged a damp rag across the rough floor. The cloth was soaked with cleaning fluid, and streaks of something darker rasped against the wood. He pressed harder, though the surface was too dirty to see any difference.

His breaths came quickly and shallow, each one a stab in his chest. He stopped, bracing himself against the wall, eyes slipping shut. The memory flared—James's face, drained of color, eyes wide with an unanswered plea. The shovel caught the faint light, then descended, filling his mouth with dirt as the screaming stopped. Tyler's bowels twisted, bile rising, but he forced it down, locking the image away. Time was moving too quickly—less than two hours until his kill switch triggered.

He checked his watch and moved to the tripod where the camera rested, its lens a dead eye pointed upward. His fingers, clumsy with adrenaline, fumbled with the buttons. The footage flickered to life, but his shoulders sank as the truth hit him: James's confession had spilled out in the woods, beyond the camera's reach. Useless. Yet Helix could twist anything. He deleted the video, then slammed the device against the table's edge. Plastic splintered, and he swept the pieces into a trash bag.

Tyler moved through the cabin's decay, wiping away every trace of himself and James. In the main room, he wiped down the chair stained with James's blood. He scrubbed the sink in the kitchen, its cracked porcelain gritty under his sponge, the rust-streaked basin resisting until his knuckles ached from the effort.

The silence bore down, broken only by the groan of the floor or a distant owl's call. The cabin felt like a trap once the hope of exposing James's conspiracy faded. He was haunted by guilt but also driven to destroy the evidence of his actions. This wasn't for him but for Emily, for the truth Helix had silenced.

At the window, he paused, looking into the endless darkness. The woods stretched out, a shroud of mist concealing James's grave. Tyler's fists clenched. He hadn't chosen this path—the world had pushed him onto it. Now, he carried the burden alone.

He grabbed the trash bag, its contents shifting, and stepped outside. The damp night air brushed against his skin, gravel crunching under his feet. He tossed the trash, the shovel, and his duffel bag into the trunk of the Tesla, then looked back at the cabin one last time. He climbed into the car, tired. The engine purred to life, and he drove into the darkness, speeding past the abandoned quarry.

The Tesla sliced through the night's stillness, its tires droning against the asphalt as Boston's skyline appeared closer. Tyler gripped the wheel tightly, eyes flicking to the rearview mirror every few seconds. At a deserted truck stop miles back, he'd discarded the broken camera, shovel, and cleaning supplies into a dumpster—a hollow clang marking their end. Now, the neon lights of the city swallowed him.

He parked in a dark lot three blocks from the twenty-four-hour Internet cafe, the engine's hum fading into silence. Pulling his hoodie tighter, he stepped into the cold, the streets eerily still except for the occasional rumble of a delivery truck. Dead leaves crunched underfoot as he approached the cafe, its neon sign flickering above a door smeared with years of neglect. Inside, the air hit him—stale coffee mixing with the smell of body odor and overheated electronics. Fluorescent lights buzzed overhead, casting shapes across the few customers slouched at their terminals.

Tyler looked around the room after paying cash for an hour's time. He moved to a corner station with the wall behind him. The stained chair squeaked as he sat, and the keyboard felt sticky under his fingers. He logged in, the screen's glow lighting up his tense face.

He pulled Emily's thumb drives from his pocket, their significance a silent accusation. He had taken them from her backpack after the apartment break-in on Saturday. He had presumed he would need evidence of the Helix conspiracy if he couldn't make James confess. When he plugged in the first drive, the upload window appeared, and he felt relief as the progress bar slowly advanced.

A voice interrupted the hum. "You good over there, dude?" The desk clerk—scruffy, mid-twenties, with a faded Red Sox cap —leaned over the counter, peering at him.

Tyler's head jerked up, startled. "I'm fine," he snapped and turned his body, shielding the screen. The clerk paused, eyes narrowing, then muttered something about porn and returned to his phone. Tyler exhaled, the tension tightening. One slip, and he wouldn't have another chance.

The upload inched along, painfully slow. He opened a blank message and began to type.

To the press: Helix has betrayed humanity. Their claim of creating gene therapies to save lives is a blatant lie. They have mastered predicting lifespans with frightening accuracy and uncovered a looming mass extinction event, yet hid both to push a sinister agenda. By selling this knowledge to wealthy bidders, they aim to control our destiny. The attached files, obtained at significant personal risk, contain undeniable proof: manipulated records, secret plans, and their "terminal gene" project exposed. You can expose their lies with a single revelation: Chronos. As always, follow the money. Spread this truth far and wide, protect the innocent, and act quickly before all is lost.

He reread his message, ensuring no clues pointed to Emily. His finger paused over the enter key, hesitating. This could destroy everything—most importantly, Emily's trust. But Helix's plan to sell the kill switch data was too important to delay. If she had heard James's last confession, she would have understood. He pushed send, and the files vanished into the void, a shiver running through him.

A customer coughed nearby, a wet, hacking sound that made Tyler flinch. He glanced over—some guy in a stained jacket, oblivious, tapping away. Still, every click of a keyboard, every shuffle of feet, felt like a spotlight swinging his way. He yanked the thumb drive free, pocketing it, then pulled his phone from his jacket. With a quick twist, he popped out the SIM card, wiping the device clean. In the bathroom, the air reeked of damp rot and cheap cleaner. He crushed the phone under his heel, then buried it deep in the trash beneath a pile of soggy paper towels.

Back in the cafe, the room's low chatter faded. The leak was out—Helix's lies finally revealed. Dread swiftly extinguished the brief flash of relief. Emily would face the fallout, and he wouldn't be there to help her. His watch glared back: time was slipping. His kill switch ticked closer.

He pushed through the door, the sounds of the surrounding city—horns blaring, voices rising. One stop remained.

Tyler lingered on the cracked sidewalk; the chilly night air calmed him. Boston's Mass and Cass district sprawled around him, a bleak patchwork of boarded-up shops and gleaming streetlights. He slid the letter into a corroded mailbox, its lid screeching as it closed. Addressed to Emily at her parents' house, it contained his last words—regret for his choices, love that would always burn bright, a quiet plea for her to keep fighting. His fingers brushed the rusted metal of the mailbox, then fell away. The act freed something inside him.

He walked past the desolate lot where his Tesla was parked, its smooth black lines standing out against rusted pickup trucks and abandoned sedans. The key fob stayed in his pocket. Looking around for any shadow that might follow, he slipped into the darkness, his footsteps scraping on the pavement covered with cigarette butts, crumpled fast food wrappers, and glass shards, as he dropped his wallet, thumb drives, and fob into a sewer grate.

The Mass Mirage Motel rose ahead, a decaying relic in the heart of Mass and Cass. Its neon sign pulsed uncertainly, casting a sickly pink glow over a facade covered in cracked stucco and peeling paint. The word "Mirage" flickered, half its letters dark.

The lobby assaulted his nose with stale cigarette smoke, mildew, and the faint scent of spilled Thunderbird. A fan clattered in the corner, stirring dust across the linoleum floor, lifting at the edges.

The clerk, a heavyset man with bloodshot eyes and a stained T-shirt, barely looked up from a dog-eared magazine with folded center pages. Tyler moved to the counter, its surface sticky from years of too many hands, and slid a wad of crumpled bills forward.

"One night," he murmured, eyes fixed on the scuffed tiles on the floor.

"Room 217," the clerk rasped, tossing a key that skidded across the counter, its chewed edges rough in Tyler's palm. "Keep it quiet."

Tyler nodded and climbed the stairs, each step feeling heavier.

Room 217 was a testament to despair. The door scraped open, revealing a bed sagging under a gray blanket blotched with yellowed stains—sweat, neglect, or something worse. A bare bulb hung from a frayed cord, its dim light failing to pierce the corners, where peeling wallpaper clung to the walls, blistered and brown. A torn curtain let the neon's erratic pulse bleed through, bathing the room in a light pink haze.

After locking the door with a sharp click, Tyler placed the paper bag with the whiskey he'd brought on the dingy green carpet. He thought a drink or two before dying might ease the pain in his chest.

He moved to the nightstand, where a battered radio rested with chipped plastic and worn dials from countless hands. A twist of the knob sparked static, then a deep voice broke through —Johnny Cash, a tribute station. The opening notes of "Hurt" unfurled, each chord sinking into the room's oppressive silence.

Tyler slumped onto the bed, springs creaking, and pulled the photo from his pocket. Emily's smile shone in the beach sunlight, her hair tangled by the breeze—the image taken from her parents' fridge. His thumb traced her face, the paper softened by wear, her eyes bright with a love he wondered if he deserved.

Cash's voice rasped, raw with grief, echoing the ache in Tyler's chest. He leaned back, the pillow crackling with cheap stuffing, and stared at the water-stained plaster of the ceiling. His watch ticked. The kill switch was only minutes away. James's face flashed—pale, dirt-smeared, eyes wide as the dirt fell. Tyler's breath caught, the memory a razor. He'd shed his soul to uncover Helix's lies, to save Emily. What was left? A man? A monster?

Emily's laughter echoed in his mind—that summer day by the ocean—her hand warm, the salt air sharp. He had dreamed of a future then—simple, unbroken. Instead, he had unleashed a firestorm with the leaked data. Helix's extinction fraud was now spreading through the press. Emily would face it alone, believing Vic or James had taken him. The letter might arrive too late to spare her the worry. Guilty, he took a long pull from the whiskey bottle. The leak would shatter Helix, giving her a chance to survive. He had carved that much out of the dark.

"I'm sorry," he whispered in the room's stillness. The photo trembled in his hand, Emily's smile flickering like a dying light. Cash's song played on, its slow rhythm echoing his own. His breath grew shallow, the grip of the kill switch tightening. The neon glow dimmed, and the radiator's gurgle faded away. He sensed it—a quiet unraveling, the world slipping sideways. His hold on the photo loosened, the paper resting against his chest. Emily's fierce, unbroken eyes surged in his mind, fueling his resolve. A final moment of peace warmed him as his chin dropped to his chest.

The music softened, Cash's voice a faint whisper. Tyler's chest stilled, and the room's edges blurred into gray. Room 217 of the Mass Mirage Motel fell silent, and he was gone.

Emily's phone jolted her awake, its shrill ring cutting through the silence. She fumbled for it, the screen's glare harsh against her eyes. Anita's name flashed. Emily answered, "What's wrong?"

Moonlight slipped through sheer curtains, casting silver patterns across faded posters on the walls. The bed creaked beneath her as she leaned on one elbow, its worn quilt a patchwork of memories. A scuffed dresser from years of use held a cracked mirror reflecting the dim green glow of a digital clock: 2:17 a.m.

"You need to see this," Anita said in a panic. "It's everywhere—news channels, social media, all of it. Someone leaked data about Helix and BioSpark. They are talking about the terminal gene and some things I've never heard of. Do you know anything about an extinction event and a network named Chronos?"

Emily sat up, the bedding slipping to her waist. Her pulse quickened, a cold knot forming in her chest. "Leaked? Who?" Her breath caught. Tyler. She scrambled out of bed, her bare feet hitting the cool hardwood, and paced to the window. The neighborhood slept beyond the glass, houses dark under a starless sky, Tyler's car nowhere in sight. "What exactly are they saying?"

Anita's voice crackled with urgency. "They've got documents —proof Helix falsified their gene therapy claims, covered up an extinction event, and planned to use the terminal gene to control people. The press is freaking out. They're calling it the Chronos conspiracy. Emily, this is huge."

Her grip on the phone tightened. Was this because of the thumb drives taken from her bag? Someone had taken them on Saturday after the break-in. Had Tyler done this? She opened her laptop on the nightstand, its surface covered with old stickers. The screen lit up, and she pulled up a news site. Headlines blared, "Helix Exposed: Extinction Cover-Up, Terminal Gene Conspiracy Sparks Global Outrage." Her stomach clenched as she skimmed the articles. The data was hers—the files she'd risked everything to download—now spreading across the world.

"Emily, are you okay?" Anita asked.

"Yeah," her throat tight. "I... I need to talk to Tyler." She hung up without waiting for a reply, her fingers trembling as she pressed his number. The call rang, unanswered. With every try, the silence on the other end grew more concerning. Tyler wouldn't run—not like this. Something had gone wrong.

She sank onto the bed, the springs groaning, and stared at

her phone. The room's familiar shapes—her old bookshelf, the scratched desk, a stuffed panda propped in the corner—felt distant, like relics from someone else's life. Her mind spun. Tyler had left to confront James, but had promised he wouldn't do anything rash without talking to her first. Had something happened? But why didn't he call her? Unless… Her chest tightened—James or that creep Vic. One of them could have hurt him before he could reach her.

The thought struck her hard. She pressed her palms to her eyes, hoping the pain would fade, but grief overwhelmed her. Tyler was missing—she had fallen asleep waiting for him, and now his phone went straight to voicemail. She didn't know how he got hold of the Helix information she had hacked, unless he had taken her thumb drives. Still, she was sure the headlines were his doing, since he had been pushing for days to expose Helix's lies. He had protected her, kept her name out of it, even as he threw himself into the fight.

She stood, walking over to the dresser where a photo sat in a chipped frame. She and Tyler grinned from a rollercoaster ride last year, his face smeared with ice cream. Her fingers brushed the glass, the memory vivid—his laugh, the summer heat, the promise of forever. Tears welled up, but she blinked them away.

"Emily?" Her mother's voice drifted through the door. "Is everything okay in there?"

Emily wiped her face, composing her voice. "I'm fine, Mom. Couldn't sleep and was talking to Anita on the phone." The door remained closed as her mother's footsteps faded down the hall.

She turned back to the laptop, the news still scrolling. Commentators debated, their voices tinny through the speakers, speculating about Helix's motives and the implications of the terminal gene. Emily's mouth tightened. Tyler's absence was a question, but whoever had released this information had ignited the fire. Someone had given her a chance to fight, not run or hide. She couldn't let that opportunity slip away.

Her phone buzzed again. Anita was sending a link to another article. Emily ignored it and opened a blank document instead. She began to type. A plan was taking shape. She needed to think things through instead of reacting. The media would be there soon, and she had to be ready. She also wanted to see how Dr. Morrow would react now that Helix's secrets had leaked. The bedroom filled with childhood memories now felt like a war room. With a tight smile, she nodded at the quote on the Einstein poster hanging on the wall. "You have to learn the rules of the game. And then you have to play better than anyone else."

She paused, her gaze drifting back to the photo. Tyler's lopsided smile challenged her, urging her to keep going. "I have to make it count," she murmured. Anguish still burned, but it was settling into determination. Helix and James would answer for this. For whatever they had done to him.

As the clock ticked toward dawn, the room's quiet remained unbroken except for the faint whir of the laptop. Emily leaned forward, her fingers moving faster, each keystroke a step into the fight.

Chapter 20

Welcome to the Jungle

The television's glow illuminated Emily's face in cold light, casting sharp outlines across the modest living room on Telegraph Hill. The screen shone with the chaos of Boston Common. "Look at this mess," Anita muttered, slouching beside Emily, her voice thick with disgust as she pointed at the TV. "They're tearing each other apart out there."

Protesters flooded the park, their shouts blending into a roar that echoed across the broadcast. Some held up signs—splintered wood painted with "GOD'S WRATH" in dripping red, while others displayed posters scrawled with "NO HELIX, NO END." Above them, augmented reality billboards read, "THE END IS CODED," or "TERMINAL GENE = JUDGMENT DAY."

Camera drones buzzed low, their lenses capturing every grimace, every fist raised in defiance, streaming live to the world.

Emily sat on the edge of the worn couch, her fingers gripping the faded fabric. Tyler's absence felt like a knife in her chest—he'd been gone over twelve hours without a call, a text, or anything. Her phone stayed silent in her lap, its blank screen reflecting her dread. Had he gotten caught up in the city's violence, or worse, was this the work of Helix?

The news anchor's voice cut through, strident. "Dr. Emily Harper, lead scientist on Helix's BioSpark project, is now the face of this crisis. Leaked documents allege a terminal gene could trigger an extinction event." Her photo flashed on screen —grainy, taken at a conference, her eyes wide with surprise. Her stomach lurched. She hadn't leaked anything, but the world didn't care.

A commentator interrupted, introducing a man labeled "Ex-Helix scientist, Dimitri Kline." His face was sharp, with twitching eyes as he leaned into the microphone. "Harper's dangerous," he said. "She rushed the research at BioSpark and ignored warnings. The terminal gene isn't only a way to determine your life span—it's a guillotine for humanity."

Emily's breath caught. Kline? She racked her brain, sifting through years of Helix meetings, emails, and faces. Nothing.

"Who the hell is this guy?" Anita muttered, sprawled beside her, already pulling up the employee directory on her tablet. Her fingers tapped furiously, then stopped. "No Dimitri Kline. Not now, not ever." Emily's heart raced. A fraud was smearing her on live TV, and the media was eating it up.

Whatever happened to innocent until proven guilty?

The screen shifted to a drone's perspective: a protester in a tattered jacket shoved another, their shouts drowned out by the crowd's roar. A wild-eyed woman yelled into a megaphone, "Helix has sold us out!"

Emily sensed the substance of their fear and anger, accusing her of being the villain in a story she hadn't written. She'd been trying to prevent this kind of chaos. Her worry about Tyler churned, mixing with guilt. Had her work on BioSpark—on the kill switch—caused this? She built the program to predict neurological threats, save lives, and not end them. But Tyler's disappearance and the city's rage hinted she had failed.

Anita's hand tightened on Emily's arm, pulling her back into the moment. "We need to move, Em. Helix is where we fight this. Get them to step in front of this madness. The CEO or the board of directors should be the face of this public relations disaster, not you."

The television blared on, showing a protester hurling a bottle at a drone, glass shattering in midair. Emily's chest tightened, but Anita's presence was a calming force, a reminder she wasn't alone. She stood, her legs shaky but her voice firm. "You're right. We need to go to Helix. We have to stop this before people get hurt." The Common's insanity filled the screen, a thousand voices screaming for answers no one had. But she'd find them for Tyler, for the truth, for a world teetering on the edge.

Emily stood near the window, her fingers trembling as she parted the faded lace curtains to glimpse the narrow street in front of her parents' home. Media vans rolled in like predators, their headlights carving through the morning gloom, tires crunching when they pulled up onto the sidewalks.

Patricia sat on the couch with her knitting, the needles clicking in a constant rhythm that masked the underlying tension. Emily had always admired her mother's ability to stay calm and keep her perspective even during stressful times.

The TV flashed Emily's face again, a looped clip from a Helix press release, her expression frozen mid-sentence. "The face of the Chronos crisis," the anchor declared, her voice cutting like glass. Emily's throat constricted. She wasn't ready for this kind of scrutiny.

A sudden, sharp knock rattled the front door, sounding like a barrage in the quiet room. Another followed, louder and more insistent. "Ms. Harper! Tell us about the terminal gene!" a man's voice yelled, raw with accusation. Silhouettes shifted behind the curtains, and camera flashes pierced like lightning. A third knock—more of a pound now—shook the doorframe, and Emily's muscles tensed visibly.

"They know we're here," she whispered.

Patricia's needles stopped, her hands still as she set the knitting aside. Her face was stern, but her eyes flashed with a hint of alarm.

"You're stronger than this, Emily," she said. "Remember when you were twelve, facing that bully who stole your science fair project? You didn't flinch. You fought. Do it now."

Emily nodded, but the pounding intensified, each thud like a hammer blow. "Harper! You can't hide!" a woman shouted. Something heavy scraped against the door—maybe a tripod, or a shoulder testing its strength.

Anita, pacing near the coffee table, froze, her dark eyes wide. "They're not only reporters. That's a mob growing out there."

Emily's phone buzzed, the screen flashing with Dr. Morrow's name. She fumbled to answer. "Dr. Morrow, what's going on?" Her voice stayed even, but her free hand clung to the curtain, knuckles turning white.

Morrow's tone was calm but tense. "The board needs you at Helix this afternoon for an emergency meeting. I'm sure you know why by now. We're sending a car with security—the media's out of control, and James..." She paused, the silence heavy with dread. "James is missing. He left the office last night but never made it home."

Emily's breath caught, her mind reeling. The CEO is missing? Like Tyler. Her thoughts spiraled—the last time she saw Tyler, he was heading to confront James.

"I'm not the leak," Emily blurted out, overcoming her fear.

"I believe you," Morrow replied, her tone softening. "But we need someone here who can bring everyone up to date on BioSpark. Stay safe."

She agreed, suspicion gnawing at her despite Dr. Morrow's reassurance.

The door shuddered again, a fist pounding harder, and a muffled shout carried through: "You're killing us all, Harper!"

The door shook violently now, the wood creaking as if it might splinter. "Open up, Harper! The world deserves answers!" a voice roared, joined by others, a chorus of rage. Camera flashes lit the curtains, and Emily's heart pounded so hard she felt it in her throat. "They're going to break in," she said, terrified.

Anita stood, grabbing a heavy brass candlestick from the mantel. "Let them try," she growled, but her hands shook.

Patricia rose, her face pale but resolute, and moved to the phone. "I'm calling the police," she said, her voice composed despite the chaos outside. "No one's getting through that door. I wish your father or Tyler were here."

Emily's gaze flicked between the TV, where her face kept looping, and the door, where the pounding had turned into a relentless assault. The voices outside grew louder, a mix of reporters and protesters, their words merging into a wall of anger.

Media vans clogged the street, pulling onto the lawn to get closer to the house. Anita grabbed her tablet and began to draft a statement. "We need to deny that you're the source of the leak. Keep it simple. Send it to Lena at the Globe. She's fair."

Emily, with trembling hands, examined the message. "Dr. Emily Harper did not leak BioSpark documents. Details will be released after a meeting with the Helix board of directors. Her commitment to Helix's safety and transparency goals remains steadfast."

They sent it.

While they were typing, Patricia finally reached the police. "We've got trespassers threatening my family and destroying my home." Emily moved to the window, peering out. A reporter in a gray coat squeezed against the glass, his camera flashing. She stepped back behind the curtains, but couldn't hide. Chronos was the threat, but somehow she had become the world's target.

On her laptop, Emily pulled up the genuine BioSpark data files she and Anita stored on a secure server to prevent tampering. The data showed: 100% accuracy in the terminal gene's predictive ability and evidence predicting a global extinction-level event in one hundred twenty years. She would present this to the board, unfiltered, along with the evidence she had uncovered about James's involvement with the Chronos conspiracy. She realized some board members might be involved with James, but transparency and confronting the situation directly were her only chances to survive.

A sleek black SUV pulled onto the lawn, pushing people aside as it approached the front porch. Its tinted windows acted as a shield from the chaos.

Security guards in dark jackets cleared a path. "Dr. Harper, let's go!" one called out. Emily grabbed her laptop, with Anita beside her. The door opened, and the media rushed forward, microphones thrust ahead.

"No comment," Emily barked, her voice cutting through the commotion. A protester lunged, shouting about the terminal gene's danger, but a guard blocked him, shoving him back. Emily and Anita slid into the SUV, the door slamming shut with a heavy thud.

Once inside, Emily's paranoia intensified—could she trust Morrow? James's absence, Tyler's disappearance, and the fake Helix employee making accusations all pointed to the conspiracy's work. But she didn't know where it started or ended. She'd face the board, not as a scapegoat for the leak, but as a scientist with the evidence on her side.

Anita squeezed her hand. "You've got this, Em. Show them who you are." The SUV sped toward Helix, the city's skyline in the distance, moving away from the safety of her parents' home. Emily's fear didn't fade, but it sharpened her purpose. She'd fight for answers, for Tyler, for a future not yet lost.

The SUV moved through Boston's congested streets, its

engine a loud rumble beneath the noise outside. Emily sat stiffly in the back seat, her fingers clenched around the leather armrest, the cool, smooth material under her palms. The air carried a noticeable smell of smoke, drifting through the vents.

Beyond the tinted windows, the city pulsed with unrest—shouts swelled and broke like waves, pierced by the wail of sirens echoing in the distance. Protesters pressed close at several intersections as they tried to see beyond the tinted windows, their faces a blur of fury and desperation. Some held hand-painted signs jerking above them. "HARPER = HOPE" was scrawled in bold black, countered by "HELIX LIES" in jagged red.

As Helix's headquarters came into view, its glass-and-steel facade gleamed cold against the overcast sky, reflecting the turmoil below. Virtual reality billboards shimmered overhead, cycling their messages relentlessly. Emily's statement flashed in neon white. A heartbeat later, urgent warnings blazed in crimson: "CHRONOS WILL END US ALL." A choked sob escaped her. The crowd's cries grew louder—some chanted her name in support, others spat it out like a curse—melding into a rumble that rattled the glass beside her.

The vehicle slowed, and the security barriers scraped apart to let them in. Protesters surged forward, their voices a wall of sound: "Emily! Emily!" A palm slammed against her window, leaving a smudged imprint. She recoiled, her breath catching, as the SUV stopped at a side entrance.

Her door swung open, and security guards in dark coats and earpieces closed ranks around her and Anita, their expressions tense. "Dr. Harper, move," one ordered, his hand steady on her arm. They advanced in a tight group, arms raised against the crowd. The air crackled with the threat of violence.

A man's shout cut through, "You can't run, Harper!"

The heavy metal doors thudded shut behind her, muffling the chaos into a distant drone. The lobby extended spaciously, all polished stone and glass. Dr. Morrow stood near the elevators, her posture composed, though her eyes flicked nervously to the entrance.

"Emily," she said, her tone even, giving a slight nod. "I'm glad you made it here safely. The board's waiting. But tread carefully. They're on edge."

Emily's throat tightened as she looked down. "Dr. Morrow, did you check the file I left you on Sunday about James and Chronos?"

Morrow's brow creased, a fleeting trace of confusion crossing her face. "File? I don't remember any file, Emily. It must have slipped my mind in all this commotion."

An icy wave washed over Emily, and her stomach clenched. She'd placed it in Morrow's hands and saw her set it on her coffee table. The denial stung, a thread of suspicion unraveling quickly. "Right," Emily replied, though her mind was racing. "I'll bring it up with the board then."

Morrow's lips pressed thin, her eyes narrowing briefly, but she remained silent. Emily turned toward the elevator, thoughts racing. *If Morrow was lying, who else might be compromised?* Tyler had warned her not to trust her, but their past relationship conditioned her to trust anyway. The burden of her purpose felt heavier. She was confronting a conspiracy orchestrated by James. And Dr. Morrow, too?

The elevator doors opened, and she stepped inside, her reflection shining in the mirrored walls—pale, unyielding, a scientist turned warrior. The numbers climbed as each *ding* pulsed with anticipation. She would reveal the truth, whatever the cost. For the world. For Tyler. The doors opened onto a quiet hallway, with the boardroom casting a shadow at its end.

Emily lingered in the hallway outside the boardroom, the quiet pressing against her like a held breath. The space was bare —smooth walls, cold marble underfoot, and the air carried a faint scent of disinfectant. The boardroom door was slightly open, a sliver of light spilling out, but she paused, drawn to a glass panel beside it.

Her reflection looked back at her, framed in the dim glow—eyes dulled with exhaustion, mouth set in a line of determination. Grief had carved lines into her face, yet she also saw strength there.

She rested her fingers against the glass, its chill seeping into her skin. "I know you're with me, Tyler," she murmured. "Wherever you are, I'll fix this."

Her phone buzzed in her pocket. Hoping it was Tyler, she quickly pulled it out, the screen lighting up with Anita's message. "You've got this." Anita's unwavering faith steadied her. Emily's lips twitched into a brief smile, and she gripped the phone more tightly. This fight wasn't hers alone—it was for everyone Chronos threatened to erase.

She took a slow breath. The board waited beyond that door, a battleground of betrayal and truth. Distrust gnawed at her—Morrow's feigned confusion, James's disappearance, Tyler's silence—but she pushed it aside. She would confront the board as a scientist armed with facts, a woman shaped by inevitability. Her reflection changed as she straightened, shoulders squared, steel in her eyes.

Her heels hit the floor with a sharp rhythm as she approached the door. The light grew brighter, angry voices erupting inside. She didn't hesitate or look back at the glass. With a steady hand, she pushed the door open and stepped inside, ready to face her challengers.

Chapter 21

Board of Betrayal

The Helix boardroom radiated polished luxury, with its large mahogany table dominating the space, its surface so polished it reflected the soft glow of the recessed lights above. Floor-to-ceiling windows framed Boston Harbor, the sky finally clearing from last week's persistent rain. The air inside was cool, with faint traces of leather from the high-backed chairs and the subtle scent of expensive cologne, unchanged since Thursday's meeting. Outside, the distant wail of sirens was barely audible through the thick glass.

Chairperson Herbert Beyer, a stern figure with wispy white hair and a commanding presence, leaned forward in his seat, his fingers steepled. His tailored suit was immaculate, but his expression was tight, with lines of worry etched around his eyes. "Has anyone heard from James? His absence is concerning."

Ms. Patel, her sharp features etched with concern, shifted in her seat, fingers tapping on her tablet. Although she was younger than most on the board and had her dark hair in a sleek bun, her usual composure was slipping.

"I tried calling him this morning. No answer. It's unlike him to miss a meeting, especially one this critical."

Emily stood, her blazer feeling too tight, the fabric constricting as she took a deep breath to calm herself. Her eyes scanned the board members—Mr. Carver's jowls tight with suspicion, Mr. Langston's swollen face colder than usual, Ms. Patel fidgeting with her tablet.

Emily's fingers twitched at her sides, a nervous habit she couldn't overcome. The weight of the leaked BioSpark files and Tyler's unexplained absence bore down on her like a vise, making it hard to breathe. Her heart pounded, each beat echoing in her ears, a relentless drum of anxiety. She wasn't simply presenting her findings; she was under attack, and the stakes had never been higher.

Beyer abruptly stood up, his chair scraping loudly against the polished floor, causing Emily to flinch. "Dr. Harper, the leaked BioSpark files have thrown Helix into chaos. The media is relentless—our stock's plummeting. Many of the board members think you're responsible for it."

Mr. Carver leaned forward, jowls quivering with anger, eyes narrowed. "You've always been hesitant about commercialization. Maybe you thought leaking it would stop us from going to market. Sabotage the project to prove your point."

Mr. Langston gripped the table's edge, his gaze cutting through Emily. "This is a serious allegation, Dr. Harper. The evidence points to you. Your access to the files and your vocal opposition to the timeline to commercialize the terminal gene—it's all too convenient."

Ms. Patel looked around the room, seeking support or a way out of the mounting confrontation. "We need to address this." Her voice faltered slightly. "But accusing Emily without proof…"

"Proof?" Mr. Carver interrupted, face reddening. "The

timing is proof enough. IT checked the retrieval logs. She was the last one to access the data before the leak."

Emily's pulse raced, heat flooding her face, but she composed herself, drawing on every ounce of resolve. "That's absurd." Her voice rang firm despite the tremor in her hands. She recalled Thursday's board meeting, her passionate pleas for caution, restraint, and more time, while Kessler and Carver had pushed relentlessly for profit at any cost. "I warned against rushing the project. I begged for more time to study the implications. This leak sabotages everything I've worked for. Why would I do that? It makes no sense."

Emily fought to keep her expression neutral. Tyler's face flashed in her mind—his evasive glances, the way he dodged her questions about his plan to confront James yesterday evening—before he vanished. The memory sent a sharp pang through her chest, but she couldn't let it show—not here, not now.

Carver scoffed, his face reddening even more, a vein pulsing at his temple. "Your warnings last week don't absolve you, Dr. Harper. Perhaps you wanted to force our hand, to delay the project indefinitely. Or perhaps you're hiding something— working with a competitor to undermine Helix."

Her silver hair catching the light from the windows, Dr. Morrow nodded faintly in Emily's direction. "Emily has always prioritized ethics over profit." Her voice flowed calmly, a contrast to the rising tension. "I've known her since she was an undergraduate, and she's not the type to act rashly."

But her eyes slid away, elusive, avoiding Emily's gaze. The support felt hollow, and Emily couldn't shake the sense that Morrow knew more than she was letting on—perhaps something tied to Chronos.

Emily held her ground, posture stiff, but the lack of solid proof made her feel exposed, like a specimen under a magnifying glass. "I didn't leak anything." Her voice rose slightly.

"But I will find out who did. This isn't about me—it's about the future of Helix, BioSpark, and the world. We can't let this destroy everything we've built."

Mr. Beyer's expression remained stern, his eyes piercing her with unwavering focus. "We expect full cooperation, Dr. Harper. This matter is far from over. We will conduct a thorough investigation, and if you are found responsible, you will face more than dismissal—your career will be over, and we will press charges. I will make sure you are prosecuted."

Emily nodded, determination strengthening inside her. She knew she was innocent and fighting influential people, but retreat wasn't an option—not now, not when so much was at stake. "I understand." She met his gaze steadily. "And I'll cooperate. But I hope you'll keep an open mind and consider all possibilities, not only the convenient ones."

As the board members exchanged glances—some skeptical, others uncertain—Emily's hands settled at her sides. The room's tension closed in around her, but she held firm. Maybe she could turn this around, expose the truth, and protect what mattered most.

Emily balanced herself, her fingertips lingering on the smooth edge of the projector's control panel. With a tap, the device activated, and holograms appeared above the mahogany table. Red-spiked graphs cut through the air, their jagged peaks glowing like fresh wounds against the dim light of the conference room. The data painted a bleak picture: a global collapse in one hundred twenty years, ecosystems falling apart, populations disappearing, all leading to a synchronized extinction event.

"The terminal gene doesn't only predict individual lifespans." Emily's voice steadied, firm despite the tremor rising inside. "It predicts an extinction event for all life on Earth. One hundred percent accuracy."

After some tense glances, the board erupted. Ms. Patel's pen twisted nervously between her fingers as she muttered, "Alarmist nonsense."

Mr. Langston slammed the table, his bulky frame taut with indignation, face flushed beneath the recessed lights. "The discovery of the terminal gene was shocking enough. Now you're telling us the world ends in just over a century? This strains credulity, Dr. Harper. It makes me doubt your earlier claims; you should have mentioned this during last week's presentation."

Carver grunted, arms crossed tightly over his broad chest, jowls quivering slightly. The greed that had sparkled in his eyes on Thursday—when Kessler had spun visions of a trillion-dollar empire—had turned sour into skepticism. "We've sunk billions into BioSpark for profit, not prophecies. This feels like a dodge."

Emily ground her teeth as she forced herself to take a slow breath. The board's angry, dismissive murmurs scraped against her nerves like sandpaper, each scoff and eye roll fueling the bile rising in her throat. She balanced herself on the edge of the projector as she stared down their skepticism.

"This isn't an evasion. The simulations are based on validated genetic markers—millions of samples, cross-checked and confirmed. The gene is universal, and in one hundred twenty years, it triggers in every species with a lifespan that extends into that time frame. We can't ignore this and hope it's a mistake."

Ms. Patel's pen tapped rapidly, a staccato beat against her tablet. "But over a hundred twenty years?" Her brow furrowed in disagreement. "That's far beyond our reach. Why should we act now?"

"Because it's real," Emily fired back, voice rising, fueled by conviction. "And if we don't start now—studying why the timing is important, countering it—we're condemning the future. This is bigger than Helix."

The holograms cast long shadows across the table, their red

glow filling the room with a foreboding light. Mr. Langston's lips were pressed in a thin line, showing his unwavering skepticism. Beyer's posture stayed stiff, his silence serving as a warning. Emily felt their doubt weighing on her, but she stood tall. The truth was her weapon, and she refused to let their shortsightedness dull its edge.

Emily's pulse thundered in her ears as she adjusted the projector's display. The extinction event graphs vanished and were replaced by a flood of files—emails, audio clips, financial records—a thread connecting James Kessler to the Chronos Conspiracy. She took a deep breath, steadying herself against the storm she knew was coming.

"This is why I believe the leak happened," she said. "Helix is compromised. James has been working with an international group of conspirators called Chronos to exploit the BioSpark data about the terminal gene and extinction event for their own agenda."

Mr. Langston sprang to his feet, his chair screeching against the floor. "Deflection!" His shout masked his rage, veins bulging at his temples. "You're pinning this on James to dodge your guilt!"

Mr. Carver knocked over a water glass that spilled across the polished wood. "Outrageous!" His roar was guttural, like a snarl. "You're framing James to save yourself. I'll see you ruined for this!"

Mr. Holt, pale and thin, drummed his fingers rapidly on his notepad, eyes flicking between the files and Emily. "These records…are they authenticated?"

"If this is true…" Patel shouted, nearly drowning out the surrounding noise. "If James is tied to something illegal…"

Emily held her ground, eyes intense. "They're real. I've traced every email and every payment. James has been diverting funds, modifying research, and secretly meeting with Chronos members to outflank this board. He's transforming the terminal gene into a weapon for control and a path to unimaginable wealth for a few."

"But, why?" Langston asked, shaking his head.

"You asked me why I didn't mention the extinction event in last week's presentation," Emily said. "The reason was that Mr. Kessler altered the data to hide it, and I only discovered it in the last few days."

Emily pointed at the information being shown. "From what I've seen in the emails, it looks like James and Chronos want to use the extinction event as leverage to control others but aren't prepared to act yet."

Dr. Morrow stood, expression composed. "I've mentored Emily for a long time." Her voice grew steady and loud, a bulwark amid the storm. "She's no liar. If she says these files are real, and James has altered the data, we need to investigate. We can't dismiss this accusation."

She had been an advocate on Thursday, but now her support felt more calculated.

Mr. Carver spun around to face Morrow, his face twisted with rage. "You're backing Harper? After the leak? She's the one we should question, not James. He's not even here to defend himself!"

Morrow didn't flinch, her gaze fixed on him. "I'm on the side of the truth. And we don't know what that is yet. We owe Helix a thorough look."

A tense silence settled as they exchanged cautious glances. Holt's tapping stopped, his hands hanging uncertainly. Mr. Langston sank back into his chair, anger simmering but no longer bubbling over.

Emily said, "I'm not here to point fingers without reason. I'm here to save Helix. If Chronos wins, they'll dismantle everything we've built—and the BioSpark data will be their scalpel."

The images hovered over the table, creating a revealing pattern of conspiracy. For a moment, Emily thought she saw a fleeting hesitation in Mr. Carver's eyes, but it disappeared, and his scowl returned. Beyer cleared his throat, his tone resentful. "We'll review the evidence, but this doesn't clear you, Dr. Harper. The leak investigation stands."

Emily nodded, jawline tight. She'd expected resistance. The seed was planted—doubt in James, fear of the conspiracy behind Chronos. It would have to be enough for now.

Emily's phone vibrated in her pocket, a sharp buzz piercing through the uneasy silence of the boardroom. She pulled it out, hoping it was Tyler. But her heart pounded as Anita's name flashed on the screen. The message was terse. "Found Q's background—Chronos puppeteer. It's who I thought!"

It stopped there, the exclamation like a shout of triumph. Her hands trembled as she gripped the phone beneath the table. The board members' murmurs faded into a dull roar, their faces blurring as her focus narrowed to Anita's unfinished message.

Beyond the thick windows, a siren wailed softly, signaling the chaos approaching Helix. If Anita uncovered Q's identity, Chronos would be fully exposed. She slipped the phone into her pocket, forcing her facial muscles to relax as she hid the fear inside her. The board was still watching, eyes sharp, waiting for a crack in her armor. She couldn't give them one.

Beyer's voice rumbled, bringing the meeting back into focus, but Emily barely heard it. Her mind raced. She needed to get to Anita. And if Q were the key, she'd use the knowledge to dismantle Chronos piece by piece.

Emily raised her chin, cutting off Beyer. "We must go public with everything—the terminal gene, Chronos, the extinction event. The secrecy's killing us. The world deserves to know what's at stake."

The chair's gaze hardened, eyes glinting like flint beneath the glow of the light. He leaned forward, hands flat on the table. "Confidentiality is nonnegotiable, Dr. Harper. Helix's survival and your own depend on silence. Push this, and you'll regret it."

Carver's chair creaked as he shifted, thick fingers drumming the tabletop. "You're overstepping." His tone roughened with disdain. "This isn't a lab experiment you can control. You're a scientist, not the one setting Helix's strategy." His jowls quivered, indignation radiating from him like heat.

Catherine Morrow sat quietly, silver hair reflecting the light as she looked at her clasped hands. The slight tremor in her fingers revealed her discomfort, but she refused to meet Emily's eyes.

Emily nodded once, her face a mask of calm compliance, but her fingers dug into her palms, a silent vow taking hold. She'd tear down their wall of silence, no matter the cost. The truth wasn't theirs to hide. *Damn them all.*

The chair's lips held in a thin line. "We'll address the leak and Chronos internally. That's final. The board will decide when and how we go public, not you," he said with a dismissive wave.

Emily's fingers uncurled, but she remained firm. The board's rejection was a wall, invulnerable for now—but not forever. Tyler had opened the floodgates, but she would find the cracks.

Beyer's palm struck the table with a sharp crack that echoed through the room. "We'll proceed to executive session. Dr. Harper, you're dismissed."

Emily stood quickly with purpose, despite the heat building in her throat. The board watched her leave—Carver with a scowl, Morrow with averted eyes, Beyer with a blank stare. Muffling their whispers, the heavy door shut as she entered the hall.

The corridor stretched out before her, marble floor cold and gleaming. At the far end, Anita waited, her back taut as a bowstring. Her dark eyes locked onto Emily's, wide with fear and urgency, and she jerked her head toward the bathroom—a silent, frantic command.

Emily's breath caught, her mind racing. Anita's unfinished

message—Q's background—flashed through her mind, tangled with the outline of Chronos and the board's stonewalling. She moved swiftly, heels clicking sharply, her heart pounding with urgency. The stakes now felt razor-sharp, cutting through any remaining hesitation to act. What had Anita discovered?

Anita pushed the bathroom door open, her shaky hand brushing the frame. Emily followed, and the door clicked shut behind them, echoing off the tiles like a vault sealing.

The bathroom's glare jolted Emily's senses after the luxury of the boardroom. Bright fluorescent lights buzzed overhead, cold light reflecting off spotless white tiles. A faint scent of pine disinfectant lingered in the air.

Anita stood by the sink, face pale, eyes darting to the door. "I think I know Q's identity." Her whisper barely rose above the buzz of the lights. "It's—"

A chill ran down Emily's spine. Anita's fear, the board's secrecy, and Tyler's disappearance all hit her, hardening something deep inside. She was no longer just a scientist. Now, she fought for Tyler, Anita, and a world teetering on the brink.

Shadows twisted as the harsh lights pulsed. As Emily's breathing settled, determination ignited within her. Whatever Anita knew, whatever Q was, she'd confront it and the board directly.

Chapter 22

Time Keeps on Ticking

Anita's hands trembled as she twisted the lock on the bathroom door, her breathing shallow. She leaned close, her voice barely above a whisper. "It's Beyer. James's uncle—the board chair. He got him the CEO spot." Her eyes darted nervously to the door, then back to Emily. "He's ruthless. Cut me off in the garage last week, almost hit me."

The bathroom's fluorescent lights cast a sterile sheen, reflecting Emily's image in the warped mirror above the sink. Her pulse quickened. "Are you certain?" she asked, skepticism evident in her tone. "He's an ass, but we can't accuse him without proof."

Anita shook her head, her ponytail swaying. "I didn't see Beyer's name, but Q's email to James was clear—they're on the board and said they can 'maneuver the sheep' however they want. That sounds like Beyer to me."

Her mind raced, replaying the board meeting: Dr. Morrow's distant gaze, her careful silences. "Morrow's been acting strange, too," Emily muttered, fingers brushing her temple. "Too quiet, too guarded."

Emily's stomach clenched. In this bleak space, the truth felt close—and dangerous. Morrow, her mentor, had guided her for years, a steadfast hand in a cutthroat world. The thought of her as Q—scheming, betraying, plotting her and Tyler's deaths—made her feel sick. Still, the pieces fit together: Morrow's evasions and Beyer's influence. Suspicion clashed with loyalty, each doubt chipping away at her trust. This moment—realizing she was close to whoever was behind the conspiracy—changed everything.

Emily pushed open the bathroom door. The fluorescent buzz faded behind her as they stepped into the hallway. They hurried to the elevators, eager to reach the BioSpark lab's secure terminals, hoping to uncover more evidence of Q's identity while the board was distracted. Emily's hand paused over the elevator call button, her reflection in the polished steel doors showing a woman on a mission.

The elevator doors closed with a dull thud, trapping Emily and Anita inside. Emily's eyes caught the blinking red light of the camera in the corner, a silent sentinel. Her face, pale and drawn, looked back with eyes dimmed by the malicious accusations from the board meeting. Her skin prickled as she wrestled with the same creeping sense of exposure she'd felt after last week's board meeting. *Were they being watched? Was Q monitoring their every move?*

Emily stood stiffly, her fingers clutching the hem of her jacket. The overhead lights pulsed, casting fleeting lines across her tense face. She pushed her back against the wall, the cold metal seeping through her blazer. The board's accusations and Anita's revelation—all of it felt like it was suffocating her.

Her gaze shifted to the floor numbers counting down, each digit bringing her closer to an unavoidable confrontation. The elevator pulled her into a deeper unknown, where trust was a luxury she couldn't afford anymore. The soft ding of the doors opening amplified her paranoia.

BioSpark's white walls glowed under overhead lights, with screens casting a bluish hue across workstations. Emily and Anita huddled at a terminal, the air filled with the soft whir of cooling fans.

Anita's fingers darted across the keyboard, pulling up fragmented files—Q's digital footprints, elusive and frustrating. "Here, you can see the email to James is from a board member. No name, but the pattern's clear."

The screen shifted, revealing a new email thread. Anita froze, her breath catching. "James tampered with your kill switch," she moaned. "After Thursday's board meeting. He shortened it—December 25th, not forty-five years. He changed your date to eliminate you as a threat."

Emily's heart raced. The numbers on the screen blurred as her vision narrowed to the stark data points. "He wanted me dead? To die on Christmas Day?" she whispered, disbelief breaking into cold clarity about James's depravity. Her fingers clenched the edge of the desk, the smooth surface grounding her as shock shifted into dread.

Anger surged at James's betrayal. He'd sat across from her in meetings, his calm smile hiding his treachery, knowing she would die on Christmas, which would devastate Tyler, Anita, and her parents. But amid the horror of the revelations, a flicker of hope shone—if the switch could be moved forward, it could be reversed.

The lab suddenly came alive, buzzing with potential. Emily looked at Anita, whose wide eyes reflected her own. While the news of her impending death was shocking, it also indicated that James had found a way to make the terminal gene adaptable. It was a new puzzle to solve. Once a place of answers, the lab now raised more questions, each more alarming than the last.

Emily typed at her workstation, alone now, as the lab's cold light cast sharp angles across her face. Anita had slipped away to get something to eat, leaving only the soft click of the door behind her. The screens glowed, their data a relentless reminder of the ticking clock inside her.

"If it can be changed…" Emily murmured, the implication a spark in her anguish.

James's betrayal, Q's shadow, Morrow's possible duplicity—these weren't mere threats; they were challenges. Her image on the monitor showed a woman transformed, eyes burning with purpose. Acceptance settled over her, not of death, but of the struggle ahead.

Tyler's face appeared in her mind—his goofy jokes and unwavering trust in her. She would unmask Q, dismantle Chronos, and rewrite their destinies. The lab was now her testing ground. Her features hardened with determination.

Emily headed to the archive room with direct access to BioSpark's data. Knowing her terminal gene had been altered, she now had a lead to follow. She swiped her keycard at the heavy glass door, and the soft beep granted her entry to a space that held the answers she needed.

The archive room's dim glow cast elongated shapes across towering servers, their faint sounds filling the air. Emily sat at a terminal, fingers poised over the keyboard, ready to explore more of Q's secrets and the mystery of her altered terminal gene. The sterile space felt alive, pulsing with urgency. Time was no longer slipping away; it was a quickly approaching threat.

Her gaze flicked to the glass door as Beyer's profile appeared, his measured steps echoing in the lab. Her pulse quickened, but fear gave way to purpose. She was no longer a cog in Helix's machine, mindlessly following orders. She was a force, unshackled and with nothing to lose. Whoever was behind Chronos they'd underestimated her. Emily's eyes narrowed. Her deadline bore down on her, but she was begin-ning to fight.

Chapter 23

Goodbye, My Love

Emily measured sugar into a saucepan, her movements stiff and her gaze unfocused. She half-listened to her mother rambling on.

The kitchen glowed with morning light, sunlight spilling through the windows and casting a soft warmth on the countertops. She stood beside her mother, Patricia, their hands dusted with flour as they prepared Boston cream pies for a charity bake sale.

The rhythmic clatter of a mixing spoon against a bowl filled the room, a sound that should have calmed her. Instead, it clashed with the restless churn of her thoughts. She stirred the custard too fast, a small splash hitting the counter.

The board meeting replayed in Emily's mind—angry voices, narrowed eyes, false accusations. Afterward, Beyer had cornered her in the archive room. "Go home, Dr. Harper. We'll take care of it." He had plucked her badge from the desk, a quiet severance from Helix. Following the executive session, her access to the building and IT systems had vanished, erased as the investigation into the leak tightened its grip.

Patricia glanced over, her brow furrowing. "You're quieter than usual this morning, Emily. Is something bothering you about what happened at work yesterday? I didn't see you when you came in last night."

Emily set the spoon down. "It's everything, Mom. The board meeting went badly. They told me to leave afterward and took my badge. They've locked me out—the building, systems, everything. There's an investigation into the leak, and they're looking at me despite the evidence I showed them of the conspiracy."

Patricia's eyes widened as her hands paused over the dough. "But you did nothing wrong, did you? They can't point fingers without proof."

"I didn't leak any information," Emily said, her voice strained. "But I was the last one with the files. And with Tyler gone..." She paused, the ache of his absence pressing on her chest. Outside, police radios crackled faintly through the window, officers stationed to keep back the media and restless crowds. Yesterday's chaos had left the city on edge, and her trip to Helix only fueled the fire. Reporters swarmed, feeding on the unrest.

Her thoughts drifted to the kill switch, the timer primed inside her, counting down to Christmas. She imagined telling Patricia—watching her mother's face crumple under the truth—but the words wouldn't form. Instead, she let the silence stretch between them.

Patricia dusted off her hands on her apron and stepped closer. "You've always kept a cool head, Emily. They'll realize you've done nothing wrong. Give it some time."

Emily nodded, though her reassurance felt thin. Patricia didn't know the half of it—the ticking clock, the reason for Tyler's disappearance, the suspicion swirling around her like smoke. She returned to the baking, the kitchen's warmth a thin buffer against the storm rising around her.

The rattle of the mail slot interrupted the kitchen's rhythm as letters slapped against the wooden foyer floor. "Could you go grab the mail, Em? Your dad is expecting a notice from his publisher, and I'm elbow-deep in this filling."

Emily wiped her hands on a towel, the flour leaving faint streaks, and then walked to the front door. A small stack was on the floor—bills, a glossy sales ad, and a plain white envelope with her name scrawled across it in a slant she knew all too well. Her pulse quickened.

She lifted the envelope. The paper was smudged and slightly creased under her fingers. Tyler's handwriting stared back at her, unmistakable even in its haste. He'd been gone since Monday night, storming off to confront James about Chronos, and now this. She turned it over—her apartment as the return address, her name in his precise cursive. Her throat tightened as she tore it open, revealing a thumb drive tucked inside a folded scrap of paper.

One word stared up at her. "Listen."

Emily stood frozen, the envelope trembling in her hand. Was this from Tyler? A message sent before or after he disappeared? Or something darker — a trap she didn't see yet? She held the drive between her fingers, confused. Tyler had always left notes —scribbled encouragements tucked into her coat pockets—but this letter was different, and it scared her.

She returned to the kitchen, leaving the sponge cake batter on the counter. Patricia whisked the cream, her movements continuous, unaware of the change rippling through her daughter. "Mom, I need to check something," Emily said.

Patricia looked up, worry crossing her face. "Everything okay?"

"It's only work stress," Emily said, forcing a thin smile. She couldn't burden her mother with her anxiety about Tyler's disappearance, not yet. The drive seemed like a stone in her pocket, a silent promise—or a threat—pulling her from the comfort of flour and sugar onto a path she couldn't escape. Her hands trembled with a mix of curiosity and fear. Every thought was tinged with anticipation and dread, knowing that what she might hear could change everything.

Emily grabbed her laptop from the counter, the cord catching briefly on a jar of stirring spoons. She took it into her father's study and shut the door.

She plugged in the thumb drive, her fingers hovering over the keys before clicking on the only file. It was encrypted and needed a password. She paused momentarily and entered the date she and Tyler got engaged—a day they often talked about. A video flickered on the screen, and Tyler's face appeared—pale, shadowed, but his eyes burned with intensity. Her breath caught, and the study faded around her as she sank into the leather chair.

"Emily, if you're watching this, I'm gone," he began, his voice low and fading in and out. "I'm so sorry. I don't have much time, so listen closely."

He leaned in closer; the camera captured the strain on his face. "My kill switch is active. I know the date and time—it doesn't matter how I found out. I have less than two hours to live. I confronted James and demanded answers. At first, he wouldn't talk."

He leaned back in the chair and took a deep breath before speaking again. "When he finally broke down, he swore you still had years left on your kill switch, and he intended to hurt you after I was gone. I couldn't allow that to happen, Emily."

Her stomach dropped, and the room felt more suffocating with every word. Tyler had no idea James had lied to him. She wouldn't have known either if she and Anita hadn't found out yesterday what might have been true initially. Instead, James had reset her switch to Christmas Day.

Tyler's eyes glistened, red and exhausted. He absentmindedly twisted the frayed leather bracelet he always wore. "So, I dealt with James. He's out of the picture now, no threat to you or anyone. But he said Q was the kingpin behind Chronos, and he was only taking orders to survive. I had to do more. I leaked the data—the terminal gene, the extinction event, Chronos—all of it. I'm sorry for the mess it's caused you, but I couldn't let them pin it on you. The truth's out there now. Even with James out of the way, they may try to hurt you, but the world is watching now."

Emily's hands pressed against her mouth, muffling a gasp. He'd torn the world apart to shield her. Tyler's gaze softened, piercing through the screen. "I love you, Emily, more than anything. I didn't want you to watch me die, to have that as your last memory. I wanted you to know I'm fighting for you, for us. Keep going, please. Expose them. Make it matter. They're behind it all, and I know that if anyone can stop them, it's you."

The video ended, his face frozen in a final, pleading look. Tears blurred her vision, spilling down her cheeks. He'd given everything—his last moments—to protect and help her, and she'd been blind to it. She replayed the part about James. Had Tyler killed him? The possibility tore at her, but the leak—Tyler's confession—cut deeper. He shouldered the blame, leaving her standing while he fell.

Her chest ached, a hollow space where love and guilt collided. She gazed at the blank screen, the sounds of her mom baking in the kitchen echoing in the distance.

Emily's knees buckled, and the laptop slid from the desk to the floor with a loud thud. She gripped the thumb drive, her knuckles whitening as sobs tore through her—raw and jagged. The study blurred—mementos on the shelves, the faint scent of dusty books—swallowed by the sound of Tyler's anguished voice still ringing in her ears.

Patricia rushed in, her apron fluttering. "Emily, honey, what's going on?" Patricia knelt beside her, wrapping her arms around her trembling shoulders. "Talk to me."

Emily shook her head. Her mother's hands gently smoothed

her hair, a constant pressure against her breaking heart. "It's Tyler," she finally choked out, her voice breaking. "He's gone. He left a message... He did it for me."

Patricia's grip tightened, her eyes filling with tears. "Oh, Emily, I'm so sorry. What do you mean he's gone?"

"He met with James about all this craziness. It turned ugly, but he recorded a video before he died." It wasn't a lie, but not the whole truth either.

"He said he leaked the information about Helix," Emily whispered, wiping her face with a trembling hand. "To protect me. I can't. It's too much, Mom." She couldn't speak of the kill switch, her countdown to Christmas. The truth remained locked inside, a jagged shard she wouldn't let cut her mother.

Patricia gently rocked her, her voice soft. "You loved him so much. I don't understand it all, but I'm here, sweetheart. You don't have to carry all of this alone."

Once full of happy memories, the study turned bitter—a space now empty because of loss. Emily leaned into her mother, her sobs gradually becoming ragged breaths. Tyler's sacrifice echoed within her, a wound too deep to understand, but Patricia's warmth pulled her back from the edge. She had to hold on —for him, for them.

Emily sat at the kitchen table, the thumb drive in front of her, its matte surface absorbing the light. Tyler's message replayed in her mind—his confession, love, and plea. She hadn't seen his pain, hadn't saved him. His kill switch had run out, but hers still had time remaining, and with it, a chance he had died to give her.

She traced the drive with her fingertip, her lips tightening. Tyler thought James was gone, but what if he'd misjudged? And Chronos and Q still pulled strings, twisting lives with their genetic timers. She wouldn't let that stand. Her hands clenched into fists, eyes closed tight. She'd carry his fight forward, turning his sacrifice into something more.

The risks still threatened her—Helix's board, the investigation, the city's simmering unrest. Chronos wouldn't hesitate to crush her, but she wasn't defenseless. Anita would help, and maybe others, too. Her time was running out, Christmas approaching fast, but that only sharpened her focus. If her remaining time were short, she'd spend it tearing down the machine that took Tyler.

Emily lifted the drive, clutching it tightly. This was her vow—to him, to herself. She'd expose them, no matter what it took. The kitchen was silent, with flour and sugar fading into the background as the fire burned hotter in her chest. She wouldn't wait any longer. She'd strike back today.

Emily stood and moved to the window overlooking the backyard, the thumb drive a keepsake and a burden in her pocket. Outside, the police watched vigilantly, their silhouettes long against the rising sun. The media stayed nearby, eager for scraps, but her fight wasn't theirs. She turned, glancing at Patricia stirring the cream, unaware of the fury hardening in her daughter's eyes.

She needed Anita—someone to help from the inside. Together, they would dig into Chronos and Q and uncover their secrets. The task cast a long shadow, like a mountain looming over her shrinking time. The sun rose higher, its bright rays streaking the kitchen floor. It was a new day, and she was ready to face it fearlessly.

Emily slipped a hand into her pocket, feeling the drive. Tyler's love wrapped tight around her, a quiet strength she'd carry into the fight. She wouldn't falter—not for him or the world he'd tried to save. She was ready.

Chapter 24

Lighting the Fuse

Emily sat motionless, her laptop open but unused, its screen dim.

Her phone buzzed, and Anita's name flashed on the screen like a warning. She hesitated before answering, her voice still husky from a restless night.

"Anita, are you okay? What's going on in the office?"

Morning light filtered through the lace curtains, casting intricate, dappled patterns across the worn oak table in her parents' kitchen. The air carried the warm, sugary scent of Boston cream pies on the cluttered counter, beside chipped coffee mugs and a half-eaten bagel. Her mother stood at the sink, scrubbing a pot with a steel-wool pad, the regular scrape of metal against metal creating a soft rhythm in the quiet.

Anita whispered, "Emily, they're tearing through the servers at Helix. IT's on a corporate witch hunt, searching every file, every log. They're hunting for proof of the leak and any alterations to the terminal gene data. A tech said he was told you had something to do with it, and they're checking everything you've touched in the last month. I'm worried they're close to finding the original files we hid on Monday."

"Take a deep breath, Anita. It's going to be okay," Emily said.

"If you say so, but I'm freaking out here," she said with a tremble in her voice.

Emily's stomach twisted, but her face remained calm. Her fingers slowly traced the worn grain of the table. The kitchen's normalcy—faded rugs, a refrigerator humming softly, the faint clink of Patricia stacking dishes—felt like armor against Anita's panic. "They're chasing their tails," Emily said, her dry humor cutting through. "Let them dig through that crazy file system. We covered our tracks well enough."

Anita exhaled, the sound crackling through the line. "The team's with you, Emily. I had a chat with Javier and Wei this morning. They trust you—your integrity and judgment. They know you're the one who can pull this off. But if they find those files, we're cooked."

Emily's lips turned into a half-smile, but her voice stayed steady. "They won't find them. They'll have to publish the files Chronos changed to reach them, and they never will. Slow down any executive directives—lose paperwork, misfile emails, anything to buy us time. And tell the team..." She paused, glancing at Patricia, who was now drying a plate, humming softly, unaware of the brewing storm. "Tell them I'm grateful for their trust. More than they realize."

Anita said, "You've got a plan, don't you? I can feel it."

The corner of Emily's smile twitched, a flash of defiance. "I'm about to light a fuse. Something big enough to make Helix's board look the other way while we gain some momentum." She leaned back in her chair, the wood creaking softly, her eyes drifting to the window where a crow perched on the sill. "Keep your head down and cut back on the coffee. We'll get through this."

"For Tyler?" Anita asked.

"For Tyler," Emily confirmed, her throat tightening at the memory of his sacrifice—his kill switch triggering, too soon, too final. She felt the crushing impact of his death and the truth that he had died defending. "Stay away from IT. I'll call you soon."

She ended the call, her fingers pausing on the phone's dark screen. Patricia turned, wiping her hands on a faded dishtowel, her brow furrowing. "Anything new from Anita, sweetheart? You look pale."

Emily forced a smile, her heart pounding, her face composed behind a practiced calm. "She was giving me an update, Mom. Nothing to worry about."

She stood, the chair scraping the linoleum, and grabbed her bag from the counter, heavy with the Helix files she'd printed. The kitchen's warmth, with its lingering pie scent and morning light, felt like a thread to a world she was about to upend. Helix's secrets—the kill switch, Chronos, and all the ugly truths they'd buried—were hers to reveal. She wasn't fully ready, but the choice had slipped away yesterday. For Tyler, for the truth, she'd take on the corporate Goliath, no matter the cost.

Emily's phone buzzed again, the vibration startling against the oak table. An unknown number flashed persistently, and she hesitated, her thumb hovering over the screen. So far, none of the media had uncovered her unlisted number. She answered reluctantly, her nerves already tense from the morning.

"Hello, who's calling?"

"Dr. Emily Harper? Lauren Chen, CNN producer." The woman's tone was sharp and urgent, cutting through the kitchen's quiet like a razor. "We're breaking a story on Helix's data leak—the extinction event cover-up. I understand you're the BioSpark team lead, the person with the evidence. You talked to a few people here this morning and said you're ready to go on record. Is that true?"

Her pulse quickened, a rush of adrenaline flooding her veins, but she kept her tone even, her fingers tightening around the phone. "That's me. And yes, I'm ready. What's the setup?"

We need you for a live segment. Helix is doubling down, denying everything—Chronos, extinction risks, the works. We want your reaction, your evidence, the entire story. Can you get to our Brookline bureau in forty-five minutes? 637 Washington Street.

Emily glanced at the kitchen clock, its hands moving past 8:15 a.m. Her parents' house was only a few miles from the bureau, and the timing still worked even at rush hour. But the leap from this cozy, sugar-scented haven to a national news spotlight felt like crossing the universe. Her mouth went dry, but she nodded and then remembered to speak.

"I can make it. How am I going to be interviewed?"

"Live, no pre-tape. Someone will anchor from Atlanta. We'll send a black SUV to pick you up. The driver's name is Chris. He's already en route. You'll be on air within the hour, so be ready to lay it all out—Helix's lies, your data, everything."

Emily's heart pounded, but her courage was a steel wire running through her. "I'm ready. Let's do this."

"Perfect. Chris will signal to you when he arrives. I'll brief you more when you're in the car." The call ended suddenly, leaving a chilling silence behind. Emily stared at her phone, its screen now blank, the moment's importance settling in. She grabbed her bag, the weight of the printouts feeling like a ticking bomb against her hip.

Patricia looked up from the sink, her hands pausing mid-scrub. "You're leaving again, sweetheart?"

"Another work thing," Emily said, her smile tight, masking the white lie. "I'll be back soon." She entered the living room and looked out at the busy street, her mind racing. Helix's lies were about to unravel, and she was ready to pull the thread. Hard.

Ten minutes later, a sleek black SUV pulled up, its tinted

windows reflecting the tidy Telegraph Hill street, where Victorian houses and leafy maples basked in the fall morning sun. Emily slid into the back seat, clutching her bag, a constant reminder of the incriminating evidence.

The driver, Chris, gave a curt nod, his eyes fixed on the road. "Dr. Harper?"

"Yes," Emily said, settling into the cool seat. The SUV roared ahead, gliding out of Telegraph Hill into Brookline Village's charming storefronts—red-brick facades, quaint cafes with chalkboard menus, and sidewalks dotted with joggers and dog walkers. The neighborhood's polished calm felt surreal, starkly contrasting to the firestorm brewing in other parts of the city.

Her phone rang again, Lauren's voice crackling through. "Emily, confirming several details. It's Harper, right? Formerly Helix's BioSpark team lead?"

"Correct, although not formerly. They haven't fired me yet," Emily said, her fingers tightening on her bag. "Although that may change after today. Who will be interviewing me?"

"Jake Tapper reporting from Atlanta. His questions will challenge Helix's denials, clarify the scope of the extinction event, and scrutinize your claims. Be prepared. He's skeptical about the allegations and will push hard."

Emily's smile wavered, her dry humor surfacing like a reflex. "Helix's creative fiction won't hold up. I've got the receipts, and they're ugly."

Lauren chuckled. "Love the vibe. Stay focused, Dr. Harper." The call ended as the SUV turned onto Harvard Street, the engine's soft rumble contrasting with the city's rising tension. Outside, a small crowd gathered near a pharmacy, their signs scrawled with "Helix Lies" and "Kill Chronos–Not Us." A man yelled, his voice muffled through the SUV's windows, while a police officer waved traffic along, her expression grim. The city's unrest was spilling over, a ripple effect of the truth Tyler had unleashed, and she was about to confirm.

Chris carefully navigated, weaving through Brookline's tree-lined streets past the Art Deco marquee of a theater and a bookstore's colorful display. The SUV pulled up to the CNN bureau, a modest brick building with an unassuming facade that blended seamlessly into the village's charm—no neon signs, no flashy logos—only a small plaque near the door.

Emily stepped out, the crisp air biting her cheeks, the street's quiet energy clashing with her racing heart. She tightened her grip on her bag, the files a deadly weapon against Helix's machine. The bureau's entrance stood out ahead, a gateway to a fight she wouldn't avoid, its glass door reflecting the morning sky and her determined face.

A segment producer, a young woman with a clipboard and a brisk stride, met Emily at the CNN bureau's side entrance, her sneakers squeaking softly on the polished floor. "ID, please," she said, her eyes flicking quickly over Emily's driver's license with practiced efficiency before handing her a guest badge.

The door buzzed open, revealing a busy newsroom alive with energy—soft chatter, the clicking of keyboards, and the glow of monitors casting a blue light across glass-walled offices. Reporters moved quickly, their voices overlapping in a constant rhythm. The stark difference from her mother's kitchen less than an hour earlier was unsettling.

The producer led Emily down a narrow hall, past a glass office where a reporter argued into a headset, her gestures abrupt. They entered a small camera room, its green-screen backdrop painted with a cityscape—Boston's skyline, soft and generic. A tech clipped a mic to Emily's collar, the metal cold against her neck, and fitted an earpiece, its wire curling behind her ear.

"Look straight at the lens," he said, pointing to the camera's unblinking eye as he adjusted the lighting, softening the harsh glare on her face. The room's sterile brightness made her skin prickle, but she squared her shoulders, forcing her breath to calm.

The producer, scanning her clipboard, spoke quickly, "Jake Tapper's anchoring from Atlanta. He'll hit you with Helix's denials, the extinction event's impact, and your evidence. Be ready for tough questions. He won't hold back. Tell the truth, and you'll be fine. You ready?"

Emily nodded, her voice clear despite the dryness in her mouth. "Ready as I'll ever be." She glanced at the monitor, her reflection pale under the lights, her long brown hair slightly mussed from the car ride. A faint smile tugged at her lips. "This lighting makes me look like a fugitive."

The producer smiled, her tension easing briefly. "You're golden, Emily. The audience will love you." She stepped back, speaking into her headset in a low voice. "Dr. Harper's set. Cue in five."

Emily's mind raced, replaying the details of the files. Helix's hidden data on the gene discovery, the kill switch, the extinction-level threat they'd concealed beneath layers of corporate denial. The Chronos conspiracy, her team's trust, Tyler's death— all converged here in this stark, high-tech room.

The tech adjusted her mic, and the faint crackle in her ear was jarring. She closed her eyes for a moment, picturing Tyler's laugh, him standing at their kitchen counter eating pizza, the way he'd pushed her to stand up for her ethics. This was for him, for the truth.

The producer's voice sharpened in her earpiece. "Live in ten. Stand by."

The monitor came to life, Jake Tapper's face appeared, and his expression was stern as he spoke from Atlanta.

"We're joined this morning by Dr. Emily Harper, BioSpark project lead at Helix, with explosive allegations about a cover-up linked to a catastrophic gene discovery. Let's dive in."

Emily stared into the camera, its lens a glass void, her heart pounding against her ribs, the studio lights blinding her.

Jake Tapper went on, "Dr. Harper, you're accusing Helix Innovations of concealing a genetic discovery with catastrophic potential. Walk us through it."

Emily exhaled, composing herself, her hands clasped tightly beneath the desk to hide their tremor. "My team at BioSpark discovered a universal gene sequence—the terminal gene— present in every living organism: humans, animals, plants. It predicts the exact moment of death, down to the second, fixed at conception. It's not a theory. We've validated it through millions of trials. Helix plans to sell this knowledge to the highest bidders—governments, corporations, elites—while concealing its devastating implications."

Tapper's eyes glinted. "This terminal gene, break it down. What does it mean for the average person watching at home?"

Emily leaned forward, her voice restrained. "It means your death is predetermined, encoded in your DNA from the moment you're conceived. No diet, no medicine, no lifestyle can change it. For the average person, knowing their exact expiration date could unravel their mental health, destabilize insurance markets, or even allow governments to profile citizens based on their lifespans. Helix wants to turn this information into profit."

Tapper's brow furrowed as he pressed, "Commercialize it how? Are you saying people could buy their death dates like a product?"

Her eyes narrowed, her tone sharp with conviction. "That's right. Helix is packaging the terminal gene data for governments and elite clients—think billionaires, private labs, even authoritarian regimes. They're promising insights into lifespans. But this isn't only about money; it's about power. Imagine a world where your employer, your insurer, or your government knows when you'll die—and uses it against you."

Tapper tilted his head, unwavering. "Helix claims you're

spreading fear, that your data's unverified. They say you're a disgruntled scientist with an axe to grind. Your response?"

Emily's expression grew tense, her eyes flashing with defiance. "Helix is deflecting. I have evidence, such as lab reports, genetic sequencing data, and internal memos. They show Helix knows the gene's implications and has buried them to protect its profits."

The producer's voice crackled in her earpiece: "Hit the extinction event details."

Emily gave a subtle nod, seamless. "The terminal gene data revealed something worse: an extinction event. Every organism's death date converges in roughly one hundred twenty years, a universal biological shutdown. It's not random—it's coded into life itself. We're facing a global collapse of ecosystems, food chains, and humanity. Helix knows this and is keeping it secret, planning to profit off the chaos."

Tapper leaned in, his voice pressing. "An extinction event in more than a century sounds distant, almost abstract. How do you convince viewers this is real, and what can they do?"

Emily met his gaze. "The data is mathematically certain. In one hundred twenty years, every living thing dies, no exceptions. The ripple effects come sooner: societal panic, economic collapse, governments weaponizing this knowledge."

Tapper's voice grew darker, his eyes fixed on hers. "There's talk of a deeper conspiracy. What's the truth about Chronos, and who's behind it?"

Emily's posture stiffened, and her tone shifted. "Chronos is not a Helix project. It's a separate conspiracy, an international cabal operating beyond Helix's board, led by powerful anonymous figures. This group—financiers, rogue scientists, ghost operatives—is using the terminal gene data for their nefarious purposes, beyond Helix's commercial plans. They aim to monetize mortality, offering the wealthy a chance to learn and possibly manipulate their genes while leaving everyone else vulnerable to the extinction event. It's about absolute control over life and death."

Tapper pushed further. "So, Chronos is a rogue operation, not Helix's profit scheme. What can people do to stop this kind of power grab?"

Her voice wavered briefly, Tyler's earnest face flashing in her mind. "Look at Chronos. They're already planning to sell lifespans to elites while the rest of us face oblivion. People need to demand transparency. Force Helix to release the terminal gene data responsibly. Push for global cooperation to research solutions, not profit-driven cover-ups. This isn't about science but who controls life and death. The public must hold Helix and this cabal accountable before they turn our future into their dehumanized playground."

Tapper nodded, his voice brisk. "Dr. Harper, thank you. We're out of time, but this story's far from over. Stay with CNN for updates." The monitor switched to a car insurance ad, its jingle jarring. Emily exhaled, trembling, as the tech unclipped her mic, the studio's glare fading into a blur.

Tapper nodded reassuringly as the tech removed Emily's mic and earpiece. The slight tug of the wire felt like an odd disconnect from what she had experienced moments earlier.

The producer gave a quick smile, her eyes shining with the segment's success, but also with a hint of fear at what Emily had revealed. "Great job, Dr. Harper. You were phenomenal. Can you stay if we need you for follow-up segments? The story's blowing up."

Emily nodded, her body exhausted, her mind still reeling from the live segment. "I'm on my cell. Let me know."

Her legs felt weak as she entered the hallway, the newsroom's buzz fading behind her. She moved through the side exit, and the glass door closed softly with a thud. Brookline's crisp air hit her like a wave—sharp and clean, carrying the faint scent of coffee from a nearby cafe. The village stretched out before her.

The sudden calm after the intensity of the newsroom was startling.

Her phone buzzed, an unknown number flashing. She answered, her free hand tightening on her bag. "Hello. Lauren?"

A low, distorted voice came through the line. "You've started something you can't stop, Doctor. Congratulations. You're on the right track, but overlooking an important detail about the terminal gene. Check your personal email." The call suddenly cut out, leaving an abrupt silence.

Emily froze, her breath catching in her throat. The village's charm suddenly seemed like a façade hiding something darker and more dangerous.

She had exposed Chronos and revealed their lies, but this voice, this warning, suggested a new thread in the web, a shadow she hadn't foreseen. Was this the mysterious Q or someone else? She looked back at the bureau's facade, its brick exterior blending into the village, then down Washington Street, where the world was waiting. Her personal email—what was waiting there? And who was now pulling the strings?

Chapter 25

The Devil You Know

E mily sipped her drink, averting her eyes from the news on the television in the cafe's bar.

The cafe near the CNN bureau in Brookline glowed softly, with pendant lights casting amber pools of light over the worn wooden tables. The aroma of garlic from the kitchen drifted through the air, and her stomach growled. She sat alone in a corner booth, her rum and Diet Coke sweating onto a crumpled napkin, beads of condensation shimmering. A half-eaten turkey sandwich was abandoned beside it, the bread soggy.

Clara, the server, approached the table with a tense smile, her name tag catching the light. She carried a tray of empty plates, her eyes occasionally drifting to Emily's untouched meal.

"You okay, hon?" she asked, her voice filled with concern. "That drink looks like it's mostly ice. Need a refill?"

Emily's gaze lifted, her anxiety flaring at the attention after the long day, but Clara's wide smile softened the tension. "I'm good," she said, her fingers tightening slightly on the glass. "Taking it slow while I wait for my friend." The cafe's chatter felt close, a flood of noise that made her tense.

Clara waited, wiping the table with a rag, using her movements as an excuse to chat. "I saw you on TV today," she said with a hint of awe. "That was you, right? Doctor Harper, they were calling you. The Helix whistleblower? Spilling all that about...Chronos?" She squinted as if she didn't quite understand what she'd heard.

Emily felt a knot tighten in her stomach. "Yes, that was me," she said, looking at Clara's face, taking in everything—her red cheeks, the nervous circles with her cloth. "It's complicated." The cafe's warmth suddenly seemed stifling, the air heavy with the scent of damp coats from the evening drizzle.

Clara leaned in closer, her voice dropping to a whisper as her rag paused mid-wipe. "You're braver than I'll ever be. Going up against a big company like that? I'd be shaking in my shoes." She glanced over her shoulder. The clink of a glass nearby made her flinch. "Aren't you scared? I mean, they might come after you, right?"

Emily's fingers clenched around her glass, her gallows humor surfacing despite the tightness in her chest. "Scared doesn't cover it," she admitted, her voice strong, a faint smirk touching her lips. "But someone had to say it. These people don't get to play God with people's lives."

After she'd spent all day at CNN, the continued attention felt like a spotlight she couldn't escape.

The day's events flooded her mind. The interview with Tapper that morning—revealing the Chronos conspiracy, the extinction event, and the genetic kill switch—played on a relentless loop. Lauren, the producer, cornered her afterward. "Where are you staying? Who's protecting you? Do you know what this means for your future?" Lauren's fixation on the predictive mortality algorithm, the idea of a set death date, had left Emily emotionally drained.

The following interviews were intense—Jake Tapper's relentless questioning, panels of scientists hurling accusations from distant studio sets. Some branded her a fraud, their voices dripping with scorn. Others saw her as an attention-seeking whistleblower.

"You did remarkably well," Tapper had said off-air, his eyes narrowing with respect.

Emily's response was reflexive. "It's easy when the truth's on your side." But now, in the cafe's dim lighting, the reality of what she had done felt like a cage she had built for herself.

Tyler's laugh echoed in her mind as she sipped her drink, bringing back memories of late-night pizza runs, his hand brushing hers as they shared a greasy slice, and his teasing grin while he held her. The engagement photo by her apartment door flashed next, its frame broken from the break-in, glass glinting on the floor. Her throat tightened, the cafe's murmur fading as grief took hold.

Anita slid into the booth beside her, pulling her out of her memories. Her glass of red wine wobbled in her hand, and her dark eyes were hazy with exhaustion. Clara stepped back, giving a quick nod before heading to the counter, her tray softly clinking.

"Emily," Anita said over the cafe's noise, "Helix is a mess. Security has doubled with guards at every door, and new keycards have been issued to all the employees this morning. I saw contractors dismantling James's office today."

Emily had exposed him, and now he was gone. Tyler's goodbye video echoed in her mind. "He's out of the picture now." She was sure James was dead, though no one said it out loud. Anita's voice wavered, her wine catching the light like blood. "No sign of him. Some say he's hiding, others...worse. The BioSpark team's scared. They're jumping at shadows because of what you said on TV."

Emily's breathing slowed. "I didn't want this," she whispered, the cafe's warmth now suffocating. "But silence would've killed so many innocent people." The familiar smell of garlic and damp wool coats kept her from succumbing to her anxiety.

Anita leaned in closer, her fingers clutching her glass. "You've stirred a storm. They're scouring archives, interrogating everyone who touched those files. Helix is a ghost town. People are afraid even to whisper your name. What's your next move?"

Before Emily could answer, a woman's shrill voice cut through the noise. "You're her, aren't you? The one who spilled it all about the terminal gene!" A young mother stood at a nearby table, her face streaked with tears, clutching a toddler's stuffed bear, its fur damp and matted.

Customers turned, their stares piercing Emily like needles. "Tell me when I'm going to die," the woman sobbed, her voice breaking. "I can't leave my baby without a mother!"

Emily froze, her mind scrambling to adjust to the sudden disturbance. The cafe's air was filled with whispers, some patrons glaring, others nodding quietly in recognition. The mother's plea was a blade of guilt twisting in Emily's gut.

Anita grabbed Emily's arm, her voice firm. "We need to go. This could turn ugly." Clara reappeared, her nervous smile replaced by a serious expression, her eyes turning to the crying mother. "Come on," she whispered, guiding them toward the back exit, her hand gentle but firm on Emily's shoulder. "People like that are why I would never do what you did. Hurry." She pushed open the door, shielding them from curious glances.

Emily's heart raced. "I should go to my apartment," she told Anita as she pulled out her phone. "Did you drive over? I need more clothes and Tyler's things, then I want to go back to my parents' house. It's safer there than my apartment."

Anita nodded in response. "My car's parked down the street." Her face was pale as they hurried into the night, street-lights casting shimmering silhouettes on the wet pavement. The cafe's soft glow faded behind them, icy drizzle on her skin, her paranoia a gloom she couldn't shake. They quickly headed toward Anita's car.

Rain streaked across the windshield, blurring Boston's neon lights into a mix of red, gold, and electric blue. The city's streets, lit up this morning by a gentle sun, now sparkled with hidden dangers, the pavement slick under a constant drizzle that pounded against the car's roof.

Anita gripped the steering wheel tightly, her breath shallow as she drove toward Emily's apartment. Emily sat stiffly in the passenger seat, her eyes flicking to the side mirror. Two black SUVs quickly took the corner behind them, their tinted windows as dark as ink, and their sudden presence felt too deliberate to be a coincidence.

Her pulse quickened, suspicion igniting like a spark in dry grass. Helix operatives? Government agents? The SUVs drew closer, weaving through traffic aggressively, their tires squealing on wet asphalt—a grating sound that made her teeth grind.

"They're tailing us," Emily said, on edge.

Anita's breath caught, her hands trembling on the wheel, her eyes wide. "What do we do? Emily, I can't—" She swerved onto Boylston Street, and the minivan lurched slightly.

They sped past protestors huddled near a shuttered pharmacy, holding signs that read "Helix Lies" and "Chronos Kills," which flapped in the wind. A halogen streetlight cast a harsh glow on their faces, twisted with rage and fear.

The SUVs matched their turn, their headlights glaring like a predator's eyes, quickly closing the gap. Emily's mind raced, cataloging details: no license plates, new models—probably the kind Helix would use for discreet operations. Her fingers gripped the door handle, its firmness anchoring her amid the rising panic and Anita's frantic driving. The city felt alive, like a beast awakening, its pulse reflected in the distant wail of sirens and the sharp honk of a nearby cab.

Anita's voice rose, high-pitched with fear. "Emily, they're right behind us! What if they—"

The minivan struggled through a tight turn onto Tremont Street. The rain intensified, smearing the windshield, while the wipers' rhythmic scrape created a surreal backdrop to the tension inside the vehicle.

"Focus on the road," Emily said. "I'll try to look up the address of the nearest police station." She scrolled through the map app on her phone. She glanced back, the SUV's grill filling the mirror. Her mind flashed to Tyler's goodbye video echoed. James, the vanished CEO, was dead. She was sure of it, and now someone wanted her dead, too.

A siren suddenly blared, red and blue lights piercing through the rain, startling Anita and Emily. A police cruiser swerved in front of the closest SUV, forcing it to brake sharply with a screech that echoed down the street. The SUVs stopped, backed up, and sped away, their taillights disappearing into the night's blur. From the cruiser, an obscured figure waved Anita to the curb, the gesture sharp despite the rain beading on the windows.

Anita pulled over to the curb, and the police cruiser pulled up behind her. Officer Mooney, off-duty, hopped out, her eyes hidden under a baseball cap, rain dripping from her hood. She approached the driver's window, boots splashing in shallow puddles. "Stay put," Mooney said. "I was in the area. Lucky break." She radioed for backup.

Emily's relief quickly faded. Mooney's repeated appearances seemed too convenient. The near-miss near the office, when Mooney's cruiser appeared after an SUV almost hit her, and the break-in response, her pointed questions about enemies, only increased Emily's growing suspicion. Was Mooney truly a protector or another player in Helix's game?

"You two okay?" Mooney asked, her tired eyes lingering on

Emily, rain beading on her coat. "That SUV's been circling the area. It seems you've got enemies, Harper." Her maternal tone felt genuine, but her probing questions about Helix and Tyler gnawed at Emily's trust.

Anita's voice trembled, tears swelling as she clutched the wheel. "Why are they after us? What did they want?"

"I'm sorry," Emily said, her calm facade cracking. "I didn't mean for you to get caught in this."

Mooney leaned in the open window. "I'll escort you to your destination to make sure you arrive safely. Protocol. Drive, and I'll follow behind."

The police cruiser was visible in the rearview mirror, its lights flashing steadily as Anita drove, warding off the city's hidden threats. Emily stared at the cruiser, her mind torn between gratitude and suspicion. The stolen evidence files in her bag felt like a truth that had marked them both as targets.

The rain grew heavier, its relentless rhythm emphasizing the city's unrest—a shattered storefront window, a protester's shout echoing down an alley. Anita's shallow breathing filled the car, her fear a heaviness Emily couldn't shake, and her distrust of Mooney a shadow that deepened with every passing block.

Emily's apartment in Jamaica Plain was a mess. Thick dust hung in the air, and the burnt smell from the break-in lingered like a warning. Books were scattered across the hardwood floor, their pages splayed like broken wings. The crooked, cracked glass of her engagement photo seemed to mock her. Her chest tightened as memories of Tyler flooded in.

Anita packed a duffel with Emily's clothes. Officer Mooney lingered by the kitchen counter, her hands wrapped around a coffee mug Emily had offered, the steam curling in the stale air. "I'm not here by chance," Mooney said, meeting Emily's gaze with an intensity that made her skin tingle. "A friend of a friend is worried about Helix's fallout. They want you safe, Harper."

"Who's this mysterious friend?" Emily countered. "I need all the friends I can get right now."

Mooney's lips squeezed thin. "I can't name them, but they know what you're up against."

Emily's distrust flared. "A friend of a friend? That's flimsy, Officer. I'm not in the mood for riddles." Mooney's sincerity—her exhausted eyes, her weathered hands—tugged at Emily, a flicker of honesty conflicting with her evasiveness. Ally or plant? The question gnawed at her, a puzzle with dangerous edges.

Anita paused, clutching a sweater, her voice pointed. "Emily, she stopped those SUVs chasing us. Maybe we should trust her. We need someone." Her hands shook as she zipped the duffel, her eyes darting to the mess in the living room.

She turned to Anita. "Trust is a luxury we don't have. Not now."

Emily's phone buzzed. It was a text from Vic, Tyler's friend from the Army. "Don't trust the police. Come to the safe spot I showed you. Charlestown Wheels."

Her heart lurched. Charlestown Wheels flashed through her mind. The abandoned chop shop in Seaport, Vic's shifty eyes when he'd shown it to them, promising a refuge. His ties to the Boston underworld made him a devil she didn't understand, but this text... How did he get her number? Tyler had shared it, she remembered, during a tense meeting outside the shop, but Vic texting now, after Tyler's death, felt like a trap set at the worst moment.

Was he watching her, tipped off by her CNN appearance? Her mind was spinning with questions. Was he Tyler's friend, trying to help her, or was he reaching out to her for someone else?

She clutched the phone, her voice hushed as she whispered to Anita. "Vic texted. He says not to trust Mooney."

Anita's eyes widened, and a sweater slid from her hands.

"Vic? That guy? How does he even know where you are? Emily, you can't trust him. We both know he's trouble."

Emily's throat tightened as her eyes flicked to Mooney, who stood still in the kitchen with her coffee mug untouched. Her eyes narrowed slightly, as if sensing the shift.

"I don't trust either of them," Emily said. "But Vic, knowing my number, is texting now—it's like he's been waiting and watching." The memory of Vic's sly grin clashed with Mooney's stable presence, her vague "friend of a friend" excuse. Both felt like traps, each a different shade of danger.

Mooney set her mug down, and the clink was loud in the quiet apartment. "What's the plan, Harper?" Her tone was calm, but her eyes were probing. "If we're done here, I'll ensure you safely get to your next stop."

"Still packing," she answered, taking a moment to think. She packed Tyler's sketchbooks, their pages filled with half-finished dog sketches, her fingers lingering on the worn covers, the paper soft and warm. Tyler's death and her role in exposing Helix crushed her, a heaviness no amount of truth could ease.

Anita's voice broke the silence, rising. "Emily, I think we've got everything. Are we headed to your parents' house now, or what? We can't stay here." Her eyes flicked to the door, the cracked photo catching the light beside it, Tyler's smile a ghostly reflection in the dimness.

Emily's eyes flicked to her phone, Vic's text still glowing. Mooney's presence made her nervous—her gaze was too perceptive, and her motives were unclear. A faint creak came from the hallway outside the front door, like a footstep testing the wood.

"We need to go," she said, her eyes fixed on the door. "But I don't know who to trust."

Mooney stepped closer, her footsteps heavy on the hard-wood. "You're scared, Harper. I get it. But I'm here, and I'm real.

Whoever's texting you, they're not." Her tone was steady, almost maternal, but her eyes held a glint Emily couldn't read.

Anita grabbed the duffel, her voice trembling. "Emily, let's go. We can't wait anymore." The creak sounded again, closer—a shadow shifting in the hallway, the noise loud in the quiet air. Emily's breath caught, her fingers clutching her bag, Vic's warning and Mooney's presence clashing in her mind, her decision still uncertain as the darkness settled around them.

Chapter 26

The Cipher

E mily, you're pacing again," Anita said, her knees bouncing as she sat on the torn couch. Her dark eyes flicked to the front door, then back to Emily, who stood stiffly, fingers twitching against her glasses.

"I'm fine," Emily snapped. She glanced at Officer Mooney, who leaned stiffly against the kitchen counter with her jacket unzipped, revealing a holster tucked against her lower back. No uniform tonight—just denim, baseball cap, and a stare that made the hair on Emily's arms stand up. Vic's text burned in her mind. "Don't trust the police. Come to the safe spot I showed you."

"I think I heard a noise outside," Emily said, her voice low, barely above the rumble of a passing truck on the street. "Check the hallway."

Mooney's eyebrow arched, but she stepped to the door, her boots squeaking on the worn hardwood. She held her eye to the peephole, her fingers lightly touching the butt of her holstered pistol. "Old guy out there. Gray beard, tattered coat. Looks like he's been living in a dumpster."

Emily's throat tightened. "What's he doing?"

Shuffling and mumbling, he held something—maybe paper or money. Mooney's hand hovered near her holster, a subtle signal that made Emily's nerves stiffen.

"Open it," Emily said, her voice even despite the tremor in her hands. Anita's head snapped up, her fingers pausing in mid-fidget on the couch's frayed armrest.

Mooney hesitated, her jaw tightening, then she unlatched the door. The hinges squeaked, revealing a small, hunched figure in the dim hallway light. The man's beard was matted, his coat patched with stains, and his hands shook as he clutched a crumpled piece of paper. His watery eyes fixed on Mooney, then Emily, wide with something like confusion.

"Is one of you Emily Harper?" His voice was gruff, thick with an accent—possibly Eastern European or Russian. He shuffled forward.

Emily nodded, her mouth dry. "I am. Who are you?"

"Ivan Petrovich." He handed her the paper, his fingers shaking as if it burned him. "The woman on the corner gave me twenty dollars to bring this, but only to give it to you." He looked nervously at Mooney.

"What woman? Describe her," Emily pressed.

"Big, dark hair. Red scarf. Deep black eyes, like she's looking right through you." His gaze flicked to Mooney and then back to Emily. "Didn't give a name. She said you'd know what to do."

She couldn't think of anyone she knew who matched that description. She furrowed her brows, considering the possibilities—Helix operative? Ally? Trap? She took the paper, its edges dirty and worn, and unfolded it. A message was written in ink, with barely readable handwriting. "Go home, Doctor, and check your email. Your phone is being tapped."

Her breath caught. She looked at Mooney, who narrowed her eyes and stiffened like a predator sensing prey. "What's it say?" Mooney asked, stepping closer, her voice hard with authority.

Emily folded the note and slipped it into her jeans pocket. "It's personal. Nothing that concerns you." Her voice was calm, even though her heart was pounding. "We're finished here. I'd like you to escort us to my parents' house in Telegraph Hill."

Mooney's jaw clenched, her gaze piercing into Emily's. Then she nodded, a brief dip of her chin. "Fine. Let's move."

Anita scrambled to her feet, grabbing the half-packed duffel bag from the couch. Her eyes were wide with unspoken questions. Emily scanned the apartment one last time—the clutter, stacks of books, the empty refrigerator whirring, the shattered coffee table—setting the chaos of her recent life in perspective.

Outside, the early-December night nipped at Emily's exposed skin, with the wind carrying the faint scent of fall from the park. Emily and Anita got into the minivan as Mooney slid into the cruiser behind them.

The city's lights streaked by, casting long, distorted shapes across the dashboard. Emily sat, feeling the edges of the note in her pocket, her mind tangled with suspicion and hope. Was Mooney's protection genuine, or was she Helix's eyes, watching her every move? Vic's warning echoed in her mind, but his evasiveness—his refusal to explain Charlestown Wheels, his warning about Mooney—left her grasping at ghosts.

The drive to her parents' house was a blur of streetlights and quiet streets. The minivan's tires crunched on the gravel driveway as Anita pulled in. Mooney parked across the street. She stayed in the police vehicle, her silhouette a dark outline against the glow of a distant streetlamp. Emily stepped out, and Mooney's eyes met hers through the window. Emily's chest tightened. Someone out there might be an ally, but every step forward felt like a gamble.

It was dark and quiet in her parents' house, and Emily and Anita slipped inside, quickly heading up the stairs to Emily's childhood bedroom. Emily threw her bag onto the bed, while Anita placed the duffel bag on the floor and disappeared. Emily pulled an old computer from the back of the closet and started connecting the cables.

"Are you sure you don't want any coffee?" Anita asked, her voice worried, as she stood in the doorway a few minutes later. The mug in her hands steamed, the smell of roasted beans mixing with the faint scent of lavender that filled the air.

Emily shook her head. "I'm already too wired." She focused on the old desktop computer wheezing to life on her battered wooden nightstand, which she used as a makeshift desk. The room felt frozen in time—faded posters of Einstein and the periodic table stained at the edges, a twin bed with a quilt her mother had sewn, and a window framing clouds heavy with the threat of rain. She yanked the curtains shut, sealing out the world that felt too close, too exposed.

Her personal email account on her laptop was a dead end, with no new messages. Ivan's note had to mean something different. This old desktop was her last hope, connected to an email address she hadn't used since college. The screen flickered, casting a faint glow across the room as she entered her password, the plastic keys on the keyboard sticking slightly under her fingers. Thousands of unread messages awaited.

She quickly sorted the content, filtering for spam and messages received within the past forty-eight hours. Among the emails, one subject line stood out; a jumble of letters and numbers, clearly encrypted.

Her stomach knotted as her curiosity battled dread. She opened the email; the cursor blinked over a block of text that looked like gibberish. A cipher, complex and deliberate. Her mind raced, parsing possibilities—Vigenere? Something custom? She grabbed a notepad, her pen scratching as she copied the first few characters, her glasses slipping down her nose.

Her phone buzzed, interrupting the stillness. Dr. Morrow's name lit up the screen. Emily froze, her thumb hesitating over the accept button. The timing felt like a trap—too perfect to be a coincidence.

She answered, "Good evening, Dr. Morrow."

"Emily, I've reviewed the documents you and Tyler left me on Sunday morning. It took me longer than I expected to sort through the details. But it seems your instincts were right about this Chronos group. It's real, and James was deeply involved."

"I wish you had said this at the board meeting," Emily said with exasperation.

"I would have, but the timing wasn't right—spilled milk, Emily. James is still missing. When was the last time you saw him?"

Emily's grip tightened on the phone. James, Helix's CEO, was dead, though she couldn't let Morrow know she knew. That would expose Tyler's involvement. It would be impossible to explain without implicating herself.

"Not since last weekend," she said. "I ran into him late one evening at the office. Why are you asking?"

"No one has seen James since Monday night." Morrow's voice was even, but there was a hint of tension, a subtle pressure that made Emily's skin prickle. "They're investigating his last movements. The badge logs show you were at the Helix offices late Saturday night. Did you notice anything unusual?"

Emily forced her voice to stay calm, relieved she had told the truth. "I hope he surfaces soon," she said. "Maybe he was running because he suspected an investigation was coming." She knew that wasn't true. She couldn't afford to let Morrow see her doubts. "He seemed distracted when I saw him," she added, carefully neutral. "Stressed, perhaps. But nothing specific."

Morrow sighed, her voice heavy with disappointment or perhaps something more calculated. "You should've waited for me to finish investigating, Emily, and not gone to CNN. This is bigger than you realize. Bigger than you, bigger than BioSpark."

Dr. Morrow had been her mentor, guiding her through the

maze of her PhD, believing in her even when she doubted herself. But this call, this loaded questioning, wasn't friendly. Emily's gaze flicked to the encrypted email, its letters taunting her from the screen.

"I didn't know who to trust," she whispered, the truth cutting deeper than expected.

"You still don't," Morrow replied, and the line went dead.

Emily set the phone down, her hands unsteady. She examined the cipher, its letters forming a puzzle she couldn't solve yet. Guilt nagged at her—had she misjudged Morrow, pushed away an ally? Or was Morrow's probing a sign of something darker, a betrayal waiting to happen? The ethics of her pursuit weighed heavily on her. Revealing Helix's secrets might save millions but also unleash consequences she couldn't predict—perhaps extinction, not salvation. Someone sent this encrypted email, knowing she was close to the truth. But who?

The desk lamp cast a harsh pool of light across the bedroom, its glow highlighting the edges of scattered papers, coffee cups, and an old cryptography book she'd uncovered from a dusty box under the bed. The clock on the wall ticked past midnight, like a heartbeat in the stillness. Anita sat cross-legged on the faded rug, her laptop resting on her knees, her fingers flying across the keys as she cross-referenced code-breaking techniques from an online archive. Emily leaned over the computer, her glasses smudged and her pen scratching furiously on a notepad.

Emily's fingers gently touched the cracked leather cover of the cryptography book, its yellowed pages fragile beneath her fingertips. The book was a relic from her college days, full of puzzles. The room felt familiar and strange, like a time capsule of a girl who believed in answers, now weighed down by what those answers might represent.

"It's a Vigenere cipher," Emily said. "The key's personal. Something tied to me."

Anita looked up, her eyes bright with excitement, her dark

hair falling loose from its bun. "Your old username when we were doing those hacking challenges in college?" She grinned, a spark of nostalgia cutting through the tension. "Remember those late nights in the library, you hunched over your laptop, arguing with randos on those crypto forums? You were relentless, Emily. DrD153, that was you, right?"

Emily's lips quivered, a faint smile breaking through her tension. The memory hit hard—restless nights at Lamont Library, the glow of her screen, the thrill of solving codes and performing penetration testing with strangers online. Anita had been there, sneaking her espressos past the librarians, her laughter a lifeline when the challenges felt never-ending.

"Yeah," Emily said, her voice softening. "DrD153." She typed the string into the decryption tool on the desktop, her fingers trembling on the sticky keys. The scrambled text unraveled, each letter realigning, revealing a message that chilled her to the bone. "Dr. Elena Volkova. Charlestown Wheels. Find her. She knows all about the terminal gene."

Volkova. The name hit like a shockwave, stirring up fragments of memory buried beneath years of corporate secrecy. A Russian-born geneticist who died in a car accident after pioneering gene-editing techniques that might change humanity's future—methods whispered about in Helix's secretive corridors. Emily's mind raced, connecting the threads. Helix's mysterious hires, projects too dangerous to name, hidden within BioSpark's history.

But Volkova had died years ago. How could she be involved in this? And Charlestown Wheels—Vic's safe spot. Her thoughts snagged on the vivid memory of Vic on a Saturday night, pointing toward a dilapidated warehouse hidden in a Seaport alley, his voice low, mentioning an old brick building where "they should come if they need help." A chop shop? A garage? The ambiguity fueled her unease, a spark that would ignite answers or burn her down.

Anita leaned in closer, her sweater brushing the edge of the computer, her voice bubbling with excitement. "This is it, Emily. This is the break we've been waiting for. If Volkova's alive, she could tell us the background on the kill switch, expose Helix, all of it."

Emily's fingers paused on the keyboard as hope battled with caution. Vic's text hadn't mentioned Volkova. Was he guiding her toward answers or leading her into a trap? However, he had also mentioned that her phone was being tapped. Perhaps he didn't want to put too much in writing.

She looked around the bedroom, its familiarity grounding her—the faded posters, the creaky furniture scarred from her teenage years, and her favorite quilt. She was reminded of the girl who trusted in truthfulness, science, and doing what was right. That girl still lived within her, but she had grown, hardened by challenges and loss, with her idealism hardened by Tyler's painful sacrifice.

Anita shifted on the rug. "You're quiet," she said, her tone softer now, probing. "What's going on in that head of yours?"

Emily exhaled, her breath stirring the dust motes in the lamplight. "I'm thinking about what happens if we find her," she said, her voice calm. "Volkova's work might save lives, Anita. Stop Chronos's plans. But if it falls into the wrong hands…"

Unlocking Volkova's secrets could be salvation, catastrophe, a cure, or a weapon.

Anita placed her laptop aside. She leaned forward, her hands clasped. "You're not alone in this, you know," she said evenly. "Back in college, you'd get this look when you were stuck on a problem—like the world was ending if you didn't solve it. But you always did. And I was there, sneaking you snacks, telling you to breathe deeply. We're still that team, Emily. Whatever this is, we'll face it together."

She met Anita's gaze, the familiar spark in her friend's eyes reminding her why she kept going. "Thanks," she said and turned back to the decrypted message. She was determined to find Volkova, no matter the risk. The truth was her only way forward, even if it meant risking everything.

"We need to move. In the morning, we'll head to Charlestown Wheels. I think I can find my way back to where Vic took me and Tyler. But we can't tell anyone, especially not Dr. Morrow or Officer Mooney."

Anita nodded. Her fingers brushed the rug, tracing its worn patterns—a nervous habit from their college days.

The path ahead was unclear, wrapped in fog, but for the first time in a week, Emily felt a spark of control, a feeling that her choices—no matter how risky—might still influence the future. She leaned back in the chair, the wood groaning beneath her, and let the silence fall, the cipher's promise burning in her mind.

Chapter 27

Decode the Lie

"G et something to eat, Emily," Patricia Harper said with unease. She stood in the dimly lit kitchen of their Victorian home, the stained-glass window above the sink catching the pre-dawn light and casting crimson and sapphire patches across the oak floor.

Emily paused by the counter, her eyes flicking to the front window. The curtains concealed Officer Mooney's cruiser across the street, its dark bulk a silent threat in the neighborhood's stillness. "I can't stay, Mom. Not with her out there."

Officer Mooney had rescued her from the chase last night and offered vague warnings, but trusting her was a gamble Emily couldn't take.

Patricia tightened her cardigan, her hair loose around her shoulders, worry deepening the lines around her eyes. "She saved you a couple of times, didn't she? You don't know she's against you."

"That's the problem," Emily said. "I don't know." She saw the familiar fear in her mother's eyes, a look that had become common in the last few days.

Anita hovered near the back door, her backpack slung over one shoulder, her breath visible in the cold air. "Emily, we should go before it gets too light," she said as she tied her sneakers. The floor creaked—a familiar childhood sound that Emily knew well from sneaking midnight snacks.

Patricia stepped closer, her hand warm on Emily's arm. "Where are you headed? You can't keep running without a plan."

"Seaport," Emily said, hesitating. "Someone's waiting— someone who knows about Chronos." *Was she really going to trust an anonymous email?* The thought unsettled her.

Her mother's lips thinned, eyes searching. "Emily, let us help. Your father—"

"No." Emily's voice softened. "I need you both safe and to keep you as far from this as possible." She glanced at the staircase, picturing her father asleep, unaware of the storm swirling around him.

Patricia pulled her into a tight hug. "Love you. Be careful, sweetheart."

Emily nodded and gestured to Anita. They slipped out through the back door, carefully avoiding the creaky floorboard. Outside, the well-kept lawn sparkled with frost, and the air bore the sharp chill of December. Telegraph Hill's brick row houses and glowing bay windows faded into shadows as they moved into the garage.

Her mother's Fiat, a small, old car with chipped blue paint, was nestled among gardening tools and stacked boxes. Emily slid into the driver's seat, keys jingling, while Anita buckled her seatbelt. The engine sputtered loudly in the enclosed space. Emily carefully eased the car out, the garage door whining as it lifted, and rolled onto a side street, headlights off to avoid Mooney's watch.

Distant sirens cut through the quiet of Boston as they headed toward the Seaport District, gliding through the sparse early morning traffic. Alleys replaced wide streets, forming a maze of brick buildings and rusted dumpsters. Emily tried to remember the way to Charlestown Wheels from her last visit with Vic and Tyler. The memory was foggy—alleys twisting, a deserted square, a faded sign under a streetlamp.

She turned down a narrow street, the Fiat's tires bouncing on cracked pavement, but the landmarks seemed different. A graffiti-covered wall appeared, but there was no square. She cursed softly, doubling back.

"Emily, are you lost?" Anita asked, tapping her fingers on her knee. "You said Vic took you there Saturday night."

"I thought I remembered," Emily muttered, turning into another alley, the air reeking with the harbor's briny tang and rotting trash. "It was dark, and we came from a bar. There was a square, an oily puddle, a sign—Charlestown Wheels. But these streets and alleys all look the same in this light."

Anita leaned forward, peering through the windshield. "Keep driving. Something will click."

They wandered deeper into Seaport's maze, the alleys shrinking, buildings leaning like weary sentinels. Anita's chatter —about her brothers' girlfriends and the harbor's smell—kept Emily distracted, their friendship a calming influence.

Finally, the alley opened onto a small, deserted square. The asphalt was cracked and stained with an oily sheen that reflected the faint glow of a lone streetlamp. Emily's breath caught as a crumbling brick building appeared ahead, its faded sign barely legible: "Charlestown Wheels."

Emily parked in a nearby empty lot, the car's engine ticking as it cooled. They stepped out, sneakers splashing through puddles. The dirty plaza stretched empty, the building's dark windows like hollow eyes. Emily crossed her arms, the morning chill seeping through her jacket.

"This is it," she said.

The memory of Vic leaning against that wall, cigarette smoke curling, flashed in her mind. He'd called it a chop shop, an off-grid stash, and told her to ask for Buckingham Flats if she needed help. The password felt absurd.

Anita scanned the square, her posture tense. "Creepy as hell. You sure about this?"

"Nope," Emily admitted, knocking on the door. "Is anyone here?"

After a moment, the metal door creaked open, revealing a large man with a thick Russian accent, his bulk filling the entrance. A shoulder holster strapped across his chest held a pistol, its grip worn. His eyes, cold and hooded, scanned Emily and Anita.

"What you want?" he growled.

Emily swallowed. "Do you know the way to Buckingham Flats?"

The man's gaze narrowed, then he stepped aside, jerking his head toward the interior. "Inside. Now." He guided them through the garage, past rusted car parts and oil-stained floors, to a hidden panel in the back wall. With a grunt, he slid it open, revealing a trapdoor. "Down there," he said, pointing to a ladder descending into dim light. "She's waiting."

Emily exchanged glances with Anita, whose nod conveyed a mix of fear and courage. The man's stance, weapon, and blunt attitude heightened the danger. There was no turning back now. Emily took a deep breath and descended the ladder first, the cold metal rungs biting into her palms.

The ladder led into a vast underground chamber, air thick with the damp smell of concrete seeping through cracked walls. Yellowed fluorescent bulbs cast soft shapes over cluttered work-benches—oscilloscopes showing green traces, yellowed paper charts stacked precariously, vials simmering under heat lamps, their contents faintly glowing. The space was a defiant relic, with tangled wires and handwritten logs standing in sharp contrast to Helix's sterile precision—a scientific haven carved from necessity.

Dr. Elena Volkova stood at the far end of the room. She was a large woman with intense dark eyes behind wire-rimmed glasses. Her stained white lab coat was draped over a black shirt. Gray streaks ran through her hair, highlighting the lines on her forehead. She held a clipboard and a pipette, her posture stiff with suspicion as Emily and Anita approached.

"I thought you'd get here sooner," Volkova said, her thick Russian accent prominent. She set the pipette down, crossed her arms, and looked at Anita. "And you brought an entourage."

Emily stepped down from the ladder, and the trapdoor closed with a thud above her. "Was that your email?" she asked. Volkova was still alive despite the local news and Helix reporting her killed in a car crash. "You have answers about the terminal gene?"

Volkova ignored Emily's questions, her eyes fixed on Anita. "Name?"

"Anita Gupta," she said, stepping forward and raising her chin. "I'm with Emily. We're in this together."

The lab's equipment emitted a constant rhythm of whirs and clicks.

Volkova nodded sharply. "Okay, sit. Time's thin."

They sat on stools around a scarred metal table, papers scattered like fallen leaves. Volkova poured tea from a dented pot into chipped mugs. Emily wrapped her hands around one, the warmth easing her stiff fingers. Anita mirrored her, blowing on the surface of the tea, her glance at Emily a silent check-in.

"Da, I sent the email. I knew only you could open it. But let me start from the beginning," Volkova said. "I faked my death. The people you call Chronos closed in, and Russian hunters never forget. I couldn't let them twist my work into a weapon."

Anita's mouth dropped open in surprise. Emily leaned forward. "What Russian hunters?"

Volkova's lips thinned, her fingers tightening on her mug. She exhaled, the sound heavy with memory. She leaned back. The stool creaked beneath her heavy frame, and the fluorescent light cast deeper lines across her face.

"St. Petersburg, a modest flat overlooking the Neva's gray waters. My father, a retired colonel, ruled with iron discipline over dreams. My mother, a doctor, tended the city's forgotten. I watched her work late nights, caring for patients with rare diseases—her patience was my first lesson."

She sighed, "At eighteen, a scholarship to Moscow State University pulled me from home. The city was vast, cold—my family's sacrifices weighed heavily on me. By twenty-five, I had a PhD, but Russia's labs stifled me, twisting research for war. I worked on a project to enhance soldiers' resilience and strength, but saw its toll. At a conference in the West, I defected after sabotaging it. I left my parents and brother behind. Guilt never fades, and Russian spies will never stop searching for me."

Emily noticed the way Volkova's fingers brushed a scar on her wrist. In America, her accent, background, and quiet menace slowed her integration, but Helix brought her on board for her expertise in CRISPR. BioSpark was her greatest achievement until Chronos's darkness undermined her.

"I found the terminal gene," Volkova continued, her voice steadying. "Embedded in BioSpark's data, a timed trigger for extinction. Nature didn't craft this alone; it's likely a remnant of ancient genetic drift, amplified by human intervention. James forced me to alter the algorithms to conceal any data that would expose this extinction event. He ran all data through a program to create a false dataset, accessible only to him. I was forbidden from telling anyone, especially the board, but I eventually confided in Dr. Morrow."

Emily's brow furrowed, her mind snagging on a detail. "When I told Dr. Morrow about the extinction event, she seemed shocked. Why would she act surprised if you already told her?"

Volkova's lips tightened, a flicker of admiration in her eyes. "Morrow was astonished you uncovered the truth so quickly. She thought James had buried it deeper—more layers of encryption, more false trails. Your speed caught her off guard, even knowing what she did."

Emily nodded. Dr. Morrow had been on her side all along.

"Catherine Morrow created this lab to oppose Chronos's plans," Elena continued. "She funded it and kept it hidden. Her wealth paid for everything. She suspected Helix's board, Beyer, and others, but had no proof. When Beyer brought in his nephew, James Kessler, as CEO, she knew I would be eliminated for not complying, just as they are now trying to remove you."

Elena shrugged and sighed as she reached the heart of her revelation. "When we discovered Chronos forming, I had to disappear to survive. I knew too many of their secrets. Catherine helped me set up a fake car crash. The name 'kill switch' for the terminal gene was our private joke, referencing both my staged death and the gene's function."

The news hit Emily. Morrow's cold distance, misdirection, and offer of security masked her rebellion. Relief eased the knot of mistrust. With its cluttered defiance, oscilloscopes humming, vials bubbling, the air sharp with chemicals, this secret lab stood as a testament to resistance born of desperation.

Anita's eyes narrowed, unconvinced. "And the one hundred twenty years? Why that timeline?"

Volkova exhaled, her voice grim. "Our best estimate points to June 25, 2150. There will be a total solar eclipse, one of the longest recorded. It's more than symbolic; it aligns with a predicted solar flare, amplified by the Moon's shadow, unleashing a mutagenic storm of cosmic rays. Earth's ozone layer, thinned by centuries of climate change, won't shield us."

Anita shifted, her voice breaking the silence. "So you're fighting Chronos from here? Alone?"

Volkova's gaze softened, reflecting a shared struggle. "Not alone now."

Apprehension grew as Volkova pointed to a chart, its dense lines showing the gene's complexity: feedback loops, environmental triggers, a puzzle of enormous scale, all the questions Emily had been grappling with.

Anita asked, "You've got a plan to stop this?"

Volkova nodded, pointing to a cluttered bench where a centrifuge spun quietly. "Methods to sever the gene's function, but it's delicate. One misstep, and we trade one disaster for another."

The lab's presence tempered Emily's hope. The ethical dilemma was intense: knowledge could save lives, but sharing it might cause greater harm. Morrow's alliance acted as a bridge, yet the truth felt like a razor, sharp on both sides.

The lab's air was thick with sharp chemical fumes and the constant hum of aging machinery. Cluttered workbenches formed a claustrophobic maze that mirrored Emily's swirling thoughts. Dim bulbs cast a dull glow, reflecting off glassware and folded notebook pages, each item a testament to Volkova's subversive fight against Chronos's control.

Volkova spread charts across the table, her fingers tracing faded ink lines smudged by haste. "The kill switch isn't a flaw," she said. "It's a genetic timer designed to trigger extinction, individual or mass, unless reset by those with the keys. I've changed it for several people, but scaling it? That's the unknown."

Emily leaned over the diagrams, analyzing complex sequences: recursive loops linked to cellular decay, triggers connected to climate changes. The data spread out, filled with notes, served as a blueprint of destruction. Her heartbeat sped up. "James reset my kill switch," she blurted, voice tight with anxiety. "I found out last week. My clock's ticking, with less than a month left."

Volkova's eyes softened with empathy, a rare crack in her

guarded demeanor. "I'm sorry, Emily. He likely used viral vector delivery. He made me engineer a custom adenovirus loaded with gene-editing tools targeting only the terminal gene. It's a Trojan horse, rewriting DNA without obvious symptoms. We planned to deliver it through something innocuous: spiked coffee, an aerosol spray, or even contaminated food in the break room to test on a few employees. The virus spreads systemically, editing cells, self-limiting to avoid detection, only activating with a specific trigger."

Emily's stomach churned, her mind racing with betrayal. James had been so close, offering her coffee in his office, sharing air in cramped meetings. *Planting expired PowerBars in the breakroom.*

She gripped the table, steadying herself. "Can you modify mine? Extend it?"

Volkova hesitated, her expression grim. "I can try. I've reversed it for others, but each case is unique. The process is risky, and we're racing against your deadline." She pointed to the vial in the centrifuge. "That's the counter-vector, but it's experimental. Are you willing to take the chance?"

Emily's breath caught, the weight of her choice crushing. Risk her life to fight Chronos's control, or let the clock run out. She nodded, voice firm. "Yes, I want to try."

"What happens if you turn it off?" she asked. "For one person or everyone?"

Volkova's gaze met hers, unflinching. "For an individual, it halts the trigger; life is preserved, no spread to others. I've tested that. But for populations? CRISPR edits could break the chain, destabilizing genomes, or cause mutations, cancers, and altered traits rippling unchecked. The variables are too vast to test beyond the deadline of the global event."

Anita's mug hit the table, coffee splashing. "So, Chronos lets the gene run, culling most, but tweaks it for their elite, loyal, and rich, making them a super caste ruling for one hundred twenty years while they prepare for the extinction event?"

Volkova nodded, her expression grim. "You understand. Their system ensures selective survival. We can counter it for individuals, but scaling up risks a catastrophe. Act, and we might save billions or doom them. Do nothing, and Chronos decides who lives."

For Emily, the ethical dilemma hit close to home, sending her mind reeling. Deactivating the gene would shatter Chronos's control, liberating humanity from a predetermined fate. But it could unleash chaos: genomes unraveling, diseases raging, power still in the hands of those who marked her for death.

Emily tightly gripped her mug. "I need to see your data," she said, voice firm, scientist and survivor at war. Her own ticking clock loomed; James's reset was a death sentence, counting down.

Volkova slid a folder across the table, pages dense. Emily examined them. "These vectors," she asked, circling a spiked graph, "are they stable? How does Chronos control the reset?"

"Proprietary codes buried deep in Helix's archives," Volkova said. "They select survivors. I recreated a modified version, but my testing is limited. They don't have the same ethical qualms." Anita leaned forward, eyes intense. "We should leak it—to scientists, the press, everyone. Let the world tear it apart."

Emily shook her head, caution mooring her. "That paints a target on all of us. Chronos doesn't negotiate—they erase. Hiding it means we choose who knows, and that power's dangerous."

"Doing nothing's worse," Anita shot back, voice rising. "People need the truth."

"Truth?" Emily's voice cracked, filled with dread. "Panic fuels Chronos. Riots, collapse—they'd exploit it. We're already seeing that now. If we tell people their kill switch can be changed, they'll tear the world apart searching for answers. We need a plan, not chaos.

Volkova's silence weighed heavily, and the lab's sounds—clinking glass, dripping condenser—intensified the tension. Emily's mind raced: save herself, billions, or risk ruin? Her fight for free will conflicted with the doom etched into her genes. But she had to protect the vulnerable, not play God like Chronos.

Anita's fingers tapped on the table. "You're stalling, Emily. We have the data. We need to act."

"Act how?" Emily met her gaze, voice rising. "One mistake and we don't save lives—we end them."

Volkova shrugged. "The choice is a tightrope. Chronos's plan is destruction by design. My edits could stop it or cause everything to fall apart. Choose, or they will."

The lab's air suddenly shifted as the trapdoor above opened and closed, heavy footsteps descending the ladder. Vic jumped down from the last rung, his athletic silhouette casting a lengthy shadow across the cluttered benches, his face guarded beneath damp, dark hair. His olive-green jacket carried the harbor's briny scent, mixed with cigarette smoke, and his eyes locked onto Emily with an intensity that immediately sparked mistrust.

Emily stood, her voice sharp. "What are you doing here?"

Anita tensed next to her, her hand gripping the table's edge. Volkova's fingers inched toward a drawer, her posture stiff.

Vic raised his hands, palms out. "To help you."

"Help me?" Emily stepped closer, anger flashing. "After you gave Tyler a gun, your cryptic texts, your games? What do you really want, Vic?"

He leaned against a workbench, the air shifting around him —salt, smoke. The lab's fluorescent light faintly reflected off a scar on his jaw. "Viktor Volkova," he said, "but my friends call me Vic. I'm Elena's brother."

Dr. Volkova nodded, her gaze piercing. "He's with us, Emily. Hear him."

Vic exhaled. "Russia and my family shaped me. Elena, my sister, was the star, always out of reach. She left early, her success pulling her away. I followed my parents' paths—Kirov Military Academy, Spetsnaz medic. Syria, Afghanistan—patching wounds under fire, using vodka, duct tape, whatever worked."

He paused, the lab equipment filling the silence, a centrifuge spinning with a faint whine. Emily watched—his jaw tight, eyes distant. He spoke of meeting Tyler Reed, an American soldier whose pragmatism saved him twice: dragging him from a burning Humvee, shielding him from a sniper's bullet. Those moments, forged in blood and dust, broke his loyalty to Russia. Elena's defection in 2018, fleeing during a Boston conference, planted the seed. In 2019, Vic seized his chance amid Afghanistan's chaos, defecting to a U.S. unit alongside Tyler, offering intel and medical skills.

"The CIA hid me," he said, voice distant. "They fabricated an AWOL story to get me out of the country. Special Immigrant Visa, 2020. Vetted me thoroughly—Elena's defection made them suspicious. I worked as a civilian advisor for the Special Forces, but the constant war wore on me. Now, docks by day, obscurity by night—smuggling, security. Keeps Elena safe, and I repay Tyler. And help you."

His motives were tangled like the lab's cables: protecting his sister from Russian mercenaries, honoring life debts to Tyler through Emily's quest, and chasing a civilian life in a foreign country. Yet his troubled life made Emily wary.

"Why didn't you tell me this before?" she asked, stepping closer. "Why did you and Tyler drag me into this blindly?"

"Tyler did not know. I did it to protect both of you," Vic said, meeting her gaze. "Chronos watches everyone. Ask my sister. Trust is a risk."

Anita interrupted, her voice crisp. "You could've told us sooner and saved us the paranoia."

Vic's eyes flicked to her, then back to Emily. "Paranoia has kept you alive."

Emily's hope wavered. His information was essential but still seemed veiled in half-truths. Empathy for Volkova and relief at Morrow's alliance clashed with Vic's deceit.

Vic's expression darkened as he looked at his glowing phone screen. "My contact texted. Chronos has found this place. We need to move."

Upstairs, gunfire cracked sharply, followed by shouts and pounding boots. The trapdoor rattled, dust falling—sounds menacing and sudden.

Chapter 28

The Trap

Emily hunched over a scarred workbench in the underground lab beneath Charlestown Wheels, her fingers racing across a keyboard to catalog encrypted drives. She grabbed the handheld radio from Elena's desk, her fingers trembling as she pushed the talk button. "Elena, we're losing ground," she said. "Are there backups for the drives? We can't lose the sequences you've developed."

Elena's voice crackled through the radio, interrupted by a burst of rifle fire. "Not everything, Emily. Core data's on the main server—redundant data is in the safe, but we don't have time to grab it all."

Emily's breath caught as muffled gunfire echoed from the garage above, followed by muffled shouts. Her pulse quickened, a cold realization settling in. Someone had found out the lab's location, and they were violently trying to breach it.

"Then we need to assess what's critical," Emily said, her mind racing. Her eyes flicked to the safe in the corner, its steel door dull under the lab's flickering lights. "Prioritize Helix's gene modification data and the kill switch overrides you've designed. We'll take those and wipe the rest."

Elena grunted, the sound of a magazine snapping into her pistol audible over the radio. "Wiping the servers means no second chances. Are you sure?"

"No choice," Emily replied. "If Chronos gets this, they'll find a way to weaponize it. Start the wipe protocol—ten minutes, max." She glanced at the monitors, watching an armed operative crumple under Vic's fire. "We'll take what we can and go."

She darted to a nearby monitor, checking a security feed Elena had set up. One grainy image showed Vic hanging at the top of the rusty ladder to the trapdoor, his pistol in hand. Another camera shot captured muzzle flashes lighting up the interior of the garage, revealing Elena's small security team— three broad-chested armed men, their faces grim as they fired at black-clad operatives breaching the metal door at the entrance.

"It has to be Chronos," Emily whispered, gunfire echoing through the camera feed. She zoomed in, catching Vic's expert moves as he dropped an operative rushing from behind a pile of tires, lunging for the ladder.

Elena, breathing heavily, hid behind a stack of crates, her gray-streaked hair pulled back. A bullet grazed her shoulder, blood seeping through her sleeve. "Not my time yet," she growled into her radio, her Russian accent thick with defiance. "Kill switch says I've got years."

Emily's stomach twisted—Elena's bravado concealed her pain, and the kill switch, embedded in their DNA, loomed over them all. Emily's remaining time was ticking down, but with weeks left, she knew today wasn't her day to die.

A wave of dread swept over her. Her survival relied on her cleverness, since she lacked a fighter's instinct. With a few keystrokes, she accessed the lab's secondary security system, her fingers rapidly locking the garage's back door to buy some time before reinforcements arrived.

Her eyes scanned a digital blueprint on another monitor, spotting a ventilation shaft in the west corner—narrow, rusted, barely wide enough for Elena's broad frame, but a potential escape route if the ladder fell. "Vic, they're circling," she said into her radio. "Back door's sealed, but there's a shaft in the west wall. Can you hold them?"

"Vent shaft?" Elena asked.

"West wall," Emily confirmed. "It's our only shot out of here."

Vic's voice crackled back, rough and punctuated by a gunshot. "Daylight raid means they've got the Boston PD in their pocket. We won't last much longer. Cops will seal off the entire area when the heat's on."

Had Vic's shadowed past—dockside smuggling, relationship with the CIA—led Chronos here? His fierce defense, another operative crumpling under his fire, held her trust for the moment.

Officer Mooney's cruiser, a constant silhouette outside her parents' home last night, flashed in Emily's mind. Its dark bulk, parked across the street in the pre-dawn light, seemed like a predator waiting to strike. Was Mooney Chronos's eyes or a cop too close to the truth? Emily pushed the thought aside, focusing on the lab's blueprint.

She hacked deeper into the security system, triggering a false alarm in the alley to divert any police responding to a nearby street. The camera feed showed an operative lifting the trapdoor, only to fall as Vic's shot hit its mark.

"We can't hold them," Elena barked. "Get the backup drives out, Emily!"

The lab's air thickened with smoke, monitors pulsing with data that could unravel Chronos's plan or doom humanity if mishandled. Bullets ricocheted off the concrete and metal, the sound relentless, vibrating through Emily's chest.

She glanced at Anita, wide-eyed and clutching a backpack

full of drives by the safe. "Stay close to me," Emily said, her mind mapping out the route to the ventilation shaft entrance.

Her thoughts racing—had someone betrayed them, or had Chronos finally been lucky enough to find the lab while Emily was here? Mooney's vague warnings and "rescues" during the chase seemed too convenient. But Emily still didn't trust Vic and his divided loyalties, despite his professed dedication to Tyler and his sister Elena.

Now, in the lab's dim light, that distrust drove her actions. She activated the secondary lock on the trapdoor, giving herself a few more moments, and memorized the shaft's route.

"We move after Vic and Elena reload," she told Anita, grabbing a second drive.

The lab's monitors glowed, their light reflecting off broken glass—a smoking monitor, shattered beakers—evidence of Vic and Elena's desperate struggle. The crackle of gunfire and the acrid odor of smoke pushed forward. She wasn't a soldier like Vic or Tyler, but intelligence was her weapon, and she'd use it to protect the data, no matter what.

Thick smoke curled through the lab, the acrid stench of melting plastic mixing with gunpowder as Vic and Elena rigged explosives amid shattered equipment. The lab's servers sparked, their screens flickering to black. Emily stood by the ventilation shaft, its rusted grate pried open, her backpack stuffed with encrypted drives.

Beside the server rack, Vic crouched, carefully wiring a small bundle of C4 taken from a hidden cache beneath the lab's floor. Elena had devised the idea—a desperate plan from their early days of resisting Chronos, back when they knew the lab's data could be a threat if it fell into the wrong hands.

"Explosives are our only shot," Vic said, scanning the lab's flickering monitors. "Blow the servers, fry the circuits. It'll also slow those bastards down and give us time to get the drives out through the tunnels."

Elena, her shoulder bleeding through her shirt, checked the timer on a detonator. "Dangerous down here," she muttered. "Ceiling could collapse. You sure about this, Vic?"

"Three minutes to clear," he replied, taping a charge to a steel lab bench. "It'll take out the electronics, maybe a few of them. We'll be down the tunnel before it blows." His confidence was firm, but Emily caught a flicker of doubt in his eyes. Did he trust his plan, or was he gambling with their lives?

Elena's voice cut through the sound of renewed gunfire above them. "After you enter the vent, take the first branch on the left. We'll take the right exit, Emily. Split up and shake them. Check your personal email later. One way, no replies." The static crackling, she added, "Vic says we're hunting Q. Whoever they are, he wants to kill the head of the snake."

Anita, clutching her pack, whispered, "Herbert Beyer? The Helix board chair?"

Vic, securing another explosive charge, snapped, "Beyer's a dead end. Q's someone else inside Helix." Emily's mind churned, worried about Vic's dependability. He always seemed to know more than he let on—his cryptic games, his connections to the underworld and the CIA—caused unease. The daylight raid, bold and reckless, revealed Elena's data was likely Chronos's target, but her doubts about whom to trust remained.

Mooney's absence during the raid made Emily feel nervous, as if there was a space where someone should have been—a silent threat. Had she followed them this morning and then revealed their location to Chronos? Emily's suspicions had led her in circles, but now, as Chronos attacked the lab, Mooney's missing presence screamed of complicity—or a deeper deception.

Vic's voice echoed through the lab again, "Get clear. You have three minutes."

"Go," Emily told Anita, gesturing to the shaft, her voice steady despite the knot in her chest.

Emily and Anita crawled into the ventilation shaft, the rusted metal scraping their knees as they moved through the tight tunnel. For two agonizing minutes, their breaths echoed in the cramped space, the clatter of their packs against the walls drowning out the sounds from the lab. Emily strained to hear Vic's voice, garbled through the radio, yelling something to Elena—orders or a warning.

"Keep moving," Emily whispered, her flashlight beam cutting through the darkness. They turned left into a wider concrete shaft, its damp walls slick with condensation, the air thick with decay. The change in space allowed them to crawl faster, but the distant rumble of shots kept Emily's heart pounding. Was Vic's plan working, or were the explosives going to seal their fate?

A deep rumble shook the lab as the C4 erupted in a fiery blast. Smoke billowed into the shaft, and the ground trembled as Emily and Anita hurried further into the damp, concrete tunnel, its rough floor scraping their palms. The radio went silent, leaving Emily to wonder if Vic and Elena had survived and were now navigating another branch of the tunnel.

Her chest tightened, memories of her parents' Victorian home flashing briefly. She had left that safety to protect them, and now the weight of the drives—genetic codes, trigger mechanisms, a blueprint for extinction or salvation—felt overwhelming. The lab's collapse echoed behind her, the ultimate act of defiance against Chronos. The tunnel's air grew dank, water dripping from cracked concrete, their breaths visible in the chill. Anita's flashlight danced across rusted pipes and faded graffiti —a scrawled "No Exit," barely readable—intensifying the claustrophobic dread.

"Think they made it?" Anita whispered, shoes sloshing through puddles.

Emily didn't answer, her mind on the next move. They paused at a junction, the tunnel splitting three ways. Emily's memory of the blueprint wavered, but a faint draft from the left suggested an exit. "This way," she said, voice even. Anita nodded, her silent support a quiet gesture of trust.

Shouts echoed faintly—were they pursuers or Vic and Elena? The tunnel's walls closed tighter, the air thick with mold and a faint sewer stench, but Emily's resolve stayed strong. She would rescue Anita and the data, no matter the odds.

Anita's flashlight wavered as she crawled, its beam illuminating a rusted pipe sticking into the narrow shaft. She halted suddenly, her breath catching. "Emily, hold up," she whispered urgently. She motioned to a faint seam in the concrete wall, barely visible in the dim light. "This looks like a maintenance hatch. It probably leads to a utility tunnel. This could be our way out if Chronos covers the main exits."

Emily squinted at the seam, her mind racing. The blueprint hadn't shown this connection, but Anita's sharp eye had caught it. "How do you know it's not a dead end?" she asked, her voice tense as distant shouts echoed through the tunnel.

"My uncle works in maintenance for the Seaport District," Anita said. "He's always going on about how these tunnels connect to the old harbor grid. If we're lucky, this hatch bypasses their perimeter. Only one way to know." She pulled a multi-tool from her pack, prying at the seam. The hatch creaked open, revealing a narrow passage lined with ancient cables, the air thick with mildew despite a faint breeze.

Emily's pulse quickened, but she trusted Anita's instinct. "You're full of surprises," she said, a faint smile breaking through. "Lead the way."

They reached the tunnel exit, climbed the ladder, and carefully lifted a lid into a rain-soaked alley.

Cobblestones shimmered beneath the drizzle, and the air was thick with the smell of harbor brine and the sour stench of trash piled in rusted dumpsters. A distant foghorn moaned softly and mournfully, blending with the sound of rain.

The sound of footsteps followed as two men passed them on the street, their radios buzzing with terse commands.

Emily's heart hammered as she grabbed Anita's arm, pulling her toward a side alley. "Market's two blocks," she whispered. "We ditch them in the crowd."

Anita nodded, her eyes wide but steady, clutching her pack. The alley narrowed, with a discarded newspaper soaked against a brick wall. "They're too close," Anita muttered, glancing back. "Think Mooney's with them?"

"I don't think they're police. That's what scares me."

They slipped into the market's clamor—vendors hawking fish, the sizzle of grills, the jingle of coins—its chaos swallowing their trail. The air carried a fishy smell, sharp and salty, as they navigated through shoppers bundled up against the late fall chill. Anita's breath hitched, but she matched Emily's pace.

The market's din faded as they approached South Station, the fishy scent giving way to diesel fumes and the low rumble of bus engines. The sensory change grounded Emily, hiding their escape in the station's midday rush. Commuters pushed past neon-lit ticket counters, their chatter a distraction.

"Stay low," Emily whispered, scanning for Chronos's hunters. A man in a dark coat lingered near a counter, his gaze too intense, his hand brushing a radio earpiece.

"See him?" Anita whispered, her fingers tightening on her pack.

"Too obvious," Emily said, unconvinced, steering them toward a busy bus platform. Using Anita's Boston University library pass, they boarded a bus to the university. The ride was tense, with their silence heavy as they scanned everyone getting on. Anita's fingers tapped her knee—a nervous habit. Emily's thoughts churned—Chronos's reach was too long, Mooney's shadow too close.

The Mugar Library was ahead. They slipped into the twenty-four-hour study area, its quiet stacks smelling of aged paper, ink, and dust. Fluorescent lights cast a sterile glow over rows of carrels, the hush a welcome relief after the chaos in the underground lab. Emily checked the drive in a secluded fourth-floor cubicle, confirming Elena's backup data was intact.

Her phone buzzed with a text from an unlisted number. "We made it. Looking for our cue." She knew Elena and Vic were safe and hunting Q.

Anita slumped in a chair, absentmindedly sketching as her pencil softly scratched the paper. Her drawing took shape—a rebellious figure holding a broken chain, symbolizing their determination to win.

"Think this place is safe?" Anita asked quietly, her eyes scanning the empty stacks.

"For now," Emily admitted, gazing at Boston's skyline through a window, its distant silhouette a faint reminder of normalcy. "It's all we've got." She opened her laptop, and the data on the drive spilled across the screen—feedback loops, cellular decay triggers, and a coded endgame.

Anita set her pencil down, the sketch half-finished. She leaned forward, her voice soft. "Emily, you're carrying this like it's all on you. The data, the kill switch, Chronos—it's not only your fight." She tapped the drive on the table, its faint whir a reminder of their burden. "I've been working with you on this project from the beginning. I know what's at stake. If we lose this, Tyler's death means nothing."

Emily nodded. "I didn't know you were that deep in the code," she admitted, her voice quieter now. "You've been holding back."

Anita's lips curled into a wry smile. "You're not the only one who keeps things close. But I'm here, Emily. I've seen the data—Helix's mods, the triggers. I can help you verify the sequences, even spot something Elena missed." She paused, her eyes steady. "You don't have to carry the burden alone. Let me share some of it."

Emily studied her, the burden of the drives and her ticking clock pressing harder. Anita wasn't only a coworker in the lab. She was her best friend. "Alright," Emily said, sliding the laptop toward her. "Start with the override sequences. If we're going to beat Chronos, we'll need every advantage."

Anita nodded, her fingers moving across the keyboard, matching Emily's focus. The library's silence no longer felt oppressive. Their shared purpose served as a shield against the threat. Emily's fingers hovered over the keyboard, the enormity of billions of lives bearing down.

Her immediate goal was to protect Anita and the data, but the most crucial and fundamental question remained unanswered. What price would humanity pay to uncover the truth?

Chapter 29

Fate and Free Will

T he smell of pepperoni grease filled the air in Mugar Library's fourth-floor study carrel, where Emily and Anita hunched over a battered wooden table.

A crumpled pizza box, its edges shiny with grease, sat among scattered notebooks and a laptop, a quiet defiance of library rules. Since midday, they had been hiding here as the late-fall dusk shrouded Boston. Their cold pizza served as dinner after the chaos in the underground lab and hours spent sifting through Elena Volkova's files. Crumbs clung to Emily's fingers, the oily sheen of the crust still present, while Anita balanced a half-eaten slice on a napkin, her other hand busy sketching.

A soft cough broke the silence. A librarian with auburn hair and a streak of purple paused at the edge of her carrel, her gaze on the pizza box. "No food or drink allowed," she said, her tone firm but softened by a faint smile, as if recalling her own rebellions. Adjusting her glasses, she noticed the glow of Anita's laptop, where jagged genetic code sprawled across the screen.

"Looks like intense work. Big project? I can point you to the bioinformatics stacks."

Emily's heart rate spiked, fingers freezing mid-type. "It's research for a paper we might publish," she said, forcing a smile. The lie felt thin under the librarian's attentive eyes.

Anita wiped her hands, nudging her laptop to dim the screen's glow. "Yeah, a real killer," she said, a smirk hinting at her pun. "We're good, thanks." Her relaxed grin softened the librarian, who laughed politely, adjusted her glasses, and stepped back into the stacks, her footsteps fading away.

Emily exhaled, pushing the pizza aside, her appetite gone. A distant door's soft thud sent a shiver through her, her mind briefly recalling the Chronos agents suddenly attacking the lab.

Through a narrow window, Boston's skyline shimmered, with a single red light pulsing among the gold, serving as both a beacon of hope and a warning of danger. The warmth of the encrypted drive holding Volkova's data—genetic sequences, kill switch triggers, a blueprint for salvation or catastrophe—felt like Pandora's box.

Anita flipped a page in her sketchbook, her pencil scratching the angular lines of a dog, its floppy ears echoing Tyler's old drawings. "Expose Chronos, Emily," Anita urged, fierce. "Get the data out—scientists, journalists, anyone who can dismantle it." Her pencil froze, eyes locking onto Emily's, blazing with grief-fueled resolve. "Tyler would've wanted it. His death can't be meaningless."

The mention of Tyler tightened Emily's throat. His laughter at his terrible jokes echoed in her mind, a fleeting memory bright against the raw wound of his loss. His goodbye video haunted her in moments of silence—his voice calm, urging her to expose Chronos. "You never told me how close you two were," she murmured, probing Anita.

Anita's fingers traced the dog's outline. "Watching Tyler

sketch encouraged me to take art classes. He loved drawing those dogs—fierce, loyal, free. They were his escape from the war's ghosts." Her voice caught. "You have so many memories of him, Emily. For me, he stays alive through drawing. You and the drawing are all I have left of him. We can't let Chronos win."

That struck Emily deeply. Anita's art, born from her friendship with Tyler, was her way of holding onto normalcy. Glancing at her laptop, which displayed code related to cellular decay triggers, Emily saw a countdown to humanity's end. "Releasing this might spark more riots," she said, voice taut. "Panic. Chronos would purge scientists, activists, us. The data's a weapon, but it could backfire."

Leaning forward, Anita tensed. "And doing nothing? Chronos decides who lives and who dies. They'll control us all with every kill switch." Her anger flared, sharpening her gaze.

Emily's nails dug into her palms. Her own kill switch gave her a few weeks. Tyler's video and Volkova's warning echoed. One misstep might unleash mutations or tighten Chronos's control over an elite group spared by the gene's timer. "I'm not saying we hide," she said, "but we need a plan. Releasing this without a strategy lets Chronos spin it—propaganda, fear, martial law."

"You sound like Dr. Morrow, always calculating. This isn't code—it's people. Tyler was the best thing that happened to you." Her eyes flicked to the drive. "You've got until Christmas. I never checked my kill switch, so I don't know my time. I say, carpe diem. Why fight if not for something bigger than ourselves?"

The question hung heavy in the library's quiet. A distant page rustled, and Anita's chair creaked. Emily's mind spun, torn between the risk of truth and the fleeting safety of silence. Her impending death, honed by Tyler's loss and his parting video, demanded action. Anita's grief and fire were her stand against Chronos's predetermined fate.

Sliding the pizza box aside, Emily met Anita's look, her voice calm despite the ache in her chest. "We'll be smart," she said, a silent vow. For everyone, this data can either save or destroy.

The laptop's pale glow cast shifting shapes across the carrel, flickering like ghosts on the bookshelves. The faint hum of the laptop fan buzzed beneath Emily's fingers. Dr. Catherine Morrow's face appeared on a secure video call, her silver hair pulled tight, eyes sharp despite the fatigue that etched her features. Static crackled through the speakers, a reminder of the risk. Her fortune had funded Volkova's lab to challenge Chronos's grip.

Emily lowered the volume so only she and Anita could hear the call. Morrow's voice was a murmur in the library's peaceful silence.

"You have Elena's data, Emily," Morrow pressed, urgent. "You're the fulcrum now. Chronos wants it destroyed or weaponized. You can't let them have it." Her gaze darted off-screen, wary, checking for unseen listeners. "I've tracked Chronos's moves before they became a formal group. Herbert Beyer brought in his nephew James to be the CEO a couple of years ago to build the group and implement the plans. He's their architect. And now he's missing. Chronos plans to use the terminal gene to protect a loyal elite, leaving the rest to rot."

Emily's stomach clenched. James's name overshadowed her own ticking clock. His change to her kill switch forced her into a Christmas deadline. "They're building a new world order."

Morrow nodded, her face grim. "Exactly. Silence hands them victory. The truth is a weapon, but only if you wield it."

Emily's chair squeaked as she leaned in closer, her voice barely audible. "So Beyer is the elusive Q leading Chronos?"

There was a long pause in the video conference. "No, I don't believe so, but I'm not 100% certain."

"Who are they then?" Emily asked. Her fingers tightened on

the drive, the name a specter from Volkova's encrypted notes. "Vic's hunting them, obsessed. Why?"

Morrow's expression darkened. "I don't believe Q is one person. I think it's a code name for a small leadership cell within Chronos—scientists, defectors, and insiders who cracked under the strain of their plans. Circles within circles. That document you gave me on Sunday was marked with an Ouroboros symbol, hidden in the metadata."

Emily gulped. "Is that a symbol of a snake eating its own tail?"

"Yes," Dr. Morrow answered. "It has several meanings, like infinity, natural cycles, or a destructive loop. Those meanings could apply to both the terminal gene and Chronos."

Emily recalled seeing that symbol in the file she'd taken from James's desk. "Then who is Vic hunting? He said he was going after Q."

"Vic's after them because they threatened his sister. It's personal. But I also suspect he's an intelligence agent—ruthless and loyal to their goals. Q's data would support government interests, but is raw and chaotic. Vic's close, and he wants Chronos to be stopped, but he also wants the data to be controlled by the United States. Like I said, circles within circles."

Emily's throat tightened. "So Q may be allies or a threat," Vic's cold accuracy when killing the operatives at the lab chilled her. She shifted uncomfortably in her seat. "How do we find them?"

"You don't," Morrow sighed. "They find you. Q leaves breadcrumbs in dark web forums and encrypted channels. If they want you, they'll reach out. But Vic's involvement means he's watching you too. Stay sharp."

Anita paused sketching, her grip tightening on her pencil as Morrow spoke of Q. She snapped a page with a flip. "What if we leak Dr. Volkova's data anonymously?" she cut in. "Get it to scientists, hackers, without our names. Or we can signal Q ourselves. If they're leaving those symbols, maybe we can use the data to get a reaction."

Morrow's eyes narrowed slightly. "A leak can be manipulated. Chronos owns the media. Their propaganda machine is relentless. They'd call it a hoax or use it to justify retribution. You need a controlled release, something that forces accountability." She leaned in closer, voice dropping. "It's your call. You're in the crosshairs."

Doubt gnawed at Emily. "I don't know who to trust other than you two," she murmured. "Not Vic, not even Elena entirely. Officer Mooney's always there, wrong place, right time. Is she Chronos's eyes in the police or something else?"

Morrow's expression softened, her voice firm. "You can't trust everyone, but trust yourself and Anita." She looked at Anita, a faint smile breaking through. "She's got fire. You need that."

Anita's cheeks flushed. She nodded with resolve. "For Tyler," she muttered, her pencil resuming the sketch.

Morrow's encouragement echoed Anita's plea, solidifying Emily's role: not a scientist but a resistance leader. The data was her weapon. Anita, her ally.

Emily glanced out the window. Boston's skyline pulsed with the small, red light. Chronos's web spread wide, into labs, governments, and lives. Publishing the data could unravel their plans or illusions of secrecy. Riots might happen, but Q's splinter cell hinted at cracks in Chronos's armor, vulnerabilities that could be exploited. How many good people like Tyler would fall if they waited too long?

"I'll think of a way," Emily vowed, adamant. She straightened as the chair creaked. "We'll hit the right targets. Maybe lure Q into exposing themselves, like Anita said." Morrow nodded, her image flickering as the call cut off, leaving the carrel dark. Anita's sketchbook was open, "Tyler" etched in stark lines with an Ouroboros, a symbol of hope amid a system of self-destruction.

The library was nearly empty, its late-night quiet broken only by the faint rustling of pages from a distant aisle. A wooden table in the corner, scarred with etched initials, held Anita's sketchbooks and empty coffee cups. The air was filled with the smell of cold pizza and exhaustion.

Outside, Boston's skyline glittered in black and gold, each light representing a life that Emily's upcoming decision would affect. A faint siren wailed nearby, its sharp whine piercing the quiet.

Emily's laptop screen glowed with data from the encrypted drive: feedback loops, cellular triggers, and a coded endgame that could save or doom billions. She drafted a manifesto, weaving Volkova's findings into a call for unity. Her fingers hurried, embedding this information into a decentralized network for scientists and activists worldwide. A beacon to dismantle Chronos's control over the terminal gene. Each keyboard click brought her one step further.

Anita sat across from her, reading a book and pondering whether people can truly make choices or if past events already determine everything. Occasionally, she jotted down a note. Anita had placed a half-finished sketch to mark a page and looked up, her exhausted eyes meeting Emily's. She slid the book, *An Essay on Free Will*, across the table. "Read this."

Emily read the section Anita pointed to aloud, "'The free will problem is this. Is it possible to reconcile human free will with a universe ruled by deterministic laws of nature?' I think he wrote that for us. The terminal gene definitely looks like a deterministic law of nature.

Emily nodded, then felt her chest tighten when she saw the sketch used as a bookmark—the sketch of an Ouroboros crushed under their boot heels. Anita had drawn it to symbolize their partnership—a stand against Chronos's control.

She hesitated, fingers hovering over the keys. What if this sparked violence, tearing cities apart? What if Anita, her friend, became Chronos's next target? Fear clawed at her, but Tyler's steady voice in her mind urged her to stay strong. "Together," she echoed, voice firm. She sent a text message to Elena, signaling the upload. No reply would come. She pressed the send button. A weight lifted, but Chronos would hunt them even harder now.

Anita closed her book, fingers brushing the cover. "They'll come for us," she said, calm despite the fear in her eyes. "But we did the right thing."

Emily nodded, the skyline's glow brighter, pulsing with possibility. "We did." Her kill switch ticked on, weeks fading away, but this defiant act gave it meaning. The data was now the world's, a spark for dreamers and rebels.

Anita's suggestion to signal Q remained. "We could try it," Emily said. "Use their Ouroboros symbol in a dark web post with some of Volkova's data, prove we're onto them, and see if they react."

"Risky," Anita replied, pencil tapping on the desk. "But I like it. Tyler would say to go for it, don't you think?"

Emily's gaze shifted to the book on the table. Its faded spine served as a subtle reminder of their fight for free will against the certainty of the terminal gene. The library's hush settled in, heavy with the scent of old paper and history. The siren's wail faded. "If Q responds, it'll bring them into the open," she said. "If not, we've lit the fuse."

Chronos's vision—kill switches controlling survival, sparing only their elite—couldn't stand.

The skyline's red light pulsed as both a warning and a beacon. Emily packed her laptop into her bag, feeling the drive's warmth fade. Anita slipped her sketchbook into her backpack along with the other encrypted drives. As they rose, a notification flashed on Emily's screen, an Ouroboros with the phrase "The cycle won't end." Q's reaction. Her pulse quickened.

They slipped away, the library's silence giving way to Boston's frigid night. Rain-slick streets smelled of diesel and salt air. They disappeared into the darkness. The manifesto was released—an ember in the darkness. The world would either burn or rise.

Chapter 30

Legacy

D r. Harper, you've turned Helix upside down," Dr. Catherine Morrow said, her voice piercing the tense silence in the boardroom. She leaned forward, silver hair catching the light, her sharp eyes softened by fatigue. "Your appearance on CNN and last night's manifesto forced investors to act. Beyer's gone, there's a nationwide hunt on for Kessler, and half the board's under investigation. You've given us a chance to rebuild...or ruined us."

Emily sat stiffly at the mahogany table, its polished surface reflecting the recessed lights above. Her hands clenched tightly, her pulse pounding relentlessly in her ears. To her left, Anita tapped a pen in a restless rhythm, her dark eyes flicking between the board members, her agitation obvious. Elena Volkova sat across the table, her posture composed, but her guarded expression revealed nothing.

Several seats around the table were vacant, and their owners, including Chairperson Herbert Beyer, were detained by the investigation sparked by Emily's leaked data. It was late

Saturday morning, and this emergency meeting had pulled Emily and Anita from their bunk beds.

They had slept at Found Boston, sharing a dorm-style room overnight and paying in cash to hide from anyone searching for them. Morrow had sent private security to pick them up from the old red-brick building that morning, escorting them through Boston's rain-slick streets to Helix's glass tower.

"I didn't act alone," Emily said. Tyler's final plea echoed. "Expose them. Make it matter." Her throat tightened, but she met Morrow's gaze, deflecting the spotlight. "Anita, Elena, Tyler —they all carried this fight."

Mr. Richard Holt, a gray-suited board member with long, thin fingers and thinner lips, scoffed, his pen twitching like a nervous tic. "Carried it into chaos," he snapped, his voice strident. He gestured to his tablet, its screen flashing news clips: protesters outside Helix's doors, their signs reading "No More Kill Switches!"

He went on, "Your leak's got powerful people on Wall Street threatening lawsuits. Stock futures are crashing around the world. You're no hero—you're a liability."

Anita's pen stopped, and her chair creaked as she leaned forward, her tone bitter. "Liability? Chronos is the liability, planning to use the terminal gene to decide who lives. Emily exposed them. Maybe thank her instead of complaining." She stared down Holt.

Dr. Clara Nguyen, a biochemist with a steady gaze, tapped her stylus against her tablet. "I apologize for missing the previous board meeting; I was traveling, but the data's out now. Protesters are chanting because of it. Look." She swiped her screen, projecting a hologram of a changing crowd outside Helix. "Emily's actions forced reform. Beyer's resignation proves it. We can't disregard her impact."

Emily's chest tightened as gratitude and guilt clashed inside her. Tyler made everything possible by taking out Kessler, sacrificing himself, and releasing the initial leak. His self-sacrifice protected her and bought time to find Elena and upload the manifesto. She pictured him in their tiny kitchen, making his famous "cowboy" coffee and laughing at his puns.

Morrow raised a hand, silencing the murmurs. "Enough. Emily's leak only sped up the investigations that devastated this board. Apparently, they've been ongoing for months. Investors forced Beyer out and made me interim chair." She tapped her tablet, pulling up a headline from the Wall Street Journal. "Helix Board Fractures During BioSpark Scandal."

"We must pivot to transparency, or we risk collapse. Emily, you've earned a place in that shift—chief science officer. Lead our research and dismantle Chronos's legacy. Ensure transparency and that we live up to our mission to serve humanity."

The unexpected offer stunned her, her eyes widening in disbelief. That position signified power: labs, budgets, a voice to reshape Helix. Emily looked at Elena, who had spent years perfecting her genetic engineering skills in the hidden lab. She'd sacrificed so much to keep the fight against Chronos alive. Elena's fingers rested on a folder of research notes, her tired features drawn but resolute—a scientist who'd defied Chronos at a tremendous personal cost.

Holt's pen jabbed the air, his face reddening. "A whistleblower as a senior executive? That's a PR disaster!" His voice rose, a vein throbbing at his temple, echoing Mr. Carver's outrage from the previous meeting when he accused her of sabotage. "She's no leader—she's a renegade. Investors won't tolerate it."

Nguyen's stylus paused, her gaze locking onto Holt. "Renegade? She exposed a conspiracy that'd kill billions, Richard." Her voice was precise, scientific, but her eyes blazed with conviction. "Emily's proven her judgment. We need her vision, not your Ivy League paranoia."

A security alert sounded through the boardroom's speakers,

its sharp chime cutting across the discussion. Morrow looked at her tablet, her expression tightening. "Protesters have breached a side entrance," she said. "Security's holding them, but they're demanding answers." She swiped the screen, projecting a live feed on a hologram. A crowd pushed against the metal barriers, their chants growing louder, sirens wailing in the distance.

Emily's breath caught, the unrest outside reflecting the storm inside the boardroom. She recalled last night's discussion with Anita. Her pragmatism had focused her then, and it kept her composed now. "I'm honored," she said, her voice clear despite the discomfort in her chest. "But I can't accept the position. Dr. Elena Volkova should be the chief science officer."

The room grew silent. Elena's head snapped up, surprise breaking through her guarded veneer. Holt's pen stopped mid-twitch, his mouth opening to protest, but Emily pressed on. "Elena's work on terminal gene alterations is unmatched. She's risked her life to expose Chronos, not for power but for truth. She's the one to lead Helix's science into the future."

Anita nodded, her voice pointed. "Emily's right. Elena fought the real fight for years. She wasn't sitting around in a fancy boardroom talking about it."

Holt's face contorted, and his pen clattered to the table. "Volkova's a defector! She's been pretending to be dead! Chronos's shadow is on her. Investors will balk. I guarantee it." His voice showed the growing frustration, but the empty chairs —Beyer, Carver, Langston, all absent—undermined his position and his usual sources of support.

Nguyen leaned forward, her stylus tapping a deliberate rhythm. "Investors will balk at collapse, Richard. Elena's appointment shows we're serious about change. Emily's endorsement seals it for me." Her gaze flicked to Emily, a nod of respect breaking through her reserve.

Morrow's eyes narrowed, evaluating. "Elena's credentials are impeccable," she said, pulling up a file. "I have to admit that the plan to have Dr. Volkova continue her research in a secret lab away from Chronos's prying eyes was done with my blessing, but this role is political and public. Emily, your manifesto made you a figurehead. Are you sure you want to step back?"

Emily hesitated, feeling the significance of the decision. Accepting the role could strengthen her fight, giving her tools to dismantle Chronos's web. But it also risked chaining her to Helix's corporate machine. She recalled Tyler's last video—his trembling hand, the photo of them, his plea to keep fighting. Her resolve hardened. "I'm sure," she said. "I'll advise Elena, consult, whatever it takes. But she's the leader. I'm here to make the world a better place and don't care about a title."

Morrow's jaw tightened slightly, but she nodded. "Let's vote. Dr. Elena Volkova for CSO, with Emily as senior advisor."

The debate broke out, with voices overlapping.

Holt argued for an outside veteran, his pen frantically jabbing in the air. Nguyen countered with Elena's research experience and understanding of the terminal gene. A junior board member, Ms. Patel, hesitated, her fingers twisting a ring as she murmured about public perception. Emily stood firm, her advocacy unwavering. The vote passed: Dr. Elena Volkova, chief science officer.

Elena stood up, her voice clipped but warm. "Thank you all. I won't forget this." She reached out her hand, her grip strong, gratitude shining in her eyes. "Emily, we'll need you. Chronos isn't finished."

Emily nodded, her throat tight. "For Tyler," she whispered. The boardroom windows framed the harbor, gray waves churning under a clearing sky. Protesters' chants grew louder, "Truth now!" Emily's choice felt right, rejecting personal gain for a greater good, mirroring Tyler's sacrifice. Yet the cost—his life—was a wound that would be raw for a long time.

As the board adjourned, Anita squeezed Emily's arm. "You nailed it," she said. "Tyler would be grinning like you'd won the lottery." Emily offered a small smile, feeling the heaviness of his absence. The fight wasn't finished, but together they had ignited the spark.

"You're the one who shook up Helix, aren't you?" a gruff voice called out loudly in the crisp air. Emily froze mid-step, her shoes crunching on the frosty grass in the park near Helix. She turned to see a grizzled man in a worn jacket, his face creased like old leather, standing beside a golden retriever that bounded toward her, tail wagging. "Saw it on the news—protesters chanting your name outside that tower." He squinted, his eyes flicking toward the distant sound of the crowd.

"Yes, that's me," she said, sinking onto Tyler's favorite bench. The oak overhead cast sharp shadows, its bare branches swaying in the breeze, carrying the scent of damp earth and faint wood smoke.

Tyler's sketchbooks rested in her lap, their pages worn— depictions of soulful eyes, terriers mid-leap, and a poodle with a hilariously puffed-up haircut.

His body, recovered from the motel, had been identified at last. Following a call from the coroner's office, his remains were cremated as per his wishes. On the way to the board meeting this morning, she had the driver stop at the mortuary to pick up his ashes. Tomorrow, she would take the urn with his remains to his parents for a small memorial. For now, this bench was her sanctuary, a bridge from Helix's fight to her lost life with Tyler.

The man, Gus, introduced himself as he scratched behind his dog's ears. "Tyler's work, huh?" He nodded at the sketchbook. "Used to see him here, sketching my Rosie like she was queen of the park." Rosie nosed Emily's knee, her wet snout cold against her jeans. "Thought you might be a reporter sniffing around. You know him?"

Emily's throat caught, a smile breaking through her tears. "Yes, he was my fiancé. He died this past week."

"I'm sorry to hear that," Gus said as he looked away. "He was a good man."

"He loved dogs," she said, opening the sketchbook to a drawing of Rosie, her floppy ears captured in Tyler's pencil strokes. "Said they kept life simple." The memory hit her hard. Tyler sprawled on this bench a week ago—when all this chaos was beginning—sketching a bulldog with a toothy grin while teasing her about the sour look on her face.

"You look like you've eaten some bad sushi," he had joked. The memory of his lopsided grin warmed her even now. The tension in the boardroom was behind her—a victory made possible by Tyler's sacrifice.

As she watched Gus walk away, Emily noticed a flicker of movement across the park. A man in dark glasses lingered near a bare maple tree, his gaze fixed on her for a moment too long before he turned away, blending into the background. Her pulse quickened, the memory of yesterday's attack at the underground lab resonating in that fleeting stare. *Was he a passerby or a Chronos agent trailing me?*

The surreal unease tightened her chest, but as the man bent down to tie his shoe, a playful dog bounding to his side, Emily exhaled, her grip on the sketchbook loosening. Not every stranger posed a threat. Tyler's full-of-life drawings reminded her to hold on to hope despite the fear.

Emily's tears fell, smudging the page. She flipped through the sketchbook, each drawing a piece of Tyler—his kindness, his zest for life. A note read, "Free spirit." The victory in the boardroom felt hollow without him. His death had strengthened her resolve to fight Chronos, regardless of the odds. Mortality and meaning clashed—his death haunted her, yet gave her purpose. *Was all of this fate or free will?*

A young boy, maybe ten, ran up, his sneakers muddy and a

scrappy terrier at his heels. "You knew Tyler?" he asked, breathless. "He drew my dog, Rocket. Taught me how to shade fur." He pulled out a crumpled drawing, a rough copy of Tyler's style, showing Rocket leaping. "Look!"

Emily's heart ached, a bittersweet warmth spreading. "He'd love this," she said softly.

She reached into her bag, her fingers brushing a small vial of Tyler's ashes she'd brought with her to the park. With a sigh, she scattered a pinch beneath the bench, the gray dust blending with the soil. The oak's leaves rustled, a gentle echo of his presence, as if he were sketching beside her.

Anita arrived, her steps crunching on the frost, her breath visible. "I figured I'd find you here." She'd slipped away after the boardroom, needing air, but now sat close, her warmth a comfort. Her eyes flicked to the vial with Tyler's ashes, her jaw tight with grief.

She pulled a small sketchbook from her jacket, her pencil moving swiftly across the page, outlining a dog—a scruffy mutt like Tyler's strays. "He got me sketching to deal with the stress," she said, her voice almost breaking. "This one's for him." Her lines were sharp and deliberate, mirroring Tyler's style, a quiet act of grief paralleling Emily's ash-scattering. "Will you put it on his memorial?"

She nodded, her voice barely a whisper. "Of course, it's perfect." The park's stillness surrounded them, with the distant rhythm of the harbor as a reminder that her life would go on without him. Her love for Tyler, forged in early morning hikes and late-night pizza runs, had driven her to uncover BioSpark's truth. The trade-off—his life for her fight—hurt, but it fueled her determination.

With a final glance at her drawing, Anita closed her sketchbook, rose, and stretched, her arms reaching for the sky. "What a week! I'm ready to go home and sleep for a year," she said with a grin.

Emily said, "Thank you for being there for me. I couldn't have done it without you."

Anita blew her a kiss, her breath fogging in the cold air, as she turned to walk across the park. Tomorrow's memorial would close a chapter, but her fight—now Anita's too—would carry Tyler's light forward.

The park was a sacred space with its weathered bench and rustling oaks. As dusk painted the park a soft purple, Boston's lights flickered on. Emily sat on the cold bench, with Tyler's sketchbooks beside her. The small urn felt heavy inside her bag. The crisp and cool air carried the scent of decaying leaves, a momentary reminder of time's unstoppable march.

She whispered to the empty bench. "I'll protect your legacy, Tyler. Helix's secrets, Chronos's lies—I won't stop." Her voice was soft, a vow forged in grief. She pictured his grin, and a faint laugh broke through her tears. "You'd laugh at me crying over a bench," she murmured.

Emily shifted on the bench as it squeaked underneath her. The memorial for Tyler, organized with his parents, was approaching, bringing a mix of sadness and closure. She had found her purpose, not as a scientist or hero but as a woman driven by compassion and pain. The park was a sacred place that connected her to Tyler's dreams—her dreams of a shared life that would never come.

She slung her bag over her shoulder and stepped into the evening. Chronos's tangle still stretched wide, but Tyler's sacrifice, Anita's fire, and her resolve were cracks in its foundation. The fight wasn't over, but she could feel the tide turning.

Chapter 31

Unveiled Horizons

E xcuse me, are you the doctor they talked about on TV?"
The voice, soft but tense, broke the chill of Boston
Common.

Emily turned, her boots crunching on dry leaves, to see a young woman holding a toddler's hand. The child's knit cap slipped over her dark curls, and her mother's wide, worried eyes held Emily in place. "I saw you on the news. The kill switch gene... Is it true we might be safe now?"

Emily's scarf, a bulky woolly thing Tyler once called a "knit fortress," caught the December gust, and she stifled a wry smile at the memory. Her glasses fogged slightly as she exhaled, her breath visible in the chill. "Please call me Emily," she said with a nod. "The science is promising, but it's early. People are working together—scientists, communities. That's where hope starts."

The mother nodded, her grip tightening on her child's hand. "Will it be enough for my daughter?"

Emily's chest ached. "We're fighting for it," she said, offering a reserved smile. The woman's shoulders relaxed, and she turned back to the crowd, her child running beside her.

Emily's journey to the Common had started hours earlier when she woke up to a text from Anita. "Check the news. They're saying your name again." The message startled her, the burden of her influence pressing down. She walked back and forth in her apartment, Tyler's absence almost overwhelming. His sketchbooks were on her nightstand, and she felt the need to be with others, away from the silence.

Grabbing her coat, she'd taken the T from Jamaica Plain, the subway's rattle a backdrop to her thoughts. Stepping onto the Common, she'd found it transformed into a hub of global importance. The crowd's energy, their shared hope and fear, fueled her.

The Common buzzed with activity, its grass trampled by boots and wheels. News vans lined the park's edge, their satellite dishes piercing the cloudy sky. A CNN reporter stood on a makeshift stage, her voice sharp through a microphone. "Global summits in Geneva, Tokyo, and São Paulo are underway, sparked by Dr. Elena Volkova's leaked data on the terminal gene..."

Portable screens glowed, drawing clusters of people, their faces lit by images of scientists in sleek conference rooms, protest signs in foreign languages, and a grainy photo of Elena, her stern face now a global symbol of hope.

Emily stood near the stage, her hands buried in her coat pockets. A scientist on-screen mentioned her name: "Dr. Emily Harper's analysis of BioSpark's flaws guided our approach." Hearing her name on the news seemed surreal, as her influence grew beyond her control. She shrank back, her mind flashing to late nights in her apartment kitchen, papers strewn across the table, coffee mugs piling up. Tyler had once said, "You're gonna solve the world's problems with a spreadsheet and burnt coffee, Em." The memory warmed her, but grief followed, as sharp as the fall air.

Around her, the crowd's murmurs grew louder. The newscaster's voice, "Dr. Harper, the whistleblower," sparked pride but also made her feel shy. She wasn't a hero, just a scientist caught in a conflict bigger than herself. She never saw any of this coming.

The reporter's voice changed as they described international efforts: geneticists debating Elena's findings, some viewing them as a way to predict extinction risks, while others warned of ethical violations. Governments pledged billions for research, and Boston's protests, which had been a roar a few days earlier, grew quieter. Emily's heart lifted, but her distrust of Chronos lingered. Was this global optimism genuine or a cover for darker motives?

She recognized a familiar face as Gus stood a few steps away. She had met Gus at the park yesterday afternoon, his worn parka covered in dirt, his golden retriever Rosie tugging at her leash, tail wagging like a metronome. His wrinkled face softened as he squinted at her, the morning sun reflecting off the ice in his gray beard.

"Aha, I thought I recognized you."

He shuffled closer, Rosie panting at his side. "Tyler would say you're doing right by him."

A flash of heartache followed. Emily nodded, her throat tight, and glanced at the screens, where her name flashed again.

"You did well, kid," he said, his voice gruff but kind. He gestured to the screen showing the Tokyo summit. "Heard your name there. You're making a difference. We need more people like you. And Tyler." Rosie nosed Emily's knee, leaving a wet spot on her jeans.

"Thank you," Emily said, her smile tight. Gus tipped his cap and shuffled off, following Rosie, leaving her alone with the crowd's buzz.

The stage microphone crackled. A city official stepped onto the stage, his voice booming through the mic, promising transparency and funding. The crowd's tension eased as sunlight broke through the clouds, but Emily's thoughts drifted back to her mother's kitchen from days ago—after watching Tyler's goodbye video, the moment she had decided to act.

With its rustling oaks and hopeful murmurs, the Common was the epicenter of her fight, but the final cost remained uncertain. She straightened, the cold air sharp in her lungs, ready to move Tyler's light forward.

Dusk cloaked Jamaica Plain in shades of bruise and amber, with the Boston skyline fading into an overcast horizon. Emily stood on her apartment balcony, the sliding door slightly open, letting in a cold breeze heavy with the smell of damp earth and wilting thyme from her potted herbs.

The living room still showed the subtle signs of last week's break-in: scratched floors and a lampshade askew against the wall. But her mother had tidied up yesterday, rehung pictures, and straightened the shelves—a quiet gesture of support for Emily. Patricia's presence lingered: a folded quilt on the couch, a vase of bright marigolds on the coffee table. Her mother's quiet strength lifted Emily, a reminder of the family she was fighting for.

A note from her landlord sat on the kitchen counter, pinned beneath a few shiny keys for the door's new deadbolt. "I'm sorry about everything." Emily cradled a chipped mug of tea, its steam curling upward as she scrolled through her laptop, its screen casting a harsh glow across her freckles. Headlines from the Boston Common flashed, "Geneva Summit Yields Breakthroughs," "Boston Protests Bring Hope."

Her phone buzzed, a vibration that sent her tea sloshing. A text from Vic glowed. "No luck on Q...still a mystery. But I have news about Mooney. Let's meet." Her heart lurched, the mug forgotten on the balcony railing.

She recalled Mooney's cruiser idling outside her parents' house, her gaze dark and unreadable. Vic's warning about rotten apples in the Boston police, some tied to Chronos, gnawed at her. Emily texted back, "Are you sure Q is real?"

Vic's reply came fast. "Q's real—but not sure if they're friend or enemy. Mooney's at the quarry with a shovel. Strange."

Emily froze, the balcony's cold biting into her skin. *What quarry? What secret was Vic hiding now? And why would Mooney be there in the dark with a shovel?*

Emily's fingers trembled as she opened Elena's encrypted files, the laptop's keys cool to her touch. She began searching for any references to Q and a quarry. Cryptic emails appeared, their language cold and precise. One from Beyer, named Q the orchestrator, manipulated BioSpark's terminal gene data to extort governments, using its timer for profit. A second message, anonymous, hinted at Q's dual nature. "Q drives Chronos, but there are fractures within. Trust cautiously."

During her search, she couldn't find any mention of a quarry. "Tyler, you'd say my laptop's glow makes me look like a mad scientist," she muttered in frustration, a snicker breaking through.

Emily's thoughts spiraled to Tyler's final days. He was determined to reveal James's role in the conspiracy and had planned to confront him. But why would they meet at a quarry? Vic clearly knew something and hadn't told her.

Vic's following text buzzed. "Q's got eyes everywhere. Quarry is key. Make sure you aren't followed. Midnight?"

Emily replied, "Midnight. What quarry? Should I bring a shovel?"

Her stomach churned when Vic didn't text her back, the tea's bitter aftertaste lingering on her tongue. Emily leaned back, the wicker chair creaking. The decision to meet Vic felt like stepping into a storm—reckless but necessary. The quarry, Q's shadow, and Mooney's riddle were pieces of a puzzle she still had to solve.

A faint noise from a neighbor's window drifted on the breeze, mingling with the clink of dishes and the distant hum of traffic. Elena's files detailed the terminal gene's mechanism, adjusting its timer using James's algorithm. Her notes promised a way to reverse the effects of the terminal gene, but it required servers—and all of Elena's equipment was destroyed during the escape from the secret lab. Emily's chest tightened; the stakes were personal. Her kill switch was a ticking clock, and time was running out.

The balcony, once a stage for her doubt, was now her crucible, and she would meet the challenge with her intellect and a fighter's heart. She'd trusted Helix, then defied it. Isolation had given way to influence. The conspiracy's scale overwhelmed her, but her love for Tyler fueled her dedication to the truth. She sipped her tea, grimacing. "Tyler, you'd say this lukewarm tea tastes like regret." The laugh calmed her.

Night cloaked the apartment balcony, stars piercing a velvet sky. Emily leaned against the railing, its chipped paint rough under her palms, the air thick with the scent of wood smoke and wet leaves. The city's distant pulse—traffic's low hum, a siren's fleeting wail, the creak of a neighbor's window—wove a tense rhythm, punctuated by the occasional buzz of a drone overhead, a dull reminder of technology's grip on humanity.

Her laptop sat closed on the wicker table, its screen dark, but Elena's files weighed heavily on her mind. She sipped the cooling tea from Anita's mug, its bold letters reading, "Keep calm and question everything."

Ten days had shattered her world. Tyler's death, an attack in an obscure lab, a media firestorm branding her a household name, and James's sabotage of her kill switch, set to end her life by Christmas. Once a trusting scientist dreaming of her wedding, Emily now stood as a reluctant figurehead, fighting not for heroism but for free will against fate's unyielding grip.

She messaged Anita, "Wanna do some gardening tonight?" A coded message about Mooney and her shovel.

Anita's reply came quickly. "Ha, sure."

The breeze carried the faint sound of a baby crying in a nearby apartment, reminding her that everyday life kept moving.

Tyler's loss burned brightly in her thoughts. She imagined his grin, his teasing voice. "If I make it through this," she whispered to his picture on the bookcase, "you owe me a warm pizza and a terrible dog pun." Humor had become her way of coping with the trauma she had endured over the past ten days. She was a scientist challenging a rigged destiny, fighting for her family, Anita, the toddler in the Common, and a world hanging on the brink of extinction.

Elena's promise to disable Emily's kill switch offered hope, but time was a thief, and the quarry held either answers or traps. Regardless of the risks, she knew she'd press on. The stars above, sharp against the dark sky, were no longer just symbols of hope—they became a challenge, daring her to take control.

She'd face the unknown not for glory but to rewrite her fate and humanity's, with a steady hand and a fierce heart.

THE END

A Note From John H. Thomas

Thank you for reading The Terminal Gene!

I have a request. Could you please take a few minutes to review it? Reviews help others discover my work. Without them, my books might be buried among many other outstanding stories.

With millions of books online, a higher-rated book becomes more visible, so readers like you can enjoy this story too! Please take a moment to share your thoughts with me and others. I'd greatly appreciate it.

- John

About the Author

John lives in the Seattle area with his wife and the world's sweetest cat: Karmann. Raised in a nomadic military family, he is annoyingly curious, a consumer of whiskey, and a political junkie at heart, but his most significant interests are his family and their collective shenanigans.

Also by John H. Thomas

www.ingramcontent.com/pod-product-compliance
Lightning Source LLC
Chambersburg PA
CBHW050022120726
47903CB00006B/1869